THE VERY FIRST NIGHT.

(nicole ryan's version)

Copyright © 2024 by NRC Publishing

The Very First Night

First Edition, July 2024

Cover design by Nicole Ryan

Edited by EKB Books

All rights reserved.

No part of this book may be reproduced in any form or by any electronic or mechanical means, including information storage and retrieval systems, without written permission from the author, except for the use of brief quotations in a book review.

The characters and events in this book are fictitious. Any resemblance to actual people or events is entirely coincidental.

ISBN 979-8-9877304-6-1 (Special Edition)

Nicole Ryan - NRC Publishing
Woodville, Ohio
nicoleryanbooks.com

DEAR READER

I have been holding onto the idea for The Very First Night for quite some time now. There is something incredibly therapeutic about exploring a part of yourself that has long been hidden away but needs to be acknowledged. People often say that every version of ourselves, past and present, makes up who we are today. This book has been a healing journey for me, mending a broken part of my soul that I cannot fully express in words.

I believe many of us can relate to Kat's journey in these pages (minus the time travel aspect, of course). Her story of resilience and finding her self-worth is one that I've found exceedingly important to share. While certain aspects were inspired by my own experiences in my youth, this is purely a work of fiction.

The Very First Night delves very heavily into learning to value one's self worth in a relationship. It also delves into topics such as parental abandonment and complex family dynamics. This story shows some relationship dynamics that

DEAR READER

may be triggering for some and should be ventured into with care. If this is not something conducive to your mental health, please feel empowered to skip this one.

My first book was dedicated to my loving husband, my second to all of you, and now this one is for 19-year-old me. For the young girl who so desperately wanted to be loved that she latched onto the wrong people and struggled for far too long to let go.

Don't worry, in a few years you find the right one.

Oh, and Go Flashes!

A Taylor Swift inspired novel wouldn't be so without an overindulgent playlist.

THE VERY FIRST NIGHT

The Very First Night
Taylor Swift

2:05 -1:15

The Very First Night
Taylor Swift

the 1
Taylor Swift — 03:29

Mr. Perfectly Fine
Taylor Swift — 04:37

The Black Dog
Taylor Swift — 03:58

The Prophecy
Taylor Swift — 04:09

ONE

KAT

I've always loved weddings.

There is something about being a part of the biggest day of someone's life that feels...monumental. Months, sometimes years of work; flowers, linens, dresses, suits, venues—dozens of choices, all culminating in a day that you're going to remember for the rest of your life.

Sure, there is typically some drama involved. Goodness knows my family would end up screaming at each other by the end of the day, but it's still worth it. My cousin Michael's wedding alone was complete and utter chaos. His mom ended up getting into a fight with the bride's mom in the middle of the first dance. Now that I think of it, I don't know that they've resolved it, and it's been two years.

Family drama aside, my opinion stands.

I love weddings—that's why I decided to get into wedding photography in the first place. My catastrophic love life aside, weddings are everything right in the world...pure, concentrated love.

CHAPTER ONE

"Can you scooch like six inches to the side?" I ask with a wave of instruction as two tall, statuesque blonde women in champagne-colored satin bridesmaid dresses step to the right.

While I understand why some couples prefer to do a first look, I still think it makes it extra special for the couple to see each other for the first time at the altar. Would a first look make photos a lot easier? Absolutely; I would have been done and on the road hours ago. However, the photos I captured of the groom seeing the bride for the first time were worth it.

"Okay, now, Richard, if you could give Annabeth a big ol' smooch, and everyone else smile at them."

The bridal party follows my instruction with ease. Richard wraps his arms around Annabeth's waist and pulls her close. She tilts her head back, eyes closed in anticipation as he leans down to kiss her. The bridesmaids and groomsmen stand close together, smiling and watching as the couple shares a passionate moment. I snap several quick shots, capturing the tenderness of the embrace, before calling out "Perfect!" and lowering my DSLR.

Sparkling white lights glimmer along the wooden beams and cast a glow on the rows of seats lining the oversized pergola. Hanging lights dangle like lanterns from the middle of each support, connected by long strands of lights. A few raindrops gather on the outer edge and add shine to the sides of the wood, making it look almost silver. The bride was freaking out about impending rain, so I'm glad that it held off long enough for their outdoor ceremony to occur and the guests to go into the hall.

I just hope that it holds off long enough for me to drive the two hours to Cleveland.

"I believe we are good on the posed shots if you guys

would like to start heading inside," I say, dismissing the bridal party so they can start lining up for the reception entrance as I pull my long, sweat-dampened brown hair away from my neck. I don't care that it's July and it rained yesterday—it should never be this muggy outside.

While typically I would photograph the ceremony and reception, this wedding unfortunately falls on the same day as my college roommate's wedding. I'm glad there is enough time for me to get there for their evening wedding, but I'm even more thankful that my friend Cheyeanne, who often assists me with weddings, is willing to shoot the reception by herself.

"What time do you have to be there by?" Cheyeanne asks as I begin maneuvering my camera into the bag already filled with other equipment such as lenses and flash attachments.

"The ceremony starts at five." I give the sides of the bag a last tug to secure the zipper and check my watch. It's two o'clock, and I'm relieved I'll have enough time to get on the road and check in at the hotel before Jenna's ceremony begins. I'm just glad that she opted to hold the ceremony and reception at the same hotel.

"Are you sure you don't need me to come, Kat?" Cheyeanne asks, twirling one of her tight ringlets between her fingers.

My mouth feels like a desert as I try to explain to my friend the dread that is overwhelming me at the thought of seeing Elijah again. We've been talking about the wedding for weeks, and it has recently become clear that he will definitely be there. It has been six long months since I've seen him, and I know it will be awkward—I mean, he is one of the groom's closest friends; of course he'd RSVP yes.

Cheyeanne has been pushing me to bring a plus-one, but

CHAPTER ONE

the harder I worked to find someone to bring, the more pathetic I felt in trying to force it to happen.

I can be around Elijah for one night. It's not the end of the world...right?

"I'm sure," I say. "Besides, I need you to finish shooting the reception."

"I could drive up afterward. I should be able to get there before the first dance."

"Seriously, Chey. It's fine, I'll be fine."

Her gaze hardens, her eyes dark and full of disbelief, as if daring me to admit I am not okay.

I hold her gaze for a tense moment before she looks away. I met her shortly before graduation, so she has seen the chaos with Elijah firsthand. I don't blame her for being worried, but I'm genuinely confident I'll be fine.

I'm twenty-five years old; I *should* be perfectly fine with spending a single night at a wedding with my college boyfriend. Now ex-boyfriend.

"Okay..." Cheyeanne clears her throat as her eyes meet mine. "Just call me if that changes, okay?"

"I will, I promise."

I secure my camera bag, laptop, and external hard drive in the trunk and get into the car. The engine starts with a throaty purr, and I pull out of the parking lot. A tight knot begins to form in my stomach as soon as I merge onto I-71.

It's not very often that I venture back to Northeast Ohio. Despite having gone to college just south of Cleveland, I've been intentional in my neglect of returning this past year. The anxious feeling in the pit of my stomach is nothing new, but I need to push through it.

This is Jenna and Marcus we're talking about—two of my

best friends since college. I can put aside my own discomfort for a few hours if it means celebrating their love.

With each mile that passes, the sourness in my stomach begins to quell, and I hope it keeps away. However, as I pull up to the valet attendant and exit my car, my eyes lock on the one person I've spent all this time trying to forget. All my apprehension comes rushing back, and I can feel my insides tying themselves in knots again.

Elijah Hanas.

His back is turned to me, but I could recognize his familiar stature anywhere. The way he stands, the shape of his body, and his signature dark, wavy hair are all too familiar. My heart aches at the sight. My body aches to move closer to him and feel that sense of home I have grown so accustomed to, but my stomach churns with nausea and holds me back. He is wearing a navy-blue suit jacket that clings to his broad shoulders, and my chest tightens as I remember how I used to rest my head there.

I need to get to my hotel room; he'll see me soon enough.

TWO

KAT

Green vines cascade over the gazebo, weaving around the intricate columns like living strings of ivy. The grass beneath my stilettos is plush and damp, my heels sinking slightly into the earth, evidence of the shower that passed only an hour ago. White chairs line the aisle, each with a deep cushion of cream, atop which pink roses have been placed. At the end of the aisle, the altar is picturesque, standing out against the lush backdrop.

I attend a lot of weddings, but the decor is exceptional. It's hard to say if it is more the work of the venue than Jenna and Marcus, but I'd venture to say it is a combination of the two. Jenna, being an interior designer, has impeccable taste, and her soon-to-be-husband Marcus is an architect, so he isn't exactly without knowledge of what looks good.

They've always been a match made in heaven. From the day they met back in college, Jenna was absolutely smitten. I still remember the way her face lit up when she told me the following morning that she met him at a welcome weekend party our junior year at Kent State. They've been inseparable ever since, and while I try not to paint any couple as perfect, they're the closest I've ever witnessed in real life.

My gaze roams over the crowd of wedding guests, searching and pausing on the fourth row back. Our usual group of college friends is gathered there, and I smile in anticipation of catching up with them as soon as possible. But in the far-left corner, I spot Elijah, his dark eyes peering out from beneath his brow as he turns toward his girlfriend, Evelyn.

My heart sinks. While I want to talk to everyone, it would be best for me if I could avoid him, at least until the reception starts.

I slip into a seat toward the back, my eyes lingering on where he sits only a few rows in front of me.

Tonight is going to be long, and not in a good way.

In the background, the musicians softly tune their instruments, plucking strings as the quartet falls into harmony. The last few guests quickly make their way to their seats as a gentle tune begins to play, its melody weaving through the space like a whisper.

At first, the idea of not having a bridal party sounded weird to me. However, as we all stand and Jenna glides down the aisle, dressed in a flowing silk gown that looks like a second skin, her golden curls swept up into an elegant bun with a cascade of flowers against her neck, I begin to see her vision. She looks like a picture from another time, and she makes her entrance look effortless.

Tears mar the tops of Marcus's cheeks as his eyes lock on his bride, the love evident in his expression. His dark eyes are

CHAPTER TWO

consumed by her, the adoration on his face an emotion that could live on forever.

I wonder what it's like to be loved so unconditionally, to have someone stand by your side through everything life could throw your way...to know they won't leave you. I want that, even if I don't know how to get it.

My dating history is limited and admittedly kind of depressing. I had my high school boyfriend, whom, if we're being honest, I'm not sure I even loved—it was a suburb of Columbus, and he was one of the few guys in my grade that wasn't entirely intolerable.

And then there was Elijah. Of course, I had other opportunities over the years, but no one quite compared in my mind. We met in college and he has weaved in and out of my life ever since.

It sounds less tumultuous when you think about it like that—weaving in and out, as opposed to coming into my life and then leaving just as swiftly.

Jenna and Marcus wrote their own vows, something most people opt not to do. As she speaks, I can see the love in her eyes and the effort it costs her not to cry. Marcus looks at her with the same expression of raw emotion, though he must be used to this by now. He has a tenderness that is instantly discernible—he's just one of those people. I couldn't take my eyes off of them if I tried.

They exchange vows so intimately that you would think they're completely alone, causing a smile to spread across my lips.

"You may kiss your bride," the officiant says, grinning from ear to ear.

Marcus doesn't hesitate as he cups Jenna's chin in his

hand and pulls her to him. A string arrangement of what I assume to be "Happy" by Pharrell begins to play and my gaze lingers on the couple, following Marcus's hand as it slides into Jenna's. They walk back down the aisle, facing each other at the end of the chairs, and I know what is coming next.

It's their wedding day; they are allowed to kiss again.

As I follow the crowd into the building, I'm faced with the most beautiful reception area I've ever seen—and that is saying something, given my profession.

Entering the reception hall, I am enveloped by the warm and sweet aroma of calla lilies. The delicate scent mixes with the faint hint of vanilla from the wedding cake, causing my taste buds to tingle. The warm, pale gray walls suffuse the space with an airy vibe as the candles on the tables flicker against the bright base of the room. Opaque white draping curtains accent the floor-to-ceiling windows, contrasted by the elegant dark-wood chairs at the large circular tables scattered throughout the space.

I catch my reflection in the vintage mirror resting against the wall next to the entrance, where table numbers are written out against the glass. While there are over twenty tables, the room doesn't look even remotely cluttered.

Scanning the mirror, I find my name spelled out in a sprawling script under the table number.

CHAPTER TWO

Table Twelve
Aaron Ernest
Regina Armacost
Elijah Hanas
Evelyn Celeste
Jeffrey Brough
Brendan Wallace
Katarina Marritt
Tanner Adler

A sense of relief sets in as I see that Tanner has opted to go solo to the wedding as well. It's not necessarily a surprise—he has never been big on dating. However, that relief quickly washes away as I notice Elijah is also at my table. It is to be expected, but it doesn't make it any less awkward.

"Hey, Kat!" Tanner saunters over to my side, a sly grin on his lips and mischief sparkling in his big green eyes. While most of the men in attendance have opted for a black or navy suit, he has never been one for the conventional. His camel-colored tailored suit brings out the warmth in his brown hair, the color a near-perfect match, his hair just a shade darker.

"Hey, Tanner!"

"I see we're both stag tonight. Be my date?" he asks, leaning in with a cheeky wink.

I can't help but smile at his playfulness, my gaze catching the sprinkle of freckles across his nose and cheeks. Despite being a notorious flirt, Tanner has always been harmless and charming, with a boy-next-door appeal.

"Fine, but you're not getting lucky," I chuckle, and playfully bump into him with my hip.

He lets out an exaggerated groan in response. "Feelings,

Kat. I have feelings. You've wounded my heart," he jokes, placing a hand over his chest in mock despair.

"Something tells me you'll get over it, my sweet, sweet Tanner." I teasingly pinch his chin between my fingers, earning an infectious grin from Tanner. He towers over me, his tall frame somehow making him seem both intimidating and approachable at the same time. His grin widens and I can't help but smile back, feeling a sense of comfort and familiarity with him.

Tanner extends his elbow toward me, encouraging me to loop my hand through. I follow his lead as we move toward our table arm in arm.

A menagerie of vases consumes the center of the table, ranging from two inches to two feet tall. Each cylinder houses water and a floating tea light, the flame flickering off of the large, ornate gold pedestal vase in the center that overflows with pink and white roses with greenery mixed in. Each place setting has a clear charger plate with gold beading detail along the edges, adding an elegant touch to the tablescape. The table number card is propped within the roses, the calligraphy a shade of gold matching the vase.

"Milady." Tanner exaggeratedly pulls my chair away from the table, bowing down as he steps backward.

"Milord," I laugh as I take my seat, Tanner pushing the chair in behind me.

The rest of the table is empty, but quickly begins to fill as Brendan and Jeff approach, followed by Aaron and Regina. Aaron and Regina have been together since our junior year of college, but Brendan and Jeff didn't meet until last year. While we've known Brendan since undergrad, Jeff went to Ohio State.

CHAPTER TWO

Comfortable conversation sets in as everyone explains what has been going on in our respective lives. Aaron and Regina live here in Cleveland and are getting married in three months. I'm a bit surprised they haven't already gotten married, if we're being honest, but they were waiting until they bought a house. They've always been the most responsible of the group.

Brendan and Jeff recently moved to Columbus and live only about a half hour from me. I see them every so often and have grown to really love Jeff. He's good for Brendan; he grounds him. The mellow guy we see today is nothing compared to the oftentimes chaotic party boy we knew in college. It's amazing what the right person can do to level someone out.

Elijah and Evelyn approach and my breath catches in my throat.

His wavy dark brown hair has been styled impeccably and not a single strand is out of place. His tan olive complexion glows as the light of the sunset shimmers through the windows. Standing just over six feet tall, he towers over Evelyn, which is only more obvious as she leans into his side. Her long blonde hair falls fluidly across his lapel, the highlights so subtle I wonder if they might just be from the sun. Her blue eyes are reminiscent of my own, but they somehow look more natural on her.

I've met her a handful of times, but I know very little about her. Her grandfather was the Governor of Ohio in the late eighties, so she's a pretty buttoned-up person. I wouldn't be surprised if I learned that is how she's been since birth—groomed for a life in the political spotlight.

"Hello," Evelyn greets the table as she sits down, Elijah pushing her chair in behind her so she is snug with the table.

A cluster of greetings rings from around the table as everyone says hello to Evelyn and Elijah, but it isn't until he is seated that he says anything. He's awkward, more awkward than normal. He can be flustered when he's uncomfortable, but most of the time he's pretty even-keeled.

It's then that I notice it. The gleaming glow radiating off of Evelyn's ring finger as she reaches for her water glass. The ring is exactly as I would expect for such an elegant woman, a modest yet impressive round solitaire diamond centered on a classic, dainty silver band.

He has impeccable taste in rings and women, yet my stomach sours as his eyes meet mine.

"Congratulations," I choke out as his eyes linger on my own.

"Thanks," Elijah mumbles. There's a sadness in his expression that no one notices...except for me.

THREE

KAT

When they say you shouldn't drink on an empty stomach, they really mean that.

By the time appetizers begin circulating, I am three glasses of champagne deep. With every glimmer of light that bounces off that devastatingly perfect diamond, I take a massive gulp.

Engaged? He's engaged?!

How is he engaged?

Okay, I objectively know how these things work, but Elijah is engaged? This has got to be a joke. My heart races as dizziness overwhelms me.

Gulp.

"Are you okay?" Tanner leans over and whispers in my ear. We're over halfway through dinner and I've taken two bites, but boy are liquid calories really doing it for me tonight.

I take a sip of my champagne and feel it burn down my throat like a slow-moving fire that leaves behind a refreshing, fizzy sensation. It radiates from the roof of my mouth and lingers on my tongue as I swallow the last bit. The bubbly liquid swishes around in my stomach, providing me with a newfound dose of confidence, causing me to sit up a little straighter.

"I'm fine." I try to put on a brave face, but my voice cracks as I force out the lie. My eyes wander, unable to meet his inquisitive gaze as he awaits a more honest response.

"Kat—"

"I said I'm fine!" I pep up with a stab of my fork into the succulent piece of chicken on my plate. As I lift it to my lips, I find the smell is anything but pleasant. It should be—it objectively smells good—but the thought of eating is not appealing. Still, I force it past my lips, chew it twice, and swallow. "See, I'm fine."

Despite his obvious lack of faith in my words, Tanner backs off. However, I don't miss the way Elijah's eyes are locked on me. My reaction really shouldn't be a surprise to him; it hasn't been all that long since that night. If anything, I'd say it would be weird for me to suddenly be chill.

That and, well...I've never been the chill type.

Finally, as dinner comes to an end, Jenna and Marcus make their way out to the dance floor for their first dance. I'm just thankful that it gives everyone, including Elijah, something to look at other than the pathetic woe-is-me expression of his now halfway-to-plastered ex-girlfriend.

I turn in my seat to watch Jenna and Marcus and it brings me a short-lived sense of calm. Jenna really does look incredible—not that I would expect anything less from her. She's always been stunning. Her tight ringlets stay firmly in place in her updo as Marcus sways her to the music, the song unfamiliar but reminiscent of Frank Sinatra. Her tanned skin has a sheen to it, the lights dancing off the

CHAPTER THREE

shimmering body lotion to which she's been loyal since we were teenagers.

She looks like a dream, a picture of Aphrodite's elegance.

The song eventually comes to an end and, once they've had their respective parent dances, the guests are invited onto the dance floor.

I'm not given even a moment to think as Tanner drags me from my seat.

"No sulking. This is a wedding, with an open bar. We're having fun!" He twirls me as we reach the center of the dance floor, the fast-paced beat managing to reluctantly pull me from my wallowing.

At least for now.

Tanner pulls me to him as I try to lose myself in the moment. However, I still struggle to pry my eyes away from Elijah and Evelyn as they stand on the fringes of the dance floor, each holding a glass of champagne.

I thought I was past this. I thought I would be more okay seeing him with her again—but I made that assumption thinking that she was simply his girlfriend, like many other women I've seen him with over the years.

After a few songs, the tempo changes, shifting to a song I haven't heard in years. A song that once filled me with an overwhelming amount of emotion now has my stomach in knots of discomfort.

Hunter Hayes's familiar tune begins to play and Tanner wastes no time in pulling me to him, still not allowing me to slip away. We've danced together dozens of times over the years, usually inebriated, but always in good fun. However, I don't feel fun, and I think he can tell.

"What's going on?" he whispers against the shell of my ear as I try to match my movements with the tempo of the song.

My eyes lock with Elijah's across the dance floor as he holds Evelyn to him, the significance of the song seemingly only a concern of mine. Every symbol, every memory, every memento...I realize they all mean more to me than they ever did to him. How embarrassing it is to know that despite knowing all of that, I still ache for him like I did at twenty years old.

"Nothing," I say, my voice cracking.

Tanner grasps the bunched fabric at the back of my dress tightly. "Katarina..."

"Please drop it. I'm fine, let it go."

And to my surprise, he does. He's never been the type to push a sensitive topic or make me uncomfortable. But I don't miss the disappointment in his eyes as I shoot him down.

I count the seconds until the song is over, at which point I gracefully exit the dance floor. Well, perhaps not exactly graceful—more like a half-sprint to the bar, then out to the garden. I need air and a fresh glass of champagne.

As soon as the crisp air hits my skin, bumps spread across it like wildfire. It feels unseasonably chilly for July, but the lake effect can be a bitch, I guess.

"What are you doing out here?" A phantom voice travels from behind me. Unfortunately, I'd know that voice anywhere.

"Getting air." I pull my champagne flute to my lips and take a long, drawn-out sip. This doesn't seem to sit well with Elijah as he slides his fingers over mine, gently grasping the crystal stem and tugging the glass away from my mouth.

"I think you need a break, Kat."

CHAPTER THREE

"And I think you need to leave me alone." It comes out far snippier than I intend it to, but I don't have the wherewithal to offer pleasantries right now.

He seems to get the hint, but his silence only lingers for a few seconds. "I didn't plan for you to find out like that..."

I scoff, earning me a glare. "How exactly did you think I would find out, since you didn't tell me?"

"Honestly? I assumed Jenna would have told you."

A few years ago, that would have made sense, but Jenna and I don't talk most days. She is still one of my best friends, but our relationship is not what it used to be. It's comfortable, and while I would like to think she would have told me, she's also been planning a wedding.

"When did it happen?" I glare down at the ground, the blades of misty grass sticking together with a glistening glow.

"About a month ago."

"You've been engaged for a month and didn't think to shoot me a text? You knew I'd be here."

"Well, the world doesn't revolve around you. Letting you know wasn't at the top of my priorities." Something in the look I give him causes him to double back. "That was shitty to say. I'm sorry."

"Yeah," I say as I reach toward him and yank my drink from his grasp, my glare not breaking, "it was."

The sound of crickets chirping and mayflies humming fills the stale air between us, but we don't move. The silence is all-consuming, but it's only because nothing needs to be said. We know each other too well now. It's not uncomfortable; it's just...sad.

Everything it could have been, everything we once were, all swirling in the air in a breath-catching haze.

A biting shiver runs down my arms as a gust of wind picks up. Elijah tugs at his sleeves, the unerring gentleman I've always known even amidst this awkwardness.

"Don't." I hold up my hand and he stops. "I'm going to head up to my room. My head is starting to hurt. I'll just text Jenna and let her know why I left."

He nods silently and walks alongside me toward the French doors leading back into the hotel.

"Can I walk you up?" he mumbles.

That feels like playing with fire, but I'd be lying if I said I didn't ache for more time with him. I know after tonight I probably won't see him for a while, so his mere presence feels in short supply.

"If you must."

We silently pass the reception hall and head toward the elevator, which stands open next to a long table filled with chocolates and flowers. The sound of my heels against the tile floor is loud in the silent space as the doors close behind us.

The elevator dings as it reaches the third floor and I step out into the hallway. I anticipate Elijah heading back down, but I'm surprised to find him tailing my steps.

"I'm not a child—I can find my hotel room without assistance," I say, struggling with the key card.

He moves toward me, forcing me to step to the side before he takes my card and swipes it, opening the door for me.

"Thanks," I mumble as I push through the doorway, stumbling slightly. When I'm only about a foot into the room, he grabs my arm.

"Kat..."

With every fiber of my being, I try to avoid looking at him, but he holds me in place until I do. "Believe it or not, I do care.

CHAPTER THREE

I'm sorry I didn't tell you; I wasn't sure how. We didn't exactly leave things on great terms."

I think back to the last time I saw him. I'd do anything to change how things went for us. When I fell in love with him all those years ago, I never would have imagined we'd end up here.

Twenty-five and him engaged to someone else.

It was supposed to be us.

I simply nod, which seems to encourage him enough to release my arm.

"Get some rest, okay?" he says softly before backing away, leaving me in the doorway and disappearing down the dimly lit hallway. I watch as he enters the elevator before I close my hotel room door.

How the hell did we get here?

Kicking off my heels, I revel in the feeling of my feet against the carpet, the ache of the day setting in despite being dulled by the alcohol.

I trudge to the bathroom, hastily scrubbing off my eyeliner and mascara with a warm cloth. I run my toothbrush over my teeth, rinsing away the day before climbing into bed. Pulling back the white duvet, I sink into the cloud-soft mattress, cocooned in silence for a few moments until the sound of laughter and music floats through the wall from the room next door. Rolling my eyes, I throw an arm over my face, trying to ignore the fact that it is only 10:00 PM.

Don't these people have any respect for other guests?

As I lie in bed staring up at the ceiling, I find myself replaying the day's events. I knew it would suck, but I didn't anticipate the level of anguish I would feel seeing Elijah again.

He holds so much power over me even though we lead entirely separate lives now.

I hope one day that goes away, at least in some capacity.

The sound of pounding bass and boisterous laughter somehow gets louder, drifting from the wall behind my bed and making it nearly impossible to hear anything else.

I sigh and grab the blanket, wrapping it tight around me as I walk out onto the balcony. The garden below is illuminated by a few small lights, but beyond that lies only darkness. The moon is hidden behind a thick bank of clouds, but stars twinkle all around, tiny pinpricks in an otherwise black sky.

The wind pushes the clouds away, revealing the full moon. Its milky light shines above me as I look up, imbuing me with a sense of peace and comfort. Maybe the full moon is why today has been so weird. I'd like to think it is something as simple as that, but it's never been simple.

Elijah and I were never simple. From the day I met him, it was messy and painful, yet invigorating and all-consuming.

Goodness—what I'd give to be able to go back. Redo it, do it differently, go back to the very first night...

Haven't we all thought that once or twice? Wished to have the ability to go back and make better or different choices?

I sway as I squint at the night sky. A tiny streak of light pierces the darkness, streaking across the velvet canvas of stars before disappearing into the horizon.

Weird.

ENCHANTED

Enchanted
Taylor Swift

3:10 -2:43

| | Enchanted
Taylor Swift | ⌃ |
|---|---|---|
| ▶ | I Think I Fell In Love Today
Kelsea Ballerini | 02:32 |
| ▶ | HEARTFIRST
Kelsea Ballerini | 03:06 |
| ▶ | Willow
Taylor Swift | 03:33 |
| ▶ | needy
Kelsea Ballerini | 03:11 |
| ▶ | Lover
Taylor Swift | 03:41 |
| ▶ | Renegade
Big Red Machine, Taylor Swift | 04:13 |
| ▶ | hoax
Taylor Swift | 03:39 |
| ▶ | The Moment I Knew
Taylor Swift | 04:44 |

FOUR

FIVE YEARS AGO

KAT

The sun filters in through the window in the worst possible way as the pounding in my head increases in pace and intensity. It feels like I'm being whacked in the back of the head with a drumstick. I don't know why I continue to do this to myself, but I've hardly ever been super smart when it comes to my alcohol consumption when out with friends.

Light, sharp as a knife, slants through the blinds and illuminates the room. The new day bursts into the space, yelling a clear sign of its arrival. Every cell in my body aches for the comfort of sleep; my eyes hurt from trying to adjust to the brightness. The constant spinning has me ready to heave off the side of the bed, the slightest movement teetering me a little too close to revisiting last night's dinner.

When my queasiness becomes insufferable, I reach for the trash can next to the bed, thankful that I had the foresight to put it there before I laid down last night. I continue feeling around until my hand bumps into the plastic bin beneath all

CHAPTER FOUR

the blankets and throw pillows. I groan before I pitch forward and barf much like Jenna did freshman year in the middle of the Manchester Hall common room.

I heave and I heave, the choices of last night a blur amidst the morning haze.

Wait.

I'm not in my hotel room.

While I'm not sure where I am, it feels weirdly familiar and uncomfortably quiet. I wipe my mouth as I gaze around the room, the space feeling eerily sterile, but with clear attempts at making it feel like home peppered throughout. The cream walls barely poke through the collage of posters littering the space—everything from Taylor Swift's *1989* world tour poster to a large print from one of my favorite photographers.

The room looks exactly how it did five years ago, right down to the unmade bed and pile of textbooks on the floor.

Overwhelming panic consumes me as I come to the realization that I am back in my past self's body.

My heart races uncontrollably, pounding against my rib cage with each beat, the sound reverberating in my ears. My body shakes violently, making it difficult to take a deep breath and steady myself. The world around me seems to spin out of control as I desperately try to make sense of this confusing and disorienting situation.

I'm in my junior dorm room.

How the hell am I back at McDowell Hall? There is no way this is physically possible. Not only was I a full forty minutes from Kent last night, but I can't imagine I stumbled upon a dorm room at Beall-McDowell with the exact setup Jenna and I created five years ago.

I gaze around the space, the door connecting my bedroom to the shared bathroom a welcome salvation as I feel last night's choices crawling back up my throat with vengeance. I dart toward the toilet, landing on the tile floor with less than a second to spare.

Time blurs. Through long passes of heaving and gagging, I faintly hear the sound of a door clicking shut from the direction of Jenna's bedroom.

Memories of last night in the future and last night in the past start to flow together, images of dancing with Tanner at a historic hotel in Cleveland meshing messily with faint memories of playing Slap the Bag at one of the sorority annexes with Jenna's friend Molly. It's a bizarre medley of past and future, and yet they seem just as recent as one another despite being five years apart.

The old hinge on the door creaks as Jenna enters the bathroom from her side of the space.

"Are you feeling okay?" she asks before reaching for a makeup wipe off the counter, only waiting a few seconds before she continues her train of thought. "It's probably all the sugar from the wine last night. We probably should stop playing Slap the Bag—I think we're getting too old."

The age-old game of chugging from a bag of cheap wine taken out of a boxed receptacle was among mine and Jenna's favorite games to play on a Friday night. Well, *is*, I guess.

For a moment I think about pretending to be okay, but instead opt for honesty. "No, I feel like shit. You're probably right," I mumble as the taste of bile crawls back up my throat.

Jenna rushes toward me at the exact moment my face plunges back into the toilet bowl, her hands cupping my long brown hair in a ball at the base of my scalp.

CHAPTER FOUR

We continue like this for about ten minutes before my back is flush with the wall, the cold bite of the tile a welcome comfort, the sweat from the exertion cooling against my skin. I've always been a morning puker and I hate it. I still have no idea why I continue to break every rule of drinking.

Don't overindulge in sugary beverages, don't mix beer and liquor, don't mix beer and wine, don't mix dark and clear liquor... So many rules, none of which I've ever diligently adhered to. I can't tell if it's the severe dehydration from drinking last night or the fact that my head hasn't stopped spinning since waking up somehow in the past, but I clearly need to get that under control if I stand any chance at not having Jenna think I'm batshit insane right now.

"How did you get home last night?" Jenna asks as she hands me a bottle of water from the counter, one I faintly remember setting there as I stumbled in last night.

"I—" I think for a moment, the memories a haze. "I walked back to campus."

"By yourself? Kat, that isn't safe."

"I'm fine, aren't I?"

Jenna seems to find this response annoying. She rolls her eyes.

"What did you get up to after I left last night?" I raise a brow, the implication of her sneaking back into our dorm in the morning not lost on me.

"I...met a guy," Jenna replies as she grins from ear to ear.

Memories of what has yet to happen are getting hazier and hazier as the moments pass by, but I'm still aware enough to remember that last night was Friday of welcome weekend. The night she met Marcus.

"A guy, huh?"

"Yes, and he's perfect." She plops onto the ground in front of the shower, a dreamy look in her eye that, up until Marcus, I had never really seen. "He's in Lambda. I don't know how I've never met him; I feel like we end up there like every weekend."

"Does he live in the house?"

"No, he has an apartment off campus. It was only a block from the Zeta annex, so we walked back there."

I raise a brow as I grin, pulling the water bottle to my lips. Knowing how things go with them only adds to the joy of seeing my best friend so unabashedly enamored. They're the real deal, but something tells me I can't tell her that. Space-time continuum and all that—that's what it's called, right?

"So...he was good, then?" I laugh.

"He was *incredible*... Lambda is having a party tonight, actually—we should go."

The memory of that night used to be seared into my brain, but the moment she mentions it is the exact second that I completely forget everything that happens. Is that how this is going to go? I know I should remember more than I do. I know I meet Elijah tonight, and the idea of that has me giddy...but I'll care a bit more later. Right now I'm just trying not to hurl.

"I'm down." I groan as I stand up from my spot on the floor, reaching for my toothbrush to hopefully rid my mouth of this god-awful taste. "But first, I need food. I haven't eaten since before we went out last night."

"Bagels?" Jenna says as she reaches for her own toothbrush.

"Obviously."

CHAPTER FOUR

We clean ourselves up minimally, but find ourselves dragging our feet, Jenna's sweatpants roughly tucked into UGG boots and mine grazing the tops of my slippers as we walk from our dorm building to the student center. We could have gone to a closer dining hall, but the food-court-style setup of the student center hits differently than yet another breakfast platter from Rosie's.

Let's be real—Rosie's is best eaten at 2:00 AM.

We step into the student center, and our noses are instantly filled with the scent of fresh-baked bagels. The line at the chain bagel restaurant is almost out the door, but I persevere in pursuit of a warm everything bagel smothered with cream cheese.

It is almost 1:00 PM, but on a Saturday in college, time is simply a state of mind and it is considered morning in my mind until I eat breakfast.

As we get to the front of the line, I'm disappointed to see that they are fresh out of everything bagels. It's not an uncommon issue, as it's one of the more popular offerings, but you would think it would drive them to make more. I opt for a sesame bagel instead, still covered in extra cream cheese.

The service is prompt and we're quickly handed our boxes. We find seats over by the sprawling floor-to-ceiling windows that look out over the "K."

The "K" is the not-particularly-creative nickname for Risman Plaza, the area between the student center and the main library on campus. The plaza is made up of a large concrete area with a giant K built into the brick, the Kent State University fountain, and a large grass section where students often lay out blankets in the spring to study for finals. It's always been one of my favorite areas on campus.

Jenna squeals, causing me to jump in my seat. My gaze darts to her, finding her staring off toward the other side of the food court over by the bookstore. Within seconds I realize why she's excited as I spot Marcus waiting by the bathrooms.

"Marcus!" Jenna yells, and he turns our way.

FIVE

KAT

Marcus looks our way without hesitation, his warm brown eyes reflecting the sparkle of adoration in Jenna's. I've never known another man who has such unadulterated admiration for a woman he was interested in from the get-go.

He strides confidently toward us, disregarding whoever he had been waiting for in the bathroom. His pace increases and a broad grin spreads across his face, exposing a charming dimple in his left cheek.

"Hey, you." He winks as he approaches Jenna.

I've seen a lot of guys over the years blow girls off the morning after. Not Marcus.

He pulls Jenna into a tight embrace, her head cradled in the crook of his neck. Her hands gently grasp his arms and she looks up at him with a smile that lights up her eyes, her joy mirrored in his expression.

"Marcus Delgado. I'm guessing you're Kat?" He turns toward me and extends his hand to shake mine, the formality of it all feeling weird.

"Nice to meet you, Marcus—yes, I'm Kat. Um, Katarina Marritt."

"Great to meet you, Kat," Marcus says with a wide grin. "Sorry for stealing your roommate last night." He chuckles as he reaches up to ruffle the hair atop Jenna's head. Her perfect curls from last night now lay in a tangled mess of a bun.

Unlike Jenna and me, Marcus looks immaculate. How men can wake up after a night of drinking and still look like the picture of health is beyond me. His deep curls are styled perfectly, yet still manage to look effortlessly tousled in a way that screams *"I didn't try too hard, it just comes naturally."*

Last night is weird to think about. While objectively I know I was at their wedding, the more time that goes by, the less real it feels. I distinctly remember walking back to our dorm last night despite having memories of an entirely different evening. I remember throwing my shoes under my desk and cuddling up next to the trash can, but I also remember Elijah walking me back to my hotel room.

It's the most bizarre feeling.

I also remember Jenna ditching me at the party, but I'm not going to turn that into a thing. In the grand scheme of things, it truly doesn't matter.

The scent of Marcus's cologne wafts subtly through the air as he shifts slightly on his feet, seemingly at ease despite his late-night escapades. Where Jenna and I both look like the walking dead, our sickly pale skin from the night of drinking is only polarized by the tanned tone of Marcus's, his pearly white smile present to provide even more contrast.

The three of us chat for a while, discussing the courses we intend to take this semester as well as our plans for tonight. The Saturday before classes start always has some of the best

CHAPTER FIVE

parties. The house parties tend to go a little harder than they should, while the bars tend to be a little livelier.

"What did you guys get?" Marcus asks as he peeks down at the empty paper box in my hand that previously housed a bagel.

"Oh, we got Einstein's. Needed the bread to soak up all that liquor from last night," Jenna laughs, and Marcus welcomes her amusement with a chuckle of his own.

Despite the conversation including all of us, I don't miss the way Marcus's eyes don't leave Jenna the entire time. It's adorable.

If only they knew.

My attention drifts away from them as they continue their borderline gag-inducing flirting, and that is when I notice him.

Elijah.

Gorgeous waves of dark brown hair move toward us. My stomach is jumbled in knots as he approaches, but I don't miss the way he doesn't look at me.

Actually, I'm not even sure he's walking toward Marcus at all.

I watch as Elijah's tall frame shifts toward the Chinese food place next to Einstein's Bagels. He settles into the long line.

While I try not to let the disappointment of him not coming over here show too obviously, I completely miss Tanner as he approaches Marcus. In a swift and unexpected move, Tanner punches Marcus in the stomach, causing him to double over in pain.

Hunched over, gasping for air, Marcus growls through clenched teeth, "What the hell, man?" His fists ball at his sides, knuckles turning white.

"That was a dick move this morning," Tanner laughs, the mask of his outrage slipping.

It becomes evident what previously looked like a fight about to break out in the student center is just a weird game between friends. I let out a nervous chuckle and relax my shoulders.

"I didn't do shit." Marcus bites back a laugh as he continues to force air into his lungs.

"Bullshit," Tanner responds. "Now she won't stop blowing up my phone. All because *you* wouldn't shut up about how in love I was with her. You and I both know I don't have shit for feelings for Rebecca. She knows that—well, she did…until you decided it would be funny to get her hopes up and make me look like the bad guy."

"Who's Rebecca?" I ask.

Tanner glances at me and his expression changes instantly. He grins before extending his hand and saying, "Absolutely no one important. I'm Tanner Adler."

"Kat." I grin up at him as I take his hand.

"Katarina, actually," Marcus chimes in, finally finding enough air to string together a sentence.

"*Katarina.*" Tanner chuckles, his tone warm and teasing. His grip on my hand tightens and I can feel his eyes studying my face.

"Just…Kat." I laugh nervously, brushing a strand of hair behind my ear. My family always calls me Katarina, but with friends and in social settings, I go by Kat. I can't control what my family calls me, but I've never liked my name.

"Kat it is." He squeezes my hand one last time before letting it go. I don't miss the way the warmth leaving feels…

CHAPTER FIVE

bad. His eyes linger on me for longer than I anticipate—I can't remember how this happened before.

I'll be honest, I don't remember meeting Tanner at all. So much of my memory about today revolved around meeting Elijah later at the party. But as I stand here with this boy who I know will grow to be a lifelong friend, I realize there are gaps in my memory from today that I can't explain.

I met two of my closest friends today, yet all I remember in five years is Elijah.

"Are you guys going tonight?" Marcus asks, pulling Tanner's attention away from me.

"Yes, we are!" Jenna's voice is significantly more enthusiastic than it was minutes ago—before Marcus came over.

I almost start questioning what they're talking about...and then I remember.

The Lambda party.

The party I meet Elijah at. Suddenly my enthusiasm matches Jenna's.

"Sounds great," Marcus says as he smiles down at Jenna, clearly not that concerned with my attendance.

Tanner's usually bright and wide smile is missing, replaced with a tight-lipped frown. His usual exuberance for parties is nowhere to be seen as he stands next to his friend. Marcus elbows him in the ribs, causing Tanner to grab his side on instinct.

"Rude," he mumbles.

"Gotta rally, man. I don't care that you didn't get much sleep."

"I didn't get much sleep because Rebecca wouldn't leave this morning. Do you remember why she wouldn't leave this morning?" The glare he shoots Marcus has me suppressing a laugh, enjoying the tension between them.

"Touché." Marcus then presses his lips to Jenna's cheek before whispering something inaudible to her. She simply nods her head before looking over at me.

We exchange pleasantries and the guys disappear toward the bookstore, Tanner going on and on about how he needs to try to get his hands on a used copy of a book for his International Marketing class.

"So?" Jenna smacks my arm with a cheesy grin.

"What?"

"Tanner," she says as she rolls her eyes.

"What about Tanner?" While I know where she's going with this, I can't for the life of me figure out why.

"He's cute."

"There are lots of cute guys on campus…"

"Yeah, but *this* cute guy seems interested."

"One: no, he's not. Two: *I'm* not interested." I glare at her and a pause settles between us.

She finally cracks. A huff passes her lips. "Ugh, fine. One day we will find you a guy that actually keeps your interest for longer than two seconds."

Little does she know that is exactly what is going to happen.

Tonight.

SIX

KAT

"Have you seen my pink liquid lipstick?" Jenna's voice carries from our shared bathroom with a franticness the situation doesn't call for. We've been trying to get out the door for half an hour, but Jenna's nervous energy keeps pulling us back inside.

I gnaw at my thumbnail as I stare down at my phone, sitting on the floor in front of my full-body mirror, scrolling through the pixelated photos from last semester littering my photo gallery. A short video of Jenna doing a keg stand during a homecoming weekend Kegs and Eggs party last year pulls a chuckle from my lungs.

Without looking up from my phone, I yell, "Didn't you have it last night?"

I remember because we both wore the lipstick and Jenna threw it in her crossbody bag for us to touch up throughout the night. It proved to be ineffective, though, as Jenna quickly disappeared from the party. Therefore, I was left walking back to our dorm with the *worst* butthole lips in existence.

Absolutely *no one* likes butthole lips.

"Oh shit, you're right!" Jenna says excitedly as she steps into my room, wearing a romper and white sneakers.

I'm so glad we abandoned the idea of wearing heels out after freshman year. Was it cute? For sure. Did it hurt worse than period cramps? Pretty damn close.

Jenna pulls the sleek tube of pink out of her bag and stands behind me, applying the bright hue with precision. The color has always looked incredible on her, the vibrant shade causing the golden strands of color in her eyes to become more obvious.

"Do you want some?" She holds out the tube, gesturing for me to take it.

"No, I think I'm going to just wear a clear gloss tonight."

"Planning on making out with someone, are we?" She smiles from ear to ear. I should be asking why she's choosing to wear a bright pink lip that is only moderately transfer-proof, but I resist the question.

"Doesn't hurt to be prepared," I say as I bite back a grin. Truth be told, I'm hopeful.

Everything from before is hazy. The longer I'm present, the harder it becomes to remember details. I remember that I meet Elijah tonight, but outside of that, everything is a blur.

Will I eventually forget the future completely? I hope not. I want that knowledge.

"Oh my god, you met a guy!" Jenna squeals.

How do I tell her I haven't met a guy, but I *will* meet a guy? That today is the last day I'll be this person?

Tonight I don't just meet a guy. I meet *the* guy. The one that changes everything.

The kind of love that they write sonnets about; the kind of

CHAPTER SIX

love that consumes you so much that you'd do anything to hold it in your fingers.

Elijah Hanas, my person.

"No...but I'm hoping to."

She doesn't appear convinced, but as she shrugs and turns around to grab shoes from her room, I know she accepts my answer.

We take the elevator down to the main floor of McDowell Hall, not wanting to walk any more than we already have to with the impending trek across campus. Deciding to live in the Twin Towers—which is just a shorthand way of referring to Beall and McDowell Halls—was a choice made based on one thing. It's not the fanciest dorm on campus, nor the most conveniently placed—it's not even the cheapest—but they are the only two dorm buildings on campus in which upperclassmen can have alcohol in their room.

We venture out into the still-humid late summer air and instantly pass a group of freshman girls, who are no doubt also walking to a party. The difference is, while Jenna and I are wearing more reasonable shoes, they're all wearing heels. They'll learn by second semester. We all have to do it; builds character.

"Cute dress!" Jenna says with a smile to a girl wearing a blue minidress with a cutout under the bust.

"Thanks!" The nameless girl looks down at her dress, her self-conscious slouch straightening with confidence.

Jenna has a way of doing that—making you feel confident with a few short words.

As we approach the Kent State fountain, the sound of splashing water grows louder. We see a young man, wearing

THE VERY FIRST NIGHT

an oversized T-shirt with Greek letters that are barely legible, stumbling through the knee-deep water.

Jenna calls out to him from a safe distance, her voice laced with amusement and concern. "It's a bit early to be that drunk, don't you think?"

The guy scoffs and attempts to climb out of the fountain, but his movements are unsteady and comical. His words come out slurred as he denies being drunk, only to be interrupted by a loud belch.

"All right, big guy, you're not drunk."

This seems to appease him, his bloodshot eyes squinting and crinkling at the corners. Pride radiates off him like heat from a fire as he believes he's successfully deceived us.

Drunk guys are weird.

We continue walking.

"Do you plan on seeing Marcus tonight?" I ask.

Jenna tries to play it cool, but she's never been great at playing anything cool. "Maybe," she sighs before allowing herself to express what she's really thinking. "He texted me twenty minutes ago. He's going to be at the Lambda party!"

The squeal she expels would be irritating if I wasn't so damn happy for her.

"He seems like a really good guy." Truth be told, I shouldn't know that. Actually, I'm not sure I *do* know that at this point. Everything is such a blur.

"Isn't he?!"

The group of freshmen from before manages to catch up with us and we watch as they huddle together, doing a terrible job of stashing the flasks they have tucked in their necklines.

"Freshman year feels like eons ago, doesn't it?" Jenna seems almost...reminiscent.

CHAPTER SIX

I can't help but laugh at her words, because that is the understatement of the year. "You have no idea."

Though it was supposed to be a closed party, we can see the house is filled with bodies from wall to wall. The brother manning the door is being loose with the list in his hand.

"Name?"

"Jenna Hannover and Kat Marritt."

I guess Jenna gave Marcus our names to add to the list. The guy seems pleased, but something tells me he's letting in any girl he deems minorly appealing anyway.

Lambda Rho has been my and Jenna's go-to place when we go out since the middle of our freshman year. It can be chaotic on a party night, but we feel comfortable here. How we went two years without meeting the guys, I don't know.

As if he can hear my thoughts, Marcus arrives by Jenna's side, slinging his arm around the back of her neck and pulling her into a hug.

Jenna melts into him with ease and little concern for the chaos surrounding them. She lifts onto her toes and presses a kiss to Marcus's cheek, then whispers something to him—knowing Jenna, I probably don't want to know what.

"I'm going to go grab a drink," I yell over the music, wanting to give them privacy but also genuinely wanting a drink.

The bass from the stereo nearly shakes the room as the guy behind the DJ table works to keep the energy up. The party is mostly centered around the spacious living room with a vaulted ceiling. People stand shoulder-to-shoulder as they chat amongst themselves, making it nearly impossible to locate a beverage.

After searching for what feels like forever, I find the

kitchen. I groan when I realize that this isn't a regular old keg party. Where I was hoping to find a big metal barrel, there is something else—in the place of the designated keg is a large storage container filled to the brim with a mystery beverage. The smell of alcohol mixed with fruit juices and pop wafts through the air, indicating that this party will be one wild night.

Jungle Juice.

Equal parts gross and effective.

"Can I buy you a drink?" An all-too-familiar voice carries from behind me. Instantly, it makes me smile.

I roll my eyes, turning around to find Tanner grinning down at me. "The drinks are free."

"Fine, if you want to be, like, a scientist about it." He chuckles as he snatches two red plastic cups from the stool beside the transparent container, which is filled almost to the brim with the unknown red liquid. He holds it out to me, seemingly posing a question.

"Sure, why the hell not?" I chuckle.

He holds our cups and dips them into the murky liquid before handing me the cleaner-looking one. I watch in disgust as he casually plucks a fruit fly out of his cup and flicks it to the side. My face scrunches up in revulsion at the sight.

"What? Extra protein."

"You're gross," I respond with a laugh.

"You wound me." He grins as he lifts the cup to his lips. "So, you're Jenna's roommate, eh?"

"Are you Marcus's?"

"Oh, ha—no. Marcus doesn't *have* roommates. Too dedicated to school. I live in the house," Tanner says as he

CHAPTER SIX

waves his hands around. "Everything the light touches is mine."

"Did you just quote *The Lion King*?"

"Oh please, it was a paraphrase. It would be absurd to quote *The Lion King* to a cute girl on our first date."

My brows raise nearly to my hairline at his words. "Date, huh?"

"If you want it to be."

"I'm not looking for anything right now," I respond awkwardly. It's not *not* a lie; it's a partial truth at best. I'm not looking, because I'm about to find it.

It's not that I don't find Tanner attractive. Hell, for a brief moment I find myself considering his words. However, it would be a waste of time.

It's Elijah—it has to be Elijah.

"I hear ya," Tanner says before swallowing another sip of Jungle Juice. "Friends, then?"

"Friends."

"Well, friend...how is your night?"

"We just got here. Jenna and me, I mean. She—" I nod my head in her direction, finding her pressed up against a wall with Marcus's tongue down her throat. "—is busy, apparently." I chuckle as I scratch the back of my neck.

Tanner's eyes follow my gaze, and a much more boisterous laugh escapes him at the sight.

"Classy."

At first I think it's Tanner responding, but my heart instantly crawls up into my throat as my eyes venture upward. Instead of Tanner's adorable green eyes, I am met with dark, piercing eyes and a cocky smirk.

Elijah.

My heart races as he extends his hand. I shake it, feeling a jolt of electricity at the simple contact.

"I don't believe we've met. I'm Elijah," he introduces himself confidently.

His strong grip makes me feel off-balance, like my whole world is tipping toward him. My stomach is swarmed instantly by a kaleidoscope of butterflies, the tiny wings pushing me closer and closer to vomiting.

Or maybe that's the Jungle Juice—it's hard to tell.

"And you are?" Elijah's grin lingers on his lips, but his eyes are filled with confusion.

I stand there, his hand still in mine, but words escape me. "Huh?"

"I didn't get your name." He nearly has to yell over the music as he leans toward me, the familiar tropical yet musky scent of his cologne filling the air around me.

"Kat—Katarina. Katarina is my name, but people call me Kat." My anxiety spills out as I stumble over my words.

"Nice to meet you…Kat, Katarina."

On instinct I think to correct him, then notice the amused expression on his lips. He finds my nervousness entertaining.

"Nice to meet you too."

I don't miss the way his hand is still holding onto mine.

SEVEN

KAT

A loud crash reverberates through the house, drawing everyone's attention toward the DJ booth. My gaze snaps to the source of the noise, my heart rate quickening in anticipation.

Tanner stands tall amidst the chaos, his arm tight around the waist of a petite blonde. He skillfully pulls her out of harm's way as two guys start throwing punches and screaming at each other about a foot in front of the DJ booth. The music screeches to a halt as the DJ jumps over the table, attempting to pull the two men apart. Tanner pushes the girl behind him, urging her to go toward the kitchen as he attempts to intervene alongside the DJ. He holds the taller of the two men back as the DJ attempts to wrangle the other, arms swinging haphazardly as one of them tries to land a blow on the other guy's jaw.

The sounds of breaking glass and thuds are drowned out by Elijah's voice as his lips ghost past my ear, pulling my attention back into the moment.

"Do you want to go outside?"

Despite my being nosey in nature, I want to be alone with him more.

"Sure," I respond, my voice barely audible amidst the chaos.

Still holding my hand, Elijah begins to guide me to the door, his skin somehow cold yet biting into my flesh as if my hand might combust into flames.

He leads me out the front door and we veer off into the yard. The further from the house we get, the quieter the air around us seems, a combination of walking away from the chaos inside and finally being alone with him after the anticipation all day.

Since waking up here this morning, I've been aching to talk to him—to talk to *this* version of Elijah, the young man who so easily managed to hold my heart in his hands before life made it too hard for either of us to withstand.

His hand doesn't leave mine and he intertwines our fingers, guiding me toward the worn picnic table set up in the side yard. Water pools atop the sun-bleached wood, but Elijah lets go of my hand to pull his zip-up hoodie off to wipe away the stagnant water and lay it out as something dry for us both to sit on.

We sit down in near-silence, the pitch-black air cut through only by the voices and music in the distance, the fight from a few minutes ago long gone and replaced with laughter.

"So, Kat," he says as he bumps his arm against mine. The contact radiates through me, causing goosebumps to form a blanket over my skin.

I don't think I've ever been as nervous as I am right now.

The fading memories of what is to come for us linger. The

CHAPTER SEVEN

exact events are a distant blur, but the emotions hang around just the same.

I've never loved anyone like I love Elijah—or *will* love Elijah.

Part of me wishes he had memories too...well, not memories, but at the very least I wish he was aware of what I eventually become to him. Right now, as he stares at what I assume he sees as a complete stranger, a nearly inconsequential meeting at a party, I sit here lost in a sea of emotion as I fumble for the right words. Trying to find the words to prevent everything—every bad thing that will happen—from happening.

Even if I can't remember what those things are anymore.

"So...Elijah." I attempt to match his flirty tone, but my voice comes out shaky. I can't tell if he notices, nor do I know if I want him to.

If I told him that I somehow went back in time to save our future relationship, we very well might never happen, in part because of all that butterfly effect stuff, but more than anything because I'd look like a raging psychopath.

"Where are you from?" he asks.

"Columbus...well, technically Dublin, but it's easier to say Columbus."

He gasps and says in a joking, mocking tone, "Blasphemous. *I'm* from Columbus. Dublin isn't Columbus."

"Seriously?" I laugh.

"Completely—like, thirty minutes from Dublin."

"Small world."

"The smallest." He lets out a soft chuckle. "Why Kent? Why not one of the tons of other universities in Ohio?"

"Why *not* Kent?"

To be honest, I didn't have a big reason for coming to Kent. I simply toured the campus my junior year of high school, liked it, and was able to get enough financial aid to cover the tuition.

"Fair enough."

"Why did you choose Kent?" I ask.

I don't miss the way his expression drops at the question. "Oh, uh, my dad went here. Actually, I'm a legacy." Elijah points to the fraternity house. "It just always made sense, I guess, to go to Kent. Look who had just as boring of an answer." He forces out a laugh as he bumps his arm into mine again.

We quickly fall into comfortable conversation. My stomach thankfully settles, the anxiety a distant memory as we laugh in near-darkness. Elijah tells me a story about some ridiculous stunt that Marcus pulled freshman year that involved the roof above the back patio of the house and a skateboard.

My face grows flush as I gasp for air, the amusement at the absurdity of the story a welcome moment of levity for both of us.

"So, Elijah. What's your major?" I ask before pulling my almost-empty cup of Jungle Juice to my lips.

"Poli-Sci with a Pre-Law minor."

"What do you want to do?"

"Oh, uh—I want to go into politics."

"That's really cool!" I've never known anyone who was in politics. However, as silence overtakes us, I find myself questioning if that was an appropriate response.

"You don't know who my dad is, do you?" His expression is reserved, tentative, and—dare I say—a little nervous.

CHAPTER SEVEN

"Should I?"

"My name is Elijah Hanas." He stares at me as if he is anticipating me to have an "*Aha!*" moment, but I don't.

"Okay..."

His confused expression from before is nothing compared to the evident amusement on his face now. "My dad is Mike Hanas."

"Am I supposed to know who that is?"

"Well...yes...you probably should." He releases a full-bellied laugh. "He is the Governor of Ohio."

I feel...so stupid, even though I don't follow politics.

How the hell didn't I know that?! I swear, the further from going back in time I get, the less I remember anything about the future.

"Wow, how did I get into college?" I choke out through laughter. "Sorry about that."

"Don't be... It's kind of refreshing, anyway...not being automatically recognized by my dad." A sadness seeps into Elijah's expression, but it melts away just as quickly. "What do your parents do?"

The whiplash of emotions has me shifting from amusement to discomfort in a matter of seconds, the previous light energy souring.

"My mom manages a restaurant in Dublin."

"And your dad?" He raises his brows in curiosity.

"He..." I clear my throat. "My mom manages a restaurant in Dublin."

My reiteration seems to turn on a light in his mind, the realization finally dawning on him.

I'm thankful when he doesn't pry.

"What restaurant? Maybe I know it," he says with a grin.

"I very strongly doubt it. It's not, like, famous."

"Try me."

"Pip's Bar & Grill."

A moment passes and I am sure he is going to respond, reaffirming that he's never heard of it. Then he says, "They have the best bacon jalapeño popper burger." He grins from ear to ear.

"I stand corrected."

"I can't believe you've never heard of my dad; he loves that place. We went all the time when I was a kid."

I don't know how to go about telling him that the reason I wouldn't know that—outside of just generally not following politics—is because I never really spent much time at the restaurant.

As a kid, my mom worked a lot. I mean, being a single mom, that's par for the course. But I spent most of my time at my grandma's, and, if we're being completely honest, I had a closer relationship with her than with my mother.

"It's not like I was sitting in the corner booth analyzing every person that walked in the door!"

Elijah laughs. "I guess that's fair. So what's your major?"

"Photography."

His brows nearly touch his hairline, a confused expression marring his lips.

"What?" I ask.

"Nothing," he says, "I just didn't realize that was a major. Do you need a degree to do that?"

"Not necessarily, but an education always helps. My minor is in business."

"Why not be a business major and minor in photography?"

CHAPTER SEVEN

"Because the goal is to be a photographer, not a business owner who happens to take pictures." I can feel myself growing defensive, but I try my best to bite it back.

He nods in response, but I can't tell if he understands what I'm saying.

You can't get much further apart than Pre-Law and Photography when it comes to majors. Actually, you can't get much further apart than me and Elijah, either. Our lives, our goals, our parents—we couldn't be more different.

However, I think it's a beautiful thing when opposites attract.

Especially when it's Elijah Hanas.

We grow quiet again and I struggle to think of what to say. I'm finding myself starting to question if, rather than providing me with a lifeline, the universe was just playing a sick, twisted joke on me by sending me back in time. I have to sit through it all again with the knowledge that nothing is as inconsequential as it seems, and with one wrong word or move, I could throw it all away. Even if I don't know exactly what happens, I know that Elijah is important. He stays important, so I'm terrified of messing things up.

"So..." Elijah breaks the silence, pulling my attention to his eyes. "What's the deal with your dad?"

My brows shoot up, but he continues speaking.

"I'm sorry. I know that was a bit crass, and if I'm being honest, I'm a little drunk right now. But I can't stop thinking about how you avoided the question."

"Because he's not important. I barely know the guy."

"Oh," he responds. He doesn't elaborate on what he is thinking.

We settle into silence again, but this time I break it. Mostly because I don't like silence.

"He had an affair...when I was a baby. I was only like six months old when it started. Anyway, he got the other woman pregnant and ended up moving into the city to be with her instead. I haven't seen him since I was eight, but even then, it was in passing at the mall."

Despite the revelation, Elijah remains silent, making it almost worse.

I keep going to fill the silence. "He didn't really want to be in my life. He didn't really want *me*. He told my mom that when I was a kid. I overheard them on the phone. Said she trapped him and that he didn't want me in the first place."

When Elijah responds, it's in nearly a whisper, an expression of utter disbelief on his face. "Damn."

"Whatever. I wasn't wanted—it's fine."

"You're wanted, and you should be able to feel wanted. It sucks that he made you feel like that wasn't true."

"It's fine." What else am I supposed to say? Should I bare my soul and scare him away? That's an awful idea.

"Where do you stay?"

The quick shift in subject nearly throws me off my axis. "What?"

Elijah seems to suppress a grin at my confusion. "Where do you live?"

"Oh, McDowell."

"That's clear across campus."

"It's August, so it's not like it's cold. It's a nice walk."

"Isn't Jenna your roommate?" he asks.

"Yeah...why?"

CHAPTER SEVEN

"Because she's halfway down the street—I'm assuming walking with Marcus back to his apartment."

My head jerks to the left, and what I see confirms that is exactly what she's doing. Jenna's hand is intertwined with Marcus's as she laughs at something he says. They are disappearing down the road, but not toward campus.

"Shit," I mumble as I pull out my phone. I see a text from Jenna from ten minutes ago.

> JENNA
>
> im going home with marcus. lmk when you get back to our room

I gnaw on my bottom lip, unsure of what to do. I've walked home by myself—hell, I did it last night—but I prefer not to. Not this late, and not when half the town is wasted. It's not safe.

"Could you..."

"Take you home?" Elijah raises a brow.

"Yeah..."

"I would, but—" he holds up his empty can of beer, "this is my eighth Coors Light. It wouldn't be safe for either of us for me to drive."

"Oh." I stare down at my hands in my lap, a pang of disappointment overtaking me.

"But I could walk you."

Oh.

"Okay," I say with a grin, trying desperately to hide just how excited I am.

EIGHT

KAT

As we head back inside the fraternity house, Elijah beelines for Tanner, presumably to tell him that he will be walking me home. Tanner responds, but I'm not close enough to hear him. However, I do notice the way he stares at me as Elijah walks toward me. He looks irritated—I wonder if it's because Elijah is essentially leaving him to deal with the chaos of the party alone. It's barely 1:00 AM and it will more than likely keep going for some time unless the cops show up.

When Elijah approaches me, I look away from Tanner and see an infectious grin plastered on his lips.

"Let's go," he says, placing his hand against the small of my back and guiding me toward the front door.

"You're a junior, right?" he asks just as we're making our way past the "K." "Why do you stay in the dorms? I mean, you could live off campus."

"We thought about it—we actually even looked at apartments...but the convenience of being on campus outweighed anything else, really." Finances were the main

CHAPTER EIGHT

reason living on campus made more sense, but I don't mention that. Being the son of a governor, I can't imagine Elijah has had a single financial struggle in his life, so I worry that my qualms might fall on deaf ears.

"That makes sense." He nods, not prying any further.

We walk in comfortable silence until we finally reach Beall-McDowell, the middle section that houses the mailroom a ghost town save for the student employee sitting behind the counter.

"Hey, Kat!" Rochelle waves as we walk in, barely acknowledging Elijah as he trails by my side.

"Hey, Rochelle! Any chaos yet for welcome weekend?"

"Not yet, it's definitely better than when I worked in Eastway."

The Eastway Center is across the street from Beall-McDowell and houses the most freshmen in one place on campus. It is home to four freshman-only dorm buildings and it is where I lived freshman year, as well as where I met Jenna.

It is also pure chaos during welcome weekend.

Freshly minted eighteen-year-olds flexing their freedom for the first time is never pretty, so I feel for Rochelle in that respect.

"Yeah, that sounds awful," I laugh.

As we pass the polished wooden counter and the generic common area with uncomfortable couches, I let out a sigh of exhaustion. We enter the elevator, and I press the "8" button before leaning against the cool metal wall.

It isn't until the elevator almost reaches my floor that I realize Elijah didn't leave once we got to the lobby. If he were any other man, I'd make a remark about it, assuming and all that. However, in this moment I kind of *want* him to assume. I would thoroughly like for him to come back to my room, despite the fact that we just met and we haven't so much as been on a date.

"Awfully presumptuous of you to come upstairs, no?" I look up at him with a stern expression that quickly melts into a grin.

"What are you implying, Katarina? I am nothing but a gentleman." He winks with a smile just before the door opens on my floor. He stands there, clearly taking what I said more to heart than I intended.

I turn around, my feet flush with the low-pile carpet in the hallway as he lingers in the metal enclosure.

"Are you coming?" I laugh.

"Do you want me to?"

I pause before I say, "Yes."

Then, as we're standing in front of my bedroom door, I start to feel the effects of the concoction of liquor.

"Are you okay?" he asks as he presses his hand to my back again, goosebumps peppering my arms at the touch.

"Yeah, just finally feeling the Jungle Juice a bit."

"Are you sure we should..."

"I'm tipsy, not wasted... Come here." I swipe my card and push the door open in one motion, pulling him into my dorm room by the hem of his shirt. Elijah follows as the door clicks shut behind us.

Within an instant, he is on me like a fly on honey, my back flush with the cold wall as his lips press against mine, the hoppy flavor of the beer on his tongue pushing me further into the abyss.

As he trails kisses down my neck, his tongue swirls and caresses the sensitive spot below my ear that always sends shivers

CHAPTER EIGHT

down my spine. I feel lightheaded as he lifts me off the ground, effortlessly carrying my weight and pressing me against the wall. My legs instinctively wrap around his waist as our bodies mold together, the heaving in my chest matched only by his own as we both struggle to find stability in a situation that offers anything but.

He shifts my weight off of the wall as he moves me toward my bed. I've never been more thankful that Jenna and I have separate bedrooms than I am right now, but then again, she said she wasn't coming home, so it really shouldn't matter.

The moment my back hits the soft cotton of my duvet, I look up at him. His intense gaze holds mine, sending shivers down my spine and setting my skin ablaze.

I want to know what he's thinking. Is he aware of who I am? Does he know how important we'll become to one another?

My mind is racing a mile a minute, but everything melts into bliss as soon as his lips are on mine again—this time with far more intent than before.

Elijah's tongue darts past my lips, caressing my own tongue. He tastes of beer and bad decisions, but in this moment, I can only think about the sensations coursing through my body and the desire for him to continue exploring me with his touch. While I know that taking things slow would be the smarter approach to yield a different result for us, all I can think about right now is the way his mouth feels as he engulfs me, leaving me a quivering mess at his disposal.

"Kat," he mumbles, my name a near-gasp as it leaves his lips.

"Hm?" I say, reaching toward him, my hand brushing against a hard bulge in his jeans.

He gasps and quickly tilts downward to look at me, his face flushed with desire. My own body responds to the unmistakable proof of his arousal as I trace my fingers along its shape.

"Fuck," he breathes. He reaches down and wraps his fingers around my hand. Tightening his grasp, he squeezes himself using my hand before releasing me, the lewd action sending a jolt of arousal to my core.

Elijah pushes me backward onto the bed, his body pressing into mine as he pins my hands above my head in a loose grip. I could free them if I wanted to, but his fingers wrapped around my wrists builds far more anticipation than I would expect.

His grip tightens as he trails a path of kisses down my neck, eliciting a soft moan. The roughness of his jaw tickles and teases my sensitive skin, sending shivers down my spine. His lips then focus on the spot just below my ear, where his tongue traces circles before nibbling on my earlobe.

"Elijah, please," I whine, wanting him to touch me, fuck me—really anything at this point—a need building in my core unlike anything I've ever felt.

"Please what?" he presses, his voice dripping with playful challenge.

I feel my cheeks heat as I realize he wants me to say it out loud. I meet his gaze and see the mischievous glint in his eyes before mustering up the courage to say the words he's been waiting for.

"Fuck me," I whisper only inches from his lips.

He swiftly unzips his jeans, letting them fall to the ground in a heap. His boxer briefs are stretched taut against his body, revealing the outline of his aroused cock straining beneath the fabric.

Reaching down, he delves in the back pocket of his discarded jeans and pulls out a foil package. He throws it onto the bed next to me, the packet landing next to my head.

The scent of clean linen invades my senses as I melt into the comforter, Elijah falling on top of me once again. His lips crash into mine with the intensity of a starved man, and he bites my bottom lip just hard enough to sting but not enough to hurt.

Then he lifts himself up with one hand and uses the other to pull his boxer briefs down. While I don't see him, I feel him as the hard, velvety skin brushes against my inner thigh.

Something in my expression must reveal my thoughts; he quirks a grin but doesn't say anything. However, his eyes linger on me for a silent moment as if waiting for the go-ahead to proceed. The second he sees me nod in approval in the darkness, he reaches over and grabs the condom. He pulls it to his mouth, using his teeth to rip the foil with one swift motion.

Elijah pulls the latex condom out of its packaging before reaching down and sheathing himself entirely with ease. The condom is slick as he presses his cock against my entrance, my breath catching in my throat in anticipation.

I feel every inch as he slowly presses inside me, the foreign stretch bathing me in a combination of mild pain and a far more intense, growing wave of pleasure. The moment he is buried to the hilt, he nuzzles his face in my neck.

A joke bristles on the tip of my tongue, but it dies as he starts tepidly moving in and out of me. Pleasing friction catapults me into a euphoric abyss, causing a quiet moan to spill past my lips, which only seems to urge Elijah forward as his pace begins to quicken.

"Oh my god," I moan loudly, earning a grunt of approval in response, right before he slams into me with far less restraint than before, shifting me further into complete and total oblivion.

The creaking of the old bedframe fills the air, mixing fluidly with the moans and grunts of pleasure as we move toward release—well, as he moves toward release. I've never really been able to orgasm with a partner, so I don't even attempt to get myself there and neither does he.

It's rushed, it's frenzied, but it's also all-consuming and feels terrifyingly like the stars are aligning.

Elijah and me.

Me and Elijah.

As it was always meant to be.

―

Light blares through my dorm room window, the aggression of the early morning sun shooting daggers through my temples. My mouth is dry and all I can think about is getting over to my mini fridge to find a bottle of water. I jerk up in bed, only to realize that there is a strong, muscular arm draped over my midsection.

It takes me no more than a couple of seconds to come back down to reality and realize that it's Elijah.

My Elijah.

As if he could feel me stirring, Elijah's eyes flutter open. A hazy grin plasters across his lips almost instantly.

CHAPTER EIGHT

"Hey, you," he says as his lips pull into a full smile, his eyes meeting my own.

"Good morning." I smile down at him. The sight of him shirtless in my bed does nothing to help the dryness in my mouth. "I need to grab a bottle of water," I say, tapping his arm.

"Okay," he mumbles, squeezing me around my middle before pulling his arm away, giving me the room I need to get out of bed.

My room is an atrocious mess, clothing haphazardly thrown around and only about half of it from the night before. I've never been a big fan of cleaning; my messiness always drove my mom nuts when I was at home.

"Do you want one?" I ask as I grab a bottle of water from the fridge, the frosty coating on the plastic biting into my palm.

"Yeah, sure," he says.

I walk toward him, almost tripping on my rug, which is bunched around the bed. When I hand Elijah the water bottle, he doesn't hesitate to grab it from me, chugging over half of it down in a matter of seconds.

I take three large gulps of my own before setting it on the corner of my desk.

"Do you have any big plans today?" I ask, awkwardly shuffling my feet.

"Nah." He doesn't elaborate, but I try not to be difficult.

Silence descends as I try to think of what to say, seeming to stretch on forever.

Elijah either thinks of something to say or finally realizes the silence is uncomfortable, and finally asks, "Do you?"

"Not really," I laugh. "I doubt I will see Jenna until later tonight. I'm sure her and Marcus are going to do something."

"Yeah, what's going on there?"

I pause for a moment before speaking with a laugh. "I actually don't know—they just met. But I don't know, I could see it being something."

"You get all of that from a couple of days of them fucking?" he laughs.

I roll my eyes. "Well, no, but it could be. I mean, anything could be. Statistically, a lot of people find their person in college."

"True, but a lot of people also get chlamydia in college. Doesn't mean we assume everybody has chlamydia."

I know why he is saying this—at least, I think I do. I wish I didn't, but what would be the point of going back in time if he was suddenly a different person?

The good with the bad.

The pessimist—but the one I'm supposed to end up with.

Anything different would be me trying to change him, and I don't want to do that.

"So...would you like to?" I ask nervously.

"Like to what?"

"Would you like to do something later? I mean, since we're both free."

Why am I so nervous? I'm just asking someone to hang out, not proposing marriage.

Silence befalls us again and I think for a split second that he very well might turn me down. My stomach knots, causing me to reach for my water and gulping down half the bottle without hesitation.

"What did you have in mind?" he asks.

CHAPTER EIGHT

I wipe the moisture off my lips, a bit flustered. "Oh, uh..." I swallow. "We could go do something or we could just hang out...I'm cool with whatever."

"Do you want to come over to the house?" he asks nonchalantly.

I struggle to maintain a calm facade, but my insides are in turmoil. I don't want to seem too eager, but I can feel my voice betraying me with exaggerated enthusiasm as I reply, "Sounds good!"

I desperately want him to like me and I'm terrified that my efforts will backfire because I'm trying too hard.

The corner of his mouth lifts into a smirk as he nods, but my stomach sinks as he stands and begins to pull on his pants.

"I'll text you later, okay?"

I nod, knowing that if I open my mouth, I'm going to make an absolute idiot out of myself.

He kisses the top of my head far more casually than I feel right now before disappearing out my bedroom door.

Despite everything going exactly perfectly, I can't help but wonder if I am still going to find a way to fuck it up.

NINE

KAT

When I arrive at the Lambda house shortly before sunset, I'll admit it is one of the weirdest experiences of my life. I've been here numerous times—I could probably map the main floor with ease—but it's always been during a party. Being at a frat house when it isn't midnight and I'm not half-buzzed is weird. While the faint smell of beer still haunts the air, the energy is different, but not in a bad way.

I step across the threshold, the remnants of the summer heat lingering on my skin. The house's air conditioning is on full blast, the vents kicking on every few minutes. Despite this, the space is a balmy seventy-nine according to the thermostat on the wall.

Elijah notices my discomfort and places a hand on my lower back, leading me toward the stairs. "We were supposed to have someone come and fix it, but they can't make it until next week," he explains with a sympathetic look. "Do you want us to go back to your dorm?"

"No, it's fine. We can hang out here, I don't mind the

CHAPTER NINE

heat." Despite my attempt at being agreeable, I internally groan at the thought. I hate warm weather, so I've always been happy when the weather turns in the fall. However, I can be not difficult for a single night.

The group of guys, usually tense and on edge in search of female attention while cramped in their crowded living room, are now lounging comfortably on the couch and floor. It is oddly comforting to see them in their natural state, laughing and joking with each other without any pretense. A football game is playing on the large flat-screen TV in the corner, but they chat amongst themselves as a replay hits the screen.

Elijah's hand sears into the small of my back as he nudges me forward, my foot brushing against the first step. "Let's go upstairs," he whispers.

I don't even get the chance to step into the living room and say hello to those gathered around the TV before we disappear to the second floor.

Stepping into Elijah's space, I brace myself for the typical frat house chaos. Instead, I'm greeted by a surprisingly clean and organized room. The floor is free of empty beer cans and dirty laundry, and every surface has been meticulously dusted. It's a stark contrast to what I expected from a college junior living in a fraternity house.

"It looks nice." I smile awkwardly.

"Thanks. I like to be clean."

As we sit in awkward silence, I scan the room for a potential topic of conversation. The low-pile carpet, showing signs of wear and tear but clean nonetheless, catches my attention. I notice the meticulously made bed with its navy-blue sheets and pillows neatly stacked on top. On the old, rickety desk sits his MacBook Pro, the only sign of life in his otherwise sterile bedroom. I let out a frustrated sigh as I struggle to find something worth talking about.

"What do you want to do?" I ask tentatively.

Met with a shrug from Elijah, my eyes continue to scan the room, but eventually he speaks.

"We could watch a movie?"

His eyes meet mine and suddenly my anxiety of being in his space unprepared is calmed, the warmth in his gaze warming my already sweat-peppered skin. "Okay."

We both sink into the softness of his bed, the crisp scent of fresh laundry filling my nostrils. The comforter, a fluffy cloud of blue matching his sheets, gently glides over my skin as I make myself comfortable.

He turns on Netflix and, with little discussion, makes a selection. I like that he knows what he wants.

Deafening explosions and adrenaline-fueled car chases fill the screen, but my excitement begins to wane. My gaze constantly flickers toward him, hoping to catch a glimpse of his reaction, but he is completely engrossed in the action-packed movie. The bright lights and loud sound effects seem to pulse through the room, my heart racing with each new scene. I've never been a fan of action films, but I am willing to give it a chance for him.

"Have you seen this movie?" I ask in a near-whisper.

"Huh?" He doesn't tear his eyes from the film.

"Have you seen this movie?!" I yell as the score grows louder, no doubt indicating an impending intense moment.

"Oh, yeah. A few times." Despite this, he still doesn't pry his attention away. He must really like this movie.

My hand hovers over his knee, hesitant yet longing to feel the warmth of his skin through the fabric of his jeans. As I

CHAPTER NINE

gently make contact, a current of electricity sparks between us. He doesn't seem to notice at first, but as my hand slowly slides up his thigh, he shifts closer to me, craving more of my touch. His leg twitches in response, a sign of his desire and anticipation. The heat radiating from his body envelops me.

Soon Elijah mirrors my movements, his hand resting lightly on my inner thigh. I can feel the heat of his palm against my bare flesh, the sensation sending shivers down my spine. He traces gentle circles along my leg, teasing the frayed hem of my denim cutoffs. The electricity between us is palpable and I hold my breath, longing for him to lean in closer.

"Elijah." I mean it to come out as an inquiry, but it's more reminiscent of a gasp, finally pulling his attention from the action flick.

"Yes?" he asks, the corner of his lips quirking upward as he continues to draw circles along the hem of my shorts. He's meticulous and intentional in his touch, careful not to let his fingers slip more than an inch under the thick fabric, no doubt with the intention of building my arousal.

Then he abandons his initial hesitation and slowly trails his fingertips upward. His gaze remains fixed on the screen, but I can feel his entire focus directed toward me. The heat emanating from his body is almost suffocating in the thick, humid air of summer. It only heightens the anticipation as his touch sends shivers down my spine.

His finger glides over the lace trim of my panties, sending electric tingles shooting through my body. I can't help but arch into his touch, desperately craving more. His nostrils flare as he struggles to maintain control, his eyes still fixed on the movie playing in front of us. With each tiny circle he traces along the damp fabric, I feel myself yearning for more intense sensations. But he's teasing me, giving me just enough to keep me wanting more.

Much to my delight, he pushes past the fabric. He shoves the lace to one side and I quake at the sensation of his fingertips dancing over the sensitive bundle of nerves.

"Please, Elijah," I moan, every bit of my reserve crumbling.

His restraint seems to waver as well, and he presses his thumb against my clit and plunges his middle finger deep inside my core.

I gasp at the sensation, realizing for the first time just how drenched I am.

As if he can hear my thoughts, Elijah mumbles, "Fuck, you're so wet."

I feel my face flush at his words, the simple action of him speaking the vulgar thought aloud bringing me to life. He pumps his finger lazily in and out of me, but I can't resist bucking my hips, chasing the sensation. As quickly as his fingers are there, they are gone, leaving me breathless and empty.

Elijah stretches his arm to the side, grabs his phone and the television remote, and places them on the bedside table. The corners of his mouth twist into a slightly mischievous grin as he shifts closer to me on the bed. He deftly flips me onto my back, causing me to let out a surprised yelp. My breath hitches as he slowly unbuttons my shorts, his fingers lingering.

My shorts and underwear are in a heap on the floor within seconds and Elijah crawls between my legs. His erection strains against the stiff denim of his jeans, but he doesn't remove them yet. His hot breath ghosts over my damp flesh, the sensation nearly causing me to buckle. I'm aware of every breath, every sensation.

So when he dips his head down and drags his tongue through my folds, I nearly lurch out of my skin.

"Oh my god," I gasp.

His mouth is hot and wet against me, his tongue moving in quick circles over my sensitive clit. Each flick of his tongue sends a jolt of pleasure through my body, encouraging him to continue.

To my delight, I actually feel that flicker of sensation start to build. I've never orgasmed from the touch—or in this case, the tongue—of another person. The mere thought electrifies me.

With every lash of his tongue, I quiver. Elijah appears to be on a full-out mission, my pleasure the only thing driving him forward. It's a foreign feeling, a partner being so dedicated to making me feel good.

My high school boyfriend never made me come—I'm not even sure he ever tried. When we had sex, we would typically just crawl into the back of his hand-me-down Chevy. There was seldom any foreplay.

But this? This is…magnificent.

The telltale sign of my impending orgasm starts to crawl up my spine, leaving me panting as Elijah sucks my clit between his lips, lapping at it with the tip of his tongue. When he pushes two fingers deep inside me, I detonate like a bomb.

"Fuck, I'm gonna—I'm gonna—"

Burning white-hot pleasure floods me, and I don't feel even remotely in control of my own body. He wields it like a tool from his very own arsenal, like my body was made for the sole purpose of him giving it pleasure.

Elijah's lips land against my inner thigh, peppering kisses against the tingling skin before he lifts onto his hands and knees, hovering over me, his cock only inches from my entrance.

He kisses me, his lips hovering for a moment before he reaches over to the nightstand. He fumbles through the drawer and pulls out a foil packet, easily tearing it open and sliding the condom on.

Holy shit.

I've never had sex right after an orgasm before. I expect it to hurt, but the bite of his thrust only heightens my pleasure, my over-sensitized core instead climbing higher and higher into oblivion.

With each push into me, he grows more frantic, as if the thought of his own release on the horizon brings out a different side of him, an animalistic side.

Wielding that kind of power is invigorating. Knowing that I'm the source of his pleasure leaves a warmth in my chest.

"God. Fuck. Kat—I'm going to…" His thrusts grow faster, more aggressive.

My head nearly hits the headboard, but I don't mind the shift. I actually think it's possible that I could come this way too, a new concept that I hadn't even considered.

Elijah's grasp on my hips tightens as he pushes into me, this time with far more purpose.

One…two…three. As his last thrust buries him deep, he lets out a groan, his cock twitching inside of me. We stay like this for a moment, panting and gasping, drenched in sweat but without a single care in the world.

And then Elijah pulls himself out of me, leaving me achingly empty.

CHAPTER NINE

He looks around the room, scanning it with purpose before his eyes land on the towel hanging on the back of his door.

"I'm gonna hop in the shower," he says before disappearing into the en suite bathroom.

I simply stare at the ceiling, giddy as hell.

TEN

KAT

After his shower, Elijah came back into the room and we finished the movie. He offered to take me home, said that it would be more comfortable for me, what with the air conditioning failing to cool the house. However, I could tell he wanted me to stay.

So I stayed.

Now, I lie in his bed, staring at the ceiling fan as it pushes hot air around. It's nearly impossible to keep my mind from racing.

The more I try to recall the future, the less I know. While I'm aware I already lived it, it's starting to seem more like a fading memory. Whatever murky future Elijah and I have, I don't remember any of it. I know he's important—that has to be enough for me to figure it out.

It has to be.

I squirm uncomfortably under his heavy arm, sweat trickling down the exposed skin on my stomach. The sound of

CHAPTER TEN

his deep snores fills the room. I carefully shift out from under his dead weight, relieved to finally have some space to breathe.

So thirsty.

Elijah's room is shrouded in darkness, but a faint glow from the streetlights outside seeps through the plastic blinds. Not enough light to see any detail, but just enough to be able to feel around in the dark with enough awareness that I won't run into something.

Fuck.

Okay, almost enough light to not run into something.

After slamming my foot into the edge of the bed, I struggle to stay quiet as I putter around the room, trying to find something to throw on—although, given how soundly Elijah is sleeping, I'm not completely sure why I am working so hard to be quiet.

Feeling around in the darkness, I finally find his dresser shoved in the far corner. I pull out a pair of boxers and tug them on quickly. I could just put on my shorts, but the thought of putting on any kind of denim with my sweat-damp skin sounds like my own personal hell. I debate pulling out one of his shirts, but decide to just wear my tank top, choosing to forgo finding my bra in the darkness. I'll be damned if I run into that fucking bed again.

I find my way into the hall, which is even darker than Elijah's bedroom, and by the grace of God and luck alone, I manage to make it down the stairs with a death grip on the banister.

I take a deep breath before turning on the kitchen light. The old bulb flickers for a few seconds, then beams with a dim yellow glow. I blink rapidly as my eyes adjust to the sudden change in brightness.

Although I've frequented this kitchen countless times, I can't recall ever seeing it in such pristine condition. The floors are spotless, the countertops gleaming, and the smell of disinfectant fills the air. It's as if someone had just finished cleaning before heading to bed, evidenced by the drying rack overflowing with sparkling white plates and crystal-clear glasses. A sponge, still damp from recent use, clings to the side of the sink.

I grab a glass from the rack and rinse it, then fill it, relishing in the icy chill of the water sliding down my parched throat as I take a long, refreshing sip.

I don't believe water has ever been this satisfying.

"What are you doing up?"

I nearly lurch out of my skin at the unexpected voice, jerking around and fully prepared to grab something sharp out of the cup of silverware drying on the counter. I reach for the handle of a steak knife, but as the velvety salvation of the black plastic lands against my palm, a much more masculine hand wraps around my own.

"Calm down, killer, it's me...and I'm far too pretty to have steak-knife-sized stab marks all over my face."

I twist around, finally connecting the voice with a face as Tanner comes into view.

He releases my hand as a chuckle breaks free, his infuriating smirk weirdly managing to quell my racing heart.

"Jesus Christ, Tanner, you scared the shit out of me."

"Yeah, I gathered that," he says as he tries and fails to bite back a laugh. "A steak knife? Really? That was your brilliant plan if somebody was actually coming up behind you to cause you harm? It would barely break the skin."

"Not if I used enough pressure."

CHAPTER TEN

"Yeah, maybe in a perfect scenario, but I could've gotten that knife out of your hand before you had a chance to even touch me."

I think on it for a second, realizing that Tanner might have a point. Whatever—it's not like I was actually expecting someone to attack me. He just snuck up on me.

"Agree to disagree," I say with a chuckle.

"Yeah, yeah." Tanner rolls his eyes in amusement before his humored expression is replaced by something else, something unreadable. His eyes travel around the room, clearly attempting to find something to look at that isn't me.

"Are you okay?" I ask with genuine concern in my voice.

"Oh, uh...yeah." Tanner clears his throat before walking over to the wall and flipping on the ceiling fan. "This house is sweltering, huh?"

"Yeah, it's pretty brutal. I don't know how you guys have been doing this for days."

"Meh, I've lived through worse."

"Is something wrong?" I ask tentatively.

"No, no...um." He gestures to my body.

I look down and notice that the sweltering heat has caused me to sweat profusely, and my camisole sits low on my breasts, clinging to my damp flesh like a second skin. The chill from the fan has caused my barely covered nipples to harden and they now unavoidably poke through the fabric.

"Oh geez," I say as I cross my arms over my chest, only to realize that covering my nipples only pushes my boobs further out. I keep adjusting myself, trying to figure out how to be a sliver more modest, to no avail. "I'm sorry."

"Oh, I don't mind. Doesn't bother me one bit. However, it seems to bother you... Here." Tanner pulls his T-shirt over his head and hands it to me. My expression must give my thoughts away as he laughs, "It's not sweaty, you big baby. I just put it on."

I pull it over my head without questioning him. I'll admit, I feel a lot better now that I'm covered up.

"Better?" he asks. I nod in response. "Good. What's got you up so late?"

"Couldn't sleep. *Someone* broke the air conditioning."

"I don't like what you're implying, Katarina."

"Just Kat," I say, attempting to be stern, but a smile invades my lips as I say it.

"Oh yes. Just *Kat*." He says my name in a way that perplexes me, like there is some other meaning to the word. "But no kidding, it's hot as balls in this house."

Tanner walks to the fridge and pulls a pint of ice cream out of the freezer door. He holds it up in question.

"Yes, please."

He reaches past me and grabs two spoons, one teaspoon and one tablespoon, before extending the smaller of the two to me, earning himself a grin.

"I've always preferred those ones," I say as I snatch it out of his hand playfully.

"Lucky guess." Tanner opens the ice cream container to reveal a fresh, untouched pint of rocky road.

"My favorite!" I immediately dig my spoon into the perfectly smooth surface of deliciousness and then shove the massive scoop of ice cream into my mouth.

He stares at me with a puzzled expression on his face.

"What?" I say through my mouthful of ice cream.

His face contorts again, except this time his lips form a smile. "Nothing, you're just really hot when you talk with

CHAPTER TEN

your mouth full like that," he says, dodging my arm as I swat at him. He digs his spoon into the other side of the rocky road.

"Shut up," I laugh.

He simply shrugs as he slowly chews through the chunks of chocolate.

We stand side by side, leaning against the cool countertop. The only sound in the room is the scraping of our spoons against the cardboard container as we try to get every last bit of the rocky road.

"I'm sorry for keeping you up," I say quietly.

"I was already up—I've always been a massive insomniac, and this heat doesn't really help. Besides, I heard someone come downstairs, so I was pretty sure there was gonna be someone to talk to." He flashes me that signature Tanner Adler smile and I know with certainty that he means it.

As the faint sound of a throat being cleared echoes through the otherwise silent room, both our heads snap toward the open doorway.

"Are you coming back to bed?" Elijah asks, a clear crease of irritation in his brow.

"Yeah, I just couldn't sleep, so I came down for some water, but then I ran into Tanner."

Elijah's usually stoic demeanor breaks as his jaw clenches and his expression morphs into one of possessiveness. His dark eyes glare daggers at Tanner. "Are you done, then?" he asks, his face softening as he looks at me.

That's new.

"Yeah, I was just going to come up." The lie falls off my tongue with ease; telling Elijah that I was actually enjoying talking to Tanner sounds like a bad idea.

He simply nods before gesturing for me to follow him back upstairs.

Without questioning, I cross the room, then turn around to look at Tanner. "Thanks for the ice cream."

"Anytime...Just Kat." He smiles, a faintly sad expression marring his face.

Trying not to linger, I walk back upstairs with Elijah, but the moment we land at the top of the stairs I notice he's sporting that same irate look he had in the kitchen—except now it's aimed at me.

Then I realize he isn't looking at *me*.

He's looking at Tanner's Blink 182 T-shirt hanging off my frame.

Oh.

ELEVEN

KAT

Exactly as one would expect, syllabus week passes with minimal work on my plate. I swear, it's like professors know that the chances of us mentally being present are slim to none. We're now halfway through the second week of classes and, to my delight, we're finally receiving homework. Nothing insanely time-consuming, but I like feeling like I'm accomplishing something.

I've always loved the start of a new semester. Fresh pencils, new notebooks—something about it has always felt like a perfect fresh start.

However, no matter how new the textbooks and the pencils and the notebooks, at the end of the day it's still the same school that you left last semester. Nothing changes; no new experiences except for the ones that you go after yourself.

So when my newly formed group of friends decides that they want to go to college night at the Dusty Armadillo, I can't help but find a poeticism in the fact that we are starting a new semester at the same line-dancing bar that Jenna and I have gone to since freshman year.

The parking lot is crowded as our Uber drops us off out front, the line around the side of the building filled with mostly freshmen in pristine new cowboy boots, undoubtedly ready for their first college night at Kent State's favorite country bar.

The guy manning the door, Darren, happens to know me and Jenna really well. Well, "know" is an exaggeration. Jenna and I have spent far too many drunken nights at the Dusty, one of which involved Darren having to pry Jenna off the bathroom floor after one too many shots. Somehow, we still didn't manage to get kicked out that night.

If we're being honest, I think Darren has a crush on Jenna. I mean, why wouldn't he? Everyone likes Jenna. If I were attracted to women, I would probably like Jenna.

As if he can hear my thoughts, Marcus pulls Jenna closer as we approach the door, not bothering with the line nearing the corner of the building.

"Hey! Wait your turn!" some girl yells.

"Are you twenty-one?" Darren asks her.

"Well, no, but—"

Darren cuts her off. "Well, people over twenty-one buy drinks. Freshmen, which I'm assuming you are, wait in line."

The girl shoots him a glare, but she doesn't bother to retort. I think she knows that it would fall on deaf ears anyway.

"There's my girls!" Darren grins as he greets us, managing to completely ignore the four guys in our group.

In the human equivalent of peeing on Jenna's leg, Marcus

CHAPTER ELEVEN

kisses her forehead. Jenna melts into him, but I can't help but chuckle at him being so obviously territorial.

Darren doesn't so much as acknowledge Marcus as he scans our group, counting and marking something on his clipboard. With a wave of his arm, he ushers us into the bar.

The dark room is lit almost exclusively by the lights behind the bar on the far wall and the ever-changing lights on the dance floor. There is a clear separation between the door and the dance floor, intentionally placed in order to allow people to mingle without getting in the way.

"Have you been here before?" Elijah asks, yelling over the music with his lips inches from my ear.

Jenna and I look at each other and exchange a knowing smirk.

"Yeah," I reply, "we used to come here all the time. Last semester not as much, but freshman year this is where it was at."

Elijah nods, acknowledging my words but not expressing his thoughts.

"You?" I ask.

"No, I've never really been a big dancer."

If he doesn't like dancing, then why did we come here?

"But I'll dance with you," he adds.

I grab his hand to pull him out onto the dance floor, but he resists.

"Later," he says with a laugh. "After I have a few drinks in me."

"Of course." I smile up at him, welcoming his lips as he leans down and kisses me.

Jenna grabs my hand and whirls me away, leaving Elijah and Marcus standing there in confusion. Brendan and Tanner join us on the dance floor, falling into the rhythm of the dance and picking up the moves with ease.

Stomp, stomp, whirl, clap, whirl, whirl, whirl, stomp.

Despite not having come here in close to a year, the dances haven't changed at all. I whirl and I whirl until I accidentally ram into Tanner.

He laughs. "Okay, killer. You're gonna knock someone over."

I simply roll my eyes before falling into step between him and Jenna, our synchronicity a pleasant surprise.

Brendan isn't quite as in sync. God love the lovable goof, but the boy doesn't have a shred of rhythm inside him. And yet he powers through, trying to keep up and fumbling through the dance, all with a grin plastered on his lips.

In a move that is most definitely not part of the choreography, Tanner grabs my hand and twirls me away from him. Before we know it, three songs have passed and we're panting from all of our laughter.

"Drink?" Jenna asks, sweat glistening on her brow.

The four of us walk over to the bar, where Elijah and Marcus are perched. I wrap my arms around Elijah's waist with ease, the quick rapport we're finding between us a pleasant surprise. He welcomes the hug, but I can't help but notice he doesn't kiss me at all. He sits ramrod straight with my arms around his waist and a glass of whiskey pressed to his lips.

"Hey," I whisper, pulling his attention to me.

As soon as our eyes meet, I can feel him relax into my touch.

"Hey." He grins, finally wrapping his arms around me and pressing his lips to my forehead.

CHAPTER ELEVEN

The cold of his glass bites into the exposed skin on my back as my shirt rides up, but I don't move, content in his arms. The smell of whiskey coats his breath, but he leans down and kisses me and any concern I had vanishes without a trace.

Upbeat line-dance music shifts through the speakers as a familiar country ballad rings through the room. I look at Jenna and Marcus as she asks him to dance and he complies without restraint. When my gaze returns to Elijah, his eyes are already on me.

I want to ask him, but I get the sense he'll turn me down. He said it himself; he doesn't dance.

As if he can read my mind, Tanner yells over the music from a few feet away. "Wanna dance?"

Just as I'm about to say "Yes," Elijah's glass meets the hard top of the bar and he's grabbing my hand. He pulls me toward the dance floor without giving me even a moment to respond to Tanner's question.

We land on the dance floor and instantly my body is flush against his. Hard, strong arms wrap around my waist and I melt into his touch.

"I thought you didn't dance," I laugh.

"I don't...but you wanted to, so." He says it nonchalantly, almost irately.

I can't help the way my stomach sours at his words. "I'm sorry," I mumble, almost too quiet to hear over the music.

As if he can already read my tells, Elijah uses his pointer finger to nudge my chin up to look at him. There's a warmth in his eyes that wasn't there moments ago. "I mean...I want to dance with you. If you want me to dance with you, then I want to dance with you."

And just like that, my anxiety is quelled.

Elijah pulls me flush to him once more as we sway to "Wanted" by Hunter Hayes. He hums along to the song, his lips pressed just above my ear, his warm breath only causing me to melt further into him.

"I want to make you feel wanted," he says, and at first I think he's singing along...but he's not. He's saying the words to me.

My chest fills with warmth at his admission, the statement giving me a sense of understanding that I've never experienced before. No one has ever expressed such unadulterated desire to make me happy.

"I do," I say as I grin up at him, my chin resting against his chest.

"Good." He smiles back, the joy in his expression causing warmth to flood my body.

Just as swiftly as the song came on, the music shifts again, this time to an upbeat Alan Jackson tune that causes the crowd to go wild.

I see the moment pass behind Elijah's eyes, but I don't let it get to me. He has his interests and I have mine. I simply have to respect that.

"Go back to the bar," I mumble, pressing my lips to his. "I'll probably be over there in a few songs. Can you get me a water?"

"Of course." He squeezes his arms around me once more before letting go. As he walks away, Jenna darts toward me, grabbing my arm and dragging me to the front of the dance floor.

I dance, I twirl, I stomp and move.

All to the beat of "Chattahoochee" reverberating in my ears.

TWELVE

KAT

The weeks after meeting Elijah are a complete and utter whirlwind. We hang out most days—sometimes at my dorm room, sometimes at his house, sometimes on campus somewhere, but always together. I haven't seen Jenna much over the past few weeks, but that isn't unusual when she's with a new guy. Marcus and her seem different, though; I could truly see it lasting.

Elijah walks up to my table carrying two large brown boxes with the bright Einstein's Bagels logo stamped on them. He sets them down on the table before sliding into the chair across from me. I quickly scan his outfit—jeans and a plaid flannel shirt—and realize he must have a break in his classes today. I tilt my head and readjust my textbooks. We smile at each other and my stomach shifts into a kaleidoscope of butterflies.

"Hey, you," I say with a grin.

While I was hoping I'd see him today, he didn't fully

commit when I asked to nail down a time. Apparently, he found time in his schedule.

He grins, his eyes lighting up as he opens one of the brown boxes. From it, he pulls out a perfectly toasted Nova Lox bagel—cream cheese with smoked salmon and capers spilling out from the sides.

I don't notice that my disgust is clear on my face until he starts laughing, immediately ready to defend his favorite breakfast dish. "It's good, I promise."

"I'll take your word for it," I laugh before reaching for the second box.

His hand lands atop the cardboard, stopping me. "Do you trust me?"

What a loaded question to pose before I open my food.

"Depends on what is in this box," I joke.

He pulls his hand away and allows me to open the box…to reveal a Nova Lox bagel piled with the same fixings as his. My eyes meet his, and I notice nervousness seeping into his otherwise confident attitude.

"If you hate it, I promise I will walk back over there and buy you something else. But…I think you'll like it."

Despite my usual dislike for seafood, I cautiously take a bite of the bagel. The creamy texture of the cream cheese and the crunch of the toasted bagel mix with the salty burst of briny capers and perfectly smoked salmon, creating a harmonious blend of flavors that leaves me pleasantly surprised.

"Good, right?" He leans forward in anticipation of my response.

I pause for a moment, wanting to respond with something snarky about him getting me food without any inkling of

CHAPTER TWELVE

whether I'd like it, but I have to give him credit. He managed to guess correctly.

"It's good," I mumble, my mouth still half full, holding a napkin to my mouth. I finish chewing. "It's really good, actually. I'm glad to have been wrong. I don't normally like fish."

A look of relief washes over him at my words. "Good." He grins before biting into his own bagel, cream cheese clinging to the corner of his mouth.

"Elijah," I say.

"Hm?"

"You've got..." I point to the corner of his mouth.

He looks confused for a split second until he reaches up and feels the cheese on his lip. He wipes it away quickly with his thumb before licking it away.

I do a terrible job at hiding the reaction my body has to that visual.

To my relief, he smirks but doesn't say anything.

"So, what class are you studying for?" Elijah leans forward in his seat to get a peek at my open textbook.

"Principles of Macroeconomics." I groan, resting my forehead against the textbook in demonstration of my frustration.

"Not going well, I take it?" he asks.

"Not going well," I confirm. "I've never been good at math to begin with, so it's proving to be...difficult."

He nods in understanding before shifting his seat, nestling up next to me to look at the page I was reading.

"What are you doing?" I ask.

"Helping you," he says, frowning. "I took this class last semester. It's still fresh in my mind, so I may be able to help."

I tilt the book toward him and he exhales. "Oh, okay. This is really easy…monetary policy focuses on interest rates and the money in circulation, whereas fiscal policy pertains more to taxation and government spending."

"Will you deal with that after you finish school?" I ask.

"To some degree. It depends on the job, but probably. If I go the law route after law school, not as much. But once I venture into politics, yes."

"Does your dad?"

He tenses at the mention of his father, Governor Hanas—who I googled after that first night with Elijah.

"Yes." He doesn't elaborate.

"And that's what you want to do? What your dad does?"

The air between us thickens, and I hold my breath, waiting for him to speak. The seconds tick by as I fidget in my seat.

Finally, he lets out a deep sigh. "Of course I do." His response is cold, and I know with certainty I shouldn't pry. I clearly made a grave mistake in asking about his dad.

My gaze flits around the room, searching for a way to steer the conversation away from the uncomfortable topic. "What are you doing next weekend?" I ask as I close my textbook.

"Next weekend is Halloween, so I guess I'll be doing that. Why?"

"Halloween is my twenty-first birthday!" I grin from ear to ear. Although I've had a fake ID since I was eighteen, I can't hide my excitement at the day finally arriving.

"Your birthday is on Halloween?" He raises a brow.

I laugh. "Yes?"

"I don't think I've ever met someone who has a Halloween birthday—it's kind of cool," Elijah says.

CHAPTER TWELVE

"It's no less likely than the other 365 days in a year."

"Yeah, but still. It's cool."

We grow quiet again, but it doesn't feel nearly as tense as before.

Elijah leans forward, grazing my thigh in the process. "I'm sorry about that. I didn't mean to get short with you about my dad. He just...that's what most people want from me, and while I know that isn't you, it still causes me to tense up."

"I understand," I say. And I do.

When people ask about my dad, I have a similar response. Sometimes there are more tears, but a pretty similar response nonetheless. No one wants to be asked about their parents all the time, whether that be because their dad left or because their dad just so happens to be the governor.

Elijah reaches over and squeezes my hand under the table with welcome warmth. "What were you thinking for your birthday?" he asks.

I shrug. "Jenna was talking about doing something at Marcus's apartment."

Elijah nods as though deep in thought, but whatever is crossing his mind, he doesn't share. As if he can hear my thoughts—the cogs turning, the whistles blowing—he grins unabashedly. "I'll be there."

And suddenly any concerns or fears I had before melt away, leaving just the two of us.

Exactly the way I want it to be.

THIRTEEN

KAT

The fall semester rushes by at an alarming pace, leaving me feeling unsteady and unprepared. It's like trying to hold onto water as it slips through my fingers, rendering me ill-equipped and out of control. Is this how the rest of college is going to be? A blur of passing moments I can't seem to hold onto?

But then, as winter creeps in and the first snowflakes start to fall, I begin to understand that perhaps this is the way it's meant to be. College is not meant to be savored and drawn out —it's meant to be a wild and exhilarating ride. The moments may be fleeting, but they are full of adventure and growth. As I embrace this realization, I realize I'm ready to let go of my expectations and simply enjoy the journey ahead.

My birthday passes pretty uneventfully. We get together at Marcus's apartment, just our small group of friends. Elijah shows up late due to something going wrong at the house before he left—or at least that's what he said. I try not to be dramatic about it, but I can't shake the fact that it effectively ruined my night.

CHAPTER THIRTEEN

Escaping the winter chill, I stamp my feet and rub my hands together as I enter the warm coffee shop. My body is still adjusting to the sudden drop in temperature, and my teeth chatter uncontrollably. The crispness of the first snowfall lingers on my skin and clothes.

"I'll have a hazelnut latte with whole milk, please," I say at the counter.

The barista puts my order into the register before holding her hand out to request my card. I hand her my payment and she takes it without a word, no doubt irritated by the now-full shop, everyone having the same idea to get out of the freezing late-November air.

"Your order will be up over there," she says shortly. No indication of when; simply...over there.

I walk over to the mob of people huddled around the pickup counter.

"Hey, Just Kat!"

I turn around to see Tanner, whose eyes are filled with delight as he peers down at me.

"Hey!" I grin.

He extends his arms, inviting me into a hug. I linger for a moment, the warmth of his body helping combat the chill in my bones. Tanner allows me to overstay my welcome, keeping his arms wrapped around me.

"So cold," I say, chattering my teeth.

He laughs at my dramatics, but doesn't say anything.

"I have a hazelnut latte for Kat!" the barista shouts with no joy in her inflection.

I reach forward, grab my coffee, and resist an eye-roll as I spot *"Cat"* written on the side of my cup.

"I swear they do that on purpose," I say with a laugh, turning the cup to show Tanner the misspelling of my name.

Tanner's order gets called right after mine, a black coffee that he proceeds to load up with cream and sugar—much less exciting than my latte. "You haven't heard that conspiracy?"

"What conspiracy?" I lean against the self-service bar as he stirs his drink.

"People think that they do it on purpose to get you to be outraged and post it on social media. One time, they wrote 'Shera' on mine. S-H-E-R-A—not even close to Tanner. I'm convinced it's intentional." He scoops his empty sugar packets off the counter and drops them into the trash can.

"There is no way it's that calculated."

"Capitalism, sweetheart. It's free marketing, and everything is calculated." He laughs.

Two girls vacate the table in the corner, leaving it just in time for me and Tanner to slide in. A girl with a laptop bag slung over her shoulder groans, no doubt gunning for a table to work at.

"Do you have any classes today?" I ask Tanner as I pull my drink to my lips.

"Just the one. I tried not to have any Friday classes this semester, but by the time I was scheduling there was only one option for my third-year design studio, so I had to take it."

"Design studio?"

"Architecture major."

"Like Marcus?"

Tanner chuckles. "No one, and I mean *no one*, is like Marcus when it comes to his schoolwork." He takes a sip of his coffee before continuing, "So, what's your major?"

"Photography with a business minor."

CHAPTER THIRTEEN

Tanner's eyes light up. "Photography? That's awesome! I'm guessing you plan to open your own business?"

"Yeah—weddings, I think. But I guess starting out I'll probably do a bunch of stuff. I take jobs on the side, but I don't plan to go fully in on it until after graduation."

"You know...I need a new headshot for this job fair the university is hosting at the end of next semester. Do you think you could?" He asks it tentatively, as if fearful I'll say no.

"Of course! Just tell me where and when and I'll bring my camera!"

"Awesome!" Tanner's cheeks redden with warmth, the icy chill from only minutes ago finally appearing to leave him.

I take a sip of my drink as a comfortable silence falls upon us. Tanner doesn't pry or try to fill the silence, and I'll admit I like the opportunity to just people-watch.

As I watch, a pair of young lovers approaches and claims the recently emptied table across from us. The boy's fingers are tightly intertwined with the girl's, and they remain so as they take their seats. They place their entwined hands on top of the wooden table, never breaking contact. It is clear they are deeply in love and don't need words to communicate their affection.

The pang that settles in my stomach is foreign, confusing. I'm happy—the happiest I've ever been. And yet I find myself wishing my relationship with Elijah was like that; affectionate, but not in the way that implies intimacy is to follow or with the intent to convey a certain message. Affection for the sake of touching the other because the idea of not touching them is more painful. I want that.

"Do you have classes today?" Tanner's voice cuts through my thoughts and pulls me back to the present moment.

"Huh?" I ask before his words catch up to me. "Oh, ha. No, I don't. I thankfully was able to forgo Friday classes this semester. I just wanted to get out of my dorm room. After this, I probably won't go out again until tonight."

The Lambda house is hosting a Friendsgiving of sorts, as Thanksgiving break starts next week. We have classes on Monday and Tuesday, but it's safe to say that most of us are already mentally checked out for the holiday.

"Are you bringing anything?" Tanner asks casually.

"I live in a dorm room. I signed up to bring pop." I laugh.

"Fair point. But...you could probably use the kitchen at the house if you wanted to...I don't know...bring something sweet and tasty." He raises his brows, almost pleading.

"Get on with it, Adler."

"I live with twenty-five guys. Most of which haven't even touched that kitchen. And...since you and Jenna are some of the only non-brothers coming..." Despite tiptoeing around what is essentially begging, amusement lingers in his eyes.

"You want me to bring pie," I say blandly.

"Actually, if you would be so kind—cheesecake."

"It's Thanksgiving. Why would I bring cheesecake? If anything, I think the traditional pie is pumpkin."

His face contorts into an expression of disgust. "Every occasion calls for cheesecake. Random Tuesday? Cheesecake. Passed your final? Cheesecake. Failed your final? Two cheesecakes."

"Fine!" I laugh at his absurdity. "I'll come over early and make a cheesecake."

FOURTEEN

KAT

Holding the printed recipe in one hand and a bag of ingredients in the other, I push open the heavy door to the frat house and am immediately engulfed by laughter and music. The thumping beat of the bass vibrates through my body, adding to the excitement buzzing in the air. I bask in the inviting warmth as I navigate through the crowded entryway toward the back of the house. The scent of cooking food and spilled beer fills my nose as I enter the bustling kitchen, where people are moving about with purpose and energy, each working on a dish for tonight's potluck dinner.

The counter is littered with dishes, quite a few of which are desserts—mostly cookies.

"Tanner!" I yell, but it comes out more of a growl.

"You rang?" Tanner appears in the entryway.

"What happened to *there will be no dessert*? Hm?"

A mischievous smirk tugs at the corners of his mouth, revealing a glint of amusement in his eyes. He shifts his weight from one foot to the other, a telltale sign of someone who has been caught red-handed.

"Tanner!"

"Did I say no dessert? That's my bad. I meant...no cheesecake. We needed cheesecake."

"We didn't need cheesecake—it's not like it's a traditional Thanksgiving dessert," Jenna interjects over her shoulder as she stirs something at the stove.

"No one asked, Jenna." Tanner sticks his tongue out at her, then turns toward me with a smile on his face. "I am sorry I deceived you. What I meant was...I needed cheesecake."

"You're an ass." I laugh.

"You love it," he says with a wink before walking over to Jenna and sticking a spoon in the pot she's stirring. "Needs salt."

"It's pudding," she says. His shocked expression causes her glare to intensify. "I'm making a trifle."

"That's pudding? Might I recommend..." He walks into the pantry and reemerges with two Jell-O instant pudding mixes. "These?"

"Kat's right—you are an ass!" Jenna laughs as she yanks the boxes from his grasp, then shuts off the burner on the stove.

Tanner walks past me and the moment our eyes meet, he shakes his head with wide eyes. "Don't eat the trifle."

I roll my eyes and find open counter space, push up my sleeves, and set to work in the cramped kitchen. I blend together cream cheese, sugar, vanilla, and the rest of the ingredients until they form a smooth, velvety mixture. The sweet aroma of vanilla extract wafts through the air, filling every corner of the room. Carefully, I pour the creamy concoction into a springform pan lined with crushed-up graham crackers and slide it into the preheated oven. Beads of sweat trickle down my temples as I anxiously wait for my first-ever homemade cheesecake to bake to perfection. With each minute that passes, my hopes rise and my prayers grow stronger. The anticipation is almost unbearable, but I know that this will be worth it in the end.

"Hey, babe." Elijah appears in the kitchen, clad only in a pair of basketball shorts. He approaches me and presses a kiss to my temple.

"Hey," I say, but I don't look away from the oven as I count the moments until I can check the cheesecake.

"Did the oven do something to you?" he whispers in my ear, providing commentary on my odd appliance fixation.

"My cheesecake is in there."

"Does the recipe call for eyes on the oven at all times?" He raises a brow, an amused smirk spread across his lips.

"Shut up," I laugh as I smack him in the arm.

He darts away and roams about the kitchen, silently perusing the fixings being prepared. As he approaches Jenna, he notices the pot sitting unattended on the stove. He does exactly what Tanner did and dips a spoon into the silky brown mixture, licking it before turning to Jenna.

"Needs salt," he says, tossing the spoon into the sink.

"Get out!" She points to the kitchen doorway, irritation plastered across her face.

As he yields to Jenna's warning, Elijah shoots me a wink. It is only then I notice Tanner silently laughing in the doorway.

"*Assholes*," I mouth to the both of them.

The two men take it in stride, smiling cheekily before allowing us to cook in peace.

With oven mitts on, I carefully pull out the springform pan and set it on a cooling rack. The crust is perfectly golden and the filling is just set with a slight jiggle in the center. A sense of relief washes over me as I admire my successfully baked cheesecake.

"It looks great!" Jenna peers at it in awe.

"Thanks!" I set the cheesecake aside to free up the oven, assuming that they need it for the turkey.

Then I look out the back window of the kitchen to see Marcus and Brendan huddled around a deep frier.

"Do they not know how dangerous those things are?" I ask no one in particular.

"Oh, they're fully aware. They're just stupid," Jenna responds, not even bothering to look up from her task.

With my cooking done, I venture out into the living room, where most of the guys—save for a few brothers in the kitchen—are huddled around the TV watching football.

"Is there a game on today?" I ask, confused.

"No, this is a replay of the Browns game from Monday," a brother replies.

I just nod, not particularly concerned with the schedules set forth by the NFL, and plop down onto the couch between Elijah and Tanner. Elijah notices my presence almost immediately, leaning into the couch and draping his arm across the back behind me.

We've settled into a newfound rhythm as of late, and I'll be honest—I love the way he's been acting. It's like the impenetrable fortress erected around his heart is slowly being removed and I adore watching it happen.

CHAPTER FOURTEEN

Especially when it is because of me.

I lean into his side as the rest of the guys hoot and holler at the game. "Did they not...watch the game on Monday?" I whisper to Elijah.

"Oh, they did." He smirks. The confusion plaguing my expression must register, because he continues, "It's hard to explain; don't think too much on it."

And that is that, I guess.

A loud crash sounds from the kitchen. That can't be good.

"I'm okay, I'm okay!" Marcus yells.

My eyes meet Elijah's and we both lunge toward the kitchen to see what catastrophe awaits us.

The turkey—the freshly fried turkey that Marcus and Brendan had been so excited about—is now on the kitchen floor. An expression I can only liken to shame plagues Marcus's face as he stares down at the bird.

Thankfully, no one—not even Tanner—is dumb enough to ask how that happened. We all just accept that we'll be having Friendsgiving sans turkey.

Well, not completely sans turkey. Marcus and Brendan are able to carve it in a way to avoid the side that landed against the kitchen floor.

We clear off the beer pong table set up in the dining room and spread a festive red tablecloth over it, atop which we arrange mismatched plates and silverware. Candles light up the otherwise dimly lit frat house. It is a warm and inviting scene, a welcome reprieve from the chaos of classes.

Almost no one reaches for the turkey. I can't help but notice the sadness in Marcus's eyes as he notices everyone's aversion to it.

"Can I get some turkey, please?" I ask as I extend my plate toward Marcus.

His eyes widen in surprise, then crinkle with joy as he reaches for my plate. "Of course!" He grins from ear to ear, piling far more turkey than I need atop my plate.

The clock strikes 9:00 PM, and despite the fact that most of us would love nothing more than to keel over and slip into food comas, the guys offer to clear the table and do the dishes.

When he's finished drying the dishes, Elijah asks, "Are you staying the night?"

I hadn't thought so far ahead, but I nod.

A smile blooms on his lips. "Good," he says before pressing a kiss to my cheek. "Head upstairs. I'll be right up."

"Okay."

The moment my head hits the pillow, I know with certainty that nothing is happening between us tonight. If I'm being honest, I'm not even sure I could manage as I'm on the verge of busting at the seams anyway.

FIFTEEN

KAT

As I enter my mom's house for Thanksgiving break, a wave of anxiety washes over me. I'm unsure what I expect, but my stomach instantly plummets when I see the note on the kitchen counter.

> *Katarina,*
> *Had to go into work, there is a frozen lasagna in the freezer. Closing, won't be home until late.*
> *Love you,*
> *Mom*
> *PS: You have mail in the basket by the door.*

I let out an exasperated sigh as I toss the crumpled note back onto the cluttered kitchen counter and make my way to the refrigerator. A quick glance reveals a sparse selection of food, but my eyes zero in on the half-empty six-pack of hard cider. With a groan, I grab a bottle and twist off the cap, letting the cool liquid soothe my parched throat.

It's not like I expected her to greet me at the door, but tomorrow is Thanksgiving. I can't imagine she plans on cooking if she's not going to get home until the wee hours of the morning, but a "Hello" would be nice.

The basket of mail in the entryway is piled high with an assortment of bills, ads, and the occasional package of coupons from the local grocery store. I quickly spot a familiar name written in bold letters on top of a bundle held together by a rubber band—"*Kat.*"

Curiosity piqued, I reach for the stack and start sorting through the mail. Most of it is junk—credit card offers, local dealerships wanting me to come in for their "special financing," a bill from the university, and...

A lump forms in my throat as my fingertips ghost over the last envelope in the stack with a "*Return to Sender*" stamp in bright red ink on the front.

I have no interest in having a relationship with my dad. The man left my mom when I wasn't even a year old to be with the mistress he'd knocked up. The irony of that is not lost on me—leaving the child you have at home to be a father to the child you don't know yet.

The sting still lingers almost twenty years later.

His address is printed in my handwriting, the same address he's lived at since leaving us all those years ago. It's where I've sent letters every fall since I was ten, hoping that he may be intrigued enough about my life to write back. The letters always go unanswered, but I liked to envision him sitting in front of the fireplace while he reads them, his shame

CHAPTER FIFTEEN

holding him back from reaching out rather than an utter lack of interest.

The big red stamp of rejection stares back at me, a clear indicator that he didn't think me important enough to give his new address.

I drop the envelope back onto the table, take a sip of my cider, pull my phone out, and begin scrolling through Instagram. Everyone is posting about their families and how thankful they are to be home for the holiday. A few people post about "Blackout Wednesday" from their local hometown bar. None of it brings me comfort.

Sinking into the couch, I remember with delight that I'm not the only person from school who lives in the Columbus area.

KAT

Any interest in coming to Dublin?

With a sigh, I switch the smart TV on and navigate to Netflix, where I scroll through potential shows to watch until my phone dings with a notification. I reach for the device.

TANNER

Text me the address

I type out the address before continuing to scroll through Netflix in search of something to watch.

Though I'm not sure where exactly Tanner is from, he shows up fifteen minutes later with a takeout bag in hand and a grin on his face.

"What the hell did you do, teleport here?" I laugh as I open the door, letting him in.

His confused expression makes me chuckle before he realizes what I mean. "Oh, ha. No, I'm from Worthington."

Worthington is less than ten minutes down the road and now I find myself wondering how I never met him before.

"Wait, where did you go to school?" I ask as he steps across the threshold.

"Kilbourne. You?"

"Scioto."

"Small world," he says with a laugh as he sets the bag on the kitchen counter. "I believe we beat you guys in football senior year."

"We were robbed!" I laugh.

"Whatever you gotta tell yourself, sweetheart."

I roll my eyes, trying not to pay his taunts any mind.

"Do you have anything to drink?"

"Hard cider in the fridge, but we also have water."

I expect it to be more awkward than it is, having Tanner in my space like this. We're friends at school, but having him at my mom's house feels…too real. However, he just reaches into the fridge to grab a hard cider before snatching the bag he brought off the counter.

"Did you want to eat in the living room?" he asks as he looks to the TV.

"Sure!" I turn on my heels with him behind me and walk over to the couch. Sinking into the plush red cushions, I sigh with relief.

Tanner begins pulling boxes from the bag and instantly my senses are overwhelmed by the delicious smell of orange chicken.

"How did you know I love Chinese food?" I gape as I

CHAPTER FIFTEEN

reach for the box. He yanks it out of my grasp with a laugh, but quickly yields when I pout up at him.

He just shrugs at my question. "Lucky guess. Everyone likes Chinese food."

I eagerly plunge my fork into the steaming orange chicken. The tangy scent and succulent pieces of meat explode on my taste buds, sending waves of pleasure through my body.

As I take another bite, I can feel Tanner's gaze burning holes into me. When I turn to him, his lips are curved in an amused expression.

"What?" I mumble.

He just laughs as he sits down next to me, balancing a box filled with beef and broccoli on his lap. "Nothing."

"What do you want to watch?" I ask.

Tanner inspects the screen as I display potential options, most of which are comedy shows. "*Community.*" He points as I scroll past the unfamiliar TV show.

"I've never seen it."

Tanner looks at me, pure shock mixed with what appears to be horror invading his face. "You've never seen *Community*? Has Childish Gambino in it? Only the funniest show on the face of the planet?" As I stare at him with a blank expression, his shock only grows in intensity. "Damn."

We settle into a comfortable silence as we watch *Community*, Tanner pausing it every so often to offer me more context.

With eager ears, I listen to every word he spills about his favorite show. How Jeff relentlessly pursues Brita, how he eventually has a period where he pursues Annie, Annie's crush on Troy in the earlier seasons. All of it. He breaks each scene down as if he's memorized the plot of the entire show.

"So, Jeff used to be a lawyer...but now he's not?" I ask, confused.

"Well..." Tanner grabs the remote and pauses the show once more, no doubt prepared to give me a full summary of Jeff's demise. "He was never technically qualified. He was practicing law, but his law degree was fake. So, he had to go back to school to get the required education before actually going to law school."

"So, he's a fraud."

"Basically."

"And we're supposed to root for this guy?" The shock that seeps into my words makes him laugh.

"Not necessarily. He's supposed to suck—it's part of his appeal. Like Dennis from *It's Always Sunny in Philadelphia*. Except...slightly less of a bad person."

I stare at him blankly.

He reels with shock again. "Don't tell me you've never seen *It's Always Sunny in Philadelphia*..."

"I...have never seen *It's Always Sunny in Philadelphia*."

"Remind me when we're back on campus, I need to get you on a stern regimen of comedy TV education."

I grab the nearest throw pillow and launch it at his face. Tanner's loud laughter fills the room as he dodges the pillow with ease. His amusement is infectious and I let out a chuckle.

"Thank you for coming over tonight," I say, my tone far more serious than moments before.

For a moment, I think he isn't going to respond. Then, when his eyes meet my own, a faint smile paints his lips, though it doesn't quite meet his eyes.

"Of course...I'll always show up for you." Tanner looks

CHAPTER FIFTEEN

down, wringing his hands with such force that I wonder if it hurts. "Was Elijah not able to?"

A lump forms in my throat at the question. "I...hadn't even thought to call Elijah. He's...busy."

"Too busy for you?" Tanner asks, but there is no jest or judgment in his voice.

"His family has high expectations. He warned me that he wouldn't be particularly reachable this weekend. I guess they do this big party at his parents' house in the city."

"And he didn't invite you?"

"We've only been seeing each other for a few months."

"Still," he says, "he should have at least asked. I would have invited you."

Silence lingers, the weight of his words not lost on either of us. He doesn't backtrack, doesn't back off; he just looks at me, his eyes fixed resolutely on my own. It should be uncomfortable—the implication should have me jumping out of my seat—yet as he looks at me, I feel nothing but comfort at his honesty.

"Thank you," I say quietly.

"For what?"

"For coming." The moment the words leave my mouth, he quirks a brow. I throw the other accent pillow at him, and this time it smacks against his cheek.

"Oh, you're going to get it," he laughs as he stands up and gathers an armful of the pillows.

I quickly dart away, placing the kitchen island between us as he adopts what I can only describe as a fighting pose, preparing to strike.

At the exact moment he moves to lift a pillow, the sound of

a key turning in the lock alerts us both to the front door opening. Tanner lowers the pillow to his side.

My mom steps into the room with little spatial awareness, looking down into her purse, searching for something. "Katarina?" she says loudly before looking up to make eye contact with me.

"Hey."

"Sorry I'm home so late—one of the cooks called in sick, so it got a bit hectic."

I look at the clock and realize it's well past 1:00 AM. My gaze darts to Tanner, who has since set the pillows gently on the couch and is now standing tall, ready to be introduced to my mom.

Oh, shit. I guess I should do that.

"Mom, this is my friend Tanner from school."

Her head jerks as she notices him standing there, a flush coloring her cheeks. "Where are my manners? I'm sorry, Tanner, it's lovely to meet you. I'm Kat's mom."

"Nice to meet you, Mrs. M—" He pauses, no doubt realizing the flaw in his thinking. "It's nice to meet you."

"You may call me Julie." She gives him a reassuring smile before stepping into the kitchen. She inspects the freezer, clearly noticing the uneaten frozen lasagna. "Did you eat?"

"Yeah, uh—Tanner brought food."

She nods, peering down at her watch. "Well, I need to get to bed. Randy called off tomorrow, so I have to work a double."

And there it is, the words I was anticipating.

She's bailing on Thanksgiving again.

She disappears into her bedroom and I stand in complete shock, though I shouldn't be surprised.

CHAPTER FIFTEEN

"Are you okay?" Tanner asks as he approaches and rests his hand against the small of my back.

"Yeah, I'm fine." I wave my hand in an attempt to feign indifference and force out a laugh. My voice cracks as I do.

"Come to my house tomorrow," he whispers so quietly I can barely hear him.

"I can't do that. That would be rude."

"It's not rude, because I'm inviting you. Come tomorrow—my mom loves meeting new people."

I dwell on the thought for a moment before turning to him. His eyes are so sincere that I quickly come to a decision.

"Okay."

SIXTEEN

KAT

I squirm uneasily on the creaky front porch of Tanner's childhood home, the scent of roasted turkey wafting out the door and teasing my senses. Nervousness tightens my chest at the thought of facing his family after being invited so last-minute. Despite Tanner's reassurance, I feel like an imposing idiot. I quickly wipe my hands on my sweater, hoping it will conceal any stains from my disastrous attempt at making green bean casserole. Trusting that Tanner's mom has the dessert covered, I take a deep breath and timidly knock on the door, wondering if I am intruding on their cherished family holiday.

The door swings open to reveal Tanner, smiling ear to ear.

"You made it!" he says as he reaches to grab the casserole dish from my hands.

He is dressed in dark-wash jeans and a cable-knit maroon sweater. Weirdly enough, it is almost the exact same shade as my sweater.

He steps to the side to allow me through the door. With his lips a mere whisper from my ear, he says, "Mine is better."

CHAPTER SIXTEEN

"You're an idiot," I say with a laugh.

"Got you to smile, didn't it?" He winks before backing away, his bare feet padding against the floor.

As I step into the kitchen, my eyes are immediately drawn to the dazzling sight before me. The pristine white marble countertops glisten and shimmer under the brilliant sunlight pouring in through the floor-to-ceiling windows. My gaze then travels to the carefully crafted Spanish tile backsplash, each tile a work of art in its own right, their hues adding a burst of vibrance to the space.

Finally, I lay my sights upon the showstopper of the room —the beautiful cabinets. Painted in a striking shade of cobalt blue, they add a touch of boldness and character to the vast expanse of this grand kitchen. It's a sight that leaves me speechless, my senses overwhelmed by the luxuriousness and elegance of it all.

"Mom, this is Kat," Tanner says as he sets my casserole dish on the counter amongst the other dishes.

"Your home is beautiful," I say in awe.

"I like you already!" Mrs. Adler's eyes sparkle with delight as she pulls me into a hug without warning. I catch a glimpse of Tanner mouthing "*Sorry*" as I gaze over her shoulder.

The instant affection is foreign, yes, but not bad. I kind of like it.

She releases me from her embrace but holds my arms with a grin as she looks me over from head to toe. "You are gorgeous! Isn't she gorgeous?"

"The most gorgeous girl I've ever seen," Tanner responds, an awkwardness in his voice that I can't quite place, but his response seems to satisfy his mom's lingering interest and she finally releases me.

A crash rings out from over by the stove.

"If you dropped the sweet potatoes, Larry, I swear to God, I will…" Mrs. Adler bustles across the kitchen without another word. As she approaches the stove, which is now coated in what looks like gravy, her expression goes from irritated to furious. "Just go." She waves Larry away and begins cleaning up the stove.

"Sorry about that," Tanner says.

"It's okay…she's nice."

"Too nice, sometimes. Don't worry, though, she can be just as mean when pushed." He laughs, nodding toward the stove as he presses his hand to the small of my back once more, gently pushing me toward the family room off the side of the kitchen.

With careful steps, we descend from the warm and inviting kitchen into the spacious room where Tanner's brothers and father are huddled around a large television mounted high on the wall. The TV gleams with vivid colors, its sharp edges casting shadows on the smooth white surface of the fireplace just below it. Flanking the fireplace on both sides are tall built-in bookshelves, lined with rows upon rows of books and trinkets.

Tanner clears his throat, but only his dad peers over at us.

"Hey, Tanner!" He barely looks at us before returning his attention to the game. After a brief delay, he does a double take, notices me, and approaches us. "I apologize. It's lovely to meet you," Mr. Adler says as he extends his hand. "I'm Tanner's father, Larry."

"It's lovely to meet you. Your home is beautiful." I smile awkwardly.

Larry looks around as if seeing the space for the first time.

CHAPTER SIXTEEN

"By golly, it is! Elaine, you've decorated our home beautifully."

"Sucking up to me right now isn't going to save the cup of gravy you spilled everywhere!" Mrs. Adler yells from the kitchen, but not an ounce of anger lingers in her words.

Larry simply laughs before turning back to us, then peering at the TV. "Please, join us," he says idly, slinking back over to the two young men sitting on the large sectional.

I look to Tanner and he just shrugs. I move further into the room and allow my gaze to rove over the bookcases. In the center of the one to the left of the television, I notice a black and white picture that looks to be a drawing of Tanner's parents.

It's stunning.

Tanner joins me and says quietly, "I drew that for their twentieth wedding anniversary a couple of years ago."

"You drew that?!"

My shock must show on my face, because his brows shoot up in surprise.

"Lack of faith, tsk tsk." He laughs before continuing, "I love to draw. It's actually a big reason I was drawn to architecture."

"Do architects draw a lot?"

"Not as much as they once did. Technology has kind of shifted things, but I like to."

I nod in understanding. His love for drawing isn't all that different from my love of photography...I just hope that I can find success in it in the same way that he's found a way to shape his love of drawing into a career path.

"Dinner is ready!" Mrs. Adler calls from the kitchen.

Larry clicks the TV off within seconds, earning a groan from the young men next to him.

"No complaining," Larry says sternly.

Tanner's brothers, Thomas and Theo, could not be more different. I can tell they're brothers, but each of them seems to have leaned toward one parent more than the other, while Tanner seems to be an equal mix of his parents, with his father's height, nose, and blasé attitude and his mother's beautiful green eyes and full lips.

As I step through the doorway into the spacious dining room, my mouth drops open in awe. The long wooden table spans the length of the room, its surface adorned with an incredible array of Thanksgiving dishes. Each dish is a work of art, lovingly prepared and arranged with precision and care. The rich, savory scent of roasted turkey fills the air, accompanied by the sweet scent of freshly baked pies. My stomach growls in anticipation as I take in the feast fit for a king, a testament to the love this family shares.

My eyes linger on the far end of the table where the desserts are laid out, a perfectly prepared cheesecake sitting amidst the otherwise traditional holiday desserts.

I chuckle, pulling Tanner's attention in my direction.

"Cheesecake," I say.

"Cheesecake." He grins down at me with a quirk of his brow.

We settle into our seats on one side of the table and his brothers find seats on the other. His parents sit at the opposite ends of the table.

Tanner's brothers eagerly pile their plates high with Thanksgiving delicacies, barely concealing their impatience for the meal to begin. Their elbows jostle and forks clink

CHAPTER SIXTEEN

against plates as they dig in with ravenous excitement, oblivious to the traditional rules of etiquette.

Tanner appears to take their lead and reaches for a massive scoop of mashed potatoes. He turns to me and asks, "Mashed potatoes?"

I nod, and he plops the scoop onto my plate before loading his own up with the same absurd amount of the fluffy side dish. We go through the same routine as he scans the table for different offerings—turkey, sweet potatoes, my own green bean casserole, cranberry sauce, and more. Every time he reaches for a spoon or spear, he looks at me to ask if I would like something.

Before I know it, my plate is piled high with more food than I know what to do with. So I do what any sane person would do—I dig in.

"These green beans are fantastic!" Tanner's dad, Larry, declares from the end of the table. Elaine informs him that I made them, causing him to turn to me with adoration. "You're an incredible cook, Kat."

"It was just the recipe from the can."

"Nonsense—you made it your own. It's delicious."

I glance at Tanner, who simply smiles at me with a shrug before digging back into his meal.

Dinner passes in a whirlwind of conversation. I learn that Tanner's brothers are fifteen and eighteen and that the older of the two—Thomas—is in his senior year of high school. He heckles me for a bit about where I went to high school, but overall the Adlers are the picture of kindness. Elaine continuously asks me questions about my life, and not a single one of them feels insincere. She asks if I'd be willing to take photos for her company picnic over the summer, and I'm giddy with delight at the prospect of another job to add to my portfolio.

As we transition into dessert, Tanner makes no attempts to hide his enthusiasm for his precious cheesecake. He piles almost half the pie onto his plate with delight before turning to me and asking if I'd like some.

When dinner comes to an end, I find myself oddly disappointed at the realization that it's over. Tanner's family are some of the kindest people I've ever met. Leaving isn't something I expected would sadden me, so when Tanner's eyes meet mine, I know with certainty that he can tell what's plaguing me.

"Don't for a second think that my mom is going to let her claws out of you any time soon."

He poses it as a warning, but I know what it is. Reassurance.

"Thank you."

"If you keep saying that, I may think you're malfunctioning." He laughs. "Seriously, Kat. I'm glad you could come. If nothing else, you gave my parents someone to dote on that isn't me."

I roll my eyes before he pulls me into a hug and whispers, "Call Elijah. I know you said he's busy, but I also know you want to talk to him and you shouldn't be made to feel like you can't." He squeezes me tightly before letting go.

I nod. "I will."

"And drive safe."

"I will."

"And—"

CHAPTER SIXTEEN

"Tanner, shut up," I laugh.

He simply salutes me as I slip into my car before disappearing into the house.

SEVENTEEN

KAT

I manage to get through finals and the blur of winter break, receiving a surprising B in Macroeconomics despite my struggles. During my stay at home, my mom barely has any free time due to her demanding job, and Elijah is constantly tied up with his father's never-ending obligations. I try to see him a few times while home on break, but he is pretty much always busy. As much as it hurts, I get it.

Now, we've been sitting at the main library on campus for hours, and despite my insistence that maybe a business minor just isn't for me, Elijah continues to attempt to explain finance to me.

My stomach growls loudly, reminding me that I haven't eaten since breakfast two hours ago. I glare at the thick textbook in front of me, the words on the page blurring together in a frustrating mess. I resist the urge to throw it out the window and take a deep breath, trying to push through my hunger and finish my finance assignment before I pass out from either anger or hunger.

CHAPTER SEVENTEEN

"Kat?" Elijah asks, clear annoyance in his voice.

"What?"

"Did you hear a word I just said?"

"You were talking about risk and return."

Something in his expression tells me that he was *not*, in fact, talking about risk and return.

"We're not even on that chapter anymore. What is going on with you?" he asks.

"Nothing," I sigh.

Elijah continues talking about various topics out of my textbook, but my eyes are practically glazed over as I stare out the window at the "K" below.

The weather has been unreliable since we returned from winter break and as snow begins to fall outside of the glass, I find myself groaning knowing I will have to walk back to my dorm in the snow.

"Kat," Elijah says, his irritation at my lack of attention resurfacing.

"What?" I ask.

"I asked if you have to take notes on chapter six too, or just chapter five."

"Just chapter five."

In what feels like my saving grace, Marcus and Jenna appear through the elevator on the other side of the room.

"Jenna!" I yell as I raise my hand above my head, earning myself a very aggressive "Shhh" and a glare from the employee sitting behind the information desk.

Jenna and Marcus spot me and Elijah sitting at the far end of the area filled with tables, our backs to the stacks. They approach us and Elijah seems to get the point, closing my textbook.

THE VERY FIRST NIGHT

"Hey guys!" Marcus grins as he approaches us, resting his arm atop Elijah's head. The glare Elijah pins him with quickly prompts him to remove his arm.

Jenna laughs at the interaction before turning to me. "What are you guys working on?" she asks.

"We were working on stuff for my business finance class, but we were just wrapping up."

"Awesome! Do you guys want to grab lunch?"

I turn to Elijah, who shrugs, a tell of indifference I've grown to know well.

"We're down."

We pack up our study supplies before heading across the street to the student center. As we approach the big glass doors, I groan, realizing the door is locked.

"What the hell?" I mutter.

"'Closed due to maintenance issues,'" Elijah reads off the paper taped to the inside of the window.

"Busted pipe," Marcus interjects as he looks down at his phone with his email open.

"But...I wanted a bagel." I pout, and Elijah laughs.

"I'm sure they have something that will fulfill your cravings over at Rosie's. Let's go." He slings an arm around my shoulders and we all start walking.

Rosie's Diner is located right in the heart of the Tri-Towers Rotunda, one of the clusters of dorm buildings on campus. It is also the only restaurant on campus that is open twenty-four hours a day, so it tends to be best eaten at two in the morning when you're slightly too tipsy. The food is better that way.

Either way, greasy diner food will always sound good,

CHAPTER SEVENTEEN

even if you're fully aware it might not feel all that great in an hour or two.

We order at the kiosk and grab drinks from the fountain before entering the campus diner, a familiar spot for Jenna and me. It's our go-to late-night hangout, where we sit at the bar-style counter facing the bustling kitchen. But today, with the bright midday sun streaming through the windows, we opt for a table along the far wall. The four of us squeeze into a booth as we await our orders to be called.

"Sooooooo," Jenna says, overdramatically dragging the word out until we all look her way.

"What?" I ask.

"What are we thinking for spring break?"

"Spring break is next month—wouldn't we have needed to book something already?" I ask.

"Not necessarily," Elijah chimes in as he leans forward in his seat, his arm resting on the back of the booth. "My parents have a beach house in Myrtle Beach; they're never there in March. We could all go there."

Jenna stares at him, her mouth agape. "How is this the first time I'm hearing about this?"

"Because you never asked," Elijah laughs.

She turns to Marcus with the same shocked expression, but he just shrugs in response.

The three of them start discussing spring break in more detail, but I can't help but feel a rush of anxiety about it. I can't put my finger on it, but the idea of going to the Hanases' beach house has me ready to vomit all over this table.

"Are you down?" Jenna asks me.

"Hm?"

"Are you down to go to Elijah's parents' beach house for spring break?"

"Oh, yeah, it sounds fun." I take a massive gulp of my pop, trying to satisfy my suddenly dry mouth.

"Are you good?" Elijah asks quietly.

I nod in response, not sure how to convey how I'm feeling. I must be having an off day.

"Fantastic!" Jenna squeals. "I'll start looking at flights tonight."

"No need—we'll drive!" Marcus says with a grin.

EIGHTEEN

KAT

Kent State is known for a few things, but no historical event eclipses May 4th, 1970. It's so highly regarded in campus history that there was a memorial garden erected on campus in the eighties.

Tucked within the bustling campus, the May 4th Memorial Park unfurls over two lush acres. A grandiose granite monument stands tall in the center, inviting visitors to reflect on this solemn day and its lasting impact. The garden draws a steady stream of alumni and students alike to the tranquil surroundings. As they walk along the memorial, their feet brush against exactly 58,175 vibrant daffodils—one for each American life lost during the Vietnam War—a poignant reminder.

As part of the mandatory curriculum, freshmen at Kent State University enroll in a seminar dedicated to the tragic events of May 4th, 1970. Each student is given a copy of the names and photos of the four students who lost their lives that day, along with details about the anti-war protest that turned deadly. The professor somberly reminds students of the importance of remembering and respecting those who passed away on the university grounds many years ago.

Even all these years later, Kent State remembers that day with clarity.

The garden also serves as one of the most beautiful places on campus and is one of the only places you won't find college students acting like idiots and causing issues. I'm glad that at least when it comes to this, students have a general understanding that we need to maintain respect.

I sit on a granite bench at the far end of the park, camera gripped tightly in my hands. I scan the surrounding trees and flowers, trying to find the perfect spot for our photoshoot but feeling the melancholy emotions that accompany this location. The memorial park is conveniently located near the architecture building, making it a convenient spot to get beautiful photos for Tanner's upcoming job fair in a few weeks.

"Hey!" Tanner yells as he approaches the park, a grin spread across his lips.

I don't know that I've ever seen him dressed up before, and I'll admit...I don't hate it.

As he strolls through the park toward me, his jeans brush against the bright yellow daffodils planted in neat rows. He wears a crisp button-down shirt with the top button undone, a navy-blue suit jacket draped over his arm. The color of his outfit combined with the flowers is a subtle nod to our university, sure to make him an instant conversation-starter at the fair.

"You look nice," I say with a smile as he halts in front of me.

CHAPTER EIGHTEEN

"So do you."

I roll my eyes as I look down at myself, clad in a Kent hoodie and leggings. "No need to butter me up, I'm already doing this for free."

He gasps with mock shock. "Attempting to butter you up? Psh, that doesn't sound like me." He winks. "Besides, I plan on paying you, so that's a moot point."

"You don't have to pay me—I already told you I'd do it for free."

"And I just told you I'm paying you either way."

"*Tanner*," I groan.

"*Katarina*," he responds with the same level of annoyance in his cadence.

"You don't have to—"

"I know that. But you work hard and you deserve to be paid for that hard work. So let me pay you."

The earnestness he conveys causes me to instantly crack. "Fine."

He smiles down at me, no doubt fighting the urge to make some shitty remark about how he won. I'm glad he doesn't, because I very well might push him down the hill into the parking lot below.

I find a cluster of flowers toward the back of the park with near-perfect lighting. "Stand here, please."

"Please. So professional, Kat." He grins and it takes everything in me not to throw something at him.

I laugh as I pull the viewfinder to my eye and smile as I admire the bright yellow flowers through my fixed lens. The shallow depth of field creates a beautiful bokeh effect, blurring the background into a soft blanket of sunshine. I am glad I invested in this lens—it's perfect for capturing moments like this, even if it did cost me most of my leftover financial aid money last semester.

"Was the outfit on purpose?" I ask as I peer through my camera lens. He squints at me, eyebrows furrowed in confusion. "You're wearing blue, and the flowers are yellow."

Tanner shifts from side to side as he takes in his surroundings. "Oh damn, they are."

I just shake my head and fail to bite back a laugh. "You're such a dork. Stand still and smile, please."

He does as I ask and we barely talk as he poses and I snap pictures. It's nearly silent, the only noise the sound of students walking to their evening classes. The garden is one of the more secluded places on campus.

"I think we got it," I say with a smile.

"Awesome!" He grins as he steps toward me. "Thanks for doing this, seriously. I appreciate it."

"No need, I am always looking for opportunities to add to my portfolio."

He nods before changing the subject. "Did you give Jenna your part of the deposit for next semester?"

We've been discussing the prospect of getting a house in the fall since getting back from winter break—Jenna, Marcus, Tanner, Brendan, their friend Aaron, his girlfriend Regina, Elijah, and me. If I'm honest, I wasn't sure it was going to work out—we'd been struggling to find a house that suits everyone's needs. We ultimately found a house about ten minutes from campus. It's not the fanciest, but it was within everyone's price range. Marcus and Jenna plan on sharing a room, as do Aaron and Regina. I wondered why Elijah didn't invite me to share a room, but was deterred from asking by the look on his face when the topic came up.

CHAPTER EIGHTEEN

"Yeah, I sent it to her yesterday. Did you send yours?"

"Last week! Are you excited to live off campus? Why do you live on campus anyway?"

"Honestly? It was cheaper than any of the apartments Jenna and I could find and it just seemed like the easier route."

"That makes sense. If it weren't for financial aid, I wouldn't be able to live in the house. Don't get me wrong, I'm not going to pretend like my parents aren't well off, but putting three boys through college is a lot." He sighs before continuing, "I'm glad you're moving off campus with us next semester." He glances at me, and I can feel my stomach erupt with butterflies.

What the hell was that?!

I clear my throat, which thrusts me into a coughing fit. Tanner stops beside me as I keel forward, my hands on my knees, attempting to control the coughing. He rubs circles on my back, no doubt in an attempt to comfort me, but as I realize why I lost it in the first place, I swat his hand away.

"I'm fine," I wheeze, standing up and stifling small coughs as I try to get my breathing back in order.

"You're sure?"

"Yeah, I'm fine." I push my hair out of my face, flushed—for a reason I refuse to think too much about.

NINETEEN

KAT

My stomach churns with anxiety as we drive through the night, leaving Kent behind and heading toward our destination. Every mile that rolls by only adds to my nervousness, and I can't shake off the feeling no matter how hard I try. The reason for my unease remains elusive, but its grip on me is undeniable.

Excitement pulses through our group as we pull up to Elijah's parents' beach house in our rented SUV, ready for a week of endless fun during spring break. The impressive beach house stands tall between two neighboring properties, its white stucco walls reflecting the bright sunlight. A large balcony stretches across the front of the house, offering a breathtaking view of the vast expanse of the Atlantic before us. As I step out of the car, the warm rays of the sun envelop me and I take in a deep breath of salty sea air, instantly feeling rejuvenated and eager to explore all that Myrtle Beach has to offer.

CHAPTER NINETEEN

Everyone darts toward the house, scrambling to claim bedrooms. Elijah and I hang back, as he already informed me that the master bedroom is off-limits to everyone but us, so we don't need to fight the masses for our room. My chest fills with warmth at his words.

Ours.

As we cross the threshold, the salty scent of the ocean is just as strong, maybe even stronger. Our feet sink into plush, sandy-colored carpet. A vase filled with seashells sits on a wicker side table next to a comfortable armchair covered with anchor-patterned pillows. Framed photographs of lighthouses and sailboats line the walls, mixed in with photos of Elijah over the years. A framed photo of him in a tailored suit next to his father at what appears to be an important event catches my eye. Elijah looks young, maybe twelve, and his father is the picture of timeless luxury.

"That's from the night my dad won the election for his first term," Elijah says as he nudges my shoulder, pride in his voice but a hard-to-place expression creasing his brow.

"You guys look really happy," I say. I can't help but think about how little I know about my dad. Do photos of my half-brother hang in his home? Does he tell people he's his only child? Is he the legacy my dad longs to have continue on? It stings to think about, so I do everything in my power to shake off the thought.

"Yeah." Elijah shrugs.

Suddenly Jenna and Tanner barrel in.

"We're going to the liquor store. You guys want to come?" Tanner says.

I glance toward Elijah, but he shakes his head. "I have to

pull the cover off the pool and hide the breakables from Aaron."

I barely know Aaron, but from the stories I've been told, he has a tendency to break things when he's drunk because he has the delicacy of a baby deer learning to walk. Apparently, he's the very reason the window in the front room of the Lambda house had to be replaced last semester.

"What about you?" Tanner asks me.

I turn again to Elijah and he just shrugs.

"Sure," I say, "why not?"

After pressing a kiss to Elijah's cheek, I follow Tanner and Jenna out the door. The three of us pile into the black SUV, which is thankfully still cool from the air conditioning. Jenna jumps into the passenger seat and reaches for the aux cord. Since Tanner's information is on the car rental, he drives, which defaults me to the back seat.

The moment Tanner notices Jenna has the aux cord, he snatches it out of her grasp. "Driver's choice, Jen." He grins, ignoring her as she flips him off. "What do you want to listen to, Kat?"

"You've got to be kidding me!" Jenna squeals in irritation, then laughs. "She's just going to want to listen to *1989*."

"That's actually not true, so—" I stick my tongue out at her.

"Fine, what do you want to listen to, then?" she asks, raising her brow.

"*Reputation*, please!"

Jenna groans before slumping back into her seat, but Tanner doesn't question it and queues up Taylor Swift's *Reputation* album on Spotify. "Ready For It" begins to play,

CHAPTER NINETEEN

instilling me with an extra dose of excitement for the week ahead of us. Tanner sets down his phone on the center console before pressing the button to roll down the windows.

A burst of warm air whips through my hair and caresses my face. The scent of fresh grass and blooming flowers fills the car, instantly calming me. I take a deep breath and feel the tension in my body melt away. It's like all the anxiety and stress from the past few days were just a result of being cooped up in cold, dreary Ohio weather. But now, with the sun shining down on us, I can feel myself relax.

As we turn into the parking lot of the liquor store, my eyes widen at the sight of bumper-to-bumper cars and people swarming around. It's no surprise—Myrtle Beach is always a hot spot this time of year. I can see groups of people loading up their carts with bottles and cans of various alcoholic beverages.

Tanner finally finds an open parking spot and quickly pulls in, carefully navigating through the chaos. We grab a cart and set out on our mission to find libations for the night.

After briefly scanning the aisles, we beeline for the vodka. Tanner grabs two bottles of Tito's vodka before we venture forward. Jenna puts two large boxes of cheap wine into the cart, one white and one red—the one thing we've never agreed on.

When we reach the coolers on the far wall, Tanner grabs two twenty-four-packs of Coors Light.

"Is all of this necessary?" I ask.

"You've never seen the amount of alcohol these guys put back on a regular basis, have you?"

Jenna approaches, struggling to balance three overstuffed bags of salt and vinegar chips in one arm while cradling a massive tub of French onion dip in the other. She stops next to our shopping cart and drops everything in, causing a loud clatter and earning puzzled looks from both Tanner and me.

"What? I've been on a kick," Jenna says. She shrugs before walking ahead.

We quickly check out at the counter. Tanner tosses two packs of Reese's cups onto the counter along with the various alcoholic beverages we've collected. Outside, we're loading up the trunk when Tanner reaches into the unbranded white plastic bag and grabs the two packages of Reese's cups.

"Here." He grins as he hands me one of the two.

"What is this?" I stare at the orange package but make no effort to grab it from him.

"Chocolate...?"

"Yeah, but why—"

"Don't you like Reese's cups?" His brows pinch together as he stares down at me.

"They're my favorite..." I continue staring at them, and he seems to register that I'm not going to grab them as he presses the package into my palm.

I don't remember ever telling him what my favorite candy was. What a convenient guess on his part.

"Thank you," I say timidly.

Jenna looks at the package in my hand and frowns. "What the hell, Adler?! You didn't get me one."

"Eat your fucking chips, Jenna." He rolls his eyes with a chuckle before climbing into the vehicle.

Jenna hops in the back seat without saying anything and I climb into the front seat. On the drive back, our words are swallowed by the rushing wind and Taylor Swift's voice blaring from the speakers. My dark brown hair whips around

CHAPTER NINETEEN

my face as I drape my hand out the window, relishing the cool breeze on my fingertips. The familiar song brings a sense of calm and ease.

So why am I filled with dread the moment we pull back into the driveway?

TWENTY

KAT

With each step down the creaky wooden staircase, the faint sounds of music and chatter grow in volume until they nearly drown out my own thoughts. I have been looking forward to a calm night of drinking by the pool with my friends, but as soon as I reach the bottom step, I am hit with a wave of energy from the crowded beach house. The guys have never been known for keeping things low-key, so it's not really a surprise that it isn't just our group of friends. Laughter echoes off the walls as people weave in and out of rooms, thankfully still sober enough that nothing has gone awry.

I navigate through a cluster of partygoers, desperate for a moment of reprieve by the pool. But even outside is bustling with people, their laughter and chatter carried on the ocean breeze, so I stay inside.

Despite the lively atmosphere, I can't seem to shake the uneasiness in my gut. Just as I begin to feel overwhelmed, Tanner materializes at my side, offering me a plastic red cup

CHAPTER TWENTY

filled with a deep red drink. Gratefully, I take a sip, feeling the coolness of the liquid soothing my nerves.

"You are a godsend," I say before taking another healthy sip of red wine.

He grabs his chest in mock shock as if I've shot him, then grins. "You looked like you could use a drink."

"Well, you were right," I reply, gulping down the rest of the drink in three large swallows. Tanner stares at me. "What?"

His gaze is intense as he studies me, and I feel a little self-conscious under his scrutiny. "Is everything all right?" he asks with concern in his voice.

"Why wouldn't I be?"

"I don't know, you've just seemed off since we left Ohio."

"I'm fine." Which I guess is true. Or it should be. I can't name a reason for the weight in my chest—I should be elated to be on spring break—so when his eyes meet mine, I just shrug. "No, I'm not. But it's just a funk. I'll be okay."

He seems to take this at face value, or at least he doesn't pry. "Well, if there is anything I can do to help...let me know."

"I will." I force a smile as he looks down at me.

Tanner grabs my cup from my hand and backs into the crowd. "I shall return."

Just as Tanner disappears, Elijah appears with two Coors Lights in his grasp. He holds one out to me and I can't find the words to remind him that I don't really like beer. I'll drink it if it's the only option at a party, but when met with options, I'd pretty much never choose it.

"Thanks," I say, grabbing it and pulling the tab on the cold aluminum can. It hisses and I take a swig, wincing at the sharp, bitter taste. Despite not enjoying it, I gulp it down as I know it will eventually have the same effect as wine.

"Are you having fun?" he asks over the music.

I force a tight-lipped smile, a facade I've become far too good at erecting. My heart races with anxiety as I watch a girl accidentally knock over a cup on the side table, causing its contents to spill onto the carpet. The liquid spreads, seeping into the fibers and leaving a dark patch behind. My body tenses at the knowledge that it will most certainly leave a stain.

"Shit," Elijah says. He hands me his beer before disappearing, presumably to find cleaning supplies.

Scanning the crowd, I struggle to find anyone I know, let alone Elijah. I'm not really sure where he ran off to. The feeling from earlier starts to creep back in, the wash of dread that fills my stomach and leaves me with nothing else to do except raise my beer to my lips.

I take a big gulp of the amber liquid, trying to hide my grimace as the bitter taste coats my tongue. My throat clenches in protest, but I force myself to swallow it down. How people actually enjoy beer is beyond me.

It isn't until I am swallowing the last bit of foam at the bottom of the can that Tanner appears in front of me with a perplexed expression on his face, holding the cup filled with wine he'd gone to fetch.

"What?" I ask as a rogue burp creeps past my lips—an effect of the hoppy nastiness—leaving my cheeks flushed with embarrassment.

"Why are you drinking beer?"

"Because it's a party and I want to be drunk."

He continues to stare at me.

CHAPTER TWENTY

"What?!" I huff, irritation creeping into my voice.

"You hate beer." He says it so matter-of-factly, like I somehow forgot that fact.

"I know."

"So, why are you drinking it?" he asks. There's no judgment in his voice; only pure, honest confusion.

"Elijah got it for me and I was thirsty," I say as I stand straighter. I know he isn't judging me, but I can't fight the urge to defend myself anyway. As if there is something to defend—which there isn't. Elijah is human; it's not his responsibility to know everything about me.

Noticing the shift in my tone, Tanner steps toward me. As he invades my space, the scent of beer and cologne overwhelms my senses. It should smell gross, but the way it mingles with what I assume to be just *him* smells...nice.

"Here," he says quietly, so quietly I barely hear him. He extends his hand between us, barely flexing his wrist as he offers the red cup to me, filled nearly to the top with red wine. He grabs the empty can from my hand, replacing it with the much-preferred beverage.

I murmur a soft "Thank you," but the words are swallowed by the pounding music and the chatter of drunk partygoers. In this brief moment, it's just the two of us—his piercing green eyes meeting mine, everything else fading into the background. The chaos of the party becomes muffled, as if we're in our own little bubble of silence.

Reaching up, I grab the cup from his hand, but jerk away quickly as the touch of his skin causes an electric current to shoot through me.

What in the actual fuck was that?

Elijah's voice breaks through the fog, shattering the moment of quiet. "I got you another bee—"

I snap to look at him and his easygoing posture stiffens, his once-soft gaze sharp and accusatory. His jaw clenches, and I can practically feel the heat radiating from his body as he glares at me with narrowed eyes.

He's jealous.

I should find it appealing how territorial he is, yet I'm starting to realize it only really happens when Tanner and I are alone together—I don't understand why. Tanner and I are friends. Hell, Tanner is *his* friend, so I can't figure out why he's so wound up about it.

Elijah's focus shifts from me to Tanner, his expression somehow even more scathing than when he was looking at me. Tanner, however, doesn't entertain it and simply grins back at him. They're nearly the same height, Tanner having maybe an inch on Elijah, so their gazes are level. Though where Elijah glares, Tanner grins.

"You got me another beer?" Tanner smiles wide before grabbing the can from him. "You're so thoughtful."

Elijah's attention shifts to the cup in my hand, realizing I already have a beverage. As if caught off guard by the interaction with Tanner, or maybe realizing he has no reason to be jealous, his lips curve upward, like he's been in on the joke the entire time.

"Of course, man. Only the best for a brother of mine."

The air feels almost metallic as I take in the false sense of pleasantry. Tension radiates off Elijah at a rate I'm not sure I've ever witnessed, yet Tanner is the picture of composure. It's almost like he genuinely doesn't care.

Then Tanner backs into the crowd with a cocky grin on

CHAPTER TWENTY

his lips, but it's not until he's nearly out of earshot that I hear him say, "I put your wine in the back of the fridge. Figured you'd want to know, since I know how much you hate beer."

If I didn't think he was taunting Elijah before, I sure as hell know he is now. And by the look on Elijah's face, so does he. His clenched jaw doesn't waver before he stalks off into the crowd in the opposite direction.

And once again I am standing by myself.

As I wander through the crowd, the pulsing bass of the music reverberates in my chest. People dance and chat in small groups, but I can't find anyone I know. Jenna is nowhere to be found. I see Regina, Aaron's girlfriend, but I barely know her.

I check my phone for any new messages, but there are none. Feeling a pang of loneliness, I grab the box of red wine from the fridge and head out by the pool.

Thankfully, the group of partygoers who were out here before have since gone inside and I find a semblance of peace. Unfortunately, without the distraction of chaos and boys pretending to be alpha-males, I am left once again with the anxious feeling flooding my stomach.

And I still don't know why.

I dip my toes into the cool, crystal blue water of the pool and feel a shiver run down my spine as a gust of wind blows in from the nearby coast. The ripples in the water dance around my feet, inviting me to take a swim. However, given everything else, I'm not sure that is the best idea.

Once I'm back inside the house, I notice that the chaos has died down, most people long gone.

"Hey, babe."

I nearly jump out of my skin as two strong arms wrap

around my waist, the smell of cheap beer consuming my senses. Elijah presses his lips to the side of my neck before whispering, "We should go up to bed."

He's drunk, but he's no longer angry, at least. I should be thankful, yet my anxiety only increases.

"Okay," I whisper.

He grabs my hand and pulls me toward the stairs.

TWENTY-ONE

KAT

The harsh rays of the sun pierce through my closed eyelids, forcing me to roll over in bed with a groan. The faint sound of the door creaking open and then closing reaches my ears. Elijah must have gotten up to use the restroom. As I lie there, still half-asleep, I feel the warmth of a body next to mine and slowly crack open one eye to see Elijah still peacefully asleep beside me.

Strange.

Shards of memories from last night come rushing back, particularly the tension between Elijah and Tanner. I squeeze my eyes shut again, hoping to block out the painful sunlight and the throbbing headache that accompanies it.

As I reach up to rub the crusty mascara from my eyes, a sharp sensation lances through my temples.

A blood-curdling scream echoes through the door, followed by a stern voice that makes my stomach churn. It's not one of our rowdy friends being obnoxious after a night of drinking.

Elijah jolts upright in bed, nearly smacking me in the head as he realizes who is yelling outside the door.

"Elijah Michael Hanas, get your ass out here. Now!"

My stomach churns and my head throbs as I jolt out of bed, my naked body reacting to the sudden rush of cold air from the early morning chill. I stumble over to the trash can on the opposite side of the room, trying to hold in the bile that threatens to spill out of me. The alcohol from last night seems to hit me all at once, and I feel like I might faint from the intensity of emotions crashing down on me.

Elijah's next words give me startling clarity as to what has had me out of sorts these past few days. I may not remember what happens—most days I don't even remember that I went back in time. However, the moment the words spill past his lips, I know with certainty that I fucked up.

"Put some fucking clothes on. That's my parents."

His parents.

Elijah's parents are here. We're at their house in Myrtle Beach, our friends spread throughout the other bedrooms, with what is sure to be a colossal mess downstairs and at least one person passed out on the couch or floor. Despite all of this, something tells me that finding Elijah and me naked in bed is what put them over the edge.

"Elijah!" The masculine voice—which I've deduced is the voice of Governor Hanas—carries through the door as Elijah rushes around the room, hastening to find his clothes and go talk to his parents. He tosses his undershirt from last night in my direction, urging me to at least moderately cover up before he disappears out the door, barely squeezing through the opening as he attempts to hide me in the room.

"What in the hell are you doing?" Governor Hanas yells.

CHAPTER TWENTY-ONE

Whatever Elijah says, I can't make it out, but I discern phrases like "I can't believe you!" and "How dare you?" voiced by a woman, likely his mother.

It is tense, uncomfortable, and impossible to ignore. I'm frozen in place, listening to every word. Where else would I go, anyway? They're in front of the door.

"This is my house, not yours. Get your friends out of this house—get that whore out. Now!"

A lump forms in my throat at his dad's words, the scathing disdain toward me only worsened by the word he used. Not "that girl," not simply "her," but *that whore.*

Normally, I don't let insults affect me, but the way he sneers those words pierces my heart and twists it in my chest. My body tenses and my hands clench into fists as I fight back the urge to lash out in defense. The intensity of his disdain is palpable, like a physical force pushing against me. It's not just the words; it's the venomous intent behind them that cuts deep and leaves a lasting impact.

He didn't know about me, or if he did...it was surface-level. Some girl Elijah has been seeing at school, but not someone who matters.

Not important. Inconsequential. *That* whore.

I objectively know that is a bizarre notion to latch onto. Hell, he called me a whore. But I don't care about that—I know I'm not a whore; I know he's not right about that. I've only been with two people. Even if it were true, it's not his place to comment on it. But *that.*

That whore.

How can someone who's only seen me once figure out the exact thought that my dad had all those years ago?

She doesn't matter... It must be pathetic the way I seem to wear that on my sleeve.

With that, the door creaks open as Elijah slips back through and I hear the sound of his parents disappearing down the hall, then down the stairs. The moment his gaze meets my own, my eyes fill with tears.

I expect him to comfort me, to tell me that they'll get past what happened, that we're in college and that they know better than to judge me after finding me naked in bed with their son once. That one day they'll learn to love me the way he does, even if he's never said it.

He does none of those things. Elijah offers me no comfort, no loving reassurances that I'm not what his dad called me, no reminder that his parents aren't in this relationship and that I matter.

Elijah says, "We need to get packed."

He grabs his phone off the nightstand, no doubt prattling off a text message to those downstairs, telling them to get packed so we can cut our trip short and head home. He then starts stuffing everything into his duffel, all while I stand there, staring at him in disbelief.

No hug, no tight squeeze to quell the tears streaming down my face. No reminder that this didn't entirely change everything about us.

He can't say that this didn't ruin everything...because it did.

TWENTY-TWO

KAT

"Are you going to tell me what happened?" Jenna asks across the table as we sit in the corner of Rosie's.

She's been prying about spring break since we returned to campus, and while I did tell her that Elijah's parents found me in bed with him, I didn't elaborate about how that went. I'm a bit surprised she didn't hear them yelling, but regardless, I'd rather not relive it by telling her.

Well, that and even I know Elijah's response to the situation doesn't make him look good.

When did I become this person? Hiding stuff to maintain *his* reputation; to ensure our shared friends still respect *him*. I'm so mad at him right now, but I have to hide it because I don't want Jenna to resent him. I want this to work—this has to work.

If it doesn't work, then what was all of this for? If this doesn't work out, I'm stuck floundering without a clue as to how I got here and with nothing to show for it. I'm aware I went back in time, but with every passing day, I remember that fact less and less. If I don't make this work, I'm repeating it all for nothing.

I just wish Elijah felt the same way. Based on how he's been acting the past three weeks, I'm getting less and less optimistic.

At one point, we saw each other at least a few times a week, but I've only seen him twice since our return from South Carolina. And even then...it was weird.

"Nothing to tell," I reiterate to Jenna. "I told you, they found me in bed with him." I stir my pop with my straw, averting my gaze even as she tries to catch my eye.

"Yes..." Jenna snaps her fingers in front of my face in an attempt to grab my attention. I look at her, but it's at best a glare. "You told me they found you naked. But that's embarrassing—it doesn't explain how you've been since we got back. I'm worried about you. Have you even been going to class?"

I'll be honest, I've spent most days in bed until at least one in the afternoon. She's not too far off about me missing classes, but all of my professors have been more than accommodating —mostly because I lied about a family emergency. I do feel bad about that, especially after Professor Augusta opened up about how hard it was for him when his grandmother passed.

"Yes, I've been going to class." The lie rolls off my tongue, but I know Jenna doesn't believe a word I'm saying. She's gone from spending every night at Marcus's to almost always coming home before bed. I'd like to think it's because she just wants to hang out, but I know it's because she's worried.

Luckily, she doesn't try to push me about the obvious lie. "Have you and Elijah talked?" she asks.

"Here and there," I say as I push my hash browns around

CHAPTER TWENTY-TWO

on my plate. Once my favorite breakfast side dish, they now just sicken me.

I don't get it. My high school boyfriend broke up with me after two years and I barely batted an eye, but Elijah avoids me for a couple of weeks and I'm in full meltdown mode.

"Kat."

I look up. "What?"

"You know you can talk to me, right?"

"Of course I know that."

"Then why aren't you?" she demands, her eyes locked on mine in a way that makes it nearly impossible to look away. "I'm worried about you."

Guilt washes over me. "I'm sorry I've been worrying you. It's not that I don't feel like I can talk to you, I just haven't wanted to talk." The pain that blooms in her expression doesn't go unnoticed and my stomach knots. "I promise if I need to talk, I'll talk to you. Okay?"

She nods before looking away. My eyes follow her gaze to find Tanner over at the kiosk, ordering food. He doesn't seem to notice us as he inspects the menu, the weekly specials offering plenty to choose from.

I look down at my food, pushing it around the plate. I don't have the energy to be pleasant, even with Tanner.

"Did this fight between you and Elijah have anything to do with Tanner?" Jenna asks, noticing me staring.

While I wouldn't necessarily call it a fight, I understand why she would deduce that.

Or *is* it a fight?

He won't return my texts; he avoids conversation when he can...did we get into a fight and I just didn't realize it?

If anyone has a right to be mad right now, it's me, and yet he still manages to make me feel like *I* messed up.

"No... Why would you think that?"

Jenna shrugs. "I don't know, maybe Elijah figured out that Tanner has been pining after you all year. I don't know."

"He hasn't been *pining*. We're friends. He's a good friend—that's it."

Rolling her eyes, Jenna again glances at Tanner, who is now walking to the counter to grab his food. "Tanner!" she yells, waving her hand.

He walks over to us with his tray in his hands. "Hey guys," he says with a grin. I don't miss the way his gaze pauses on me before he turns his attention to Jenna. "What's up?"

"Nothing, I just thought you might want to sit with us."

I think about what Jenna said. Tanner has not been *pining* after me. Sure, I knew he was interested when we met, but once I told him I wasn't interested, he let it go. He's a great friend and that's what I need right now. I don't need another man in my life toying with my emotions.

Tanner sits down next to me. If he notices that my eyes are puffy and that I've been wearing this sweatshirt for three days, he doesn't mention it. He simply shoots me a grin before saying, "You look pretty," without an inkling of sarcasm in his words.

I'll admit, I'm a bit taken aback by his compliment, mostly because I know it couldn't be further from the truth. Despite this, I smile and say, "Thank you."

Tanner nods before turning back to look at Jenna. "Do you by chance have the notes from Global Architectural History from Tuesday? I think I might be going crazy because I can't find the file on my laptop."

"Yeah, I can email it to you."

A laugh crawls up my throat for the first time in days. "Why are you taking Global Architectural History?" I ask Jenna.

She shrugs. "It counts toward my fine arts requirement and I figured Marcus could help me with it."

"I guess that makes sense," I respond before sticking my fork into my hash browns and lifting it to my lips.

"So, what's *your* excuse for taking Survey of Rock Music History last semester?" Tanner raises a brow.

A grin crests on my lips. I set my fork down. "It sounded fun."

"Exactly."

I roll my eyes and reach for my fork again, this time taking a bite and surprisingly not feeling like it's the most disgusting thing on the planet.

The rest of our meal goes by in a significantly less depressing manner. We discuss finals coming up, Flash Fest next weekend, and how the semester seems to be getting away from all of us.

After spring break in Myrtle Beach—if you'd even call it that since we were there for less than a day—the entire group has been rather quiet. While it was beyond traumatizing for me, I know that having Elijah's parents show up as mad as they were shook everyone up a little bit. I just wish it hadn't shaken Elijah to the point of barely talking to me.

It's not like I did anything. We were *both* there, yet it's like he's punishing me for it.

Every time I try to see him, he has an excuse, and that's only when he responds. Most of my texts go unanswered these days, but the conversations that we do have leave me unable to let go.

My stomach feels way better now that I've eaten, my now-empty plate a welcome reminder that not everything is bad all the time. Except for the bacon—that was rubbery as sin.

"Here," Tanner says. He grabs my tray and walks it over to the trash can.

Jenna stares at me.

I pin her with a glare. "No."

"Why not?" she asks.

"Because I'm with Elijah."

"Are you, though?" She winces as her words come out, like she didn't intend to say it. As if her thoughts just tumble out without preamble. And yet...she's got a point.

I've spent so much of this past school year trying desperately to make things work with Elijah, but now I realize that we've never actually had a conversation about what we are. I mean, we were together most days for a long time, but recently it almost feels like he is expecting it to just fade away. You don't ghost a real relationship, so where does that leave us?

I refuse to breathe life into that possibility, so I just continue to glare at Jenna. "Yes."

Tanner reappears next to me, grabbing his backpack off the back of his chair. "I just noticed the time; I have a class in Taylor Hall in fifteen. I'll text you later, okay?" He looks down at me with anticipation.

"Okay," I respond quietly.

Tanner says goodbye to Jenna and hurries out of the diner.

Jenna gives me another look.

"Shut up," I growl.

TWENTY-THREE

KAT

If I didn't just fail that exam, I will be surprised beyond measure.

Okay, that was a bit dramatic, but I will genuinely be shocked if I get anything better than a C. Despite dreading receiving that grade, I am relieved that this means the semester is now over.

Due to a freak rainstorm nearly flooding campus last weekend, Flash Fest was pushed to this Friday. What is typically a moment to let loose right before finals week will now be an opportunity for a final hurrah before people leave for the summer.

Flash Fest is an outdoor concert held on campus every year and, while the bands are seldom my taste, it's still a lot of fun. Last year, Third Eye Blind came, which was kind of iconic.

I find myself excited as I walk back to my dorm room because, for the first time in a week and a half, I get to see

Elijah. I can't say things have gotten better, but I just know that if we spend some time together, he'll sort out his feelings.

The air is thick and humid with the heat soaring well above ninety degrees. The sudden heat wave has left me dreading the long months ahead, wondering if this is just a glimpse of the punishing summer to come. If it's hot here, it will more than likely be hot back home.

Sweat beads on my forehead and trickles down my back, reminding me that I am at the mercy of this blistering sun. Normally, I enjoy strolling across campus, but between my exam having been all the way in Franklin Hall and the sweltering heat, I can't help but yearn for the mediocre air conditioning in my dorm room. Even though it's old and not very efficient, it's still much more bearable than my current situation.

I can't help but let my mind travel back to that night in the fall when the air conditioning at the Lambda house was broken—when I spent the night with Elijah anyway just because I wanted to spend time with him. Everything seemed so much simpler back then—back when my biggest concern in my relationship was his unsubstantiated concern about Tanner.

As I stroll across campus, my eyes glaze over and I barely register the excited chatter. I can't help but wonder if any of this was worth it. I might not be able to remember what happens in the future, but I sure as hell know that all of this must have been something I was trying to stop from happening.

Isn't that the way it always goes? The more you want to prevent something from happening, the quicker it comes to fruition? Or maybe I messed it up even more this time around.

CHAPTER TWENTY-THREE

As I unlock the door to my dorm room, I hear faint music seeping out from Jenna's room. Inside, she is curled up on her bed with a thick textbook lying open in front of her. Her eyes are focused intently on the page as she scribbles notes in the margin. She had mentioned having an exam for her psychology class today, but part of me assumed she would be cramming at Marcus's place.

"What time is your exam?" I ask.

"Three-thirty," she responds without looking up from her textbook. "I think I'll be fine. I'm just trying to cram a little bit more information in before I head over there."

I look down at my phone to see that her exam starts in about forty-five minutes, but that doesn't explain her being here.

"What's Marcus up to today?"

When her eyes meet mine, you would almost think I struck her. "He has two exams today, why?" she asks.

I start going through the contents of my bag, mentally cataloging what books I should try to sell back to the campus bookstore. "Don't know; you just haven't been around much."

I expect her to get cagey about it, so when the words tumble out of her mouth, I look up at her.

"I'm sorry," she says quietly, her head hanging in shame. "I've been a really shitty friend."

"No, you haven't—"

"I have," Jenna interrupts. "I've been so wrapped up in stuff with me and Marcus that I completely missed how you've been feeling...with Elijah."

Her comment catches me off guard.

Elijah and I didn't have issues until spring break, I think, but I don't say it out loud.

"It's okay."

Jenna peers at me for a few beats before her eyes shift back to the textbook in front of her. "How did your exam go?"

I shrug. "I'm pretty sure I passed."

I'm typically the type to study for weeks before a final, so the fact that I barely cracked a textbook says something—something I'm sure Jenna is reading on my face. However, I'm thankful she doesn't say anything about it.

"Well, C's get degrees, right?"

"Exactly."

We continue to catch up for a few minutes before Jenna closes her textbook and hops off her bed. I wish her the best of luck on her last final before ducking into my own room.

When Jenna returns from her exam, I am already three hard seltzers deep into pre-gaming.

"How did it go?" I ask.

"Nailed it!" she says with a grin plastered across her lips. As quickly as the smile appears, though, it's gone again, replaced by a disappointed expression. "You started without me."

"I'm sorry," I say, walking over to my mini fridge to grab one of the long, skinny cans and holding it out to Jenna. "What time do you want to go down?" I ask.

Jenna shrugs before popping the tab on her can. "I don't really care about the opener, but it could be smart to go early so we can get a good spot."

―――――

As I stumble out of our dorm building with Jenna at my side, the world starts to swirl and my steps become unsteady. I can

CHAPTER TWENTY-THREE

feel the warmth of alcohol spreading through my body, but I try to brush it off as just a slight buzz. However, as we start walking toward the concert, my gut starts churning and I realize the effects of drinking on an empty stomach are hitting me hard.

"Are you okay?" Jenna asks, genuine concern in her voice.

"Yeah, for sure." I lift my hand to my mouth as I swallow, quelling the unease in my stomach for the time being.

When we approach the crowded concert grounds, Jenna grabs my arm and leads me toward a brightly lit food truck. She glances at me with concern, knowing I've had a few too many drinks already. "Come on, let's get you something to eat," she says.

Soon I have a corn dog in hand with a healthy slathering of ketchup, and I scarf it down in fewer bites than should be physically possible. Thankfully, eating instantly seems to help the discomfort in my stomach and within twenty minutes I feel slightly more alert.

"The guys are here!" Jenna peps up, darting forward and colliding with Marcus, who wraps his arms around her tight.

As I watch them from across the field, I can't help but feel a pang of envy. Their fingers intertwined, their eyes locked in a deep gaze, and their smiles genuine and full of love. Even at our best, Elijah and I have never been like that, so effortlessly entranced by one another.

I want that.

Brendan ambles toward me, his hands tucked into the pockets of his worn jeans. Tanner follows closely behind, holding a bottle of beer in one hand and waving with the other.

"Hey," they say in unison as they reach me.

"Hey," I reply, exhaling deeply.

I can't help but notice that Elijah isn't with them. He said he was coming, so why isn't he here?

Something in Tanner's expression tells me he's about to say something that I don't want to hear. This isn't just Elijah not showing up for the concert—this is him not saying goodbye before he leaves for the summer.

My heart races as hordes of people start crowding around me. My palms grow clammy, and the smell of alcohol on my own breath only intensifies my anxiety. The ground beneath me seems to sway with each passing second, and I struggle to catch my breath as a wave of panic washes over me.

"Hey—"

A calming voice cuts through the noise, but I can't seem to latch onto it.

As the crowd gathers in front of the stage, I frantically search for him. My heart races and my hands shake as I realize he isn't here. The opening band starts to play and I feel a wave of panic wash over me—he promised he would be here.

He should be here.

"Hey, Kat." The same male voice from before attempts to soothe me as the panic sinks its claws into me.

"Kat." Another masculine voice carries to my ears, but I don't respond.

"Hey." A comforting hand lands on the side of my cheek, forcing my head upward.

My vision blurs, and my fists clench as I struggle to catch my breath. Tanner's eyes are fixed on mine, his brow furrowed with concern. His calm demeanor is a stark contrast to my panicked state.

"Can you breathe with me?" he says softly, following his

words with slow, deliberate inhales and exhales. His strong palm shifts from my cheek to my shoulder.

"Kat, look at me," Tanner demands, and, to my surprise, I listen. "Breathe with me. Inhale for four seconds." I watch as he demonstrates before doing the same. "Then out for four." He exhales and I follow suit.

We continue this rhythm for an unknown amount of time. As I focus on my breathing, my hand on my chest moves up and down at a steady pace. My racing heart gradually slows, matching the rhythm of my breaths. The tension in my body melts away gradually.

"Are you okay?" Tanner asks, the pinch in his brow far from gone as he holds tightly to my shoulders.

I don't give him reassurance; I simply ask, "He left, didn't he?"

Tanner swallows as he stares at me, and I watch as he struggles to respond. Finally he nods, causing a tear to break past my waterline.

"Are you okay?"

I shake my head from side to side, and his eyebrows furrow in concern. He pulls me into an embrace, his strong arms enveloping my body. The pressure of his hug should make me feel suffocated, but instead, I feel a sense of peace wash over me. I close my eyes and take in the scent of his cologne as he holds me tightly.

Tanner whispers against the top of my head, so quietly that only I can hear. "No one would judge you if you left. You don't have to stay. I get why you would want to, but if you can't…we get it."

It's as if he can read my mind, because the moment I look

around at the sheer quantity of people crowded around me, waiting for the band to take the stage, I know with certainty that I can't stay here.

I don't know what will help, but this isn't it.

When I nod, he squeezes me tightly for a few seconds before releasing me. The lost warmth of his embrace leaves me feeling chilly despite the heat.

"Go get some rest, okay?"

I nod again, backing away and heading toward my dorm building. I don't bother finding Jenna to tell her I'm leaving; I don't even wave goodbye to Brendan, who stands beside Tanner with a worried look on his face.

I just leave.

After I step into my empty dorm room and shut the door behind me, I collapse against the wall. Tears stream down my face as I try to catch my breath, a flood of emotions crashing over me. My knees give way and I sink to the ground, cradling my head in my hands.

This is it—I am finally alone and the dam breaks, releasing every emotion I've been holding back.

These past couple weeks.

This entire school year.

Probably the future too.

Everything hits me at once.

At first, I think I'm hearing things as the door that connects mine and Jenna's bedrooms creaks open, so I don't look up. It isn't until she slides down the wall to sit beside me that I look at her.

"What are you doing here?" I ask through strangled sobs.

She stares at me, a pained expression that I can't quite

CHAPTER TWENTY-THREE

place persisting for a split second before it morphs into an equally pained smile. "Tanner said you might want some company."

And in this moment, I've never valued him more.

BETTER MAN

Better Man
Taylor Swift

2:56   -2:01

⏸	**Better Man** Taylor Swift	⌃
▶	**right where you left me** Taylor Swift	04:04
▶	**Would've Could've Should've** Taylor Swift	04:19
▶	**How Do I Do This** Kelsea Ballerini	02:50
▶	**You Should Be Sad** Halsey	03:25
▶	**The Smallest Man Who Ever Lived** Taylor Swift	04:04
▶	**it's time to go** Taylor Swift	04:14
▶	**Lose You To Love Me** Selena Gomez	03:26
▶	**Delicate** Taylor Swift	03:51
▶	**Friends Don't** Maddie & Tae	03:07
▶	**Gorgeous** Taylor Swift	03:29
▶	**Just To See You Smile** Tim McGraw	03:35
▶	**Feather** Sabrina Carpenter	03:05
▶	**Labyrinth** Taylor Swift	04:07

TWENTY-FOUR

KAT

As the ticking of the clock on the wall grows louder and more insistent, I shift uncomfortably in my armchair. My therapist, Janet, sits across from me, her pen poised over a notebook as we near the end of our session. I can practically feel the minutes slipping away, and I find myself anxiously glancing toward the door, wondering when I can escape this confined space.

"How are you feeling about going back to school next week?" she asks as I sink further into my seat, the plush red fabric doing anything but providing me comfort.

Talk about a loaded question.

I'm beyond excited to see my friends. Tanner and I have kept in constant contact through text messages this summer, and we even went to the zoo together twice. As for Jenna, we have been texting every day, but unfortunately I haven't had the chance to see her in person. She has been interning in Ann Arbor, and her visits have been few and far between. Despite the distance, our friendship remains as strong as ever.

CHAPTER TWENTY-FOUR

Still, I can't shake the anxiety I feel every time I remember that we'll all be living together this coming semester. While I'm brimming with excitement over the prospect of all of my friends under one roof, the constant reminder that Elijah's name is also on the lease makes my stomach churn.

I shrug slightly in response to her question and find myself picking nervously at my cuticles. My nails dig into the tender flesh, leaving behind ragged edges and painful reminders of my inability to control the bad habit.

"Are you excited to see Jenna?"

That question causes me to perk up as I'm reminded that while, yes, Elijah will be living in the house, so will Jenna and Marcus. No more Jenna disappearing to stay at his apartment—we'll be under one roof. Honestly, I'm still a bit shocked that we managed to convince Marcus to live with us. He's always been diligent about having a quiet environment with minimal distractions to get his schoolwork done—it's why he moved out of the Lambda house, after all—but I think the trade-off is the exact reason Marcus and Jenna claimed the attic, which is separated from the chaos of the rest of the house.

"I'm excited to see her," I say. "Her internship kept her really busy this summer." Which, of course, my therapist already knew. Whenever the topic veers too close to what is really bothering me, I always manage to shift the conversation back to Jenna.

Jenna is a safe topic; I can handle talking about Jenna.

"And Tanner?" Janet prompts.

"Of course. I saw him a few weeks ago, but it'll be fun to see him more," I reply, and she nods before jotting something down.

My gaze diverts to the clock on the wall. How has it only

been three minutes since I last looked at it? I'm hardly a conspiracy theory nut, but I'm starting to think the clocks in therapist offices are slow. Snail-speed slow.

"How are you feeling about seeing Elijah again after last semester?"

And alas—the question I knew she was building up to. Except I still can't formulate an answer. She asks me in almost all of our weekly sessions, but I have so many mixed emotions about him right now that I can't quite place how I'm feeling.

Once again, I shrug, and once again she scribbles something on her pad.

After Elijah didn't show up to Flash Fest, it wasn't pretty. I'll admit, I cringe a bit when I think about who I became in the weeks following what was essentially a full-on breakdown at the realization that he ended things by simply leaving.

Yet, despite all of that, I still kept trying to contact him. I couldn't even tell you the amount of unanswered text messages I sent; after a while, I deleted the text thread out of sheer humiliation.

He never reached back out.

With every text message or the occasional call that went unanswered, I slipped further and further into what I can only describe as a hole of despair.

I didn't leave my bedroom for weeks. Even my usually oblivious mother couldn't ignore the state I was in. She all but forced me to call her old therapist from when I was a kid. At the time it felt invasive, like she was forcing me to do something I clearly didn't need to do. However, once I started therapy, I knew my mom was right.

I just wish I didn't *need* to. How embarrassing is it to be so

CHAPTER TWENTY-FOUR

distraught over a breakup that you essentially have a nervous breakdown and are strongly encouraged to seek therapy?

"Have you looked into the on-campus therapy options like we discussed?" Janet asks, pulling my focus away from the clock.

After last week's session, she gave me homework and told me to look into the therapy options provided by Kent State's health center, but I failed to follow through.

I don't say anything, but based on the look she gives me, I'd venture to say she knows what my answer would be.

"I took the liberty of printing these off of the Kent State website. They have a few different therapists on staff for students in crisis or even if they just need a therapist when theirs is back home. Read it over."

"I'm fine," I say as I grab the papers she proffers, pretending to thumb through the pages.

"I know. You're leaps and bounds from where you were a few months ago. However, I worry that without the outlet of seeing me every week that maybe one day you might not feel so great."

It takes everything in me to not roll my eyes at her assumption. You have one bad breakup and suddenly you're the kind of person who needs a therapist.

As if she can hear my thoughts, Janet clears her throat. "It's not shameful to see a therapist, Kat. Most people would benefit from it. Heck, I see mine every single week."

"But you're a therapist..." I say questioningly.

"Therapists need therapy too, Kat." She looks down at the watch on her wrist, signaling that our time for today is over. "Please at least call to learn more about what they offer. It doesn't hurt to call."

Staring down at the papers in my hand, I nod.

"And remember what we've been working on. Boundaries are important, Kat, even with the people we love...especially with the people we love. You deserve to feel valued in your relationships—boundaries help."

When I step out of my therapist's office, the summer heat blankets my skin instantly. I'll be relieved when the weather shifts to fall, but given how the past few years have been, we probably have another few months of this hell.

As I open the mailbox in front of my house, the scorching metal handle nearly burns my hand. I quickly retrieve the mail and rush inside, relieved by the coolness of the kitchen. I set the warm envelopes on the counter before pouring myself a tall glass of ice-cold water.

Mom isn't home, but that is to be expected as she told me this morning that Randy, her coworker, called off again. To my surprise, she hasn't been working as much this summer as she usually does. Whether that is because she has wanted to spend time with me or has just been that worried about my mental health, I don't know. However, it's been nice having her around.

Setting my glass on the counter, I begin sifting through the mail. Mostly junk—credit card offers that go straight in the trash, a bill from my dentist appointment last month, a letter from the bursar's office listing out my financial aid for the semester—and then there is a simple white envelope, unassuming but somehow compelling. I turn it over in my hands, feeling inexplicably drawn to its contents.

I stare in awe at the name in the upper left-hand corner.

CHAPTER TWENTY-FOUR

Patrick Marritt.

Ripping open the envelope with little reserve, I pull out a single piece of college-ruled paper.

Hey Kat,

I hope you're doing well. This is weird, I know this is weird. My dad, or I guess our dad, gave me this big green chest to take to college with me last year and I don't think he even realized it, but I found a letter from you at the bottom with some old documents. It's dated a couple of years ago, but you said it was your freshman year of college, so if I'm doing the math right I think you're a senior? I've been trying to figure out how to reach out. I'm a sophomore at OSU, I'm studying mechanical engineering. Sorry, I'm not sure what to say.

If I'm being fully honest, finding that letter was the first time I found out you existed. You probably hate me for never reaching out, but I promise that I would have had I known. Being raised an only child, I would have loved to have a sister...and I guess I do. I understand if you want nothing to do with me. Hell, I wouldn't want anything to do with me if I were you.

But...I hope you do, because I'd really like to get to know you.

I brought you up to my dad. He was an ass about it—if I'm being fully transparent he's always an ass—but even more so when it came to this. My mom died about five years ago from cancer. I don't know what she knew, but I want to think she didn't know about you and your mom. I'm pretty good at math and I can guess that there was probably some overlap. I didn't ask him about that, though. Just about you, but he didn't have any information to give.

So with that being said, if you'd be willing to...and I completely understand if you don't... I'd like to get to know you. The address on the envelope is to my apartment in Columbus. I hope you write back...but, like I said, I get it if you don't.

Your brother,
Patrick

As I stare down at the paper, I don't have the slightest idea of how I feel. I thought about my brother a lot when I was younger—about what it would be like to have a sibling. I always assumed that the reason I didn't know him was the same reason I didn't know my dad; I assumed he simply didn't *want* to know me.

I came to terms with that a long time ago.

CHAPTER TWENTY-FOUR

Yet, as I stare down at the letter, I struggle to come to terms with the fact that something that I accepted as truth years ago was anything but.

Dad didn't even tell him about me? How the hell do you keep that knowledge from your child? Then again, how does he do anything he does and manage to sleep at night?

The reminder of how inconsequential I am to my father stings, but it's par for the course. Outside of the court-mandated child support when I was a kid, I didn't matter and I still don't. Once I was eighteen and he didn't have to send the minuscule checks anymore, I guess I stopped mattering in that regard, too.

Patrick, though—Patrick cares. Even if he bears the same name as his dad and my glorified sperm donor, he cares. Or he wants to, if I'll let him.

I just spent the summer putting myself back together after the hellscape of last semester; do I really want to rip open a new wound?

The sound of the key in the front door causes me to stuff the letter under the papers from my therapist. When my mom appears in the doorway, her apron slung over her arm as she drops her keys on the table by the door, she smiles over at me.

"How was therapy?" she asks.

"It was good," I say. I couldn't even tell her what Janet and I talked about if I wanted to, not with Patrick's letter searing into my palm.

As if she can tell where my attention is at, my mom looks at the papers. "What are those?"

"Just some information Janet printed out about therapy options when I'm back at school."

She nods, and I almost think I catch a glimpse of approval. "Good."

TWENTY-FIVE

KAT

Gazing at the spacious two-story home we toured last spring, my heart begins to race and my palms start to sweat. Memories and an overwhelming sense of anxiety fill me as I stare at the bright red door, a feature that made me fall in love with the house now like one big sign warning me not to go past the threshold.

Why did I think it was a good idea to live with Elijah this semester? Even if we were together, it was a bad idea. Now, all I can think about is how uncomfortable this is going to be.

At least I'll have Jenna, even if she isn't coming until tomorrow afternoon.

With a box teetering precariously on the edge of my foot, I hoist another onto my shoulder and carefully balance both as I make my way toward the stairs. My arms strain under the weight, but I'm determined to minimize the number of trips I have to make. That, and I'd like to get everything into the house so I can avoid leaving my room for the rest of the night. I have no idea when Elijah is supposed to arrive, or if he's already here. I deeply hope he isn't.

My arms strain under the weight of the heavy boxes, but I finally manage to drop them onto my bedroom floor. Turning around, I don't notice the tall figure standing directly in front of me until it's too late. My hands instinctively fly up to protect my face as I collide with a solid wall of muscle covered by a tight cotton T-shirt that belongs to someone I used to know; someone who still holds a piece of my heart.

My chest tightens in discomfort as I look away, feeling his gaze upon me. I hastily choose to pay exponentially more attention to the crown molding above my head than it calls for.

"I didn't realize you were here," I say, shifting my attention and picking at my cuticles, the all-too-familiar nervous tic giving me a semblance of calm, though I'm still ready to jump out of my skin.

"I got here this morning," Elijah says after clearing his throat.

"Did you need something?" I ask coldly.

He stands in the entrance, his broad frame blocking my escape. I shift uncomfortably, avoiding eye contact until finally I muster up the courage to meet his gaze. His face is a blank canvas, but I can see the gears turning behind his eyes as he ponders something. Is it contemplation? Disappointment? The unknown is almost more agonizing than the awkward energy filling the space between us.

He's always been hard to read.

"I was hoping we could talk..."

Talk—talk?! He wants to talk *now*? After a summer of radio silence, he finally wants to talk?!

CHAPTER TWENTY-FIVE

"About?" I try to feign disinterest, but my irritation is bubbling up to the surface.

"Kat, please." If I didn't know him better, I would think it genuine anguish in his tone. I, however, do know him better, and I'm not falling for it again.

"You want to talk? Talk." Crossing my arms over my chest, I pin him with a glare.

He appears to realize something—what I can't be sure, but whatever it is causes him to cower backward. "No, it's fine. We can talk later."

The old me would have gone after him, chased him down the hall, demanding an answer, asking him to talk to me. It's all I ever really wanted, anyway: for him to talk to me.

However, I'm not that girl anymore. At least, I don't want to be. So I let him leave the room, and as he disappears down the hallway, I feel a weight lift off my chest—a giant boulder that I didn't even realize was there until it's gone.

After spending hours locked in my room, I finally gather the courage to venture out again. As I carry the last few boxes and bags up to my bedroom, I can't help but feel grateful for my decision to bring most of my belongings from home. After three years, I've learned that having familiar possessions around me makes this foreign place a little less intimidating. And as I settle into my senior year, I know one thing for sure: I don't want to be here without everything I need.

That, and I have a tendency to find comfort in familiarity—something I desperately will need, given my living situation.

"Katarina Marritt, as I live and breathe," a warm and familiar voice intones from my bedroom doorway.

The moment I turn around and find Tanner grinning back at me as he leans against the doorframe, any sort of irritation from before is gone. Gone and replaced with nothing but elation.

"Tanner!" I squeal, lunging across the room and wrapping my arms around his neck. Despite my sweat-dampened skin, he squeezes me tightly, lifting me off the ground in the process. "I thought you weren't heading up until tomorrow!"

"I wasn't, but my brother broke the garage door, and given how pissed my dad was, I figured it best to dip out a little early."

The memory of his family's love and kindness at Thanksgiving fills me with so much joy. Despite the present issue between Tanner's brother and dad, I know with certainty they'll bounce back. I long to experience that kind of family, where you know without second-guessing that any sort of fight or argument will be resolved because they love you.

I know my mom loves me, and in most cases I know she'll come around if we get into an argument. However—and this has nothing to do with my mom—there is still always that nagging feeling in the back of my mind that one of these days I'll manage to do or say something that wakes her up to the fact that maybe she'd like to leave too.

I wouldn't blame her if she did.

"You should come downstairs and hang out," Tanner says as he releases me from his grasp.

Mentally recoiling, I look up at him. "I will...but right now I just need to get unpacked." It's a disingenuous response and we both know it, but he doesn't call me out.

"That's fine. We can hang out in here!" He then proceeds to jump onto the bed that I just made with about as much grace as you'd expect from a baby deer.

"You want to hang out in my bedroom?" I pose the

CHAPTER TWENTY-FIVE

question with a barely stifled laugh. "You don't think that's a little weird? Just the two of us hanging out in my bedroom...on my bed." I raise a brow and he laughs.

"Why? Are you worried you can't resist my natural charm?" he says as he lifts his hand to his chest in mock affront. "I am but a gentleman—I would never. Besides, I'm saving myself for marriage."

Given the three girls who have very boastfully and enthusiastically shared with me that they've slept with Tanner, I know this isn't true. I throw a pillow at his head.

"Idiot," I say, and we both erupt into laughter, me collapsing onto the bed next to him.

Just as we are adjusting to sit on the bed, there is a knock on my bedroom door.

"Come in!" I yell.

The door creaks open to reveal Jenna holding a giant pizza box and a two liter of Coca-Cola.

"Room for one more?" She smiles as she sets the pizza and pop on my dresser.

"Jenna!" I shriek before I leap off the bed.

We embrace each other tightly, our laughter filling the room. Finally, my two favorite people are together with me.

"What the hell? You told me you weren't coming today!" I smack her arm, then approach my dresser to investigate the pizza.

She just shrugs. "I only managed to survive a few days at home after my internship before wanting to strangle my mom, so I decided to come early."

I fight off the urge to call both her and Tanner out on their answers that are almost undoubtedly excuses to be here the day I get in, but I know that it comes from a protective place.

How can I question it when that kind of love is all I've ever wanted? Even if it only ever comes in the form of friends.

"Thank you," I say sternly to both of them, fighting off the emotion venturing into my words.

"For what?" they ask in unison.

"For coming today. It helps."

Jenna nods in response, recognizing my appreciation while still managing to hold onto her plausible deniability.

However, when my eyes meet Tanner's, he just stares back at me with an unreadable expression on his brow. As quickly as it's there, it's gone, and he breaks into a smile. "I haven't the slightest idea what you're talking about—I just wanted to get away from the crossfire between my dad and Theo."

"Who's Theo?" Jenna asks.

"His youngest brother," I say as Tanner says, "My youngest brother."

Jenna's brows lift, but she shakes off her confusion as she steps to my side. She gently lifts the lid of the pizza box and a tempting smell wafts through the air, making my mouth water. The rich, melted cheese stretches and oozes over the smoky pepperoni slices, the tangy tomato sauce peeking out between each piece. My senses are overwhelmed by the delicious scent.

We each grab a piece—or, in Tanner's case, three pieces—and sit cross-legged on my bed.

Jenna fills us in on how her summer internship went and Tanner tells us about what actually happened to the garage door. Apparently, Theo gravely misinterpreted the difference between the gas pedal and the brake.

I'm thankful when they don't ask about my summer...even if I know it's because they're both well aware of how it was spent.

CHAPTER TWENTY-FIVE

We spend a disproportionate amount of time discussing Brendan's new haircut and how someone needs to tell him it doesn't look good. Jenna and I both agree that, of the three of us, it should be Tanner, but he insists it is weird and that we should just wait until it grows out.

"People are going to make fun of him," Jenna says, stuffing her last bite of pizza in her mouth.

"He'll be fine."

The sunset passes and we continue to talk incessantly about the most random topics, but it isn't until Jenna is standing up and stretching her arms—the telltale sign that she is ready for bed—that I realize this is the first time in months I've truly felt at peace.

"I'm gonna head up to bed." Jenna yawns and I can't help the disappointment that washes over me.

"Oh, uh—okay."

Silence creeps in before Tanner speaks. "Do you want to watch *Community*? I seem to recall you agreeing to watch it with me last semester and we never picked it back up."

Jenna relaxes her shoulders when I say, "Sure."

She kneels, her arms encircling me in a warm hug. She whispers "Good night" before she slips out of my room, leaving Tanner and me alone. The silence is heavy and suffocating.

He quickly turns on the television, opens Netflix, and queues up the show. Within minutes, booming laughter fills the room as we watch the episode where the crew plays Dungeons and Dragons.

"No, it one hundred percent makes him an asshole. Why would Jeff call him Fat Neil?" I ask, holding my hands up to emphasize "Fat Neil."

"Because it's Jeff—he is inherently an ass, but it doesn't mean he hates him more than any other character."

"Jeff is the worst."

"Not as bad as Dennis from *Always Sunny*."

"Dennis is also a predator, and probably a serial killer."

"See! So you agree Jeff is tame by comparison!" His voice elevates as he tries not to laugh.

"Two wrongs don't make a right."

"I don't think that applies here." He finally breaks and laughs at the absurdity of the argument.

I can't help but fall into the same laughter before smacking him in the arm. "Forget Jeff, *you're* an ass."

"You know what they say, you are what you ea—"

"Tanner!"

We both burst into uncontrollable laughter as I shift to hit him with a throw pillow, but Tanner manages to jump off the bed just in time to evade it. He walks over to the pizza box and sets our empty paper plates atop the cardboard. He leans down to grab a water bottle from my freshly stocked mini fridge before nodding in my direction. I nod back, and he grabs a second cold bottle.

"Milady," he says with an overly dramatic inflection—the term of endearment used in Jeff and Annie's interactions throughout the show—and he bows, holding the water out to me.

"Milord." I grab the bottle and he plops down on the bed next to me again, this time laying his head against the pillow.

We stay like that, lying on the bed, watching the equal parts hilarious and perplexing show he initially forced me to watch last year, except now I'm deeply entranced...and I've never been so content.

TWENTY-SIX

KAT

The sun peeks through the sheer curtains, casting a soft glow on the tousled sheets. As I stir from my slumber, I feel warm breath tickling my neck and strong arms holding me close. My eyes widen as I realize it's not just a dream—there is a body pressed against mine and fingers gently tracing circles on my stomach.

My eyes snap open in a moment of panic, my heart racing until I remember that Tanner and I must have fallen asleep together after our late-night marathon of *Community*. I try to sit up and remind him that this is not something friends do, but the comforting warmth of his arms around me makes it hard to move. It's been so long since I've felt this sense of closeness with someone and it feels nice.

So, I do what any reasonable woman would do...I pretend I'm still sleeping.

As I sink back into him, allowing myself to fall into the sated state between sleep and awake, I feel his muscular arms tighten around me. My heart nearly leaps out of my chest as my stomach erupts with butterflies, but I'm far too tired to delve into the implications of what that could mean.

Warmth washes over me as I close my eyes, the sun's gentle rays warming my skin. I drift back to sleep, the room fading away behind my closed eyelids.

"Kat."

A groggy whisper ghosts past my ear and the warm breath causes goosebumps to erupt all over my skin.

I ignore the voice in an attempt to hold tightly to my last bit of sleep.

"Katarina." The voice is playful, amused, and says my name in an almost singsong tone.

I groan, lifting my arm to cover my eyes, a flimsy attempt at hiding myself from the day, the sunlight impossible to escape now.

He laughs. "It's noon—we should get up."

"Noooo...we sleep," I mumble through a yawn, inching back against him without much thought for the action.

This time, he groans. "Kat, we need to get up."

The pained voice urges me into consciousness as I remember exactly who is in bed with me. Not some guy I met at a bar, not even Elijah in a drunken, terrible decision, but... Tanner.

Go figure: this is the exact moment I realize that, while Tanner is clearly as awake as the sun, so is...*little* Tanner. His morning erection is pressed firmly against my ass, and if I were more awake, I would probably jerk away. However, my sleepy state and lack of awareness leaves me with no filter.

"You have a boner," I say matter-of-factly, not even bothering to open my eyes. I expect him to jerk away at my spoken observation, cower into the teenage version of himself,

CHAPTER TWENTY-SIX

humiliated by his morning wood, but he does none of those things.

He...he...laughs. Not in a mocking way, but with pure, unadulterated amusement.

Tanner releases his hold around my waist before messing up my hair—which is more than likely already catastrophic—and gets out of bed.

I sit up and glance around the room. I know I should feel weird about waking up in Tanner's arms; I should be reiterating that it can't happen again. And yet...it felt good to be held, far better than I'd like to admit.

As if he can hear my thoughts, Tanner looks down at me with his brow quirked.

"What?" I ask.

"Are you spiraling right now?"

I definitely *feel* like I should be spiraling, or at the very least verbalizing that it meant nothing—because it *did* mean nothing. However, I simply shake my head. "I'm fine. We fell asleep together. I've done much more with Jenna."

If I thought his brows were strained before, they now nearly hit his hairline as his mouth splits into a shit-eating grin. "Please, do elaborate. I'm a visual person, but a very detailed description would do, given that Jenna isn't here..."

When I swat his arm, he breaks into a bellowing laugh, and I can't bite my own laughter back any longer. "You're an idiot!"

I stand up, adjusting my shirt to cover my partially exposed stomach. I don't miss the way Tanner's attention lingers on my navel. We both look away awkwardly.

My cheeks flush as I peer around the room before grabbing an oversized flannel out of an open box. I feel like I need to cover up, put a barrier between us—as if I wasn't nestled in his arms only seconds ago.

"I'm gonna head down and grab some food. You in?" he asks. He's so casual—a level of casual that I can't seem to muster.

"Sure."

Tanner leads us out of my room. As we start to walk toward the stairs, Elijah exits his room. I instantly clam up at the proximity and the pinched expression on his brow, fighting back the urge to inform him nothing happened between Tanner and me. Frankly, it's none of his business.

So I do what any rational—but maybe a little petty—woman would do...I pretend we didn't make eye contact as I follow Tanner.

As we descend the staircase, the aroma of freshly brewed coffee and sizzling bacon wafts up to greet us. We reach the spacious kitchen, where Brendan, Regina, Aaron, and Jenna are gathered around the massive island in the center.

We all agreed the kitchen was the selling point when we signed the lease—with its sleek granite countertops, stainless steel appliances, and ample space for cooking and socializing, it's no wonder why. We're a little farther from campus than most of us would have preferred, but it was far nicer than the beat-up houses near school.

"Where's Marcus?" I ask Jenna as I grab a piece of bacon off the plate sitting next to the stove.

"We ran out of milk for the scrambled eggs, so he went out to get some."

I nod before grabbing another piece of bacon, but Jenna quickly swats it out of my hand. "That's for breakfast, you heathen. It'll be gone before he even gets back if you guys don't stop."

I notice Tanner had the same idea as me when I see him pause with a strip of bacon halfway to his lips. The pause only lasts a millisecond before he shoves the entire strip into his mouth. It doesn't seem humanly possible, but he manages to do it nonetheless.

"You're an idiot," Jenna says as she rolls her eyes.

"Seems to be the mantra today." He laughs, grabbing a paper towel to wipe the grease residue off of his hands.

Marcus appears in the doorway with a gallon of two-percent milk and Jenna all but tackles him when he walks across the threshold. She wraps her fingers around the handle of the jug, but he doesn't let go of the bottle.

"Nope. Pay the piper, my dear." He puckers his lips dramatically, earning an eye roll from Jenna, though it's crystal clear she isn't the least bit annoyed as she lifts onto her toes and places a gentle kiss on Marcus's lips before grabbing the bottle from his hands and beelining for the stove. She swiftly starts mixing the ingredients needed for scrambled eggs as we begin chatting around the kitchen island.

"How are you?" Regina asks me timidly, pushing her long auburn hair over her shoulder.

I've only met her a handful of times, so the awkwardness she probably feels is evident in her question. Either way, I appreciate her inquiry. It's no secret that I had a rough summer and an even harder spring. I spent a long time pulling myself out of my hole, but I'm proud I got out.

"I'm good!" A forced kind of pep seeps into my words, so I repeat myself, correcting the borderline psychotic enthusiasm. "I'm good. Tired, but good. I have to go to the campus bookstore today, which isn't fun because I know it's going to be a madhouse. But I'm good."

"Good."

Jenna says, "Wait, you're going to the bookstore today? Can I tag along? I need to pick up the textbooks I ordered."

I'm not sure why she even asks—we've gone to get our books together since we started rooming together.

"I actually do care; I don't want you in my car."

"Well, bite me, because I'm going anyway." She laughs, shutting off the stove as she pulls the pan away from the heat. "Food's ready!" she yells, though there is only one person who isn't in here already.

I try to tamp down my irritation at the reminder that I'll have to coexist with Elijah for the next eight months as he appears in the doorway and walks over to the stove.

"Looks great, Jenna," he says softly before walking over to me. "Can we talk?"

I freeze. I don't want to talk to him, but also...I do? It's the weirdest feeling and I don't know what to do with it. How the hell are you supposed to navigate the mixed emotions of hating someone with every fiber of your being but at the same time holding so much love for them that they're constantly at odds?

Being a human is ass.

"Yeah, sure." I swallow hard, stepping toward the doorway, but suddenly Jenna appears at my side.

"No can do, E," she says brusquely. "Kat promised she'd take me to the bookstore, like, right now, so you'll have to talk later."

He pins her with a glare but doesn't say anything.

It's abundantly clear she just pulled the bookstore excuse

CHAPTER TWENTY-SIX

out of her ass, as there is a plate piled high with freshly cooked, untouched eggs.

I love her for that, really.

"Oh yeah. Um." I swallow before glancing upward to meet his eye. "We can talk later, okay?"

Elijah simply nods, and I can't tell if he is irritated or relieved. My guess is he's probably a little bit of both.

TWENTY-SEVEN

KAT

Stepping into the student center, I find myself ruminating on memories from this time last year—the day I met Marcus and Tanner, and then, later that evening, Elijah. It doesn't give me the sense of nostalgia I expected. What used to be a day I remembered with reverence and joy is now a source of anguish and I absolutely hate it.

Had I done things different a year ago, I wouldn't be in the mess I am now. Then again, I probably also wouldn't have the friends who have become my only source of strength in recent months. Even if Elijah is a necessary evil in that regard, I don't like thinking about the fact that all of that was meant to happen. As I find myself wishing I could go back and this time not pursue a relationship with him at all, I remind myself what a horrible idea it was to have come back in time in the first place.

I feel changed, but I can't put my finger on how. Thinking back on everything that has happened, I can't wrap my head around the idea of wanting to pursue things with Elijah again

CHAPTER TWENTY-SEVEN

so badly that I managed to bend the laws of physics. I mean, time travel? That's next-level pathetic.

And that's what I've always felt like with Elijah—pathetic. I refuse to let him make me feel that way again.

"So, do you want to?"

Jenna's voice interrupts my thoughts, causing me to look at her blankly.

"What?"

"Do you want to get food?"

"Oh, uh, no—if that's okay. I'm wiped. I kind of want to just head back to the house." Even if what sits back at the house is exactly what has me distracted in the first place.

Maybe Janet was right, and I should find a therapist on campus. I've been here for less than two days and suddenly I feel like none of the work I put in this summer was worth it.

Then again, what's the point if all the hard work of the past three months can be undone by the mere existence of my ex?

I store that thought away for later; I can't even begin to think about finding a therapist right now.

"Okay. Do you want to grab something to go, though? We didn't exactly get to eat breakfast."

After Jenna concocted her excuse to get me out of talking to Elijah, we all but sprinted out of the house. I didn't even have the opportunity to grab another piece of bacon—I'm still wearing my sleep clothes, for crying out loud.

"Sure," I say.

We walk into the tiny convenience store inside the student center, each grabbing a twenty-ounce pop and a bag of chips. Breakfast of champions, even if it is sure to wreak havoc on my stomach this afternoon.

As we make our way to my car, my mind instantly travels back to this morning with Tanner. That should have been weird, right? I should have felt weird about that—but the more I think about it, the less weird it feels, and I am almost positive that isn't normal. Friends don't cuddle like that, and friends certainly don't press their boners up against their friends while they're sleeping and then act like it's just another fucking Saturday morning.

Or maybe they do, I'm not sure. Admittedly, Tanner is the closest male friend I've ever had. Maybe people do that, but I know that *we* can't. Things like that could potentially derail our friendship, and he doesn't see me like that—and it's not like I'm in the place to get involved in anything anyway.

"So you and Tanner," Jenna says suggestively.

For the love of God—is this woman a witch?

"Been playing with those tarot cards again, Jenna?" I laugh, intentionally ignoring the question.

"What?" Her forehead furrows. "No. Well, yes, but this has nothing to do with it...why? Were you thinking about him?" She raises her brows, a bemused expression on her face as she stares at me.

"Nope."

"You've always been a horrible liar." She grabs my arm, jerking me to a stop. "Oh. My. God. Did something happen between you guys after I left last night?!"

The smile that spreads across my lips is inescapable. "No."

"Liar!"

"I'm serious, nothing happened. We fell asleep watching *Community*, that's it."

"He slept in your room?"

"Yeah." When the confirmation leaves my lips, Jenna

squeals with delight. "It wasn't like that, we just slept. Although, we might have woken up cuddling and I might have...felt something." I whisper the last two words, partly because I can't think about it without my cheeks flushing, but also because I am prepared for Jenna to freak out entirely and I would like to avoid that.

"Oh my God! You felt his dick?!" she all but screams—right in the middle of the walkway, causing not one but *two* people to stop dead in their tracks to look at us. Jenna's mouth hangs open—then, as if she suddenly becomes situationally aware, she looks around and steps closer to me. "Okay, but... how was it?"

"One," I say as I hold up a finger, "I never said that I felt his dick." I clear my throat before continuing, holding up a second finger. "And two...it was big."

"How big?"

"I don't know—I didn't exactly look at it. But it felt...larger than average."

"Bigger than Elijah's?" I glare at her, causing her to lift her hands up in surrender. "You're right, I'm sorry. That was a dick thing to ask. But...you felt Tanner's dick."

"Stop saying that."

"Fine. You're intimately acquainted with his co—"

"Jenna!"

We both burst into laughter as we get in the car. To my relief, the tension from earlier finally leaves my shoulders.

The moment we step into the house, it's eerily quiet. Too quiet. I half expect someone to jump out of the laundry room and maul us.

But no—the guys are just in the middle of their afternoon nap. Copious amounts of bacon and eggs will do that to a man.

I yawn before turning to Jenna. "I'm going to go lay down for a bit."

Dragging my feet, I make my way up the stairs with my new textbooks in tow. Stepping into my bedroom, I instantly drop the books on top of my dresser before kicking my tennis shoes off with a sigh.

"Hey."

A voice carries from my bed, startling me so much that I nearly scream before my gaze lands on the man sitting with his fingers intertwined on the edge of my bed, a solemn expression on his face.

Elijah.

TWENTY-EIGHT

KAT

"What are you doing here?" I ask Elijah coldly. "In my room, I mean. Why are you in my room?"

"I want to talk."

"Well, I don't. So please leave."

He stands, and at first I am hopeful that he's heeding my request, but then he steps toward me instead. "We need to talk."

"No, we don't. You forfeited your right to talk to me when you decided to break up with me by not showing up to Flash Fest and leaving town." Even thinking about that day makes me feel nauseous.

"Technically, we weren't."

"Technically weren't what? Finish that sentence, Elijah."

He appears to realize the error of his words, but still forges onward. I don't miss the way he guards his groin as he speaks. "We weren't...well, I mean, yeah, we were *together*, but we never labeled it." My glare must prompt him to backtrack because he instantly continues, "I just mean, at the time I didn't think it needed to be a conversation. I know now that I was wrong. I'm sorry."

"I didn't know you knew how to do that."

"Do what?"

"Apologize."

"Ouch, Kat. A bit harsh."

I shrug as I walk past him, ignoring the pang in my chest at his pained words. I don't care, or at least I shouldn't care, but when I accidentally make eye contact with him, I know instantly that it's a horrible idea.

"You really hurt me," I say, my voice cracking.

Elijah nods. "I'm sorry."

"Wow, twice in one day." I notice the bite in my words, but I do my best to own them fully. He doesn't deserve my kindness, even if it's my natural instinct to give it to him.

It's a weird feeling, the cognitive dissonance that is necessary to love someone who you also hate deeply. How does that even work—is it really that there is still love there, or is it just the memory of who I thought he was?

God, I need to get a new therapist.

"Can we be adults about this?" he asks.

Yeah, fuck no. This man doesn't deserve my kindness.

"Get out of my room." I try with the little might I have in my body to be stern, unmoving, as I point to the door behind me, but he doesn't move. "I said get out."

"We need to talk."

"We talked."

"You're not listening to me!" He raises his voice.

"What? Can't handle me not doing as I'm told?" Crossing my arms over my chest, I hold my ground.

CHAPTER TWENTY-EIGHT

"That's not what I fucking meant and you know it. You're twisting my words."

"No, I'm really not. Get out."

"You're acting like a child."

"Don't care."

"Please." Elijah's voice breaks through the tense air, pleading and desperate. He reaches out and takes my hand in his, his grip gentle but firm.

My mind tells me to pull away, to not give him a chance, but I'm frozen in place. It's as if his touch is a spell over me, rendering me unable to move or speak.

"Fine," I snap, "talk."

He doesn't let go of my hand, nor does he say anything. I just stand there, my hand in his, as he looks down at me.

Then he says, "I'm sorry. I don't say that as a means to manipulate the situation or get you to talk to me; I'm just sorry. I was horrible last semester." As if he expects me to provide him with some sort of comfort, he pauses. However, when I don't say anything to reassure him, he keeps going. "I should have talked to you. I've never been good at that—talking. When everything happened on spring break with my parents, I freaked out. It wasn't right, but it's true. I didn't know how to handle it, so I didn't. I should have. I'm sorry."

"Did they know about me?"

"Huh?"

"Did your parents know about me when that happened? Because it didn't seem like it." *Understatement of the fucking year.* His dad's words are still seared into my brain when all I'd like to do is scrub that day from my memory.

Elijah sighs. "Kat, don't do that."

"Do what?"

"Make it into a bigger issue than it was. It wasn't about that." As if those are the exact words I need to grow a goddamned back bone, I yank my hand away. "Kat, c'mon."

"No. You don't get to talk to me like that. Like you get some kind of ownership of what happened."

He glares at me, the loving and pleading man from before nowhere in sight. "You changed."

I know he sees it as a bad thing—like the summer from hell that he so graciously gifted me by leaving campus without a word ruined me but somehow wasn't his fault.

"People do that."

"When did you become this person, Kat? You've never just refused to listen to me."

I contemplate throwing one of my brand-new textbooks at his head. "Stop demanding I listen to you. You're not my father. I don't have to listen to you. My time is a privilege—one you no longer get."

He scoffs, then...laughs. A boisterous, all-consuming, bellowing laugh. What about this scenario would drive any sane person to laughter?

"What?" I ask, but he continues. "What?!"

Elijah manages to rein in his laughter before he looks at me again. "Awfully cocky, aren't we? A 'privilege'...time with you is a privilege, huh?" He steps toward the door, his hand on the knob. "If your time was such a privilege, maybe your dad would fucking want it, eh?"

And then he's gone. Walking out my bedroom door without having offered the apology he came in here to dish out, the kind and empathetic man nowhere in sight. Only the cruelty—the hate in his heart—lingering in the air.

TWENTY-NINE

KAT

With every step I take, the throbbing in my head intensifies. My eyes are red and swollen from crying and all I want to do is crawl back in bed, but I'm starving after skipping dinner. Silently, I tiptoe down the creaky stairs, careful not to wake my sleeping roommates. It's been silent for a while; I've been sitting in my room, waiting to make sure I won't run into Elijah in the hallway.

I can't believe he would say something like that. I had already disabused myself of any misaligned perspective of who he really is, but he's never been that mean to me. Not in so many words, at least. Whenever he said something that hurt my feelings, it was covert or subtle, so much so that at the time I convinced myself I was making it up.

Now I'm starting to realize that is exactly what he wanted.

It's a bizarre feeling—it makes me feel legitimately crazy. I've listened to "Haunted" by Taylor Swift twelve times over the past few hours, and yet every time I hit replay it fills me with rage just the same.

What did I ever see in that guy? I find myself wishing for the guy he was when things were good between us, yet, as I make my way through pitch-black darkness, I can't think of a single time he made me feel genuinely appreciated—not in a way that didn't require doing mental gymnastics.

So why the hell do I care?

That's the eternal question, isn't it? Why does anyone continue to care deeply for someone who doesn't care at all?

I approach the threshold to the kitchen and pause as I notice a soft glow emanating from within, cutting through the otherwise dark house. My eyes squint as they adjust and I catch sight of a faint silhouette moving around. My heart leaps up into my throat.

I swear, if it's Elijah, I might actually lose it.

Tanner appears from behind the white door of the fridge with a bottle of chocolate syrup in one hand and a pint of rocky road tucked under his other arm.

"Hey," I say quietly.

Despite my timid approach, he jumps in surprise. "Jeez, Kat. Don't sneak up on people like that!" He laughs, but when his eyes meet mine, his amusement shifts to concern in a matter of seconds.

"It's nothing," I say before he can even ask the question.

"You've been crying. Sit." He motions toward the stools lined up along the kitchen counter before grabbing two spoons from the drawer, one of them a small spoon for me. This man manages to remember every minute detail.

I sit on the stool and he sets the pint down before walking over to the fridge and grabbing a bag of frozen peas from the freezer. At first I'm perplexed, but then he holds the bag to one of my swollen eyes. It stings on contact and I wince.

CHAPTER TWENTY-NINE

"Sorry," he mumbles.

"Don't be—it's a smart idea." I hold the peas there and Tanner sits down next to me.

"Do you want to talk about it?"

I genuinely can't figure out what to say. Elijah shouldn't bother me anymore; his words shouldn't hurt because, after all these months, I shouldn't still be giving him power over me. Yet I do, without hesitation. I do, despite the fact that I spent my entire summer trying to put back together what he broke—despite the fact that he's given me every reason under the sun to not trust him or want to be around him.

And yet I cried myself to sleep for the umpteenth time because he managed to eviscerate me with a few shitty words. How pathetic is that?

"Not really," I reply quietly.

Tanner nods and doesn't pry.

I dig my spoon into the pint of ice cream before taking a bite, appreciating the midnight-snack tradition we've somehow wordlessly established. A laugh breaks past my lips as Tanner holds up the Hershey syrup with his brows raised high—a question, a dare, a distraction from the turmoil swirling around in my brain since I read Patrick's letter last week.

"So, what's it gonna be? Wanna take a walk on the wild side?"

"I'd hardly say adding more chocolate to a chocolate ice cream constitutes 'living on the wild side,' but sure."

He drizzles the sugary syrup over the top layer of our shared container of ice cream, then waits for me to take another bite. As I usher a spoonful into my mouth, my taste buds are greeted with a burst of bittersweet dark chocolate chunks, perfectly balanced by the sugary syrup. He watches me with a satisfied smile as I savor the delicious combination.

"What?" I ask with my mouth full.

He just shakes his head. "Nothing."

We proceed like this for a while, a comfortable silence washing over the silent kitchen, a somber energy hanging over us that is a far cry from the first time we did this last year. It's weird how things are with Tanner. I don't feel this invasive need to fill the space between us with words just to evade the awkward feeling silence brings.

Because it's not awkward—not in the slightest. It's comfortable.

"Elijah and I got into a fight," I say with a sigh as I push a marshmallow from my side of the pint to Tanner's. He's always liked the chunks far more than the ice cream base anyway.

Tanner nods. "I didn't realize you guys were talking again." His gaze stays on the ice cream. "Have you guys been... you know?"

It takes everything in me not to scoff as I say, "Do you really think that little of me that I'd do that after what he did?"

"No." He sets down his spoon. "I don't think that little of you. I didn't mean it like that. You—" He sighs and looks at me. "You have an immense capacity to see the best in people, and that guy...you'd *have* to have that ability to see the good in him. I didn't mean that you'd be pathetic to do it, not at all."

"Isn't he your friend?"

"No. Not really. Casual acquaintances who exist in the same friend group at best. That guy? He's an ass."

"Oh." I look back down at the tub of ice cream, no longer hungry.

CHAPTER TWENTY-NINE

"Is that what had you crying—the fight?" He picks up his spoon and scoops a lump of chocolate chunks into his mouth, his tongue languidly licking the creamy dessert off his spoon before he digs it back into the tub.

"Yeah. He said something that got under my skin. It's fine, I've just been sensitive."

"Don't do that." His words are stern, demanding, something Tanner very much is not.

"Don't do what?"

"Reduce him hurting your feelings to you just being too sensitive. You're not too sensitive. As I said before, dude is an ass."

I quickly find myself wanting desperately to divert the conversation away from Elijah, so I change the subject. "I got a letter from my brother."

This catches Tanner's attention. His eyes dart from the ice cream to meet my gaze. "Your brother...like, your dad's kid?"

"Yeah, I guess he found one of my letters that I sent my dad a few years ago. He, um—Patrick didn't know about me."

"Patrick is your brother, I'm guessing?"

I nod. "Well, technically it's also my dad's name."

"He named him after himself?"

I nod again.

"Fucking prick. Are you gonna write him back?" Tanner asks.

"I don't know, I don't even know what I'd say. He wants a relationship."

"And you don't?"

"I don't know what I want," I say with a sigh. "I mean, how am I supposed to have a relationship with the brother who is the reason my dad left in the first place? He left a baby at home to be a father to someone else...who the fuck does that?"

"A piece of shit does that," Tanner says seriously. "But...your brother didn't know that. You said it yourself; he didn't know about you. Wouldn't you like to know what he's like outside of the random Facebook stalk sessions?"

My brows shoot up in surprise, earning me a chuckle.

"I know you, Kat. There is no way in hell that you wouldn't be curious about him. So why not get the information from the source? At the very least, it might give you closure about your dad."

I hate that he's probably right. I hate that, despite it not being Patrick's fault my dad left, I still resent him for taking him away. Yes, I'm aware that isn't how the world works and people can't be forced to do anything, let alone by a fetus. But...it's there, the resentment.

There is also that nagging voice in the back of my mind that maybe Elijah is right—maybe my time isn't all that important—and the second Patrick learns that, he'll leave too.

"I hate that Elijah still gets to me." I stab my spoon further into the ice cream. "We broke up months ago and I honestly thought I was fine. But the second he cornered me to talk, the second he was remotely mean to me, I was instantly a mess."

Pain creases Tanner's brow. He shakes his head. "It's because you loved him. That doesn't just go away. You might want it to, but it doesn't just vanish. Give yourself some grace. Time will help...among other things."

"Like what other things?"

"You know what people say," Tanner chuckles. "The best way to get over someone is to get under someone else." As he swallows, I can't help but stare at his bobbing Adam's apple.

CHAPTER TWENTY-NINE

"Find a rando and get laid. Prob doesn't help that you haven't been with anyone since."

"I don't like sleeping with people I don't know. While I realize some people can do it…I don't know, it makes me feel icky."

"So have sex with someone you *do* know."

"I don't want to use someone I care about like that—that isn't fair to them. I'd need to find someone who knows it means nothing, and even then it still feels wrong." I stuff more ice cream into my mouth, relishing the sweet flavor.

"Then use me." Tanner says it as if he just told me the sky is blue, or that classes start on Monday. Something as mundane as the stucco siding on the back patio.

Immediately I break into a coughing fit, nearly choking on the bite of ice cream I just took. As I finally catch my breath, I turn to him and ask, "I'm sorry, what did you just say?"

Any other man would cower away and backtrack, take my response as a clear indicator that I am not interested. Not Tanner, though.

He grins. "Use me. I'm down for casual sex, you trust me, I know it means nothing. So use me." He scrapes his spoon against the bottom of the cardboard pint, chasing the last bits of ice cream.

I drop my spoon on the counter with a clink. "You don't date," I say with my jaw agape.

"And we wouldn't be dating." With a wink, he continues, "What? Are you too worried you'll fall in love with me or something?"

I smack him in the arm. "No, but wouldn't it be weird? I mean, me and you…ya know."

"Fucking? Me and you fucking? You have no issue saying

the word any other time—fuck fuck fuck fuck fuck. Us fucking."

"Jesus Christ, Tanner. I get it."

He laughs as he tosses the empty pint into the trash can. "If you don't want to, it's fine. I'm serious, it's not a big deal. But if you change your mind, you know where to find me." He disappears out of the kitchen without so much as a "Good night."

How the *fuck* does someone say that and then go to bed?

Fucking serial killer, man.

THIRTY

KAT

The person sitting next to me taps their pen against the desk in a steady rhythm. Each tap echoes throughout the crowded lecture hall, making it hard for me to concentrate on the professor's words. I try my best to focus on the front of the room, but the tapping continues, growing more and more irritating with each passing minute.

Whatever—it's syllabus week anyway. I stare down at the paper in front of me as it spells out the rest of the semester bullet point by bullet point. Social Media Strategies was one of the few remaining options to fill my major's final communications class requirement.

Although I set up social media accounts for my photography business, I haven't posted yet. Most of my portfolio is either stuff I've done for school or random headshots like the ones I took for Tanner last semester, so I don't have much to share.

Tanner.

God, what he said the other night still has me reeling and I can't figure out how I feel about it.

Yes, he's hot. I'd have to be blind not to see that—even Marcus will admit Tanner is hot and he's a heterosexual man. Some things are as much a fact as "the sky is blue." But sleeping with Tanner? That sounds like a one-way ticket to ruining our friendship, and I can't let that happen. He's far too important to me to risk everything for the sake of getting laid.

So it's decided: no having sex with Tanner.

Why am I weirdly disappointed by that decision? Oh, right—because it's all I've been thinking about for the last four days.

My thoughts wander to Tanner's other suggestion from that night, the part that should cause me anxiety but by comparison feels strangely safe.

Tanner had a point when it comes to my brother. It isn't Patrick's fault that our shared parent left me to raise him, even if that knowledge lingers in the back of my mind every time I read his letter, which I've done roughly thirty-three times since it arrived a week and a half ago.

Professor Montoya's bellowing voice rips me out of my thoughts. "In preparation for Friday's class, please create an Instagram account and a Facebook page for your business. It doesn't have to be real, but it can be if you are on the entrepreneurial path. Just be sure to have both set up before Friday morning's class, as it is necessary for your next assignment."

I step out of Franklin Hall just as rain starts to drizzle down from the sky, thankfully barely a peppering of water atop my head as I make my way back to central campus.

Jenna meets me in the student center for a quick bite

CHAPTER THIRTY

before we head back to the house. We've been debating whether we want to go to the Dusty Armadillo tonight, since it's the first Wednesday night of the semester and, thus, resident college night. We still haven't decided, but if I'm being honest, I don't know if I'm even up for going out.

"Did you talk to your mom about that wedding she wanted you to shoot?" Jenna asks as we near the front of the line to order the same basic bagels with cream cheese that we've been getting since freshman year. If it isn't broke, why fix it, ya know?

I don't look away from my phone as I respond to my mom's text message. "Peeking at my phone, are we?"

Jenna laughs. "Usually, yes. But that was just a lucky guess. So, are you going to do it?"

"Yeah, I think so. She just needs to confirm my rate with the bride." We approach the counter and I order an everything bagel with cream cheese while Jenna orders a plain bagel with strawberry cream cheese.

We find a table against the far wall of windows, thankful that the rain held off until we were inside. The light drizzle has transformed into a complete torrential downpour.

"So, what's the plan for tonight?" Jenna asks before shoving almost half her bagel in her mouth.

"Are you afraid the bagel is going to run away if you don't eat it in three bites?"

"Fuck off, I'm hungry," she mumbles. "Answer my question—did you want to go to the Dusty tonight?"

I shrug, taking a normal-person-sized bite of my own bagel.

"By all means, move at a glacial pace. You know how it thrills me." She does her best Miranda Priestly impression.

I roll my eyes. "I don't know. I'm not really feeling up to

it." I intentionally avoid eye contact as I take another bite of my bagel.

"Kat." She snaps her fingers in front of me, an annoyed yet concerned expression on her face.

"What?" I say.

"You didn't go out with us at all this weekend. It's our senior year. I'm not going to push you to do something that you're not comfortable with, but I also don't want you to regret letting our last year of college pass you by because Elijah is an asshole."

She has a point, but I still find myself searching for another reason to tell her no. When I can't think of anything, I do the next best thing: I deflect.

"Tanner told me he wants to have sex with me."

Jenna's eyes go wide, wider than I think I've ever seen them. Her voice squeaks, pitching upward as she all but yells, "Katarina Emma Lyn, way to bury the goddamned lead! He said that? Like, he told you, 'Kat, I want to have sex with you'?"

"Well...no."

"So, what did he say?"

"He said that the best way to get over someone is to get under someone else and that if I need to use someone to get past this stuff with Elijah, then I should use him."

Judging by the gleam in Jenna's eyes, you'd think it was fucking Christmas. "Are you going to?"

"Going to what?"

"Fuck Tanner. Are you going to fuck Tanner?"

I chew on my bagel dramatically slowly. "I don't know. I haven't decided yet. It sounds like a horrible idea."

"It sounds like a fantastic idea! Tanner is a smoke show.

CHAPTER THIRTY

And from what I've heard, his perfect proportions extend past his jawline."

"Jenna."

"What?"

"You're gross."

"What? It's vital information that you should have. Or would you prefer it if you didn't know that Rebecca Ramirez said he has the biggest dick she's ever seen and accidentally pass that up?"

She's not wrong; it's good information to have. So why does my mood sour the moment she reminds me that Tanner slept with Rebecca? Honestly, I don't love thinking about anyone he's slept with...because he is my friend. That's the only reason.

"Either way, I don't know."

Jenna huffs before shoving her final bite of bagel into her mouth. As soon as she's finished chewing, she continues talking. "Well, I think you should do it. Both for reasons of determining whether the rumors are true and because I think it would be good for you to get back out there."

"I'd hardly call having sex with one of our best friends 'getting back out there.'" I say, idly toying with my napkin. "Besides, like I said, I haven't decided what I want to do yet."

"And the Dusty?"

"Bite me."

Jenna smiles wide. "So, is that a yes?"

I sigh before popping the last bit of my bagel in my mouth, forcing Jenna to wait through my chewing. By the time I swallow, she's glaring at me, waiting for a response.

"Fine—it's a yes."

THIRTY-ONE

KAT

As we approach the Dusty Armadillo, an eerie sense of déjà vu washes over me. It feels unusually similar to when we came here around this time last year for our first night of line dancing of the semester, except this time it's just me and Jenna. She tried to get Marcus to come, but he and Tanner already got slammed with a ton of homework for one of their architecture classes, so they're both stuck at home.

I'm weirdly happy about it—not that Marcus and Tanner couldn't come, but because there is something about it just being me and Jenna that brings me calm. We haven't had a night like this in a while, and it used to be what all our nights were like. The two of us going to parties and campus events, just us.

Darren, manning the door to the Dusty, smiles at us. "There's my favorite girls," he says before looking around. "What, no boyfriends tonight?"

"Nope, just us tonight!" Jenna responds with a grin as she loops her arm through mine. "Girls' night."

CHAPTER THIRTY-ONE

Darren nods and grins. "Like the old days." He opens the door, and instantly we're embraced by the sound of a familiar George Strait song and boots stomping on the dance floor.

The rustic wooden floors creak under our boots as we twirl and kick to the beat of the music. The smell of leather and sweat mingles with hints of whiskey and beer in the air. I've lost count of how many times I have come here to dance without even touching a drop of alcohol. It has been a place where we can let loose and have fun without being pressured to drink or conform to the typical college party culture. This country line-dancing bar has become our sanctuary, our escape from the chaos of college life.

However, tonight is not the night that we choose to abstain. Tonight, we are drinking.

Jenna and I decided that, since neither of us have morning classes on Thursdays, we're all in. So naturally, the moment the song comes to an end, we beeline straight for the bar.

"Two shots of Jack Honey, please!" Jenna says with a grin, and the bartender slides two small glasses filled with amber liquid toward us across the smooth, polished wood of the bar. We each grab one and raise them in unison. The fiery burn of the alcohol as it travels down my throat causes me to wince, but I quickly recover and let out a satisfying exhale.

"Jeez—" Jenna breaks into a coughing fit. She's never been great at taking shots, and yet she always insists on them. Once her breathing is back to normal, she reaches for the tall glass of water the bartender swiftly set in front of her.

Once we're back on the dance floor, the music shifts to "Any Man of Mine" by Shania Twain and we both squeal in delight. Everyone on the dance floor flows together in an all-too-familiar dance, Jenna and I among them, each move like muscle memory.

After the third song, we decide to take a break from dancing and grab another drink, at which point Jenna insists we each order another shot alongside our mixed drinks. I still wince as I swallow the fiery liquid, but it's nowhere as bad as the first shot.

By the fifth shot an hour and a half later, I barely feel it coating my throat, and by the looks of Jenna, she's just as drunk as I am.

"Should we call an Uber?" Jenna yells over the loud music as the clock on my phone reads 1:30 AM.

"Probably," I respond. I pull up the app, but there are no Ubers available. Our pick-up estimate is over forty-five minutes out and I might actually keel over from exhaustion if we wait that long.

Jenna groans as she looks down at my phone, then says, "You should text Tanner."

"Why?"

"So he can pick us up?" she responds.

"What about Marcus?" I ask.

"Marcus has an early class, and Tanner is always up late."

She's not wrong, and I realize with startling clarity there are a few things I'd like to do beyond just *seeing* Tanner. Ever since he suggested I get over Elijah by quite literally getting under him, it's all I can think about.

It makes it rather inconvenient when I'm trying to get my footing with a new schedule of classes.

"Fine," I mutter, attempting to appear more irritated than I am.

CHAPTER THIRTY-ONE

KAT
Tannnnerrrrrr :)

TANNER
What do you want? Lol

Any chance you can come get us from the dusty?

I watch with bated breath as three dots appear, then disappear, then reappear again.

Pleeeeease

Im grabbing my keys, I will be there in ten

A sigh of relief falls past my lips as I turn to Jenna. "He's on his way."

Ten minutes later, Tanner's black SUV pulls up to the Dusty Armadillo, its tires crunching over gravel. He parks in the first available spot and jumps out of the driver's seat, his black T-shirt hugging his muscular frame. His dark gray basketball shorts are wrinkled and his tousled hair suggests he was sleeping. I feel a pang of guilt for inconveniencing him as he approaches us with a yawn.

"Thank you!" Jenna yells. She darts toward the vehicle, then all but throws herself into the back seat face-first.

"Heyyyy," I say, grinning and stumbling slightly as I approach him.

Tanner smiles down at me, not a hint of irritation in his expression. "Hey, you. Did you have fun?"

"Loads."

"Good."

I lean toward him and my fingers tingle as they trace the

defined ridges of his abs through the thin fabric of his T-shirt. I can't resist the urge to wrap my arms around his waist. It's like I'm noticing his muscles for the first time, even though I've always known deep down that he's attractive. But now, he's more than just hot—he's James Lafferty as Nathan Scott in *One Tree Hill* hot.

He doesn't recoil as I squeeze him tightly; he simply wraps his arms around me and hugs me back. "Kat…"

"Yes?" I say, sated and bordering on sleepy as I rest my head against his chest.

Tanner seems to fight off a laugh as he asks, "How much did you drink?"

"A few, why?"

"You smell like you bathed in whiskey. Let me guess, Jenna wanted to take shots?"

"Biiiingo."

Tanner just chuckles as he releases my waist and begins pushing me toward his SUV. I climb into the passenger seat and buckle myself in before turning my head to find Jenna not just lying in the back seat face-down, but sleeping. Full-on, not a care in the world, snoring with her face pressed up against the leather interior.

When we arrive at the house, Jenna is still out cold, so much so that Tanner has to carry her inside. I knock on her and Marcus's bedroom door twice before he appears in the doorway, wiping sleep from his eyes.

"Sorry, man, your girl had a little too much to drink," Tanner whispers.

Marcus nods before hoisting Jenna into his arms and kicking the door shut behind him.

As Tanner and I walk down the hallway, our footsteps are

CHAPTER THIRTY-ONE

the only sound echoing through the quiet house. I glance at him, noticing the tension in his jaw and the way his fingers flex by his side. The air feels heavy with unspoken words as we reach the end of the hall and stand outside our separate bedrooms, which are positioned directly across from each other.

Neither of us moves or breaks the silence until suddenly we both speak at the same time, causing an awkward overlap of words.

Tanner says, "Do you need anything?" right as I say, "I think we should."

"What?" Tanner asks.

"Huh?"

"What did you just say?"

"I...what did *you* say?"

"What I said doesn't matter. What did you say?"

I swallow hard as I look down at the hardwood floor, my socks tattered and mangled from the night of dancing. When I finally muster the nerve to say it again, it comes out in a single breath. "Ithinkweshouldhookup."

One corner of Tanner's lips tips upward, but he doesn't say anything. He just moves toward me, encroaching on the little space that remains between us. I tip my head back to meet his eyes, and the moment I do, it all feels abundantly obvious. He's glad I said what I said and I'm just realizing now that I don't know if I've ever felt one-hundred-percent sure that a guy was being honest—ever.

I desperately search for a way to express how much I want him, and my body takes the lead. I rise onto my tiptoes and brush my lips against his. He leans into the kiss, then suddenly pulls back as I try to deepen it with my tongue. His hesitation only fuels my desire and I reach up, tangling my fingers in his hair and pulling him closer.

"Kat, no." His voice sounds pained and I don't think I've ever been so confused.

"But I thought you wanted—"

"I do," he reassures me. "But you're drunk and I'm not that guy."

"I'm not that drunk."

"I don't care."

Stepping backward, I fix my eyes on the floorboards between us again, attempting but failing to keep the tears at bay as the humiliation of rejection washes over me.

"Hey, hey," he soothes, his voice pleading and tender as he steps toward me, tipping my chin up so my eyes meet his. "I don't want you to take me saying no to you tonight as me saying no. Trust me, it's taking everything in me right now not to give you exactly what you're asking for. But you're drunk, and I would never *ever* want to take advantage."

I try to interject and reassure him that it wouldn't be taking advantage—that I want this—but he presses his pointer finger against my lips to shush me. He actually shushes me, and I know that I should be bothered by it, but something about the motion turns my insides to water.

He continues, "I don't care if you don't think it would be taking advantage. I don't want there to be even the tiniest part of you that regrets it when we have sex for the first time. So we can talk about it tomorrow...when you're sober and don't reek of whiskey."

"I do not reek!"

"Oh, you definitely reek. You smell like you've been bathing in the barrel."

CHAPTER THIRTY-ONE

"Asshole," I giggle as I push his shoulder. He grins from ear to ear as my eyes meet his. "I understand. We'll talk tomorrow."

"We'll talk tomorrow," he repeats. "But in the meantime, go to bed. I'll grab you some water...and a bucket."

"I don't need a bu—"

"Katarina. I don't think I've ever seen you drink where you didn't throw up at least once the next morning."

Ugh, I hate it when he's right. I fight back the urge to argue more, to tell him I have both water in my mini fridge and a trash can in my room, and instead say the only reasonable thing left to say.

"Thank you."

THIRTY-TWO

KAT

To say I have been riddled with anxiety today is an understatement. I can't believe I said what I said to Tanner last night.

Not to say I regret it—actually, the more I think about it, the more I start to believe in the concept of "drunken words are sober thoughts." The liquid courage from the alcohol seemed to have unleashed all of my pent-up thoughts and feelings toward Tanner, but now that I'm sober, I can't help but feel embarrassed by my outburst.

I wouldn't be surprised if he tells me today that he's changed his mind and that he didn't actually intend for it to go as far as I suggested. Who hasn't known a guy to say something stupid, then later realize he didn't mean it? I can name quite a few.

Upon returning to the house after classes, I let my backpack fall against the hardwood floor of the entryway, the scent of rich tomato sauce with garlic hitting me instantly. Kicking off my white sneakers, I make my way to the kitchen.

CHAPTER THIRTY-TWO

Jenna's vibrant red apron is splattered with a creamy white sauce and flecked with splashes of rich tomato puree as she skillfully extracts a gigantic dish from the oven. The smell of melted cheese and pungent herbs wafts through the kitchen. The lasagna is large and enticing enough to feed a small army.

"What's the occasion?" I ask with a laugh, leaning against the counter.

"Why do I need an occasion to cook?" she counters without looking at me, sifting through drawers, clearly searching for something.

"Because you hardly ever cook when you're not stressed."

She shrugs as she finds a large chef's knife sheathed in a plastic guard. "Long day of classes. I figured we might like a nice dinner all together."

I can't tell if she's being wholly truthful. Jenna has never been a forthcoming person when it comes to what is bothering her. At least, not until after the issue subsides. I would pry, but it's Jenna—I know that would get me nowhere with her.

"Makes sense. How did you feel this morning?" Our night of drinking clearly hit Jenna like a freight train, evidenced by Tanner having to carry her in from the car.

I breathe a sigh of relief as the corner of her mouth quirks upward. "I felt fine. I don't usually get a hangover. What about you, Miss Pukes-a-Lot?"

That joke wasn't funny the first time she said it three years ago, and it's not funny now.

"I've been thinking about cutting back on drinking, actually. I swear it's like the more time passes, the less alcohol I need in my system for my body to decide it needs to expel it immediately," I mumble. I grab a paper towel and wipe up a rogue dollop of red sauce on the kitchen counter.

"You're not pregnant, are you?" Jenna asks, half-joking.

"You and I both know that that would be physically impossible without being glaringly obvious," I sigh. Jenna knows just as well as I do that I haven't had sex in over four months, not since that night on spring break, the night before everything changed between me and Elijah.

"What's not physically possible?" Tanner's voice carries through the kitchen as he appears with Brendan at his side.

"For Kat to be pregnant."

He nods as if this information is nothing new. "It's been a minute, hasn't it?"

"Dude, why would you even know that?" Brendan asks, clearly perplexed at the idea that Tanner would have any insider knowledge about my sex life—or lack thereof.

Tanner just shrugs, not entertaining Brendan's confusion, and it takes a total of two seconds for Brendan to stop caring about it.

"Anything we can do?" Brendan asks Jenna.

"Actually, yes. Can you guys set the table?" Jenna responds.

"Sure, how many?"

"Uh, everyone." And suddenly I know what had Jenna so spooked moments ago. She's avoided Elijah just as much as I have since moving into the house; she swears she wouldn't even breathe the same air as him if he wasn't one of Marcus's best friends.

I understand, though, why she still loosely associates with him despite being my best friend. I wouldn't feel comfortable

CHAPTER THIRTY-TWO

asking her to cut him off and subsequently throw a wrench in her relationship with Marcus.

As soon as the table is set, Jenna begins cutting the lasagna. "Guys! Dinner's ready!"

Within minutes, everyone is filtering into the kitchen, each person individually complimenting Jenna on the beautiful dinner. Marcus approaches her, whispers something in her ear, then kisses her temple.

It isn't until we're all seated at the table with the baked pasta dish in the center that Elijah joins us. He sits down next to Marcus and I don't miss the way he barely looks at me.

We haven't spoken since our argument, if you'd call it that. I suppose it's better categorized as him attempting to apologize, then—when I didn't lay down and thank him for his kindness—turning on me instantly.

It's a weird feeling, disliking someone so much but also holding onto the memory of who you thought they were. Still, I can't figure out what would have driven me to go back in time and fix things with a man like that. The holes in my memory of what's yet to come only leave me more frustrated as I make decisions.

I like to think I'm doing things differently, but it's impossible to say.

"It looks great," Elijah says to Jenna, and she smiles softly and nods in response.

We all dig in immediately and begin chatting about our classes. Most of my classes have been pretty slow so far, but apparently that isn't the case for everyone.

"Have you thought of any ideas for the spring fashion show?" Jenna asks Regina.

"I have a few concepts I've drawn up. Thankfully, I don't have to start working on it quite yet, but it's on my mind."

Regina is a senior in Kent State's fashion design program, the most competitive fashion program in the state and top five in the country. Every spring, the Kent Fashion School puts on a fashion show that serves as their senior showcase, where they show off their individual designs and are judged by a panel of industry critics.

"I was actually wondering, would either of you be willing to walk in it?" Regina asks, looking between Jenna and me. My eyes nearly bug out of my head as Jenna's light up with delight. "I know it's a tall ask, but most everyone has chosen their models already and I know that if I wait any longer to ask people, I'll end up with the reject pile of models."

"Of course we'll walk in the show for you!" Jenna squeals before her eyes meet mine. "Won't we, Kat?"

All eyes shift to me, putting me on the spot with little opportunity to think it over. It's not that I am completely averse to being in the spotlight, but I've always gravitated toward being behind the camera, not in front of it.

"Sure," I respond, then quickly shove a bite of food into my mouth.

"You two will look beautiful," Tanner says, and now all eyes drift toward him.

He's said stuff like that to me on many occasions, but seldom in such a group setting, and I am unsure if he's ever said it to Jenna. I try not to read into it as we still haven't talked about last night.

Tanner seems to notice all the attention on him, and he laughs. "Complimenting your female friends shouldn't be so foreign. Have some respect, man."

CHAPTER THIRTY-TWO

Idiot. I laugh to myself.

Brendan suddenly jumps up and heads into the kitchen. We hear the clinking of bottles and glasses and a faint whirring noise as he blends something. He emerges with an almost fluorescent green liquid in hand, declaring it to be his newest concoction. I can smell the sharp scent of alcohol emanating from it, and my stomach turns at the thought of drinking any more after last night's heavy indulgence.

Politely, I decline his offer to try it.

"Do you need any help cleaning up?" I ask Jenna.

"No," she says with a laugh before turning to the table of mostly men. "*You guys* get to clean up."

I take the opportunity to grab my backpack from the entryway and escape up to my room, thankful to excuse myself.

THIRTY-THREE

KAT

If I keep pacing at this rate, I very well might end up wearing away a line straight down the middle of my bedroom into the hardwood floor. It's been two hours since dinner and Tanner and I have yet to discuss last night.

I don't necessarily expect him to bring it up as polite dinner conversation, but I did expect him to want to talk. I heard him come up to his room about half an hour ago and he has yet to text, knock on my door, anything—so I do what any person who is pathologically opposed to conflict does: I pace back and forth instead of walking the measly few feet from my bedroom to his.

What if he regrets saying anything about it? What if last night confirmed to him that the idea of being intimate with me sounds far more appealing in theory than in reality? Or—worst-case scenario—what if he was kidding and I attempted to jump his bones all over a joke between friends?

Did I manage to ruin our friendship beyond repair because I simply couldn't keep it in my fucking pants?!

CHAPTER THIRTY-THREE

The thought leaves me reeling as I find my feet moving of their own volition toward Tanner's room, not a single thought in my brain outside of wanting clarity on what is going on. The longer I'm left to my own devices, the further I feel myself slowly slipping into insanity.

Without even knocking, I barrel through the door to his bedroom.

As I step inside, my eyes take in the bare light gray walls and stacks of boxes in the corner. It's clear that he hasn't fully settled into his room quite yet. The sheets on his bed are a faded heather gray, with textbooks strewn about haphazardly. A faint scent of laundry detergent hangs in the air.

Tanner sits in the middle of his bed with his textbooks arranged in front of him. He scribbles notes onto a spiral-bound notebook with a mechanical pencil. Gone are the dark-wash jeans and old faded polo he wore down to dinner, replaced with low-slung jet-black sweatpants and...nothing else. My eyes linger on the sight, momentarily forgetting why I came in the first place.

When his eyes meet mine, his face morphs from the stressed expression of someone studying for a high-level class their senior year of college to the smile of a man genuinely delighted to see the person who just walked in. At least, that's what I want to believe I'm looking at.

I walk up to the edge of his bed, on a war path.

"Hey, you," he chirps, and I instantly thaw.

"Hey."

"What's up?"

I can't help but wonder what he's thinking right now. I had all these things I wanted to say, and yet I'm standing in front of him with what I can only assume is the dumbest expression known to man on my face.

"Nothing. I—uh...what are you doing?" I ask.

He glances up at me with tired yet hopeful eyes. "Just trying to get ahead on my homework," he says, gesturing to the pile of books. "But I have some time before my next class on Tuesday." He tilts his head to the side as he asks, "Do you want to hang out? We can binge-watch *Always Sunny*."

It's as if nothing happened yesterday—as if I didn't all but throw myself at him less than twenty-four hours ago.

I feel self-conscious under his scrutiny, but manage to respond, "Sounds good."

He packs up his textbooks, closing them without even grabbing a bookmark or dog-earing the pages. Once he's cleared the bed of any obstacles, I climb up, noticing he hasn't rolled out a comforter yet, no doubt because up until today the weather has been balmy at best and smoldering at worst.

Crossing my legs underneath me, I settle against the headboard as he turns on *It's Always Sunny in Philadelphia*. It starts to play one of the show's eccentric but entertaining cold opens, this one involving Frank and Charlie getting into yet another crazy scenario.

"I love this one," Tanner says, his attention entirely on the show.

We stay like that, focused on the forty-five-inch flat-screen TV sitting atop his dresser, following along as Dee's antics cause her to be left out by the core group of guys yet again.

"Serves her right," I chuckle.

"Wait, why? All she's asking is to be a part of their scheme. Don't forget, one of them is her brother—she just wants to feel included."

CHAPTER THIRTY-THREE

I feel a sting in my chest at his words, not because they are harsh or rude, or even left up to interpretation, but because my mind instantly goes to Patrick. The brother I could have if I wanted; the brother I have never met. Is it worth pursuing a relationship with him at almost twenty-two years old, or has the ship sailed since our most formative years have come and gone?

"I think I'm going to write Patrick back," I blurt out.

Tanner nods, still staring across the room at the television, but it's quite obvious his attention isn't wholly on the screen anymore. He reaches for the remote and hits pause, then lays on his side, facing me. "What made you decide that?" he asks.

"Honestly, I didn't fully decide until right now," I say. "I don't know, I just feel like I'll spend the rest of my life questioning what it would be like to know him if I don't."

"I think it's a good idea. For you to write him, I mean. It's not even to say that it means you have to have a relationship with him, but I think it'll be good for you, at the very least to get some answers so you can have closure about your dad."

I lean against the headboard, fidgeting with a loose thread sticking out of the flat sheet. My inner cheek stings from biting it so hard, trying to hold back. But despite our conversation about my family issues, one thought keeps nagging at me: how can he sit here and talk to me like this without addressing what happened last night? The memory of my brazen actions and his response plays on a loop in my mind. How can he just ignore it?

Maybe because he wishes it never happened.

"Kat..." Tanner's voice grows stern, gravelly, and I perk up at the sound.

"Hm?"

"I can hear you spiraling from here. What's up?"

What's up? What's up?! I don't know, Tanner, what's up with you?! I internally scream, but I know that saying what I'm really thinking right now will just result in me looking like an obsessive crazy person, so I just say, "Nothing."

"Talk to me." As I look up and meet his eyes, his expression is every bit one of concern. "What's going on in that pretty head of yours?"

"Why haven't you brought up last night?" I ask in a rush.

Whatever he is expecting to come out of my mouth, it isn't that. *Oh God, he's trying to figure out how to let me down easy.* He totally regrets suggesting it. He hasn't said anything because he's been hoping to walk it back and didn't know how to do it without ruining our friendship, and now I'm the one doing it. How could I be so stupid?

Tanner's hand lands on my bare thigh and gently squeezes. His words come out firm but compassionate as he says, "Kat, look at me."

I do, despite every instinct in my body telling me not to. As I lock eyes with him, a fluttering sensation erupts in my stomach, sending butterflies soaring in every direction. His earnest gaze holds me captive and my heart races erratically in response.

He continues, "I haven't brought it up because I wanted to give you an out if you wanted it. You were drinking last night, and you didn't seem too keen on the idea prior to that. I never want you to think I'm pushing you toward something you don't want simply because I want it."

A lump lodges in my throat. The words I want to say are all stuck, caged in without anywhere to go. "You…want it—you

CHAPTER THIRTY-THREE

want...me?" I try not to sound completely shocked by the revelation, but he chuckles anyway.

"Yes, Kat. And here I thought I was being abundantly obvious, so here it goes." He clears his throat, shifting to face me head-on. "I want you, Kat, more than I think I've ever wanted anyone." He squeezes my thigh again, determination in his eyes. My heart races as his words sink in, sending shivers down my spine. "So, yeah, if you want that too, *sober*, then that's what I want. I ask you this once, and I promise that if you have changed your mind it will never get brought up again: Have you changed your mind?"

"I haven't," I mumble before clearing my throat to speak more clearly. "I haven't changed my mind. I stand by what I said last night."

His tortured, borderline pained expression morphs into a grin—an entirely mind-boggling grin that has me ready to do whatever he asks. How did I never notice it before? He squeezes my leg, but this time his hand creeps toward my inner thigh, my skin pebbling at the sensation. "Good. So... when would you like to explore that?"

I can barely think as his pointer finger draws circles against my flesh, the slight chill in the air doing nothing to cool the heat that blooms all over my body at the simple touch. "Now, preferably."

A chuckle breaks past his lips at my enthusiasm, but he doesn't pull away. "Okay."

Tanner climbs off the bed, briefly leaving me with a cold sense of foreboding until he pushes my legs apart and climbs between them.

I anticipate his kiss, mentally begging for it as if it's the last shred of salvation at my disposal; as if it's the only source of oxygen in the room.

However, rather than kissing me, he forces me to meet his gaze. "Before any of this happens, I need to make one thing clear. The most important thing about this arrangement is that you know that you never have to question what I'm thinking. I promise I will always tell you how I'm feeling. If the way I feel about this arrangement changes, I will tell you. I realize that you've been in situations that left you feeling like information is always being withheld, but that isn't the case here. So, Kat?"

"Hm?"

"Breathe." He exhales as if he needs to show me what that looks like and I follow suit, letting out a deep breath that I didn't realize I was holding.

We continue for a few short moments, taking deep breaths in unison, his eyes never leaving mine. It's not until my heart rate normalizes and I don't feel like I very well might faint that he stops his exaggerated breathing.

Then, without restraint or reservation, his lips are on mine.

THIRTY-FOUR

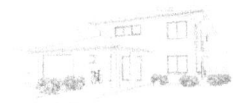

TANNER

There are few things I want more than anything in this world: my parents to live long and healthy lives, my brothers to get into good schools and grow out of being the little shits they are, to find a good job after graduation, and to know what it feels like to make Katarina Marritt orgasm, ideally more than once.

Since the day I met her in the student center, it's all I can think about. Well, maybe not so specifically. But I so badly want to be able to touch her freely, to feel her soft skin against my palm without restraint, to know the way her tongue tastes as it grazes my own.

I'm thankful that I no longer have to wonder what it's like to feel her.

Elijah never deserved her—the thought of them together actually makes my skin crawl. However, it was never my choice to make; never my place to lure her away from him simply to be able to touch her when she clearly loved him.

I'm not that guy. I'll never be that guy.

That's what makes this new advancement just that much

sweeter. She wants this, she wants me...even if it's just for the sake of wiping him from her memory.

I can work with that.

My lips press firmly against hers, my tongue flicking out to tease her own. Kat lets out a soft gasp, her body relaxing into mine as she eagerly responds. I deepen the kiss, our tongues dancing and exploring each other's mouths. Her hands find their way to my hair, pulling me closer as our bodies become one in this passionate moment.

I want to relish it, savor it, because I very well might not get this again. It's possible she wakes up tomorrow and decides that once was enough to pull her out of this Elijah Hanas-induced haze. While the thought of that is about the last thing I want, I'd respect it. We had a deal, so if this is all she needs from me, I'll gladly hand it over.

In an effort to more literally follow through on our deal, I tighten my grip on her waist and pull her toward me, away from the headboard. With a swift movement, I flip her over so that she's lying on her back under me. Her body tenses and she gasps as I maneuver her into position.

Kat's eyes meet mine for the first time since I kissed her, and I can't help but inspect them. While I'll be the first to say this is just sex, just something she needs, I can't help but find myself clamoring for reassurance that this is the right move for us, for her. The last thing I'd want to do is push her too far.

As if she can read my mind, Kat whispers, "Tanner." Her voice is raspy in a way I've never heard before.

"Hm?"

She inches closer, her eyes locked on mine, and I can smell the hint of mint wafting from her breath. "Kiss me," she demands, and I eagerly oblige.

CHAPTER THIRTY-FOUR

Our lips meet with a force that sends sparks shooting through my entire body. I wrap my hand around the back of her neck, pulling her closer. She tastes like spearmint, which must mean she snuck away to brush her teeth after dinner—a smart move considering the heavy dose of garlic Jenna used in the sauce. But even with the refreshing minty taste, all I can focus on is the warmth of her lips against mine and the electricity between us.

My lips trace a path of gentle pressure over her collarbone, leaving a trail of soft kisses. Kat's breath hitches as I continue my slow descent, my tongue gently teasing the sensitive skin beneath her ear. I can feel the heat radiating from her body, matching the fire building within me. Her moans grow louder with each pass until a gasp escapes her lips and she wraps her arms around me tighter.

Goddamn, that sound.

She tangles her fingers into the hair at the nape of my neck before yanking my head backward. It stings, but in that intoxicating way that drops you on the edge of something even more pleasurable than you could ever think possible.

Our mouths crash together once again before she reaches down to slip her fingers just slightly below the waistband of my sweatpants.

Yes, fuck yes, but not yet.

When I yank her hand away, she whimpers in protest, but all I can do is grin at her insistence.

"Have some patience—it's a marathon, not a sprint." I return to kissing her neck, except this time I venture lower. As I press my lips against her soft skin, my tongue dances over each raised goosebump on a trail toward the edge of her thin camisole. My bottom lip grazes the fabric as I continue to explore every inch of her body.

I tug the fabric downward to find she isn't wearing a bra. Admittedly, I was hopeful when she appeared to have changed into pajamas after dinner, but I couldn't be sure.

Slowly and lightly, I circle the pad of my thumb over her rosy pink nipple, in complete awe at every new discovery of her body. I've envisioned what she might look like beneath her clothes a million times over, oftentimes in situations that made me feel like anything but a gentleman, late into the night after she's gone to bed when I still taste rocky road on the tip of my tongue.

Every inch of her skin is new and thrilling to discover. I can't believe my luck.

Dipping my head lower, I close my lips around her sensitive nipple and lap my tongue against it with precision, toying with the sensitive peak as she gasps. I can't fight the grin that creeps across my lips at the sound, so I look up at her.

The flames that burn in her eyes make me wonder if she's as turned on as I am. Her skin tastes of honey and spice and all I can think about is what other parts of her taste like.

What her pussy tastes like.

And here I am telling her about the virtues of patience... The irony is not lost on me.

I hook my fingers on either side of her pajama shorts to find a cherry-red thong hidden beneath. My grin widens at the sight as I bite my lip with delight. "Did you come in here knowing this would happen?"

Her face reddens and she shakes her head. "No, but I hoped it would."

Good answer. Good fucking answer.

CHAPTER THIRTY-FOUR

Pressing a soft kiss to her lips, I pull away, scooting down the bed to bring my face level with the apex of her thighs. Kat squirms against my sheets, but she doesn't say a word. I take this as the go-ahead and dip downward, allowing my hot breath to ghost over what I hope is wet skin below the thin scrap of fabric before pressing a kiss atop the red barrier.

"Tanner, please," Kat moans, and it takes everything in me not to strip off my sweatpants and drive deep into her right this second. However, I am a gentleman, and Katarina Marritt deserves to know what it feels like when a man is fully driven by her pleasure and nothing else.

"Yes?" I mumble. I press my lips to her inner thigh and she trembles.

"Please," she says, her moans shifting into whimpers.

I chuckle, bringing my lips back against her pussy with only the thin piece of fabric keeping me from licking her senseless. "Please what?"

She glares at me playfully and I know instantly that I've toyed with her enough.

I grab the edge of her soaked panties and pull them down, exposing her glistening skin. The scent of her arousal fills my nostrils, and without hesitation, I trace my tongue from her entrance to her swollen clit, never breaking eye contact as she watches me intently.

"Goddamn, sweetheart. You taste incredible," I mumble against her sensitive core.

When I return my attention to her bundle of nerves, she lets out a guttural moan and arches her back, begging for more. I wrap my lips around her clit and suck hard, making her grind her perfect pussy against my mouth.

I focus on her throbbing clit, delicate and swollen between

my lips. Her moans grow louder as I suck and flick at it with my tongue. She arches her back, pleading for more, and I eagerly oblige, sucking hard while using my other hand to part her and expose her perfect pussy.

She rocks against me, grinding her hips and urging me on. Eagerly, I plunge two fingers deep inside her, feeling her sex grip them tightly. With each thrust, she bucks and writhes, pushing herself closer to the edge of pleasure.

But I'm not done yet. I continue to pump my fingers in and out of her while maintaining my assault on her sensitive bundle of nerves. She cries out in ecstasy, unable to contain her pleasure any longer. I revel in the power as I bring her to the brink again and again until she finally succumbs to her orgasm.

Gently, I press featherlight kisses against her inner thigh, giving her a moment—but just a moment—of reprieve.

THIRTY-FIVE

KAT

Oh. My. God.

My entire body tingles and trembles as I slowly come down from the most intense orgasm I've ever experienced in my life. Tanner's touch is like nothing I have ever felt before, his hands and tongue on my body working magic that I'm still not sure is humanly possible. My thoughts are muddled and my legs feel weak as I struggle to catch my breath. The only other person to ever bring me to climax is Elijah, but Tanner has somehow unlocked a new level of pleasure for me, one I didn't even know existed.

I can feel my legs trembling and my breathing becoming more labored as I collapse onto the bed, completely spent but bathing in the intoxicating anticipation of what comes next. Tanner appears to be waiting for my cue as he continues to softly brush kisses against my inner thigh, devoting an attention to my needs I never realized I was missing.

"Hey." My voice, raspy and quiet, rings through the air.

"Hey," Tanner responds, matching my inflection.

"Can you come here?" My voice cracks, but not with sorrow. To be honest, I think it's because my vocal cords are so fried from how loud I was.

Oh my God, could someone have heard us?!

Tanner appears at my side, resting his head in his hand as he gazes at me, his brows pulled together in concern as he asks, "Are you okay?"

"Why wouldn't I be?" I watch as tension physically leaves his form before he flashes me the very smile that I know so many women have gone feral for. "Thank you, by the way."

He laughs. "You know, it isn't exactly customary to thank someone after they give you an orgasm, but you are very welcome. How would you rate my services? We all hope for a ten out of ten, but I am also humble enough to know that we can all improve at everything."

"Asshole." I giggle and smack his shoulder. "I mean thank you for being willing to do this."

His brows pinch together in confusion. "It's hardly a hard sell, Kat. Have you seen you?"

My nose wrinkles at his compliment, feeling a mix of both pleasure and embarrassment. I quickly brush it off, leaning in to press my lips against his. As our mouths move together, I can taste the remnants of my arousal on his tongue, igniting a fire within me. The heat spreads through my body like wildfire, making me crave him even more.

Whimpering against his lips, I whisper, "I want you inside me."

Tanner's hands dart to the bedside drawer without a shred of hesitation, pulling out a gleaming gold packet and tossing it on the bed. As he moves to remove his sweatpants and slowly slides them down his hips, I can't help but will

CHAPTER THIRTY-FIVE

him to go faster. My heart races with anticipation as I watch.

The moment he springs free, a knot tightens in my throat. Heat rushes to my cheeks as I take in the sheer size of his cock, wondering how it could possibly fit inside me without causing discomfort. It's almost unreal, like a prop from a pornographic film brought to life. But here it is, mere inches away from me, stirring up a mix of excitement and nervousness that I never expected.

As I stare at him stroking himself from root to tip, my mouth falls open and my brows furrow in disbelief. "You're..." I stammer, feeling a bit intimidated by his size. "I don't think that will even fit inside of me."

"It'll fit," he says before he pushes my hair away from my face. "I would never push you to do something you don't want to do, but for what it's worth, I know you can take it."

He lowers his free hand and lightly grazes my clit, tracing small circles with his fingertips, his other hand stroking himself in perfect sync. The pleasure builds with each stroke, sending sparks of desire through my body.

"So, what's it going to be? Do you want me to stop?"

No, *fuck* no. That is about the last thing I want. As intimidating as his size might be, the mere thought of him stretching me, filling me so thoroughly, has me ready to come on the spot.

"No, I want you to fuck me."

Tanner grins, grabs the condom off the bed, rips it open, and sheaths himself with ease. I hear him whisper, "That's my girl," but it's so quiet I don't think he intends for me to hear. I instantly melt at the words.

As Tanner lines himself up with my entrance, we both

suck in a deep breath. As our gazes lock, I'm mesmerized by the intricate patterns of gold in his bright green irises. A warm wave of calm washes over me, melting away any lingering doubts or fears. Our fingers interlock, fitting together like puzzle pieces, and I feel a sense of safety with him that I've never experienced before.

As he slowly enters me for the first time, an electric current sparks between us, igniting a blazing inferno throughout my entire body. Despite my initial hesitations, I feel completely at ease in his embrace. Tanner presses deeper into me, his eyes never leaving my own, the strange level of intimacy completely distracting me from the slight twinge of pain as he stretches me so thoroughly. He's gentle and accommodating as we work in tandem to acclimate me to his size, and by the time he's fully seated inside me, it's taking everything in me not to explode.

The sensation of being so full is indescribable, especially after not having had sex in months. Even if it hadn't been so long, I feel like my body would be reacting just the same.

Tanner's movements are slow and deliberate at first, his body pressing against mine. The warmth of him sends shivers down my spine, igniting every nerve and setting my skin ablaze. As his pace quickens, the slight burning sensation fully gives way to intense pleasure, causing my entire body to tremble with desire. I can't help but let out a moan, trying to stifle it as best I can by covering my mouth with my hand. But Tanner doesn't seem to mind the sounds I'm making as his hand reaches between us to tease my sensitive clit with his thumb.

With each thrust, the pleasure grows more intense until I'm practically screaming from the overwhelming sensations

CHAPTER THIRTY-FIVE

coursing through me. My legs tremble as Tanner continues to move, each thrust more powerful than the last. He is relentless in his pursuit of our mutual pleasure, slamming into me with abandon while never faltering in his skilled touches that drive me closer and closer to the edge of ecstasy.

He never breaks eye contact, which somehow makes it even more intimate. I should find it daunting; I should find being this physically and emotionally exposed terrifying, but I don't.

It's Tanner. The friend who has stood by my side through the last year without asking for a single thing in return. The friend who invited me to his family's house for the holidays last year because I didn't have anywhere to go. The friend who offered to help me get over someone else by being what I need in the moment.

I truly don't deserve a friend like him.

Typically, friends don't do this. However, if anyone can navigate the complexities of being friends with benefits, it would be Tanner. He's the kind of guy women melt for, and he's probably indulged far more than I know about.

Why does that bother me to think about? And why in the fuck am I thinking about him with other women when he's inside of me?

"Hey," he whispers, slowing his movements, a concerned look etched in his brow.

"*Hey*," I say, but no audible sound comes out except for a faint moan that creeps past my lips.

"Are you okay?" Tanner asks almost timidly, like he's afraid that he's hurt me or done something he can't undo. He doesn't stop moving, but I can tell he's worried.

"Yeah, why?"

"Because you went from covering your mouth to keep quiet to staring at the ceiling."

Oh.

Well, I sure as hell can't tell him what I was thinking about. Jealousy isn't allowed—that isn't our arrangement. It's not like he sits there and makes a stink over me having a past. Hell, that's what got us here in the first place.

Feeling tongue-tied and unsure of what to say, I lean upward and firmly press my lips against his. His mouth opens eagerly, inviting me in. In this moment, all I want is to lose myself in the taste and feel of him.

His jaw clenches, the muscles in his arm bulging as he increases the intensity of his thrusts, slamming into me with unbridled force, causing my body to arch and quiver. I can feel him losing control and I want nothing more than to be his undoing. He buries himself inside me, each push coasting me closer and closer to release.

Fuck—I don't think it's ever felt this good. I didn't know sex like this could actually exist outside of porn. Didn't know a partner could be so hyperaware of your body's needs that they can play it like a fiddle.

As if he can hear my thoughts, Tanner returns his thumb to my clit, this time circling it with far more urgency.

"I want to feel you come on my cock, Kat. I need to feel you squeeze me."

Ho-ly shit.

Where the hell did this man come from? Because this sure as hell isn't the friend with whom I watch *Community* and share a pint of rocky road. This man...this man is...sexy.

As if he commands it into existence, my orgasm sneaks up on me like a freight train ready to go off the tracks. Every

CHAPTER THIRTY-FIVE

muscle in my body tenses and waves of pleasure radiate from my core as I reach the peak of my climax. My hips buck uncontrollably, and I let out a primal moan as my orgasm crashes over me in a powerful wave. I clench around him as I ride out my pleasure, and he lets out quite possibly the sexiest sound I've ever heard.

Forget living a long and healthy life; forget goals, forget graduating. I have lived a full life knowing that sound on his lips—knowing that I'm the one who put it there. Knowing the moan of pleasure that escapes him as he succumbs to his own pleasure is only amplified by the sound of my name on his lips.

I'm good. Universe, take me now.

As we come down from oblivion, his body goes limp and he collapses. We both gasp for air, my chest rising and falling with each ragged breath. Our bodies are slick with sweat, sticking together as we struggle to catch our breath.

"Holy shit," I gasp.

Tanner's lips crack into a smile as he pulls out of me and tosses the condom in the trash can. He rolls onto his side to face me. "Good, then?"

"Just cataloging some information for later."

He laughs. "Oh? And what's that?"

"Apparently, sex with friends leads to mind-blowing orgasms."

THIRTY-SIX

KAT

My body feels like Jell-O—like actual Jell-O.

I'm not sure that I've ever been quite this exhausted. Spent doesn't even begin to cover it.

Twilight seeps through the blinds, casting a subtle shadow over the messy bed. I fight against the heavy weight of sleep and find myself tangled in sheets and Tanner's limbs. His strong arm is wrapped around my waist, pulling me closer to his warm body. I know I should leave and go back to my own bed, but it's so comfortable here. I remind myself that this is just a physical arrangement between us, but it's hard to resist staying for a few more moments of blissful rest in his arms.

Just move, Kat, I order myself. Right now might be great, but what about in a few hours when we wake up? What about when morning fully comes and we're met with the realization that we didn't just sleep together, but actually *slept together?*

After having sex, things are even more complicated and confusing than before. The memory of him inside me makes my thighs clench together, and the lingering soreness serves as a constant reminder that what happened between us cannot be undone.

The most terrifying part is that I'm not even sure I want to undo it.

Something shifted between us, and I can't help but think about what comes next.

Except for the fact that what comes next is me getting out of his bedroom immediately.

Gently I wrap my fingers around his wrist to lift his arm so I can slip away, only for him to tighten it around my stomach. My bare stomach.

Oh my God, we're both still naked. We must have passed out immediately afterward.

Fuck. Me.

I try to move his arm again, but Tanner holds firm, the heat from his body enveloping me in a calming cocoon.

"Nope," he mumbles against the back of my head. "You're not leaving. This is part of the deal."

"I need to go to my own bed."

"Nope." He says it so matter-of-factly, like him simply *saying* it's not happening suddenly makes it so.

I make one last attempt to pry his arm away, but he's hard as steel.

"Kat," he huffs, clearly irritated. "*Please* stay in here. Just for tonight."

"It's practically morning."

"And you can leave in a few hours, but for now just let me hold you."

Tanner Adler doesn't plead; he doesn't ask women to stay the night. From what I've heard, he seldom stays the night with the women he beds. It is taking everything in me right now not to read too much into that, but given the past year, I can't let myself impose meaning onto a man's words.

If it meant something to him, he would have told me—we made a deal. Just sex, no feelings. That's what we agreed upon.

Yet he's so warm. My bare back against his torso as he curls around me is probably the most comforted I've felt in years and, even though I know it's best for both of us if I go, I can't find it in me to deny him exactly what he wants.

"Okay," I whisper.

Tanner presses a light kiss to the back of my head before letting out a sated sigh.

Comfortable and warm, we both drift back to sleep.

When the morning sun blasting through the blinds is impossible to ignore, I rub my eyes, wiping away any remnants of sleep as well as the mascara I forgot to wash off last night. It all happened so fast that I didn't even think to remove my makeup—luckily I wasn't wearing very much of it.

I yawn as I look around the room, which looks different cast in the warmth of the morning sun. I can finally make out the words scrawled on each cardboard box stacked against the wall: "Art Supplies," "Bedding," and "Books" are just a few that catch my eye. Stretching my arm across the bed to rouse Tanner from his slumber, I feel only cold sheets.

At first I think he may have just gone to the bathroom, but based on how cold it is, I know he's been gone more than a couple minutes.

A familiar knot of anxiety tightens in my stomach. I knew

CHAPTER THIRTY-SIX

I had been right to want to stay in my room. This was just a casual hookup, but even knowing that, part of me yearns for something more. The realization that he grabbed his shoes and left without a second thought washes over me as I pull the blanket to my chin. My chest feels heavy with sadness and I can't shake the feeling that I was just another fleeting encounter for him.

We're friends—friends don't have to tell each other when they're going somewhere, so why should Tanner? It's unfair for me to hold him to a standard completely at odds with what we're doing, yet I can't stop thinking about what this could mean for us.

Tanner is one of my best friends. Did I really just manage to ruin that over a single night of great sex? I was so worried about Tanner knowing that this is just sex that I forgot to remind myself.

I push the blankets off of me and search for my clothes from last night, finally finding my tank top and pajama pants fanned out haphazardly on the floor. Quietly, I sneak back over to my room and sit down at my desk, suddenly thinking about the one thing that could distract me from whatever this is with Tanner.

The letter from my brother sits on top of my desk. I've decided to write him back, but what does someone say to the brother they've never met, let alone the brother who was the reason your dad left?

Am I supposed to be like *"Hey man, don't sweat it, it's not your fault you ruined my life"*?

Because really, it isn't his fault. From the sound of it, my dad wasn't so great to him either.

My hand trembles as I reach to grab a pen and the spiral-bound notebook out of my backpack.

A firm knocking echoes through my bedroom, making me jump and let out a small yelp. I hear Tanner's deep laugh from the other side of the door, his presence unmistakable even before he speaks. Frustrated, I groan and try to focus on the paper in front of me, refusing to acknowledge his presence just yet.

"Kaaaat," he says in a singsong tone.

"Come in," I call out. I'm so not ready to have the conversation about how last night shouldn't have happened, but even I know it's necessary for the sake of our friendship. I also know his attempts at getting my attention will just get more and more outrageous the longer I ignore him.

The old door squeaks as it creaks open.

"Hey," Tanner says, his voice raspy and relaxed, his hair disheveled. He looks perfect. The asshole always looks perfect.

"Hey," I sigh, then realize he's holding a drink carrier with two large coffee cups as well as a small white paper bag, the kind you'd get at a restaurant.

"Why'd you come in here?" he asks, setting the carrier and bag on the edge of my desk.

"You left, so I figured I should come to my own room."

"I went to get coffee—"

"Look, if you regret last night, I get it. We can just pretend it ne—"

"Kat."

I hate the way my body reacts to the stern tone of his voice, the way every nerve comes alive.

"I went to go get coffee," he repeats. "I had to go to the

CHAPTER THIRTY-SIX

place downtown because Brendan decided the creamer in the fridge was 'close enough' to half-and-half for him to make White Russians last night. Spoiler alert, it wasn't."

"Oh."

"And since I know you are incapable of drinking coffee that isn't at least fifty percent creamer and a quarter sugar, I thought it best to just go pick us up some." His previously serious expression melts into a soft, comforting smile. "No, I don't regret last night. Do you?"

"No," I mumble.

"Good." He reaches into the carrier and extracts a steaming cup, placing it gently in front of me.

The smell of rich hazelnut instantly envelops my senses, confirming that he remembered my usual order. I can't hide the smile that tugs at the corners of my mouth as I read the label: *Hazelnut latte, extra hot.* "Thank you."

"No problem. Now, what are you working on?"

"I was thinking about writing my brother back."

Tanner nods in understanding as he opens the bag, setting one of two chocolate eclairs on a napkin next to the paper. "What do you think you're going to say?"

I realize that beyond saying hello, I have no idea what to say to Patrick. How do you write to the brother you've never met who didn't know you existed until he was the ripe old age of twenty-one?

"I...don't know."

Tanner pulls a chair up next to me and we spend the next hour working together to craft a letter.

A letter to which even a man with the same name as the father who has never wanted to know me might want to write back.

THIRTY-SEVEN

KAT

Three times.

The mailman forgot to pick up our outgoing mail not once, not twice, but *three times*. Who does that? I mean, it's not like most people tend to have a ton of outgoing mail in a day, but after the third time he simply *forgot* to grab my letter despite the little flag being up, I just ended up grabbing it with the intention of taking it to the post office myself.

That was a little over three weeks ago.

It's not that I'm scared to mail it; it just hasn't been convenient. Of course, I could have taken it with me to campus and dropped it at the post office in the student center, but that is beside the point.

Ultimately, I've decided to just send it while home for the weekend, since my mom's house is right next to the post office.

Or I could drop it off at his apartment. I mean, I have the address—but that would be weird.

Post office it is.

CHAPTER THIRTY-SEVEN

My hand slips from the worn handle of my weekender bag, and it thuds loudly against the polished hardwood floor. I quickly toss my camera bag onto the nearby credenza before heading toward the comforting smell of dinner cooking in the kitchen. As I turn the corner, I find my mom standing at the counter, cutting onions. I take in the array of ingredients laid out all over the countertop and notice a thick steak sizzling in a cast-iron skillet on the stove behind her.

"Hey, Mom, whatcha makin'?" I ask, inspecting the ingredients more thoroughly.

"Hey, honey. I was thinking we could do steak salads. I picked up your favorite house dressing from the grocery store."

"It smells great."

My mom's eyebrows raise in surprise and a grin slowly spreads across her face, causing the slight wrinkles around her eyes to deepen. "Thank you," she says, her voice soft and sincere. I can see the corners of her lips quivering slightly as she speaks. "Do you have any plans for tonight? I know the wedding is tomorrow, but I wasn't sure if any of your friends from high school were in town."

I don't have the heart to remind her that I don't talk to many people from high school anymore—it's just another reminder of how little we talk these days. "Um, no. No one is home. I figured we could just hang out tonight."

Her grin grows into an undeniably infectious smile. "I would love that."

Butter sizzles and pops in the pan on the stove, filling the air with a rich aroma. We both turn our heads toward the steak, worried that it might burn.

"Shoot. Can you baste that steak for me? I don't want it to

burn, but it should be ready soon," she requests, handing me a spoon.

I carefully drizzle hot butter over the meat, making sure to cover every inch of its surface. When the steak is done cooking and resting, I begin slicing it into thin pieces to be added to the salad my mom is expertly preparing in a huge wooden bowl. The salad could easily feed at least six people, even though it's just the two of us. However, we've both proven to be bottomless pits when it comes to salad.

"Do you want to eat in front of the TV?" my mom asks.

"Sure," I say with a smile.

She grabs the plates and forks as I grab the salad and our respective bottles of dressing because we've never been able to agree on one we both like.

"What would you like to watch?" She begins flipping through the cable channels.

"It doesn't matter," I reply, shoveling salad onto my plate and drenching it in dressing.

She continues searching through the television guide for a minute or two before settling on one of those obscure channels that absolutely no one has heard of that happens to be airing old episodes of *Buffy the Vampire Slayer*.

When we've both settled into the couch with our salads in our laps, she asks, "So, how is school?"

I shrug. "It's been great, actually. My classes have been good so far." We're only a little over a month into the semester, so it's not like that is untrue, but my classes are far from what has been on my mind since I returned to school.

"And how is Tanner?"

A lump lodges in my throat at her question, which I wasn't

CHAPTER THIRTY-SEVEN

expecting her to ask. I fight the urge to grill her on what would possibly motivate her to ask such a question. "Why?"

She furrows her brow, the corners of her mouth turning down in a look of confusion. It's almost comical, except for the fact that I can't shake the feeling that she knows something has shifted between Tanner and me. "Because other than Jenna, he is the only friend of yours that I've met from off at school."

Oh. That makes significantly more sense than the fear that was brewing—the fear that I somehow have the words "*I had sex with Tanner Adler*" written across my forehead in permanent marker.

It's been weeks since that happened, yet somehow things have been entirely normal between us. Almost as if we never had sex at all—and I don't know why, but it bugs me beyond reason. I would have expected at least some level of weirdness, some indicator that it had any sort of meaning.

I guess normalcy is the best-case scenario, even if it doesn't feel that way.

"He's really good!" I say enthusiastically before shoving a bite of food into my mouth, trying to forcefully will the conversation away from the friend who has recently become far too intimately acquainted with my lady parts.

However, my mother's confusion only morphs into concern. "Is everything all right? Did you ever go talk to the campus health center about therapists?"

The idea of having to recount everything to yet another stranger so they can psychoanalyze me isn't even remotely appealing. "No—I haven't needed to."

"Have you checked with Janet's office to see if she is able to do telehealth appointments? Maybe you could just keep seeing her while at school." My mom rests her hand on my knee. "I understand that you're doing fine right now, but it doesn't hurt to do everything in your power to make sure that you stay that way."

I can hear the words she is not saying, and I cringe at the memory. I'm not the only one who struggled with my breakup last spring. My mom missed out on a lot of work because she was too scared to leave me alone.

"I'll call Janet's office."

This appears to appease her worries as her pinched brow disappears and a smile sets in. "Good."

We both shift toward the television and begin watching the old show my mom has loved since I was little. I don't totally get it, but even I can admit…Spike is hot.

———

I affix my old zoom lens to the front of my camera in preparation for the posed photos. While I'm still figuring out my process, I have decided that the zoom lens is the only one appropriate for the ceremony. When I can control my distance from the subject a bit more, a fixed focal-length lens with a wide aperture is always better when shooting posed shots.

At least that's what Google told me.

When my mom told me that one of the girls at the restaurant was getting married and needed a photographer that didn't cost an arm and a leg, I'll admit I was far more excited than the two hundred dollars I'm making for a full day of shooting plus editing should justify. I probably would have done it for free. However, if I've learned anything from my mom, it is that you should never work for free.

The sun casts a warm glow through the slats of the barn's

CHAPTER THIRTY-SEVEN

walls, illuminating the lilac fabric carefully draped from the rafters. The intimate wedding party gathers around a small, rustic wooden table at the far end of the barn, bejeweled with wildflowers and flickering candles. As the bride and groom exchange vows, a gentle breeze carries the sweet scent of lavender from the open field outside.

The groom and his groomsmen are dressed in dark brown suits, pressed white shirts, and no ties. I've always loved when men wear suits outside the standard black, gray, and blue. There probably isn't a science to it, but I like to think more uniquely colored suits add an extra little something.

All the bridesmaids wear light purple dresses, almost the exact shade as the drapery hanging above us. The bride's dress is simple yet elegant and her fiery red hair is swept up in a tight bun atop her head, giving her an effortlessly glam look, accentuated by the bright red lip she is sporting.

With my finger pressed firmly against the shutter button of my camera, I am determined to capture every angle and detail as the elated couple concludes their vows. As they embrace in a passionate kiss, I snap away, capturing this moment of pure love and joy forever in time. The sunlight flowing in through the barn door creates an ethereal sight and makes me hopeful that I'll have less editing to do in post.

The bridal party exits the barn to a cheerful song that I can't quite place—I think it's from *The Parent Trap*. I follow them out into the field of wildflowers. Everyone is cooperative and understanding that I'm learning and am incredibly nervous. At first the bride is a little apprehensive, but when I show her a few of the photos from the ceremony on the viewfinder, her anxiety is instantly quelled.

I begin packing up my equipment, as they didn't ask me to

photograph the reception. Just as I zip up my camera bag, a beautiful woman with light brown skin and tight, bouncy curls framing her face approaches me. Her hair is expertly styled into a soft bun, not as tightly pulled back as the bride's. She's one of the bridesmaids.

"Hey, thanks for doing this. I know Rachel was insanely nervous about finding a photographer in her budget. You really are a lifesaver," she says earnestly.

"Of course—I was happy to help. Everyone has to start somewhere, so I'm happy for the experience for my portfolio."

She doesn't say anything else at first. However, just as I sling my camera bag over my shoulder and prepare to say a polite goodbye and walk away, she speaks again.

"I'm Cheyeanne. I know this is weird because you don't know me, but I've always wanted to pursue photography and I was wondering…if you ever need a second shooter or anything, I'd love to give you my information. I might not have any formal training, but I promise I don't suck." She smiles awkwardly with a nervousness in her voice that I recognize all too well.

"Like I said, everyone has to start somewhere, right?" I say with a smile, sifting through the side pocket of my camera bag. "I have another wedding I'm shooting in November in the area. I swear, everyone at Rachel's work is getting married right now. I was planning on shooting it alone, but it might be a good opportunity for you to get your feet wet since it's a small wedding. Are you available November seventh?"

"Yes!" Her face brightens with joy. "Yes, I am available."

I try not to chuckle, because I get it—I was similarly enthusiastic when my mom mentioned Rachel needed a photographer for her wedding.

CHAPTER THIRTY-SEVEN

I smile as I finally find and hold out my brand-new business card. "Sounds great, Cheyeanne. Text me your portfolio and if I like what I see, we can go from there."

She says thank you before skipping back toward the bridal party to head into the reception and I can't help but shake the feeling that I just met someone who will become a lifelong friend.

THIRTY-EIGHT

TANNER

As soon as we step foot inside the Dusty Armadillo, the unmistakable thump of boots hitting the wooden floor and the twang of country music sweeps over us. The dance floor is a sea of cowboy boots and hats, swirling and moving to the lively beat. The thick smell of beer and sweat mingles in the air, transporting me to a honky-tonk time warp. The dimly lit walls are embellished with vintage signs and neon lights, adding to the rustic atmosphere.

I've been here a handful of times over the years, but most of my experiences in this bar were at the hands of Jenna and Kat dragging us out for college night, despite both Marcus and I having early classes on Thursday mornings. However, tonight isn't college night, and while the line-dancing bar is significantly less crowded than usual, it's still chaotic.

We all had midterms this week. They were hard—really hard—but being prepared definitely paid off. I got a 92% on my physics exam, which has easily been the hardest class this semester. It's not to say that I don't understand physics, but

CHAPTER THIRTY-EIGHT

Professor Stanton is older than dirt and can't stay awake for half the class, yet expects us to know all the material anyway. In all honesty, I'm not even sure he knows how to upload our grades into the portal; his TA handles most of that shit.

Gotta love tenure.

My hand rests against the small of Kat's back as we get pushed closer to the bar by a group of people who apparently haven't ever heard of personal space or manners.

My fingers trace the delicate curve of her spine below her crop top before I quickly pull my hand away. She blushes, and I can't help but admire the subtle flush that sweeps across her cheeks. I mutter an apology even though I would do just about anything to keep that rosy hue on her face.

We haven't hooked up since that first night, and while I would like nothing more than to do it again, I also don't want to push her to do anything she doesn't want to do. The sex was incredible—so incredible that I'm a bit embarrassed by how often it comes to mind when I'm jerking off.

When Jenna came barreling into my bedroom earlier to inform me that we were all going out to the Dusty to celebrate the end of midterms, I was admittedly...apprehensive. With what happened between Kat and me well over a month ago, I've been avoiding Elijah like the plague. Not because I give a shit what that prick thinks of me, but because I don't want to say something that puts Kat in a weird position.

Elijah is a fucking dick who never deserved her, and I stand by that. However, her decision to stop caring what he thinks needs to be hers and hers alone.

To my delight, however, the dickhead isn't here. He was invited, but he has some campaign dinner for his dad's reelection tonight and I say good riddance. If I'm being totally honest, I doubt Jenna really wanted him here anyway. Dude's an absolute buzzkill, and after everything he did to Kat last year, I'm pretty sure Jenna would love nothing more than to dump him in Lake Erie and watch him sink to the bottom.

Actually, I'm not sure anyone particularly likes him outside of Marcus, and even then I think they've just been friends for so long that it's a friendship of obligation. That's fine with me, though; it's Marcus's obligation, not mine.

Jenna squeals as some old Shania Twain song comes on and instantly yanks on Kat's arm. The upbeat country song reverberates through my body as I lean in close to Kat. The smell of her floral perfume carries on the warm air and I can't help but brush my lips against her ear as I ask, "Do you want a drink? I can order it for you while you're out there." A small smile creeps across my face as I feel her shiver in response.

Kat hasn't been drinking much, so I've been cutting back too. Honestly, I kind of wish I had eased off years ago because I feel like a million bucks. That, and the idea of having a beer gut by twenty-five makes me want to throw up.

Kat glances at Jenna—who is growing noticeably more irritated as her favorite song's precious few minutes waste away—before she looks at me. "Yeah, can you order me a vodka cranberry, please?"

"For sure." I smile before she disappears onto the crowded dance floor.

Leaning against the bar, I order us both drinks, setting my ID and credit card down on the epoxy-covered wood. My eyes follow Kat as she moves on the dance floor in tandem with the crowd.

How these girls know every single one of these dances, I will never know.

CHAPTER THIRTY-EIGHT

As the sound of a fiddle and Shania Twain's signature voice fill the room, Kat twirls and stomps in perfect synchronization with Jenna. Every step is fluid and precise, as if their bodies are made for this beat. She beams at me from across the dance floor, her dark brown hair bouncing with every step.

I'll get out there with them soon. I always struggle to keep up with the basic line dance moves, but I do it anyway just to make Kat happy. Dancing might not be my forte, but seeing her smile is worth it all.

Kat continues to dance and I am completely transfixed as the soft white cotton of her cropped T-shirt rides up slightly, revealing what I can only assume is the black lace of her bra underneath. When she turns around—as I presume the choreography dictates—it is somehow an even better sight.

When Kat left the house earlier in a pair of denim cutoff shorts, I admittedly thought she was nuts, seeing as it's mid-October. However, I can't help but appreciate how her toned ass cheeks peek out from the frayed hem of her shorts with her every step.

Thank you, universe, for Kat's bold—if not mildly unconventional—fashion choices.

Brendan's bellowing laughter forces me to pry my eyes away from the intoxicating woman on the dance floor, but the moment I see him looking at me, I want to smack him upside the head. I glare at him as I grab my drinks from the bartender and drop a five-dollar tip on the bar.

"What?" I snip.

Brendan chuckles. "Oh, nothing...except you clearly want Kat."

He is fully aware of what happened between Kat and me.

We never agreed to *not* tell people, and I would bet money she most definitely told Jenna.

"Of course I like Kat—other than you, she's my best friend, you ass hat," I say as I smack the top of his brown suede cowboy hat that he insisted he had to buy for tonight.

"That isn't what I meant and you know it. If you want to fuck Kat again so bad, just tell her. By the way, she was just looking at you. I imagine she'd happily oblige."

It's not about obliging, and he should know that. The entire reason we had sex in the first place was to help her get over Elijah. While I don't know the inner workings of her mind, especially not when it comes to why she would ever care about that douche, she seems to be doing well. So, why would I choose to fuck that up by making things any more complicated for her?

"Nah, man, we're just friends," I say, though we both know it's a boldfaced lie.

Regina and Aaron weave through the energetic dancers, their cowboy boots tapping out a rhythm on the wooden floor. They reach Kat and Jenna, who are still laughing and twirling in the center of the crowd. Regina says something to them and they all turn to look at us, then start heading toward the bar. I hand Kat her drink and she grins gratefully before taking a sip.

"Hey, Katie?" Aaron leans over the bar to wave down the bartender. He holds up seven fingers and mouths "*Fireball.*"

"No shot for me," Kat says awkwardly, causing Aaron to look at her funny.

"Are you pregnant or something?" he scoffs.

"Aaron, I am literally holding a drink right now."

He furrows his brow and nods, the corners of his mouth

CHAPTER THIRTY-EIGHT

turned down in a deep frown. His eyes flicker with confusion and he scratches at his head, ruffling up his already messy hair.

Since Aaron appears to be shorting out, I say to the bartender, "He'll have *five* shots of fireball."

"You too?" Aaron groans. "You guys are no fun—it's our senior year, for God's sake."

"I'm not feelin' shots tonight, man, stomach is off." I can tell by the look on his face that he doesn't believe me. Whatever—he doesn't have to believe me. All that matters is that Kat doesn't feel singled out.

She leans against my side with her straw between her lips and whispers, "Thank you."

"Of course." I smile.

As the night wears on, Aaron and Marcus down more drinks, their movements becoming increasingly unsteady. Jenna and Regina proceed to do three more rounds of shots and I don't know where Brendan is for most of the night. By 1:00 AM, I know it's time to call it a night. Our group stumbles out of the bar, and I feel grateful that I only had two drinks all night as everyone clumsily piles into my SUV, Aaron slurring his words and laughing uncontrollably in the back seat.

By the time we pull into the driveway, everyone but me and Kat in the front seat are passed out cold. Luckily, unlike that time Jenna passed out in my back seat, I feel much more comfortable being an asshole tonight.

"Hey, fuck face, we're home." I reach behind me and smack what feels like a male head—I'm unsure whose, but also don't really care.

"What the fuck, man? That hurt!" Brendan groans. His

loud response stirs the rest of the drunken idiots and, to my delight and relief, they start climbing out of my car.

THIRTY-NINE

KAT

The moment I reach my bedroom, I pull off my sweaty shorts. I don't care that it's October; I'm sweating like a roast hog.

Shucking off the rest of my clothes, I pull an oversized T-shirt from Taylor Swift's *Red* tour over my head, a bit thankful that they were out of all the smaller sizes by the time my mom was able to order it online for my Christmas present that year.

It was nice going out with everyone—without Elijah. It was nice to get a glimpse of how things could be if he just wasn't around.

Surprisingly, Elijah isn't the one occupying my thoughts this evening. Instead, I found myself constantly drawn to Tanner's gaze. It could be wishful thinking, but it seemed as though he was looking at me frequently throughout the night. Every time I turned in his direction, his eyes were already locked on me. His intense gaze made me feel simultaneously seen and vulnerable, like there was a spotlight shining on my every move.

Or it could simply have been the fact that the dance floor

tends to be where most people look in a line dancing bar and I am simply reading into it; it's hard to say.

As I enter the kitchen, the chilly air from the refrigerator hits me. I see Tanner leaning against the counter, his bare chest and tanned skin on display. He takes a spoonful of rocky road ice cream and brings it to his lips, closing his eyes in enjoyment. The dim light casts shadows on his face, making him look even more alluring.

"We've got to stop meeting like this," I joke as I walk over to the cracked refrigerator and grab a bottle of water before closing it tight.

Tanner's lips curl into a playful grin as his eyes roam down my exposed legs, taking in every inch of skin before traveling back up to meet my gaze. "I have to admit," he states, "I quite enjoy it, actually." His voice is low and husky, sending a shiver down my spine.

"Oh, and why is that?" I take a deep breath and feel a surge of unfamiliar confidence coursing through me. I'm not the usual anxious mess I've become around him lately, fearing rejection, but rather stride toward him with determination, his eyes seeming to fuel my forward movement.

He just shrugs, his smirk never leaving his lips. "Well, for starters…"

My stomach jumps in anticipation of what he's going to say. I try but can't will myself to pry my eyes away from those lips—those lips that have proven to be everything but "just a friend" when pressed against my skin.

"Ah, never mind." He shrugs again.

Despite his nonchalant response, I can't ignore the prickle that rises on the back of my neck as his eyes rake down my body once more, this time lingering on my chest.

CHAPTER THIRTY-NINE

"No, tell me," I say breathily. "What makes you enjoy it?"

Tanner considers for a few seconds before setting his bowl of ice cream on the counter. He doesn't move closer to me, just crosses his arms over his bare chest as he leans against the counter. His intense gaze roams over my body, causing a shiver to run down my spine. My nipples harden under the soft cotton of my shirt, betraying my growing arousal as he takes his time to fully appreciate me.

"I enjoy seeing you like this."

I can't shake the feeling that my skin is completely engulfed in flames. "Like what?" I whisper.

"Like no one is going to see you. Like...I get a glimpse of the you that has no plans of being perceived." He clears his throat before slowly appraising my body once more. "It's... intoxicating."

"Oh."

"Oh." A faint grin curves his lips. He reaches for his ice cream and raises the spoon to his lips as though he really is completely unaffected. However, before I can descend too far into spiraling over the perceived rejection, he opens his beautiful mouth. "Would you like some ice cream?"

I furrow my brows, my mind racing to understand his question. "Ice cream?"

Tanner chuckles as he says, "Yes, ice cream..." He studies my expression for a short moment before his voice shifts, the sound of his words causing goosebumps to erupt across every exposed expanse of skin. "Come here."

I do as I'm told without a second thought of protest until I'm inches in front of Tanner. All my confusion melts away as he dips the spoon into the bowl, scooping out a small amount of sugary goodness.

"Open."

When I again obey, he gently pushes the spoonful of ice cream between my lips. The rich chocolate and marshmallow flavors flood my taste buds, momentarily distracting me from the intense arousal plaguing my body. I savor the sweetness as we stand in silence, each lost in our thoughts.

He doesn't allow my focus to slip for long, though, because as soon as I move to lick the remaining ice cream from my mouth, Tanner is there, grazing his tongue over the cold, pillowy flesh of my bottom lip, causing my breath to hitch as he takes every last remnant of chocolate for his own.

"Yum," he grumbles as he reaches for the bowl again, but he doesn't offer me a bite. This time, he presses the cold spoon to the pressure point below my left ear. The sudden chill sends shivers down my spine and I can't help but let out a small yelp. Within seconds, the cold sensation subsides as he licks and swirls his tongue over the sensitive spot, making my skin tingle with pleasure. He sucks lightly on the tender flesh, the ice cream long since gone.

Instinctively, my head lolls backward, giving him more access. He doesn't take advantage, though. He just...stops. He ceases kissing my neck and steps back to lean against the counter once more, moving to take another bite of ice cream.

My mouth grows dry and for the first time probably ever, I don't know how to react. Negative, positive, jump his bones, be offended that he randomly decided to step back... I am genuinely perplexed, and, based on the look he's giving me, he can tell.

"Where's your head at, Kat?" he asks, the calm, domineering man from before nowhere in sight, replaced momentarily by my friend—the one who, no matter what, will

CHAPTER THIRTY-NINE

always focus his energy on reassuring me and ensuring that whatever he's doing is exactly what I want.

"I'm wondering why you stopped doing that."

The corner of his mouth quirks up. "Well, there was no more ice cream on your neck." I pin him with a blank expression and he instantly laughs. "What? Was that not the purpose? Your neck simply making a lovely way to eat ice cream?"

"I do not find you funny."

He winks before stepping toward me with a smile. "I'm a little bit funny."

Hastily abandoning his half-eaten bowl of rocky road on the kitchen counter, he grabs me and presses his lips against mine. The strong flavor of chocolate lingers on his tongue, sending waves of desire coursing through my body.

Without missing a beat, Tanner's strong arms reach around me, pulling me close to his chest as he lifts me effortlessly. I wrap my legs around his waist, feeling the warmth of his body against mine. His bare chest is peppered with hair, something that I didn't have time to notice the first time we were together.

He turns us around to set me on the edge of the kitchen counter, but he doesn't separate our bodies. As soon as my bare ass is flush with the cold countertop, Tanner is pressed firmly against my core. The sensation of his hard length pressed against me leaves me whimpering, wordlessly pleading. He begins kissing down my neck and his hands snake up my thighs to rest against the tiny string attaching my thong on the sides.

Before, it felt like we had all the time in the world—like we could spend hours tangled between the sheets. However, as I feel his cock strain against his sweatpants, pressed flush against the tiny scrap of fabric that is my underwear, my silent pleading shifts.

"Please, Tanner. I can't take it anymore."

He gasps slightly as he pulls his mouth away from my neck. "Damn it," he says with a sigh as he rests his forehead against my shoulder.

"What?"

"I don't have a condom down here. They're up in my room."

Fucking hell. While the idea of him inside me without a barrier is quite possibly the most erotic thought I can imagine, I also don't want him to feel like I'm pushing something that he's not comfortable with. I've never had sex without a condom, but I've been on the pill since I was sixteen and my mom found out my boyfriend and I had sex in the back of his old Nissan and demanded she take me to the doctor, citing something about refusing to allow accidental pregnancy to derail my life.

But we're friends. Friends who fuck, but friends nonetheless. We made the decision to do this under the pretense of keeping it cut-and-dry. Fulfilling a carnal need with someone you trust. I can't imagine that, with that in mind, he'd be open to the intimacy of having sex without a condom.

Despite this, I find the words falling past my lips anyway. "I'm on the pill."

He goes almost completely still and I wish desperately that I could see his face, but it's obscured with his forehead still on my shoulder. Slowly, he pulls away and his eyes meet mine. "I've never had sex without a condom."

CHAPTER THIRTY-NINE

There it is: the realization that maybe I'm too far in this; that we have drastically different expectations of what this thing between us is. I pushed too far.

"But I'm down to try it," he adds. "I'm clean, I got tested a few months ago before we had sex the first time, after I brought up the idea. I didn't want there to be any concern about that."

"I got tested over the summer...and you know just as well as I do that I haven't been with anyone else since."

"I haven't been with anyone else," Tanner reassures me, and all I can think is...*What?*

We never discussed being exclusive. Hell, until tonight I genuinely thought it might have been a one-time thing. I try not to read too much into what that could mean, because it probably doesn't mean anything, even if I want it to.

"Then it's decided." I laugh before looking at him with a stern expression. "Get inside me."

Tanner doesn't miss a beat. He peels my underwear down my thighs, reaches into his waistband, and pulls out his cock. It's been months since the first time and I had almost convinced myself that maybe I'd imagined how big he was.

He moves himself against me and, as his thick, throbbing erection presses against my entrance, I gasp. The anticipation of being filled by him makes my heart race and my body quiver. I can feel the heat radiating off of him as he positions himself between my lips and I know without a doubt that his size was not just my imagination.

I can feel him tremble as he presses past my entrance, but as he pushes deeper into me, any semblance of awareness of my surroundings instantly leaves my mind. All I can think about—all I can feel—is him inside me. The way every nerve ending is set ablaze as he stretches me, the way his fingertips bite into my thigh as he squeezes tight in an effort to not lose control...all of it has me teetering on the edge faster than I ever thought humanly possible.

Once he's buried to the hilt, I watch as his jaw clenches and he stops. "I'm sorry, I—I need a sec." The realization that he's just as affected as I am causes my pussy to clench, which causes him to groan loudly. "If you keep doing that, I am going to come inside you far earlier than either of us would like."

"Sorry," I say as my cheeks flush. I'm not, though—I'm not sorry, because the confirmation that I have that effect on him is enough to detonate me like a bomb.

He begins moving again, though tentatively. Circling my clit with his thumb, he increases his pace, but it's still far more reserved than the last time. It's as if he's trying to savor it, like he's trying to hold onto whatever sliver of control he has to make this last as long as possible.

I press my lips to his, nipping at his bottom lip before releasing it with a *pop*. Tanner groans, his pace quickening and the circling of his thumb intensifying, yet I can still feel him holding back.

"Tanner?" I ask.

"Hm?"

"Fuck me. I want you to fuck me. Hard."

He pauses to look at me. "If I do that, I'm going to come really fast, and you haven't."

"And I'm telling you that if you let go, I will come in like two-point-five seconds. I'm right there, so *fuck me*," I demand.

This seems to be all he needs. To my delight, he gives in to his carnal desires and thrusts into me with desperate fervor.

CHAPTER THIRTY-NINE

My body responds immediately, my limbs quivering as pleasure pulses through me like an unstoppable force.

With every thrust, I grow louder, so much so that Tanner lifts his hand to cover my mouth at the exact moment I bite down on my lip to stifle a scream. The intensity builds, threatening to consume us both. Within seconds, my orgasm washes over me, thrusting me into complete and total oblivion.

Tanner's hands tighten on my hips as he follows me over the edge, his quickening pace matching the frantic beating of my heart. With a final thrust, he buries himself deep inside me and I feel the pulsing release of his climax. The sensation is new to me, but in this moment, there is nothing else more erotic than feeling Tanner lose control and spill himself inside me without holding back. It is an intimate act that bonds us in ways I never thought possible, and while I know I will more than likely freak out over what it could mean tomorrow, right now...*holy shit.*

"Fuck," he says with a groan as his head collapses against my chest.

"Yeah," I gasp.

We stay like this for a few moments before he slowly pulls himself out of me, the sensation of being so thoroughly full replaced by the foreign sensation of his cum dripping out of me. He seems to notice it too, because the moment his eyes find my pussy, the expression on his face is undeniable.

Pure, unadulterated possessiveness.

Tanner pries his eyes away from me and hurries to find an old kitchen towel—one I guarantee we will be throwing away instead of washing and returning to the drawer—and runs it under warm water. Once the towel is sopping wet, he wrings out the excess moisture into the sink and kneels before me.

It's weirdly intimate, having him clean me up after what we just did. It's an aspect that I never would have considered, but as he gently wipes the warm cloth over my oversensitive core, I can't shake the thought that I *like* this.

I like this a lot, and the idea of telling him that and potentially blowing this whole thing to shit is terrifying.

"We should go to bed," I suggest.

Tanner nods in agreement and quickly wipes away the remaining evidence before throwing the towel into the trash. Taking my hands, he helps me hop down from the counter, and together we make our way upstairs.

At my bedroom door, just as I reach for the doorknob, exhausted and ready to collapse into my sheets, I feel Tanner's arms wrap around my middle. Goosebumps erupt on the back of my neck as he presses his lips to my ear, his hot breath instantly rendering my body prepared for round two.

"I don't think so, sweetheart. My bed, now."

He wraps his muscular arms around me, lifting me easily off the ground and setting me in front of his bedroom door in the nearly pitch-black hallway. I can't help but giggle as he playfully swats my behind, urging me toward his bedroom. The door opens with a creak and I can feel the anticipation building as we step inside, the scent of his cologne filling the air, and it's becoming abundantly clear that he doesn't care about me being loud one bit.

FORTY

KAT

I sit at my desk, fidgeting with the miniature figurines and trinkets scattered across its surface, including a framed picture of Jenna and me freshman year at Flash Fest with a corn dog in each hand. My laptop is open in front of me, displaying the virtual therapy session that will begin in mere minutes.

Janet, the therapist I've been seeing since summer, appears on the screen. Despite our previous sessions, I feel a wave of anxiety wash over me as I realize I will have to confront and share my feelings for the first time in months.

"Hello, Kat. I was so happy you called to schedule." Janet smiles softly.

It's admittedly weird to be talking to her through a webcam, but it was either this or find someone in Kent, and the idea of having to find a new therapist made me feel sick.

"Hey, Janet," I reply politely as I sandwich my hands between my legs and lean toward the screen.

"So, tell me—what made you want to schedule an appointment? The last time we spoke, you said you planned to look into on-campus options but didn't seem too keen on it. Explain to me what brought you here."

I proceed to tell her everything. Well, mostly everything. I recount the conversation between Elijah and me earlier in the semester and how that ended—what he said to me and how it impacted me. We discuss the letter I received from Patrick, how I wrote him back, and how, despite everything, I can't shake the invasive curiosity when it comes to my father.

"Would you ever consider talking to your brother about connecting with your dad?"

I shake my head. "I don't know, probably not. I mean, I spent over twenty years trying to get that guy to want a relationship with me. So, I've just decided I no longer care."

"Kat, it is completely okay to admit you care. Your ability to care has to do with you, not him. It's a completely human response and I wouldn't blame you if you were still curious about him."

"Well, I'm not," I snap.

"Understood." Janet jots something down on her pad of paper. "Are you open to meeting your brother?"

That very thought has recently invaded my mind on more than one occasion. I know it's not my brother's fault what our father did, nor does it sound like he even likes the guy, but I can't shake the lingering resentment over the fact that my dad left me to be Patrick's dad. Is that fair to Patrick? No, I know it's not, but it's the truth.

"I don't know," I admit, "maybe. If he asked, I would, but I'm not going to be the one to bring it up. I've spent enough time trying for that man."

"You tried to have a relationship with your father. Patrick isn't your father."

CHAPTER FORTY

I obviously know that—I'm not a fucking moron. Patrick isn't to blame for anything our father did, but it doesn't change the fact that he's still a part of him. To a degree, he represents him, at least to me.

"I'd consider it," I respond, desperate to change the topic.

"And what about you and Tanner?" Janet asks.

"What about me and Tanner?"

"How is that going? I know he was an important support system for you over the summer. How has it been living in the house with him?"

"It's been great," I say simply. *Great* is an understatement, but the idea of telling my therapist that one of my best friends has now given me multiple mind-blowing orgasms feels weird. So I keep it relatively neutral. "We've been spending a lot of time together. He's a great friend."

Apparently, the flush in my cheeks at the mere mention of Tanner transmits to her screen and she fights a smile. "Just a great friend?"

"Yes."

I have never been this snippy with Janet before. Even during our first therapy session last summer, even when she pried into my relationship with Elijah, I was never this defensive.

I'm just tired of the implication that Tanner and I are more than friends. Jenna does it constantly even though I told her the sex is nothing but an arrangement we made to fill a need. However, the more time passes, the more I find myself questioning if I'm trying to convince others, or if I'm trying to convince myself.

"How has it been since your fight with Elijah? It can't be

comfortable living in a house with someone who hurt you like he did."

"It's been fine, actually. He hasn't been around as much as I would have expected. His dad is up for reelection, so he's been back in Columbus a lot."

She nods, making more notes. "That's good. You seem to be doing a lot better than the last time we spoke, but Kat…"

"Hm?"

"I hope you consider meeting more often than once in a blue moon. While I realize this semester has been a lot less painful than the spring semester, it might not always be like that. Think of therapy as preventative medicine. It's there when you're in crisis, but it's also there to help you through the less hectic days so you can handle the harder ones a little more easily. Everyone can benefit from regular therapy…even you."

Letting out a sigh, I say, "I know." Because I do. Despite my invasive desire to avoid my therapist like the plague when I'm not in crisis, if the last few months have taught me anything, it's that even the most mundane issues can result in needing to talk to someone.

"Thanks, Janet."

"Of course. And Kat?" She sets her pen down and gives the camera her full attention.

"Yeah."

"Over the next month, I want you to focus on being kinder to yourself. You can't change what your dad did, nor can you change what Elijah did. You can only control what you can control. Give yourself some grace. You're only one person—you are inevitably going to mess up—but if you surround yourself with people who know your intentions…it's not so bad."

CHAPTER FORTY

I nod, really taking her words to heart. "I will work on that, I promise."

"Good. Well, we are about out of time, so is there anything else you wanted to discuss while you had me?"

"No, I think we touched on everything." *Ya know, other than the fact that I'm terrified that I think I'm slowly descending into madness and I'm actually moderately falling for my best friend and will absolutely send my entire life nuclear if I don't figure out a way to get that under control.*

With a speculative expression, Janet looks at me, but doesn't say anything. She isn't necessarily the prying type, at least not since learning that I don't exactly respond well to that sort of therapy. "Well, I hope you have a lovely birthday, and I will see you in a month."

"See you next month." I sigh as the screen goes black and I close my laptop.

Despite the fact that the house is normally and consistently chaotic beyond reason, when I go downstairs to grab the mail, I'm surprised to find it almost completely silent.

Weird.

Once I've collected the mail, I start shuffling through it. It's mostly junk mail, a few letters from the university—one for Brendan and one for Regina—and a pale blue envelope. I tear it open immediately.

Hey Kat,
I was happy to receive your letter. I'll admit, I wasn't entirely confident I would even hear back from you and I would have completely understood if I didn't. To be frank, our dad is

an absolute asshole. But I really would like to get to know you. While letters are great and all, I think we would benefit from not communicating solely by snail mail. I've attached a separate piece of paper with my number, email, etc. I hope you reach out.
    Patrick

As I pull the additional scrap of paper out of the envelope, the familiar sound of someone clearing their throat carries from the kitchen doorway. I'm hopeful it's Tanner, or Brendan—or, honestly, anyone besides who I know it to be.

"What?" I grunt, looking up from the paper to find him awkwardly standing in the doorway with his hands in his pockets.

Elijah clears his throat. "Can we talk?"

I look back down at the paper in my hand, barely paying any attention to it as I respond. "Nope."

"Kat, c'mon. You have to talk to me at some point."

I slowly lift my gaze to meet his, but instead of the familiar rush of love, I feel nothing but resentment. I used to think that just seeing him would make my heart skip a beat, but now it's filled with a newfound sense of liberation. It's a strange and unexpected freedom, this emancipation from my own heart.

I shake my head. "No, actually. I don't. I may not be able to help the fact that you live here, but I sure as hell don't have to talk to you."

"What I said during welcome week was fucked—I'm not going to deny that. But don't you think this is a bit ridiculous? I

CHAPTER FORTY

mean, fuck, Kat, we're roommates. Shouldn't we at least get along?"

"Nope." I clench my jaw and force my way past him, deliberately avoiding eye contact. I'm exhausted from constantly trying to appease him and avoid his disapproval. But I don't care anymore. If he hates me for not pretending everything is okay, so be it. In fact, part of me hopes he does hate me now.

FORTY-ONE

KAT

When I was a kid, my birthday was without a doubt one of my favorite days of the year. It was the one day other than Christmas that my mom would take off from work and we'd spend the day together. We seldom did anything too crazy, usually spending the last day of the season at the local pumpkin farm, after which she'd take me trick-or-treating.

People often say having a birthday on a holiday ruins the day because of other expectations. Not for me, though—my mom always managed to figure out a way to make me feel like the most special girl in the world.

As I've gotten older, my birthday has become progressively less exciting. Once your mom isn't slaving to ensure your birthday is the best day ever, you suddenly realize that to the rest of the world it really is just another day.

After last year, I hate my birthday.

Jenna bursts into my room with two massive balloons, each shaped like a giant "2," nearly knocking over my lamp. I

CHAPTER FORTY-ONE

can already feel the headache coming on as she giddily announces, "Surprise!"

My hopes for a quiet and low-key birthday celebration vanish.

I let out a low, frustrated groan as I struggle to pull the heavy blanket back up over my head. Bright light streams in the window as Jenna so graciously opens my brand-new blackout curtains, which *were* intended to keep my bedroom pitch-black in the middle of the day.

"Go away," I groan, holding tightly to the comforter as Jenna tries her best to yank it off my body.

"Happy birthday!" Jenna ignores my blatant lack of enthusiasm and only tugs harder, eventually pulling the plush fabric away from my face. "We're going shopping."

"No, we're going back to sleep." I roll back over and bury my face in my pillow, trying and failing to block out the invading sunlight.

"Kat, you're twenty-two! It's, like, the holy grail birthday for a Swiftie like yourself. Now get up," she says with determination. She grasps my arms, trying to yank me from my cozy spot.

Despite my desire to crawl back into my hole, I sit up. "Has anyone ever told you that you are incredibly annoying?"

"All the time—now get up," she demands, thrusting a pair of black leggings and an oversized flannel into my arms and pushing me toward the bedroom door. "Go shower."

I know better than to argue with her when she's like this, so I obey, annoying as it is.

When I'm done getting ready, we rush toward the door. I take a long-awaited sip of the coffee Tanner had waiting for me downstairs and feel its warmth spread through my body, calming my nerves and easing my irritability for the day ahead.

We drive into Cleveland, as there aren't many shopping options around the Kent campus. As we're parking, the question that's been lingering at the back of my mind bursts out. "What are you planning?"

Jenna pauses after she puts the car in park. "I haven't the faintest idea what you are talking about."

I know Jenna—some days I'd argue I know her a little *too* well. While, yes, she loves a good shopping day in the city, she also hates driving with a burning passion. There is no way she would drag me out of the house to drive forty-five minutes into Cleveland to go shopping unless she is trying to get me away from Kent for a few hours.

"Jenna..." I glare at her.

She avoids eye contact for a few seconds before looking at me. "It was Tanner's idea."

The groan that escapes my lips is far more dramatic than the situation calls for, but I'm irritated. I've told her on numerous occasions over the past few months how much I don't want a birthday party.

"It's your twenty-second birthday. Arguably the biggest birthday in a Swiftie's life."

"You don't even *like* Taylor Swift."

"No, but *you* like Taylor Swift," Jenna says, shifting in her seat to face me head-on. "You've been talking about this since we were freshmen. I realize that your birthdays since then haven't exactly been great..." She sighs before she mumbles, "Despite my attempts at changing that."

The look she's giving me right now makes me feel like an

CHAPTER FORTY-ONE

asshole. All she's doing—all she's ever done—is try to make my birthday special for me. I can't fault her for that. "Fine."

She perks up. "Fine?"

"Fine," I reiterate. "But what do you have planned?"

"Costume party."

"Jenna," I sigh, trying harder to ease my temper. "I don't have a costume."

"Already covered, sweet cheeks."

When we pull into the driveway back home, Jenna and I have three bags of clothes each and Jenna is carrying a gigantic art print she found in an old boutique that she swears will be perfect above her and Marcus's bed.

It's almost 7:00 PM by the time we're walking into the house and, despite knowing a party is happening, I still manage to be surprised when we walk in the door and everyone yells "Surprise!" from the rooftops.

The living room has been transformed into a shimmering wonderland. Silver and gold balloons float along the ceiling, sparkling confetti covers every surface, and strings of fairy lights garnish the walls. It is clear that this party is not just a repackaged Halloween party—it is a celebration of my love for Taylor Swift. Posters and album covers plaster the walls. I can't help but smile at the thoughtfulness and effort put into making my birthday party extra special.

Everyone is decked out in their best Halloween costumes. Well...*best* might be an exaggeration, judging by the bizarre combination of items Brendan wears.

"What on God's green earth are you wearing?" I laugh.

He looks down at the seventeen-ish layers of clothing, then looks back up at me. "I'm Joey. From *Friends*." He clears his throat before continuing, "'Could I *be* wearing any more clothes?'"

The scene he is referencing invades my memory and I chuckle. "Solid choice, my friend, solid choice." I smack him on the shoulder, only to feel exactly no shoulder, as it's so thoroughly padded with clothing.

Tanner is dressed in a khaki-colored sheriff's costume, complete with a badge and shiny boots. However, the tight short shorts and tiny shirt that is taut across his muscular frame make him look more like a stripper than an actual deputy.

It takes me a few moments to register, then I remember his recent obsession with the comedy show *Reno 911!* "Oh my God," I say between giggles, "you're Dangle, aren't you?"

He grins from ear to ear. "I don't know what you're talking about—this is my typical choice of attire."

"Uh-huh."

"But..." He winces as he tugs at the shorts, trying to adjust for what is clearly a tight fit. I can't help but stifle a laugh at his predicament. "I'll only wear these until Jenna takes her picture," he explains, "then I'm switching to the pants that came with the costume. Frankly, I can't feel my balls in these."

"Well, unluckily for the rest of us, we can see everything you can't feel right now," Jenna snickers.

Tanner stands tall, unashamed of his exposed body. With a grin, he responds, "You're welcome."

Jenna turns to me. "Go get changed. Your costume is on your bed."

I again feel a warm flutter in my chest at my roommates' thoughtfulness. Despite my initial reluctance, my anticipation

CHAPTER FORTY-ONE

is building. I can't wait to see what surprises and delights the evening will bring.

The moment I reach my bedroom and see the costume Jenna selected, I can't help but smile from ear to ear.

FORTY-TWO

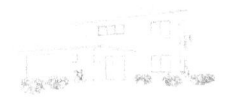

TANNER

I raise an eyebrow at Jenna as she squirms under my gaze, avoiding eye contact. "You didn't tell her, did you?"

Jenna scratches her head and stammers out a denial, but her body language betrays her true feelings. I know she's lying, and she knows that I know.

"Come on, Jenna," I urge, using my most persuasive tone.

"Okay, fine! She guessed," Jenna admits, unable to keep the secret any longer. It is no surprise to me—Jenna is terrible at keeping secrets. I was a little shocked she managed to hide the party-planning from Kat as long as she did.

We've been planning this day for weeks. Kat had been noticeably quiet about her birthday, and we knew we had to fix that. She deserves a great birthday, even if the devil incarnate insists on being home tonight. Like, seriously, why is it such a hard ask for you to stay at the Lambda house when you know your presence makes her uncomfortable?

Oh, right, it's because you're Elijah, and you are a self-centered, egotistical prick.

CHAPTER FORTY-TWO

As if he can sense the tension in the room, Elijah saunters through the front door with a petite redhead on his arm. My stomach churns at the sight; seriously, what is wrong with this guy? In what world does it make sense to show up to your ex-girlfriend's party—where it's abundantly clear that no one wants you there—and bring another woman? It's like he's actively trying to ruin her birthday.

I clench my fists, fighting the urge to confront him and throttle him for even showing up here. It's like he does this shit on purpose to hurt her, and I will not stand for it.

"Hey guys," Elijah says with a confident grin on his face. Despite the clear instructions to wear a costume, he's dressed in a simple red cable-knit sweater and dark jeans. It's a stark contrast to the short redhead clinging to his bicep like it's her lifeline, who is dressed in a tight, bright purple dress that barely covers her ass.

In any other situation, I wouldn't even bat an eye at the display of skin and blatant disregard for the theme of the party. But this? This is Elijah being calculated. He's always calculated, but this seems too far for even him.

I don't even look at him before walking away. I can hear him scoff at my dismissal, but I really don't give a fuck. I spent years pretending to like him for the sake of keeping face. But now, after all the shit he's pulled with Kat, dude can get fucked.

Despite the clear awkwardness of the situation, Marcus appears at my side with his pirate hat and sword and a grin plastered on his lips. "Are you a...stripper?" he asks, inspecting my bare legs.

"*Reno 911!*" I reply flatly, too irritated to indulge anyone.

Attention soon shifts away from Elijah and the girl he

brought the moment Kat descends the stairs. Jenna had said she had Kat's costume covered and that it had something to do with Taylor Swift, but otherwise I know nothing. Now, as Kat reaches the bottom of the stairs, grinning from ear to ear, I'm confident Jenna made the exact right choice.

Kat is wearing a white T-shirt with block lettering spelling out the words "NOT A LOT GOING ON AT THE MOMENT" in all caps. Atop her head sits a black flat-brim hat, and covering her ass is a mouthwatering pair of tight black yoga-style shorts. Admittedly, the outfit doesn't make a lick of sense, but judging by Jenna's squeal of delight, I'm almost positive it's a matter of me just not getting the reference.

Once Jenna is done fawning over Kat, she approaches me quietly. "Were you able to get the cake?" she whispers.

"Yeah, I picked it up a couple hours ago. It's in the fridge."

"Perfect. Go grab it and I'll bring everyone into the kitchen."

I do as Jenna tells me, drill sergeant that she is, and struggle to walk back to the kitchen in my horrible shorts.

Grabbing the crisp white box from the fridge, I lift the lid to inspect the cake for damage before closing it again. The amount of effort that went into acquiring the same cake Kat's mom has been getting for her birthday since she was a kid far exceeded what I anticipated. Luckily, my mom was more than happy to assist me in getting it from Kat's mom and driving halfway to Kent for me to pick it up.

Everyone begins filtering into the kitchen. As Kat walks into the room, she gasps, her eyes immediately drawn to the familiar cake box sitting on the table. Her fingers reach out and trace the smooth white cardboard, taking a moment to linger on the familiar logo as a small smile forms on her lips.

CHAPTER FORTY-TWO

With a gentle lift of the lid, she reveals a perfectly baked chocolate cake covered in rich chocolate frosting and embellished with delicate pink letters spelling out *"Happy Birthday Kat!"*

I don't know what to expect, but it's definitely not the tears glistening in her eyes. She stares down at the cake with an unreadable expression before she looks up. "Who did this?" Her voice is steady, but her hands tremble as she waits for an answer.

Shit.

Her eyes linger on Jenna, who shakes her head in response, then her gaze lands on me.

I frown and sigh. "I'm sorry. I just—I remembered you saying how much you missed the cake that Rodrigo from Pip's would make for your birthday every year when you were a kid. So I got ahold of your mom and my mom went to go get it."

Tears begin streaming down her cheeks and I instantly curl in on myself. How the hell could I have fucked this up so colossally?

"Kat, I'm so sorry. I just thought—"

Before I can finish apologizing, she lunges into my arms, squeezing me tightly with her arms around my neck. The familiar scent of her body wash—the delicious scent of toasted coconut I've grown to love—invades my senses as I tighten my arms around her waist.

"Thank you," Kat whispers, and I breathe a sigh of relief. We stay like that for a few seconds before she loosens her grip and I hesitantly release my hold on her.

"Seriously, guys, thank you for all of this." Her voice is significantly steadier as she looks to her best friend, who is beaming with pride.

However, I'm momentarily distracted by the scowl directed at me from the back of the room. The girl Elijah brought tries and fails to garner his attention, but it's no use—he's entirely focused on me.

The old Tanner would have shrugged it off, made a joke to lighten the growing tension between us. Hell, that's what I've always done when it comes to this unspoken issue between Elijah and me. Not now, though—not now that she's finally away from that sleazeball. He doesn't deserve my diversion. Instead of lightening the tension, I lift a brow at him, which causes him to clear his throat and look at the redhead he brought.

Yeah, it would probably do you some good to pay attention to your date, you fucking prick.

Kat moves to grab a knife out of the drawer to start cutting the cake when Jenna smacks her hand. "We need to take a picture!" she says. "Gather around the counter. We're going to take a picture!"

Everyone does as Jenna says, even Elijah—but when the mystery girl he brought moves to join, Jenna hands her her phone. "Can you take this?"

The girl nods awkwardly as she steps backward.

After four different tries, we finally take a photo of which Jenna approves, at which point I am elated, because it means I can finally take off these shorts that have my balls in a vise-like grip.

As I step back into the living room, I let out an irritated sigh. Music blares from speakers while people sway and dance in various corners of the room. My eyes scan the crowd, trying to find familiar faces among the sea of strangers. Jenna and I had agreed that it would just be our friends and those who live

CHAPTER FORTY-TWO

here, but it's clear that word of our party has spread far beyond that. There must be close to fifty people packed into our house, spilling drinks and laughing loudly. My stomach drops as I realize this is not what we planned for at all.

"What the hell?" I ask Jenna.

She pins me with a glare. "I didn't do it, ya dick. I don't know who did, but I'd bet someone posted about it and people just assumed it was a free-for-all."

Great—just fucking great.

Within a couple hours, most everyone is hammered, and I find myself silently regretting following Kat's lead in only lightly drinking. She's had two spiked seltzers and has been nursing a third for close to an hour. It is almost guaranteed to be warm.

"Are you having fun?" I ask when I find her alone in the kitchen, picking at a piece of cake from earlier. Seeing her hiding away from it all causes a pang of pain in my chest.

She nearly jumps out of her skin, then realizes it is me and lets out a sigh of relief, which I appreciate more than I would like to admit. "Yeah, the party is great."

As the only other sober person here, I'm far more aware of her inflections than even Jenna at this point. Without giving it much thought, I step up behind her at the counter and gently place my hand on her lower back. Her breathing quickens as I softly trace my nails up the outside of her thigh, causing a visible shiver to run through her body. A faint smile tugs at the corners of her mouth as she leans into my touch.

"Are you sure you're enjoying the party?" I whisper against the shell of her ear. As I slide my hand up from her thigh to rest on her stomach under her cotton T-shirt, she shivers against me, melting into my touch.

"It's okay." She gasps as my fingertips trace the waistband of her skin-tight shorts. "A lot more people than I'd prefer, but it's fine."

"Yeah, that wasn't the plan. I think Brendan posted it on Twitter."

"Makes sense."

"We could always go upstairs," I suggest, my lips grazing the sensitive spot just below her earlobe.

Kat's eyes flutter closed and she bites her lip, considering my suggestion.

"Well, isn't that just adorable." The smarmy voice that carries from the doorway causes my skin to crawl and I know without looking up exactly who found us alone in the kitchen.

I feel Kat tense against me.

"It's none of your business, Elijah," I say without looking at him. Despite the awkwardness of the situation, I refuse to pull away from her.

Elijah made his choices—some shitty ones, at that. Kat has made it crystal clear since this semester started that she isn't interested, but he hasn't seemed to catch the hint.

"The fuck it's not," Elijah spits with vitriol as he strides into the kitchen.

I look up—his date is nowhere in sight, but Marcus and Jenna suddenly appear in the doorway.

Elijah sways slightly on his feet, just in an undershirt now. The smell of alcohol wafts off of him as he slurs out a string of curses. "So that's why you won't talk to me then, huh? I mean, I figured you'd fuck someone else eventually after how pathetic you were, but Tanner?" He laughs mockingly.

"Elijah, that's enough," Marcus says in a low voice, but as

CHAPTER FORTY-TWO

Elijah steps further into the room, it becomes clear there is no calming him down.

Lucky for me, I don't give two shits about the trust fund baby's feelings. I release my hold on Kat and walk around the counter to face him. "Where's your date? Or did she come to her senses too?"

Elijah lets out a big, bellowing laugh, but judging from the look on his face, he is anything but amused. "Come to her senses? Please. I'm Elijah fucking Hanas. And who the fuck are you? Oh, right. Some scholarship nobody whose parents had to take out student loans to get you into a *state school*."

It's not the first time he's made comments alluding to the fact that he feels he's better than me because my parents are upper middle class and his dad is *the great Governor Hanas*. The part he fails to consider, though, is that there are few opinions in this world I care about less than his.

"Guys." Marcus tries again to put a stop to things before it gets out of hand, but Elijah doesn't back down and I'm sure as hell not giving him what he expects—for me to bow down to him.

I don't pay him any mind; that's how little his words matter.

Except he keeps going. "Sounds like my parents were right after all, though, right, Kat?" His lips curl up into a smirk. "Just another whore from Dublin like your mom. I'm sure you'll spend your life working at the same sad little diner. It's pathetic."

There are a lot of things Elijah Hanas has said over the years in an attempt to get under my skin, most of which I never batted an eye at. However, hearing him call her a whore has me seeing red. My feet start moving of their own volition.

Elijah's head snaps to the side as a tightly clenched fist collides with his jaw with a loud crack.

It takes me only two seconds to process that the punch I was planning on landing never happened because someone else beat me to it.

Jenna now stands hunched over with blood streaming from her balled fist. A whine breaks past her lips.

It all moves rather quickly after that. I rush over to Kat, who appears to be in shock, her mouth hanging open as she stares at the man who's hurt her so many times.

"Go upstairs."

I expect her to fight me on it, to say she doesn't need coddling, but she just nods and does as I ordered.

"What the fuck!" Elijah yells before splitting blood onto the kitchen floor. "Marcus, your bitch just—"

"Get the fuck out!" Marcus, who I have never seen yell—ever—gets in Elijah's face and shouts, "Get the *fuck* out of this house. I want your shit out before the end of the weekend, but for tonight, *leave!*"

"You can't kick me out. I'm on the lease."

"And I know enough about you to tank your dad's campaign for reelection. You want to play chicken? Because I promise you, tough guy, *you'll lose*. You and I will talk tomorrow, but right now you need to go."

Elijah either realizes Marcus is right or simply decides this isn't a battle worth fighting. Either way, within seconds he's out the front door without even looking for the girl who came with him.

FORTY-THREE

KAT

How? How did I just stand there and say nothing?

Elijah actually said that, and I said NOTHING.

I know I should be more focused on the fact that Jenna actually decked him in the face, for which she deserves a big hug and maybe a nice steak dinner, but I can't stop thinking about how I just stood there and said nothing. I froze, like a frightened deer caught in the blinding beams of headlights. I was paralyzed, unable to move or think, and now all I can think about is all the things I should have said.

Fuck you, for one.

I can't help but recount what just happened. As I stand in my bedroom, staring at the blank wall, replaying every word over and over in my head, the tears dry on my cheeks and I am left feeling empty. The sound of doors slamming and voices shouting has died down, indicating that everyone has gone home. But I am still stuck here, unable to shake off the numbness.

I jump at the sound of knuckles rapping against my

bedroom door, followed by Tanner's familiar voice. "Kat? Do you mind if I come in?"

At first I don't say anything—not because I don't want him to, but because I'm silently questioning if I even remember the sound of my own voice. It so clearly failed me downstairs, so why would now be any different?

"Kat, open the door, please."

My hands tremble as I fixate on the sound of his voice. My heart aches to let him in, to feel his warm embrace and the comfort that comes with it, but an invisible barrier holds me back.

The door begins to creak open and Tanner slowly steps through, an ice roller in one hand and a glass of water in the other. I notice that he's changed, now significantly more comfortable in a pair of gray sweatpants and a tattered old Kent State hoodie. He doesn't say anything as he approaches me, just sets the water down, followed by the pink roller.

My swollen, teary eyes lock onto Tanner's as he stands over me. I long to reach out and feel his warm hand in mine, but my body freezes with indecision. My mind races, questioning why I can't even ask for help when it is so desperately needed.

Luckily for me, I don't need to ask for him to know what I need.

Tanner kicks off his slippers under the edge of my bed, then climbs onto it and settles against the headboard, his disheveled light brown hair falling slightly into his face. For a moment, he sits in silence, then reaches over to grab my arm. He slowly pulls me toward him until I am nestled beneath his chin, his strong arms wrapping around me in a protective embrace.

CHAPTER FORTY-THREE

And that's it—that is the moment all of my walls come crashing down. The tears that I had been desperately holding back now flood free. It's as if his touch has unlocked the floodgates of emotion inside of me and now I can't cage them back in.

As he holds me close, his lips brush against the crown of my head and his voice whispers in my ear, trying to calm me. But the sobs continue to wrack my body, each one a flood of emotion I can't control.

"Shhh, it's okay. He's gone, you're okay," he murmurs against my hair.

He doesn't let go of me. If anything, the harder I cry, the tighter he squeezes, as if by pure might he can rewind the absolute hellscape this evening has been.

I thought there wasn't a way Elijah could fuck up my birthday more than by not showing up, but I was so wrong.

We stay like that for a while, Tanner propped up against my headboard, his strong arms wrapped around me as I lay pressed against his chest. His long legs stretch out on the bed, creating a makeshift cocoon. I get the sense he would be willing to stay like this for hours if it means easing my pain. He doesn't know it, but he is about the only thing keeping me from completely falling apart.

He shifts slightly to the side to grab the pink ice roller off the bedside table and hands it to me.

"What's this?" I ask.

"It's an ice roller?" he says questioningly. He's seen me use Jenna's on far more occasions than I'd like to admit to soothe my swollen, tear-stung eyes.

I blink at him. "But Jenna's is blue."

"I bought you a new one last week. Figured it can't be

sanitary sticking that on your eyes after Jenna does God knows what with it."

A pained chuckle spills past my lips as I grab it from him and press it to my left eye. "You're an idiot."

"Got you to laugh, didn't I?"

"So he really left?"

Tanner nods, but he looks straight ahead, a clear discomfort surrounding him that I wish so desperately I could remedy.

I hate that while this group—the people in this house—have become some of the most important people in my world, I've managed to completely throw off their lives by simply existing in them.

Maybe that was the point; maybe that's why I came back in time and I just assumed it was to fix things with Elijah. Maybe, after all that pain and effort, the point was that I was supposed to walk the other way and never become their problem.

"I'm sorry about earlier," I murmur.

"No." Tanner's voice is stern, almost angry as he pries his gaze away from the far wall and looks me in the eye. "Don't apologize for that. That was not your fault, not even in the slightest. I seriously hate him even more for the fact that you've been conditioned to think you need to apologize for his actions."

Part of it is Elijah, I'm sure, but that fucked-up habit started long before Elijah Hanas stepped into my life. I've spent my entire existence trying to be the right amount of pleasant and understanding to keep the people I love in my life—to get the people who didn't love me back to see my value.

CHAPTER FORTY-THREE

"Well, I'm sorry I made it your problem," I say. "Had I known he would do something like that, I would have been more careful."

"Stop that," Tanner snaps.

"Stop what?" I ask.

"Apologizing for things you didn't do, especially apologizing for the actions of men. I came up behind you downstairs—I put my arms around you. That, downstairs? That was nothing but a pissing match between Elijah and I that he felt necessary to drag you into. That was *not* your fault. Do you hear me?" He slides his finger underneath my chin and presses upward, forcing my eyes to meet his. "Katarina, do you hear me?" His stern voice does things to me that this situation could not possibly call for.

"Yes," I whisper.

"Good." He sighs, pressing a kiss to my forehead.

Butterflies swarm in my stomach as he reaches out to gently stroke my cheek. I lean into his touch, and he pulls me close, holding me tightly against his chest. In the quiet moment that follows, I can hear the steady beat of his heart. And then he speaks, his voice soft and reassuring.

"Do you want to watch something? A distraction might be nice for you right about now."

While I could most definitely go for a distraction, the last thing I care to do right now is laugh. It might help him after a shit day, but it just feels disingenuous. I'm not happy—I'm not amused. So I shake my head.

"Okay. Is there anything that I can do to salvage your birthday? We have most of the cake left; I can go grab you a piece and—"

I close my eyes and press my mouth against his, savoring

the tingling sensation that spreads through my body. My mind swirls with a hundred different thoughts and distractions, but all I want is to lose myself in this moment. To forget everything else—the pain, the chaos, the uncertainty—and just be present with him. As our kiss deepens, I can feel it all slipping away, if only for a little while.

He slowly pulls away, his eyes heady with lust as he says, "Kat, we don't have to."

I reach out and grasp his hand, clinging to it as my heart pounds inside my chest. I whisper, "I want to."

The warmth of his palm soothes the ache in my chest. I know that giving into these feelings will only bring temporary relief from the pain, but unpacking and dealing with them is a daunting task for another day—a day I'm not quite ready for yet.

As Tanner leans toward me, the faint scent of peppermint lingers on his breath. His soft lips graze against mine, sending shivers down my spine. "Okay," he whispers before slowly pressing his mouth to mine in a gentle yet firm kiss. The warmth of his touch spreads through my body and I can't help but melt into the moment.

So I do—I melt. I let every fear about the future and what it means for Tanner and me melt away. I welcome the reprieve from Elijah ripping open my biggest, most withstanding insecurity tonight. For once, I surrender completely to the love that has been simmering beneath the surface for I don't even know how long.

I know I'll have to face everything soon, but right now I just want to pretend we aren't just friends who sometimes fuck.

FORTY-FOUR

KAT

The drive from Kent to Columbus has never felt as long as it does right now. However, I'd much rather drive home and meet the brother I've never met than exist in that house.

No one has said anything or gone out of their way to make me feel bad, but it just feels like people are angry with me for Elijah having to move out. Jenna has reassured me on more than one occasion that I'm seeing a response that isn't actually there—that most of them are relieved to have him gone—but I can't shake the feeling that I've managed to fuck everything up.

Including Jenna's relationship with Marcus.

Paper-thin walls haven't helped ease my guilty conscience when I can hear my best friend and her boyfriend arguing well into the night. I appreciate Jenna's steadfast loyalty, but I'm not going to pretend that I don't understand Marcus's perspective. Elijah and Marcus have been friends since they were kids, and while they didn't get close until college, Elijah has been a fixture in Marcus's life since the third grade. It would be insane to ask him to cut Elijah off, but that's what Jenna has been doing. I know I need to talk to her about it, tell her that I genuinely don't care if Marcus is friends with Elijah—just that I can't be around him right now—but I have so much on my mind that simply leaving for the weekend is the only means of maintaining my sanity.

The tires of my car screech against the curb as I attempt to parallel park in front of the quaint diner in Columbus. My heart thunders in my chest with a mix of nervousness and disbelief at the thought of finally meeting my brother in my early twenties. Taking shaky breaths, I slowly open the car door and step toward the unknown.

A neon glow cascades over the worn brick, the diner's sign flickering and buzzing, casting an eerie glow over the sidewalk as I make my way toward the entrance. Every step feels like a mile, and I can feel my palms sweating as I reach for the door handle. As it swings open, a rush of warm air hits me, along with the smells of greasy burgers and freshly brewed coffee. I take in the checkered floors, vinyl booths, and an old-fashioned jukebox playing in the corner.

When Patrick selected this diner, I expected it to be a significantly more pretentious place. Though I've never met my dad, I've pieced together a picture of him through limited information. According to what little Google has revealed, he was once a successful and powerful lawyer. The thought only fuels my anger further—knowing that while my mom worked tirelessly at the restaurant, often doing double shifts just to make ends meet, he had the means to help but deliberately chose not to. It's like a slap in the face, knowing that he could have made our lives easier but instead turned his back on us without a second thought.

CHAPTER FORTY-FOUR

After seeing the "self-seating" sign by the front door, I seek out a booth toward the back of the restaurant. Patrick texted me about ten minutes ago to let me know that he was running a few minutes behind, so I shoot him a message.

KAT
Seated toward the back

PATRICK
Sounds good. Be there in 5, bus was late

Sounds good

I never would have pegged Patrick as the public transit type, but maybe he's just immersing himself in the college student lifestyle.

My nerves are a jumbled mess, my freshly painted nails tapping relentlessly against the smooth, polished surface of the lacquered wooden table. The steady ticking of the clock on the far wall seems to mock me, each second tauntingly counting down to the moment I've spent weeks agonizing over.

My anxiety continues to build as I sit there, surrounded by the chatter and clatter of other patrons. The smell of coffee and greasy breakfast food swirls around me, making my stomach churn even more as I wait for what feels like an eternity.

The bell above the door dings. My foot anxiously taps against worn tile as a young man in an old Ohio State hat walks toward me, his hands tucked into the front pockets of his jeans.

"Hey," he says timidly as his eyes meet mine—they're the same shade of blue I've seen in the mirror for the last twenty-two years.

"Hi." I smile up at him cordially.

Still tense, Patrick pushes a wayward strand of dark brown hair away from his face as he inhales deeply. "Do you mind if I sit?"

"Not at all, sit." I gesture awkwardly.

Patrick nods before sliding into the booth. The light above us flickers, casting his face in a harsh shadow.

We sit in uncomfortable silence for a while, neither of us making eye contact. I nervously peel at the skin around my nails while Patrick studies the faded menu, its edges frayed and corners curled from years of use. The tension in the air is palpable as we wait for the waitress to come take our order.

"Have you been here before?" Patrick asks.

"Huh?" I clear my throat as the question registers. "Oh, I mean, no. I've never been here."

Patrick nods, still inspecting the menu. "It's good. I used to come here as a kid with my m—" He stops mid-thought.

Awkward and unnerving as it is, I try to clear the air. "You don't have to censor yourself about her."

"I know, I just figured it would be weird for me to talk about."

It's true—discussing his mom seems almost as uncomfortable as talking about our shared lineage. Except that's the entire reason we're here.

My eyes wander to the menu and I idly pick at the corner, feeling the rough edges of the lamination under my fingertips. "So, how's school?" I finally ask, trying to steer the conversation away from uncomfortable territory.

We talk like this for a while, discussing the easy stuff—the comfortable stuff. The kind of topics you'd be more than happy to broach with your Great Aunt Sylvia at a family

CHAPTER FORTY-FOUR

function because you haven't seen her in seven years and she wants to be informed of everything. It's formal, it's safe, but it all feels painfully surface-level.

My heart clenches with a sharp pain at the reminder that I have this brother—the one person in this world who should have insight into the person I am because we are so similar—and yet I'm left staring at a man I don't know.

The server approaches our table with a warm smile and a notepad in hand. She asks if we're ready to order, but we both glance down at the menus once more, indecisive despite how long we've been staring at the choices. I request a cup of hot coffee and Patrick follows suit.

Once she returns with our coffees, I fill mine haphazardly with far more cream and sugar than one person should consume in a single sitting. I've always been more of a latte girl, seldom drinking straight coffee without my favorite hazelnut creamer in it, but I don't want to be difficult, so I choke down the burnt joe with heaps of sugar and stale half-and-half.

"So..." Patrick breaks the silence, awkwardly leaning toward the table with his hands sandwiched between his legs. "Um." He clears his throat. "Dad is sick."

As his words sink in, a strange mixture of emotions floods my body like a tidal wave. I can't bring myself to feel any sadness over the news of him being ill, nor can I muster up any happiness at the prospect of him finally being gone. Instead, I am consumed by an overwhelming sense of numbness and guilt, a heavy weight pressing down on my chest.

The memories of his absence and neglect come crashing back, causing a swell of bitterness within me. Yet, there is also a slight twinge of relief knowing that soon he may no longer be able to hurt me or anyone else. It's a complex and conflicting mix of emotions that leaves me feeling lost and unsure how to process it all.

The only words I can manage sound cold and uncaring, but they're all I have. "How?"

Patrick clears his throat. "Prostate cancer," he replies quietly.

Suddenly, any residual resentment tainting my response evaporates at the realization that while I am sitting here trying to dissect my lack of emotional response to learning my father is sick, Patrick is having to watch yet another parent wither and fade away as cancer takes them.

I may resent the man who gave us both life, but no child deserves to have to watch that happen twice.

"I'm sorry." The words tumble out of my mouth. It's a shitty way to comfort someone, but they're the only words I can figure out how to string together.

"Thank you," Patrick responds politely. "I don't want you to think this is the only reason I reached out over the summer. I actually didn't even find out until after I sent the letter."

It hadn't occurred to me that he might have contacted me out of a sense of obligation to share the news about our father rather than a genuine desire to connect with me.

I nod, my mind a flurry of thoughts.

Patrick appears to be deep in thought, his gaze fixated on the steaming mug of black coffee cradled in his hands. He seems restless, and I can't help but wonder what's going through his head. I've spent most of my life trying to understand the motivations of others, and Patrick is no exception.

Then he says, "I think you should meet him."

FORTY-FIVE

KAT

As the wedding ceremony comes to an end, I begin to pack up my camera bag. The weight of the equipment is a familiar comfort, but my mind is filled with a jumbled mess of thoughts. Memories from yesterday's conversation with Patrick swirl through my brain, the request he made before politely leaving. I understand his wanting to make a swift escape after the way my face probably contorted, but asking me to meet our father is a steep ask, even given the circumstances.

But amidst the chaos, one thought remains constant—the state in which I left things with Tanner back home. A knot tightens in my stomach as I recall the last night we spent together, and guilt creeps in like a dark cloud threatening to overtake me as I realize this arrangement between us has gone too far. I fucked it all up by catching feelings.

With a heavy sigh, I zip up my bag. I'm bracing myself to head back to my mom's empty house when my phone lights up with Elijah's name for the first time since my birthday.

THE VERY FIRST NIGHT

ELIJAH
Hey Kat. Im sorry about what I said on your birthday, that was fucked up. Can we talk?

As I read his apology, I roll my eyes and delete the message without responding. He's pulled me into his deceitful web too many times for me to believe any genuine change in him now.

My agreement with Tanner had, at the very least, provided what I needed to get past my lingering infatuation with Elijah. Despite our agreed-upon rule to not let emotions get involved, I can't deny that I have developed feelings for him, much to my surprise and dismay. It's like trying to clean up a massive mess while realizing you've been slowly falling into it all along. I know with certainty I need to put a stop to it before it gets to a place that we can't come back from.

The thought of losing Tanner in any capacity isn't something I can stomach. It's not an option.

I walk into my childhood home, dropping my camera bag onto the entryway table and contemplating only how to fix whatever divide I've unintentionally sewn between Tanner and me.

Sex was never worth potentially ruining my friendship with him—one of the most important people in my life. But how the hell am I supposed to undo that? Outside of going back in time to fix it—which I am fully aware at this point does absolutely nothing to prevent things from happening—how can I backtrack in a way that results in our friendship remaining the same?

I fumble for my phone, fingers shaking as I open the messaging app. My heart races with uncertainty as I type out a message to one of my best friends—to the one person who

CHAPTER FORTY-FIVE

makes me feel alive. The person I very well could be in love with...if that wasn't such a horrible idea.

> **KAT**
> We can't keep doing this. I appreciate you, so much, this was exactly what I needed to get through everything with Elijah. But, I'm good now, and my feelings have gotten muddled and I know we agreed not to let that happen, I fucked up. So, in an effort to not ruin everything, we need to stop.

Hastily, I shove my phone into my pocket, my fingers trembling. The words I just typed out and sent burn a hole into my mind and I desperately want to erase them from memory. I need to forget it.

I spend a solid two hours on my hands and knees, scrubbing the kitchen floor with a stiff-bristled brush. As I work, sweat beads on my forehead and drips onto the floor. My fingers turn black with grime as I dig deep into the crevices. Eventually, I wipe my brow and survey my work—the grout is now a bright white instead of dingy gray. But as I stand up and stretch my aching back, I notice the dirt caked underneath my fingernails and sigh in frustration.

When I'm finally finished admiring my handiwork, I shuffle over to the sink and turn on the hot water, vigorously scrubbing at my dirt-caked nails. Despite my efforts, some of the grime stubbornly clings to my cuticles.

Suddenly the doorbell rings, causing me to jump slightly. I grab a nearby towel and hastily wipe the suds off my hands before rushing to answer the door, my heart pounding from the startle.

The moment I twist the doorknob, a rush of familiarity

overwhelms me. A head of tousled light brown hair bursts into the house. The expression on Tanner's face is one that I have only seen a handful of times before, though never directed toward me. His usually bright eyes are clouded with anger and frustration, his jaw clenched tightly. A sinking feeling settles in my stomach at the realization that it's more than likely my text message that has him all out of sorts.

"What are you doing here?" I ask as I close the front door behind him.

"Seriously, Kat? What is this?" he asks, holding up his phone with my text message from two hours and fifteen minutes ago displayed on the screen.

"Shouldn't you be in Kent?"

"*Kat*." He says my name in that gruff, reprimanding tone that reduces me to putty, except this time, it feels anything but sexual. His voice is frantic and I don't know what to do with that.

"It's a text message."

He glares at me.

I try again. "I...it got complicated."

"*How* did it get complicated?"

"Don't make me say it," I plead as he steps into my space.

"Say it," he whispers. His breath mingles with my own, his lips only a hair's breadth from my own.

"I think I'm in love with you."

FORTY-SIX

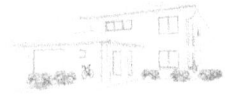

TANNER

It's as if my brain ceases to function when I hear those words from her lips.

I think I'm in love with you.

Katarina Marritt, the girl whom I've spent more time than I'd like to admit wishing would see me as anything more than a friend. The girl I fell for instantly the moment I met her in the student center with her hair disheveled and dried cream cheese on her chin after scarfing down a bagel.

The girl I went back in time for.

My heart races as I lean in, pressing my lips against hers. I can feel her heat and breath mingling with mine. For a moment, the world stands still as I gather the courage to speak the words that have been burning inside me for so long. I kiss her, if for nothing else than to buy myself time to figure out how to tell her not only that I love her too, but how *much* I love her.

She doesn't seem to grasp my intention, though, because

after a few seconds of allowing herself to melt into me, Kat pulls away. "Tanner, we can't. You said—"

"I don't care what I said. I don't give a fuck what I said—I never have. Kat, I love you. I've always loved you. I mean, fuck, I came back in time because of how much I love you." As soon as I say it, I realize how colossally I just fucked up.

A small, tentative smile creeps onto her lips, but it quickly vanishes as she processes my words. Her eyes widen in a mix of disbelief and confusion. With a trembling voice cracking slightly with emotion, she asks, "You…what?"

The air around us seems to hold its breath as she waits for my answer, the tension palpable between us.

"I…I said I love you."

"Not that part."

My mind races as I try to backtrack, but my heart pounds so loud it's hard to think. "What part? I don't remember a different part," I say, trying to sound casual and failing miserably. Sweat beads on my forehead as I desperately search for a way out of this without sounding like a lunatic or a liar.

She doesn't seem angry, just confused, and I don't blame her. Without context, what I said makes no sense. But even so, I can't think of a single plausible reason to give outside of the truth.

"Kat, I—"

Her eyes widen as she gazes at me, her mouth slightly agape. "You…went back?" she asks, her tone a mix of surprise and understanding that I can't quite decipher.

"I—no—I just mean—"

"No, explain. Please," she pleads.

I want to tell her everything—what got us here, or what

CHAPTER FORTY-SIX

little I remember of it—but I can't imagine it would be received well.

"It wasn't anything, I—"

"Stop lying!" Her voice fully breaks as the words rush past her lips in frustration. "I know you meant something, so tell me."

"It will sound insane."

"Try me."

And so I tell her, despite the fact that she very well may think me insane once I'm done. I tell her everything. I tell her how I'd read on a forum that, during a meteor shower, if you make a wish, it might actually come true. I had only hoped that one meteor would be enough.

I didn't think it would work. It's insane, right? To even think that you could go back in time and change anything. Yet one year ago, I woke up back in my college fraternity house with a girl who very much wasn't Kat in my bed.

What I wasn't prepared for was that no matter what I did, Kat still got together with Elijah. No matter how hard I tried to show her that it could be me, I couldn't stop it. Short of manipulating her, which is something I would never do, it wasn't enough to stop her from going down that path with him.

My only hope is that, now that I've heard her tell me she loves me, maybe it will be enough—even if she very well may tell me to fuck off.

As I finish recounting the whole truth to Kat, she slowly moves to sit on the couch, motionless, her eyes fixed on a distant point in front of her. There is no visible reaction on her face. No signs of distress or anger, just a blank expression that clues me into the fact that she is processing everything silently.

It's as if time has frozen, allowing us to linger in this moment before moving forward.

My throat tightens, my palms slick with sweat. "Please, can you say something?" I beg, desperate for any response other than the one I fear.

But she remains silent, her eyes unblinking.

"Kat, please."

Silence washes over us as I pace back and forth, waiting for her to shake free of whatever is coursing through her mind in this moment.

It is only when I'm just about to tell her I can go that her voice, much more timid than I've ever heard it, quietly carries through the room.

"I went back too."

Whatever I anticipate her saying, it's not that. Actually, for a moment I think I might have misheard her. However, when she looks up at me, I know.

My legs give out and I drop onto the couch next to her, my hands trembling as I try to process this onset of information.

How is it even possible?

"I...I didn't know that you'd be sent back too," I choke out. "If I had known that...I promise I would never take away your free will like that."

"You didn't—I think I wanted to go back too. Not for the same reasons, but I wanted to go back."

"To be with Elijah?" Even the thought stings, but I can't fault her. She's spent years—twice over—wanting things to work with him.

Kat's shoulders slump as her lips twist into a bitter expression. "Yeah, to be with Elijah." Her voice cracks, revealing the pain she has been hiding. She opens her mouth

CHAPTER FORTY-SIX

to speak again, then closes it immediately, as if the thought holds far too much weight.

"What were you going to say?" I ask.

She slouches back into the couch, fiddling with a loose thread on her sweater. I wait patiently, watching her struggle to form sentences. She lets out a long sigh before finally speaking.

"I don't want that anymore," she says quietly, shaking her head.

"What do you want?" I ask, admittedly a bit fearful given what started this conversation. She wanted to end things with us; maybe she still does. Maybe it's all too much.

I've always been comfortable with silence, but as the seconds tick by without a response from her, my heart begins to pound in my chest and sweat forms on my palms.

My hands clench into fists as I fight the urge to ask her again. I can see the tension in her jaw. Her eyes dart around the room, avoiding my gaze. I know she heard me, but is she going to answer? I don't want to push her, but the silence is unbearable.

Finally, she clears her throat and I find myself questioning if I've somehow managed to manipulate time again. Before, I never would have considered it, but weirder things have clearly happened.

"I meant what I said." Her gaze shifts to meet mine as she says with confidence, "I love you, Tanner. I don't know why I wouldn't have seen that before, but I do now. I don't care how we got here anymore."

Air leaves my lungs in a rush as I release the breath I've been holding. I press my palms against her cheeks, my fingers threading through her hair. I lean in, determined to taste every inch of her. Our lips meet with a desperate urgency, our breaths mingling as we pour every ounce of longing into the kiss.

It takes every ounce of self-control I have to pull away and press my forehead to hers. Our gasps mingle as I attempt to muster up the words to ask, "Is your mom coming home tonight?"

"Yes, but not until at least one. She's closing at the restaurant."

"Good," I say before pressing a gentle kiss to Kat's lips, then standing and scooping her up into my arms. She starts to laugh uncontrollably as I walk her toward her bedroom, toward the bed against the far wall that I find great comfort in knowing Elijah has never touched. It will always be a goal in my life—as long as she'll have me—to erase every memory she has with him, good and bad, and replace it with nothing but love.

FORTY-SEVEN

KAT

Tanner gently lowers me onto my plush, queen-sized bed with practiced ease. His expression is a mix of determination and tenderness, a rare combination for him. Usually, he exudes confidence in all things sexual, and I must admit, it's well-deserved. He knows how to make me feel good in ways that no one else ever has or could. In this moment, though, I can tell he wants to make sure I feel safe and loved above all else.

His eyes read only one thing: pure, unadulterated love—and God if I'm not a ball of putty at his disposal. I've spent the better part of the last six months working to break the habit of allowing Elijah—or any man—to make me feel less-than. I thought that would mean not allowing myself to be vulnerable anymore.

But I was wrong. So, so, so wrong.

It's almost as if Tanner has found a way to bypass all of my barriers, no matter how hard I attempt to keep him at a distance. He effortlessly breaks through the walls I put up and

THE VERY FIRST NIGHT

I'm tired of fighting it. I know I should be more freaked out about his big reveal.

Even if I can't remember anything about the future beyond the night we went back, I know with absolute confidence that it happened exactly the way it was supposed to.

My mind is consumed with thoughts of Tanner and the revelations about my father brought to light by Patrick yesterday. My conflicted emotions swirl within me like a storm, each one vying for dominance over the others. On one hand, I know that my dad is sick and it's only natural for me to feel some level of concern. But on the other hand, there's a sense of detachment and even resentment toward him that I can't shake off.

I wonder if this makes me a terrible person. Shouldn't I be showing more compassion for someone who is battling cancer? Yet, deep down, I can't help but feel that Patrick Marritt Sr. doesn't deserve my tears or sympathy.

Despite this knowledge, I can't ignore the nagging curiosity in my chest—the intense desire to meet the man who fathered me, even if it's just out of morbid curiosity.

But now is not the time to dwell on everything my father isn't.

Tanner leans over me, his brows furrowed and lips pressed tightly together. His body feels tense and rigid against mine, the opposite response one would hope for when the man they love hovers over them after declaring their feelings. He seems stressed, not elated.

"What?" I ask.

"Something is going on in that pretty head of yours. What's on your mind?"

CHAPTER FORTY-SEVEN

His unnerving ability to effortlessly navigate and control my emotions is steadily becoming more and more terrifying. It's as if he possesses a unique level of insight and understanding that no one else in this world has. It's both mesmerizing and unsettling in equal measures.

"Noth—" I clear my throat, failing to find confidence. "Nothing, just a long day."

A sigh falls past his lips as he settles next to me on the bed with his head propped on his arm. "What made it such a long day?"

I don't know. Could it be the fact that I met my brother for the first time yesterday only to find out that my father, who's never cared to know me, has cancer? Is it the bridezilla who made the wedding I was photographing earlier an absolute nightmare? Or could it be that I almost tanked whatever this is between Tanner and I without a second thought because I was overwhelmed and didn't know what else to do? It really could be anything, so I settle for the simplest response.

"Nothing, I'm just tired." I reach out to pull him to me, to press my lips to his in hopes of steering this scenario back toward where it needs to go, but he doesn't allow me to do so.

"Kat," he growls, his hand gripping my hip tightly. It's a tone that always makes me weak in the knees, but this time I sense something different. His voice softens as he reaches up and caresses my cheek with his thumb, his piercing eyes searching mine for answers. "What's wrong, Kat? Talk to me." My heart races as his expression transforms from intense to loving in a matter of seconds. It's so uniquely Tanner, confusing and comforting me at once.

Ignoring my every instinct, I do exactly as he asks. I tell him everything. I tell him about how the bride wanted her maid of honor removed from the premises. I tell him how Patrick confided in me about our father's cancer diagnosis, sending my mind into chaos.

Tanner's voice is calm and curious, void of any judgment as he poses the question: "Do you think you're going to meet him?"

"Would it make me horrible if I didn't want to?" The dichotomy of emotions that exists within me at the prospect of seeing my dad threatens to overwhelm me.

"No, it wouldn't make you a horrible person." Tanner positions his pointer finger underneath my chin, nudging it upward so my eyes meet his. "It makes you human. He's done nothing to deserve your kindness, and if it were purely about him, I wouldn't even think to encourage you to do it. But I think meeting him might give you some closure you might not have thought about."

I know Tanner is right, but I can't help the cowardice that washes over me at the thought of meeting the man who sired me.

I smile up at Tanner, causing his eyes to soften. "I'll think about it."

All he does is nod before his lips land on mind. His kiss is soft and tentative and everything I need right now. It's not outright sexual, but it leaves me rubbing my thighs together just the same. More than anything, I just want the comfort that being touched by Tanner provides. He's about the only person in existence who can take me so fully out of my own head, and I need that right now.

He pulls away from the kiss for a split second as his eyes rake over my expression, searching for any objection to him

CHAPTER FORTY-SEVEN

continuing. He won't find apprehension on my face, though, only complete and utter encouragement.

I gently tug at the hairs at the nape of his neck and, with his hand gently cupping the side of my jaw, he slants his lips over mine once more with a relieved sigh. I taste peppermint on his lips as he deepens the kiss, his tongue teasing mine and igniting a fire in my belly. My spine arches toward him, craving more of his intoxicating touch.

Tanner's touch is featherlight as he traces the buttons of my oversized button-down, his hands moving with a tenderness I have never experienced before. Each button comes undone with agonizing slowness, and I can't tear my eyes away from the sight of this man who has so completely consumed me. He moves to hover over me, his breath warm on my skin as he reveals more and more of my body with each unfastened button. It is intoxicating and mind-boggling all at once.

With each tug of his fingers, the buttons give way and the panels fall open like a flower blooming. My heart races as his eyes focus on the delicate black lace that covers my breasts. The anticipation builds as he slowly reaches out to touch me, gently tracing the outline of the bralette with his fingertips before ghosting his pointer finger languidly over my hardened nipple, obvious through the sheer lace fabric.

As his fingers brush against my skin, my breath catches in my throat. A wave of heat washes over me, and I can feel the dampness between my legs. It's impossible to ignore and all I can think about is how incredible it will feel when he reaches lower.

Leaning downward, Tanner flicks his tongue over the thin scrap of fabric separating him from my breast before latching his mouth over the hardened peak. He bites down gently, causing the breath that was previously lodged in my throat to break past my lips with an intoxicated moan.

"God, I missed that sound," Tanner mumbles as he presses a kiss to the scalloped edge of my bralette.

A laugh crawls up my throat. "It's only been a week."

He nods. "Yeah, but I know you. I could tell you were overanalyzing it and I was worried."

"Don't be," I whisper in an attempt to reassure him. "I've never been more sure of anything."

This appears to appease him as he peels back the dainty fabric to expose my wet, pebbled nipple to the crisp air before his lips wrap around it, the warmth of his mouth causing my head to fall back against the pillow.

Patience in the bedroom is something that Tanner and I have yet to find a middle ground on. While he loves to draw everything out, to savor every last moment, all I can think about is how badly I want him buried inside me. We can savor it later.

"Tanner," I whimper as he presses featherlight kisses from my chest to the waistband of my black leggings.

"Hm?" he responds, but doesn't stop his advance and begins prying the thin fabric away from my skin achingly slowly.

"Tanner. Please."

"Please what?" The laughter he's holding back is almost enough to make me combust.

"You know what," I grit out through my teeth.

He pauses as he drops my leggings and panties onto the floor by the bed. His eyes meet mine as he cups himself through his strained jeans. It would be an erotic sight if I didn't know that he is more than likely trying to keep himself in check.

I don't want him to keep himself in check, though—I want him to let go. Every desire to joke with my best friend about the situation melts away when his eyes meet mine again; the most beautiful green I've ever seen.

"Please, make love to me."

The weight of my words lingers, the stark difference between what we've been and what we are now clear to both of us for what might be the first time. However, despite everything that's happened—despite the breadcrumbs I accepted from Elijah for so long, all the pain he caused—despite the instinct to back away, I stand firmly. Even though my brain won't stop screaming *"Danger!"* I don't pry my gaze away from his.

Slowly, Tanner reaches for the button on his jeans and pops it open, then swiftly pulls down his pants and boxers, revealing his muscular thighs. His cock is hard and I can't help the warm wetness that pools between my thighs at the thought of him inside me.

He crawls back onto the bed, his body hovering over mine. I spread my legs eagerly, hoping he'll finally satisfy the ache between them. But instead of plunging inside me, he teases me with his cock, brushing it against my wetness as I squirm and beg for more. He leans in closer, pressing his chest to mine and locking eyes with me, a small smile forming on his lips. I can feel every inch of him against me, but he doesn't give in to my desperate pleas just yet, teasingly grazing my slick entrance. I beg for more, but he remains calm and in control, taking his time to savor every moment. His eyes lock on mine as he reaches up to brush away the hair plastered to my forehead.

"Kat?" he whispers against my lips.

"Yeah?"

"I love you."

It's vulnerable and emotional and, for the first time ever, I'm not terrified of what's to come. Actually, I'm excited for it.

"I love you too," I whisper back, and he takes this moment to push past my entrance devastatingly slowly. I gasp as he enters me with excruciating leisure. My body responds eagerly, adjusting to his girth and clenching tightly around him. Wave after wave of pleasure crashes over me as he moves inside me, igniting every nerve ending in my body.

When he's seated fully inside, he pauses for a moment, his body still and steady. I feel every inch of him pressed against me, every muscle tensed with anticipation. But it's not just the physical sensations that hold him back—when our eyes meet, I can see the intensity in his gaze. He's relishing this moment, allowing himself to fully indulge in the pleasure and connection between us. And so I do the same, letting go of any inhibitions and simply reveling in the sensation of being fully united with him.

Time seems to stand still as we both bask in the raw intimacy of our bodies intertwined.

Intimacy in a way that I've never experienced before; true intimacy with the man I love...and, for the first time in my life, the man who loves me back.

BEGIN AGAIN

Begin Again
Taylor Swift

2:56   -1:02

◀◀   ▶   ▶▶

	Begin Again Taylor Swift	

	How You Get The Girl Taylor Swift	04:06

	Daylight Taylor Swift	04:52

	You Are In Love Taylor Swift	04:26

	The Alchemy Taylor Swift	03:16

	emails I can't send Sabrina Carpenter	01:44

	Bless the Broken Road Rascal Flatts	03:53

	End Game Taylor Swift, Ed Sheeran, Future	04:03

	She Stayed Alexandra Kay	03:15

	invisible string Taylor Swift	03:15

	Leave Me Again Kelsea Ballerini	02:58

	Long Live Taylor Swift	05:17

	Paper Rings Taylor Swift	03:42

FORTY-EIGHT

KAT

Jenna's feet shuffle to a sudden halt on the pavement, her heels grinding against the rough concrete. With a sharp turn of her body, she faces me and demands, "Okay, tell me what happened." Her arms flail in an urgent gesture, but I just roll my eyes.

"I told you—once we get to the library."

Jenna has been asking me about this weekend the entire walk from Franklin Hall to the library on campus. I know I'm slowly torturing her, but I probably would have told her ten minutes ago if it wasn't so entertaining watching her freak out.

She grips my arm tightly and drags me along the main walkway, not caring about my struggling feet. "Come on, you're like the slowest walker I know," she huffs, impatiently pulling me along.

Once we're in the library, she turns to me, irritated impatience marring her brow.

"Nope," I say, "gotta get upstairs. I don't want to walk and talk about it."

CHAPTER FORTY-EIGHT

She all but screams in frustration as she yanks me toward the escalator against the far wall. Once we've made it up three sets of escalators and barrel past one seriously irritated library worker, Jenna and I are finally comfortably seated at our favorite table overlooking Risman Plaza.

"Spill," she demands.

Part of me wants to drag it out longer, in part because it's clearly driving Jenna nuts not having all the information, but also because I don't know how to put into words what happened without sounding like a crazy person. I've told Jenna almost everything about me and my life from the moment I met her, except when it comes to the whole *"Hey, I went back in time"* of it all. There are some things that are just outright insane, and even I don't think Jenna would be entirely against having me committed.

I opt to tell her everything minus that little tidbit.

"I told you; he showed up at my house." I pick up my cup of coffee, now lukewarm and unappealing, and take a sip.

Jenna's eyebrows furrow and creep up toward her hairline. "Then what?" she asks and I just shrug, which causes her to groan in exasperation. "Kat, just tell me!"

The employee behind the desk ten feet away shushes us.

I bite my lip. "I might have told him I'm in love with him and he said it back," I mumble against the lip of my disposable cup.

Jenna's jaw drops. "Way to bury the fucking lead, Marritt!" Swatting my arm, she leans in, resting her chin against her open palm. "Then what?"

Then...then we had a long conversation about how the hell we ended up here, both metaphorically and physically. However, I decide to tell her about Patrick instead.

Jenna's voice trembles and her eyes glaze over with sadness. "Wait, your dad has cancer?" she asks, the previous excitement in her tone now replaced by heavy melancholy.

"Yeah, but it's fine." I wave my hand in dismissal, causing her brows to pull together.

"Kat."

"What?"

Jenna's teeth sink into her bottom lip before she nervously chews on the inside of her cheek. She looks up at me, a sympathetic glint in her eyes. "It's okay to feel upset about this," she says softly. "It's okay to not be okay about it. I know your relationship with your dad—"

"I don't have a relationship with my dad."

"Fine." She clears her throat. "I know your *lack* of relationship with your dad makes things complicated, but if you have any emotions about this news, know that no one will judge you for it." Her tone softens and she reaches out to lightly touch my hand in support.

I know Jenna is right—that my reaction to this news is much more about me than him. However, whenever I think about it too much, I just find myself growing more and more angry.

I don't want to be angry; I've spent far too much time being angry.

The day I mustered up the courage to stop sending letters to my dad was like ripping off an old band-aid, bringing a sharp sting but also a sense of relief. For so long, I chased after the elusive man I thought he could be if he just cared enough to try. But as the years passed by, it became clear that being a dad to me would always take a back seat to his own selfish

CHAPTER FORTY-EIGHT

desires. And so, I made the difficult decision to let go of that burden and move on with my life.

Yet, even now, the thought of him passing away without us ever having a conversation weighs heavily on my heart. The ache in my chest serves as a constant reminder of what could have been if only our relationship had been different.

"It's fine." I raise my lukewarm cup to my lips and swallow the last bit of hazelnut latte.

Jenna nods as she stares down at the table, then looks up at me. "Well, if that changes, I'm here."

I swallow hard and nod in response, the only acknowledgment I can offer.

"Soooo..." Her tone again shifts. "You and Tanner."

"We're good." I smile, thankful for the shift in topic.

"Good." Jenna grins from ear to ear before clearing her throat. "Oh, and Kat?"

"Hm?"

"I told you so."

I resist the urge to roll my eyes, but a small smirk betrays me. I can't deny that she was right, though it pains me to admit it. Jenna has spent the better part of the time we've known Tanner saying he has wanted me since the day we met. If only I could tell her just how true that is.

I simply nod. "Yeah, yeah, I know."

The path here has been grueling, but I'm starting to see the value in it all. As painful as it's been, I don't know that Tanner and I would be where we're at if not for the tattered road that got us here.

"Thank you, by the way," I say. "I haven't had the chance to say that since my birthday."

The topic of Elijah has been one I haven't wanted to

broach over the last week and a half. However, given what Jenna did for me, I feel like it needs to be acknowledged.

"It's nothing," Jenna replies as she waves her hand to dismiss me, drawing my attention to her still-bruised knuckles.

"No, it's not." I pause until her eyes meet mine. "You didn't have to defend me like that, but you did. At the risk of your relationship. That isn't nothing."

Jenna shrugs and starts pulling her notebook out of her backpack. "You act like it was such an altruistic thing for me to do, Kat. I've wanted to deck that guy for a long time. So really, did I hit him for you or because it sounded like a really fun idea?" With a playful wink, she flips open her worn notebook and scribbles down a few words, seemingly unrelated to the conversation. "Besides, Marcus was on your side. Him and Elijah have talked; they're fine. Marcus was crystal clear about why he kicked him out. Marcus gets why I did it and I don't personally give a shit what Elijah thinks of me, so. It's not a big deal."

"Well, it is to me."

She quickly diverts her attention elsewhere, but I can see the faint flicker of uncertainty in her eyes. Despite trying to play it cool, she can't hide the hint of anxiety in her voice as she responds, "If that's how you truly feel, then you can buy me lunch."

"Deal," I chuckle.

Her shoulders relax and a grin spreads across her face. "Deal," she says.

FORTY-NINE

KAT

My mom's apron is crumpled and stained with coffee drips. She sighs as she grabs it off the entryway table, her fingers deftly wrapping the rogue strings around her checkbook, which is nestled inside. "I really wanted to spend Thanksgiving with you two," she says, her voice heavy with disappointment. "But no one else would volunteer to work today."

"Mom, it's fine."

Tanner sits at the kitchen table, savoring the last of his bacon and eggs. He smiles and glances up at my mother. "Thank you for cooking, Julie—it was seriously delicious," he says.

She had scolded him for being so formal with her and insisted on being called by her first name when he arrived this morning, and while at first it felt like a weird reprimand, I think I quite like the casual energy between my mom and boyfriend at this point.

While our relationship might be new in its present

capacity, there is something about Tanner and me that feels oddly timeless. It's as if we were always meant to find our way to this place, no matter what obstacles stood in our way.

My mother expressed a similar sentiment last night when I returned home for Thanksgiving break. Despite her jaded experiences, she has never let go of her romantic ideals, and she was more than elated to learn Tanner and me are now together.

I just wish she didn't learn that by finding him sneaking out of my bedroom to get a glass of water in the middle of the night two weeks ago when it all happened. Not that she took issue with it, but man does that woman know how to make things awkward when she wants to.

"Thank you, Tanner." My mom, heading off to work, tells me what time I can expect her to be home.

I nod, only half listening.

Yes, I've met Tanner's parents before. It was exactly a year ago on Thanksgiving, and the memory floods back with a rush of emotions.

But this year, everything feels different. The air is heavy, weighted with anticipation and anxiety. As we pull up to his parents' home, I can't help but feel the gravity of the situation.

Last year, spending Thanksgiving with his family was easy—I was just a friend, casually tagging along. I didn't have to worry about impressing anyone because I was dating someone else at the time. But now, as we enter this new phase in our relationship, my nerves are on fire. Every interaction feels like it could make or break their opinion of me, and I can't shake off the weight of their expectations hanging over my head.

"Kat?" Tanner questions as he puts the car in park. He

CHAPTER FORTY-NINE

turns to face me and cups my chin between his fingers. "What's going on in that pretty little head of yours?"

At first I don't say anything—not because I don't have anything to say, but because it's such a weighted question. I'm damn near spiraling at the prospect of seeing his family again and I don't know how to verbalize it. I've had to deal with the consequences of a guy's parents not liking me, and it was brutal.

Tanner is so good—*we* are so good, so the idea of everything imploding because I've managed to say or do something colossally stupid has me in a tailspin.

"Sweetheart." Tanner's voice is tender and calm, everything I need without me having to say a single word. I don't understand how he does that; how he knows exactly how to talk to me.

"Hm?"

"Breathe. I can see your gears turning from here..."

"What if they hate me?" All my insecurities spill out without restraint. "What if they realize that I'm actually the worst possible person to be with their son and they opt to dump me in the pond out back?"

"One? My mom will take great pride in you thinking she could be even remotely capable of murder. Two? They're quite literally obsessed with you, Kat. My mom thought I was lying about us being just friends last year, but when I told them that we were finally together, she actually cried. Like, tears."

"Tears of utter devastation?" I smirk.

"Tears of joy, sweetheart. Tears of joy."

"So...they like me?" My voice cracks but I don't make any effort to hide it.

"They *love* you. Almost as much as I do."

His reassurance shouldn't carry as much weight as it does. His eyes are filled with love and concern as he tries to soothe my anxious thoughts. Tenderly, he lifts my chin and presses his lips against mine, sending a wave of tranquility through my body. As I surrender to his embrace, my racing heart begins to slow.

When he pulls away from the kiss, Tanner presses his lips to my forehead, then asks, "You ready to head in?"

As my gaze falls upon the magnificent brick house, looming larger than any residence I have ever called home, a sense of calm washes over me. The familiar nerves and anxieties I felt at the thought of facing his parents again seem to dissipate like mist in the morning sun. The house stands tall and proud, adorned with grand columns and elegant windows that glint in the sunlight. It exudes an air of wealth and sophistication, but also warmth and comfort. If nothing else, Tanner's family has been a stark reminder that not all people become horrible people when money comes into play. They may not have old, political legacy money, but they're clear proof that having comforts in life doesn't automatically make you an asshole.

"Let's go."

Tanner's warm, callused hand envelops mine as we approach the door, warm and reassuring. His fingers tighten around mine as he pushes the door open, his touch offering a sense of security in the midst of chaos.

"I love you," I whisper as we approach the kitchen, a sense of déjà vu setting in but providing comfort rather than distress.

He doesn't answer me, but I don't miss the smile that lights up his face.

CHAPTER FORTY-NINE

"Tanner!" His mom's hands freeze and the knife she was using clatters onto the wooden cutting board. She turns and squeals with delight, quickly approaching him with open arms. He hugs her back tightly while still holding my hand. Once she releases him, she turns to me, beaming from ear to ear and pulling me close. Only then does Tanner release my hand, allowing me both arms to hug his mother back.

Tanner's mother slowly unwraps her arms from around me, and I see the glistening tears in her eyes. My stomach drops as I realize I must have done something to upset her. *Oh God, what did I do?* I must have done something.

Elaine leans in close, her voice barely audible as her warm breath tickles my ear. "Thank you," she murmurs, her eyes shining with unshed tears. I look at her questioningly, and she continues, "For bringing such joy into my son's life. I'm sure you know he's always had a soft spot for you, and seeing him so smitten makes me grateful." She squeezes my hand in a quick gesture of gratitude before she pulls back, a small smile on her lips.

The weight of what she just revealed is not lost on me, except for the first time I don't cower at the realization that Tanner has talked to his mom about me, presumably long before we were involved.

God, I was such an idiot.

"Larry! Tanner and Kat are here!" Elaine yells into the other room, from which I hear the television being turned off and the audible groan of two teenage boys who want nothing more than to keep watching the game. Within seconds, Tanner's father and two younger brothers appear in the kitchen, Larry far more enthusiastic than the younger men.

Theo, the younger of the two brothers, has grown

THE VERY FIRST NIGHT

significantly since I last saw him. He still has a boyish appearance, but his features are starting to resemble those of his brothers more closely. His braces, with their red and silver bands proudly proclaiming his college football team loyalty, are gone. He now sports a faint dusting of hair above his upper lip, and there is something in the way he carries himself that hints at pride over this new physical development.

I look at Larry, whom Tanner informed me has been spending significantly more time assisting his wife in the kitchen. Apparently, this change was brought about by a heated conversation between them after I left last year. It seems that Larry, much like his son, is acutely attuned to Elaine's needs and will go to great lengths to keep her content, even if it means confronting his own blind spots.

I smile at the gentle clinking of pots and pans as Larry moves around the kitchen, carefully assisting his wife with precision and care. A sweet fragrance wafts through the air, a blend of spices and herbs that add depth to the already mouth-watering scents emanating from the oven. It is clear that Larry's dedication to his wife's happiness extends far beyond their verbal exchanges.

Tanner sets the last dish down on the table in the dining room, an array of savory smells filling the air. The scent of roasted turkey—perfectly golden and crisp on the outside yet tender and juicy on the inside—mingles with the rich scent of melted butter cascading over the mashed potatoes.

My stomach grumbles in anticipation as I take in the spread, thankful I get the opportunity to enjoy a traditional family Thanksgiving dinner for the second year in a row, even if it is Tanner's family. My mouth waters as I imagine sinking my teeth into each delectable dish and savoring every bite.

CHAPTER FORTY-NINE

It isn't until everyone is seated with their plates stacked high that anyone speaks.

"So, Kat," Larry begins. "Tanner tells me that you've photographed a few weddings this year already. It's important to build up those connections now for after graduation. Smart move."

I try but fail to hide the blush that creeps over my cheeks. "It really isn't a big deal; they were both coworkers of my mom."

"Don't be silly—it doesn't matter how you get clients. Using your network isn't just smart; it's necessary in business. Speaking of, do you have a portfolio? Vern from accounting's daughter is getting married next fall and I believe she is still looking for a photographer. I could pass along your information. Do you have a website?"

Despite the overwhelming nature of his questions, I still find myself completely consumed with pride at his support. I haven't even thought about setting up a website—I wouldn't know where to begin. School has taught me the legality of everything, but not so much the practice of setting things up.

"We're working on getting her website live over winter break," Tanner responds before shoving a piece of dark meat into his mouth, followed by a euphoric groan. "Mom, you really outdid yourself this year. This is fantastic."

Elaine beams at her son's compliment before turning to her husband. "I would like to take credit, but the turkey was actually your father this year."

As if she just told him that the gravy was made with chicken feed, all three of their sons drop their forks and display nearly identical slack-jawed expressions.

"Dad...doesn't cook," Theo explains when he sees my

confusion. "I thought he was just helping you move it and get it out of the oven, Mom."

Thomas swats his arm. "You're not supposed to say that out loud, idiot," he whispers loudly before turning to their father. "But Theo is right—since when can you cook?"

Larry flushes. "I had a lot of help from your mother. I was basically just the muscle."

This answer seems to placate the boys, who begin shoveling food into their mouths once more, barely pausing to chew between bites. The only break in their ravenous feasting occurs when Theo lets out a loud burp, causing both Tanner and Thomas to burst into laughter.

"Pigs," Elaine chuckles under her breath, and I laugh too.

FIFTY

KAT

Leaving the warmth and comfort of Thanksgiving dinner, Tanner and I step out onto the porch and are immediately hit by a gust of frigid November air. I hurry to the car, but stop at the door and instinctively bury my face into Tanner's thick wool coat, grateful for its warmth. He pulls me closer, wrapping me up in his arms and shielding me from the harsh cold.

"Why didn't you bring a coat again?" he chuckles against the shell of my ear, the warm breath a welcome comfort.

"You really want to rehash this right now?" I laugh. Earlier, I adamantly insisted that it wasn't that cold outside and my only outerwear option would clash with my outfit. He had rolled his eyes and shook his head, but thankfully didn't push the issue any further. I knew he thought it was silly, but he let me make my own mistakes.

But my choice was indeed a colossal mistake.

"You ready for me to get you back home?" Tanner whispers.

THE VERY FIRST NIGHT

My stomach twists at the realization that today is coming to an end and I won't see Tanner until Sunday evening when we head back to school. Not bringing my car home was a questionable choice, but when he offered to carpool, I couldn't resist spending a few extra hours alone with him.

Does that make me entirely pathetic? Probably. However, recently I've stopped caring if I look needy or pathetic when it comes to Tanner, as foreign as it feels.

I nod up at him before he reaches to open the passenger-side door. "Milady," he says with a cheeky grin.

I can't help but smile and play along. As he takes my hand to help me into the car, I respond teasingly, "Milord."

We both laugh as we settle into our seats and buckle up for the fifteen-minute drive to my mom's house.

As we're pulling away from the house, my eyes lock on the brand-new garage door attached to their house. I laugh at the memory of Tanner telling the story of Theo's mistake, a bit thankful that it didn't come up over dinner and turn into a point of contention.

"The new garage door looks great."

"Should've told my dad that—would have been a riot," Tanner laughs.

I hunch in my seat with my hands wedged between my thighs, desperately trying to warm up my frosty fingers as my body adjusts to the warmth of the car.

Tanner glances over, sees me shivering, and, without a word, takes both my hands in his warm right palm. His piercing green eyes meet mine and he gives me a small smile before returning his attention to the road in front of us.

"Did you have a good time?" he asks.

"Yeah, it was great seeing everyone."

CHAPTER FIFTY

"I'm glad. They were all insanely excited to see you again."

Heat blooms in my cheeks, but I fight the natural instinct to scoff at his words. "Good."

Our car ride doesn't last very long and soon we're pulling onto the street of my childhood home and the small, weathered house comes into view, its faded blue paint peeling off in some spots. It is a far cry from Tanner's luxurious family home with its perfectly manicured lawn and grand entrance. Our driveway is cracked and uneven, barely fitting one car, while Tanner's could fit three comfortably.

Tanner pulls into the driveway and turns off the ignition. He reaches over to unbuckle his seatbelt, then hesitates. We have already discussed our plan for the weekend: he will walk me inside and then spend the rest of the holiday weekend with his family, including an early-morning Black Friday shopping trip with his mom.

But as our eyes lock, I can't stop myself from blurting out, "Why don't you stay the night?" My heart hammers in my chest at the thought of him leaving.

I wait for Tanner's response, feeling as though time is moving at a snail's pace. A knot forms in my stomach as I worry he will think I am the most selfish person alive. I know that family responsibilities should always come before relationships, so why did I even suggest otherwise? The weight of guilt settles heavily on my shoulders, and I feel like I am drowning in regret.

"Okay," he says.

"I...I'm sorry I asked," I stammer. "I know you have plans with your mom early—that was a dumb question. I wasn't thinking."

"Kat...I said yes. I want to stay the night."

"Yeah, but your mo—"

"My mom will understand. Besides, Theo was planning on going with her too. We can meet them for breakfast once the chaos winds down."

He's reassuring me, but I can't shake the feeling in the pit of my stomach that says this could be a turning point for us.

"Sweetheart?" Tanner prompts.

"Hm?"

"I love you. My mom loves you. I want nothing more than to stay with you tonight. I can see those cogs turning in that pretty little head of yours and I need you to know none of it is true. This isn't a big deal and I genuinely hate that you've been conditioned to think that it is. It isn't selfish to ask your partner for what you need. I never want you to stop expressing that, okay?"

My voice cracks when I reply, "Okay."

"Okay." Tanner smiles and squeezes my hand. "Now, let's get inside. I might want to spend the night, but I don't want to spend it in my car."

As soon as we step inside, I make a beeline for the thermostat on the far wall. My fingers twist the knob to the right, pushing the temperature higher and higher until it clicks at just the right spot. This old house is tricky when it comes to heat, and I know from experience that a little boost to start will make all the difference.

I kick off my sneakers and slip into my cozy, bright orange slippers.

In the kitchen, Tanner rummages through the freezer, standing with his back to me, searching for something sweet. "Do you have any ice cream?"

CHAPTER FIFTY

"You just ate like half a cheesecake."

"Correct."

"Shouldn't you be all dessert-ed out?"

His eyebrows furrow in confusion as he stares at me, his mouth slightly agape. "I had *cheesecake*...ice cream is different."

"If you say so," I say with a laugh.

Tanner reaches into the freezer and pulls out a frosty container of mint chocolate chip ice cream. "Besides, I quite enjoy the thought of all the things we can do with ice cream."

My cheeks heat up, betraying me as my mind races back to the last time we indulged in a pint of ice cream together. The memory of his tongue against my skin, swirling my hardened nipple between his lips as he lapped at the last remnants of rocky road causes me to squirm under his gaze, feeling a familiar wetness pool between my thighs.

Tanner approaches me and sets a bowl of freshly scooped ice cream and two spoons on the counter, then presses his body against mine, sandwiching me between him and the chilly tiles of the countertop. His breath tickles my ear as he whispers, "What's on your mind?"

"Nothing." My body betrays me, arching into him. "I just —ice cream sounds nice."

"Does it?" Tanner's voice is gravelly and intoxicating, so much so that I feel myself growing lightheaded at his proximity.

"Yes," I gasp. Our breath mingles, his lips only a whisper from mine, but he doesn't close the gap.

My mouth waters as Tanner dips the smaller of the two spoons into the bowl of ice cream. He lifts it to my lips. "Open," he demands, his eyes sparkling with mischief.

I can't help but comply, eagerly taking a bite of the cold, sweet treat.

Once the cold metal lands against my tongue, the combination of creamy spearmint and rich chocolate explodes on my taste buds, sending shivers down my spine. I barely have a second to relish the sweet flavors of the ice cream before Tanner's warm lips meet mine in a delicate kiss, his tongue playfully dancing between my lips before retreating, causing an intoxicating blend of sweetness and anticipation to wash over me. When he pulls away, I whimper, desperate to taste him again.

He steps back with a grin and sets the bowl on the counter. "What time is your mom supposed to be home?"

"Not for at least another five hours." My stomach leaps as I smile at him, anticipation flooding my mind. Every nerve in my body tingles with electric energy, waiting for his next move.

"Good." Tanner shoves a spoonful of ice cream into his mouth before stepping toward me. "Take off your shirt." His voice is commanding and urgent.

I quickly comply and shed my white turtleneck sweater, the rush of cold air drawing prickles along my exposed skin. I'm set ablaze under his piercing stare. The thin fabric of my cotton bra does little to hide the hard peaks of my nipples, straining against the soft material.

His lips press together in a tight line, and I can see the muscles in his jaw clenching as he bites down on his bottom lip. His breaths are quick and shallow, his eyes dark with desire. My attention is drawn to his mouth, the one that has brought me so much pleasure over the past few months. I can almost feel his tongue against my skin, the way it expertly

CHAPTER FIFTY

teases and pleases me. Memories of him eagerly lapping at my core flood my mind as I watch him struggle to contain himself, and I rock back and forth on my feet in an attempt to quell the needy sensation building within me.

"What are you thinking about?" he asks me.

"You."

Tanner nonchalantly leans against the counter, his fingers gripping the edge, his eyes glittering mischievously. "Pants."

As I heed his demand and slowly slide my fingers under the waistband of my black leggings, feeling the softness of the fabric against my skin, he casually takes a bite of the ice cream. It isn't until the black ball of fabric is at my feet that his gaze abandons its comfortable raking up and down my legs to meet my eyes.

"Come here." He beckons me with his hand, the low, raspy tone of his voice sending a tingle down my spine.

I cross the cool tiles of the kitchen floor, goosebumps erupting on my skin. As soon as his hands graze my bare hips, a surge of heat spreads through my body like wildfire, igniting every nerve.

As he leans in, the chill of his recent ice cream indulgence lingers on his lips, but as soon as our mouths meet, warmth floods through me like an inferno. I taste the faint sweetness of mint and feel the intensity of his desire with every stroke of his tongue against mine. His hand cradles the back of my neck, fingers tangling in the strands of hair at my nape and pulling gently.

Tanner's grip on my hair tightens, pulling me closer to him as his lips trail down my neck. The sharp sting of his teeth on my skin elicits a gasp from me, and he tugs slightly harder, causing my head to fall back in pleasure.

Just as I'm about to give in completely to his touch, I stop him with a gentle push on his chest. "Wait," I say breathlessly, needing a moment to catch my breath, gather my thoughts, and muster up a sliver of courage to take charge.

He suddenly recoils, his eyes widening in concern. "Did I hurt you?" he asks frantically, his hands trembling. "I'm sorry, I just got carried away," he stammers, his voice filled with guilt and regret.

"You didn't hurt me," I reassure him.

"Oh." He lets out a sigh of relief. "Then why did you stop?"

"I—" I know what I want, I know what I want to do, but when my mouth opens to speak, nothing comes out.

"Kat, talk to me. What's wrong?" His brows pinch together.

My mouth feels dry as I lean in, my heart pounding. "I want to go down on you," I say, my voice barely a whisper.

His eyes widen and he lets out a sharp breath, his body tense with anticipation.

"If that's okay, I mean." My cheeks burn as he erupts into laughter, his face turning slightly red as he struggles to control himself.

"I mean, of course I'd love that! If I ever say otherwise, just assume I've been bitten by a zombie or something because… yes. Definitely yes," he says, still chuckling.

Relief washes over me and I sigh, a bit embarrassed by my assumptions. "I don't know, you've never seemed to want me to—it's always been about me and, I don't know, I started to think you might just not want me to do that."

Tanner lifts his hands to cup my cheeks. He says, "I love you, Kat," then presses his lips to my forehead. "First of all, I

CHAPTER FIFTY

love making you feel good, so jot that down." A smile spreads across his lips as he continues, "I've never pushed that topic because I'm honestly fine if you don't want to, but more than anything my goal has been to make *you* feel valued."

"I do feel valued."

"I know, because I am an absolute catch. But Kat?"

"Yeah?"

Tanner's warm breath tickles my ear. "I've fantasized about your lips wrapped around my cock countless times," he whispers.

I can sense the pulsing wetness between my thighs. The anticipation builds, my spine turning to silk as every inch of my body yearns to make his fantasy a reality.

Without a second thought, I boldly reach down and gently cup him through his now-snug jeans. His breath catches, his every muscle tensing, his arousal evident. The fabric strains against the growing bulge as I trace my fingers over it, eliciting a low groan from him.

My hands tremble with excitement as I grab onto his muscular waist, my fingers digging into the rough denim waistband of his jeans. The metal button gives way easily under my touch, and I eagerly unzip his fly before dropping to my knees on the chilly kitchen floor. I pull down his jeans to reveal his bare legs, then look up at him. He towers above me, his eyes filled with desire.

As I slowly peel off his snug-fitting boxer briefs, my body tangles with a mix of arousal and fear. The memory of the initial sting of his impressive size returns, and the thought of him sliding effortlessly down the back of my throat has me swaying on my knees. Every inch of his exposed skin radiates heat, drawing me closer to taste and explore. The anticipation builds as I gaze up at him, eager to take all of him in and please him in every way possible.

The expression on his face mirrors my intense excitement. With determined resolve, I gather every shred of courage within me and envelop the head of his cock with my lips. The taste of salt lingers on my tongue as I lap at the bead of pre-cum before welcoming him deeper into my mouth. Each movement is met with a gasp or a moan from him, encouraging me to continue. I am overcome with desire and pleasure, completely lost in the sensations coursing through my body.

I've given head before, but never has it felt so intimate. The taste of his skin, the rhythm of his body, and the way he moans drive me to give him nothing but pure ecstasy. With each touch and kiss, I am consumed by an intense craving to please him in any way possible. This moment is more than just physical pleasure, and if this is any indication of what he meant before by being content with my pleasure alone, I get it now.

With a determined grip, I take him deep into my mouth, pressing my lips tightly around him. His moans start deep in his chest and escape through clenched teeth, a sound I've never heard before. It sends a jolt of pleasure through me, and I continue to take him in even further, desperate to hear that sound again.

"Fuck, Kat. If you keep doing that I'm going to—"

Despite his warning, I see it as a challenge and push myself, taking him deep into the back of my throat. The taste of him fills my senses and I involuntarily swallow, causing him to let out a deep, guttural moan. This time, I know it's a sign that he's close to climaxing, and with that knowledge, I become even more determined to make him unravel in my

CHAPTER FIFTY

hands. With an intense focus, I continue to push my limits, determined to bring him to the brink and watch as he gives himself over to pure ecstasy.

"Kat, I'm gonna—" He releases with a guttural moan and his pleasure spills into my eager mouth.

The taste ignites a primal desire inside of me. I have never swallowed before, but with Tanner it feels like the most natural thing in the world. As he pulls out, I meet his gaze and swallow every last drop of his release, feeling a sense of satisfaction wash over me at having pleased him completely.

With a gentle touch, he wipes away a drop of his cum from my bottom lip.

I can't help but beam up at him, completely captivated by the look of pure adoration that fills his face. "Was it everything you dreamed of?"

A chuckle falls past his lips before he says, "You have no fucking idea."

FIFTY-ONE

KAT

ELIJAH
Can we talk?

KAT
About?

What happened on your birthday. I'm really sorry.

Disgust churns in my stomach as Elijah's name blinks on the screen, but I refuse to humor his latest attempt at an apology. I sigh and shove my iPhone back into the front pocket of Tanner's faded gray hoodie I'm wearing.

I'm done with the toxic Elijah situation—the constant cycle of hurt and shallow forgiveness. I'm grateful for finally coming to my senses. He always expects me to forgive him, but I know deep down he hasn't changed. It's just about appeasing his guilty conscience. He doesn't care about truly making things right with me; he just wants the comfort of knowing I forgave him, even if it isn't sincere.

CHAPTER FIFTY-ONE

I used to constantly think about him, every word he said and every gesture he made. But now, sitting at this table crowded with laptops and textbooks, surrounded by my close friends, the memory of Elijah Hanas feels distant and unimportant. It's been six weeks since he unleashed his cruel words on me during my birthday party in this very kitchen, but as I look around at the people who truly matter in my life, he dwindles into insignificance.

A year ago, I would have said he was everything. But not anymore.

"Hey, everything okay?" Jenna's concerned voice breaks through my thoughts as she leans in to get a better look at my phone, still glowing brightly beneath the fabric of my hoodie.

I sigh and pull the phone out, showing her the text messages.

Her brows shoot up. "Big yikes," she says as she reads the short text thread, noticing the long string of unanswered apologies above it. "Does Tanner know?"

"That Elijah has reached out? Yeah, he knows. He trusts me to handle it."

It's true—Tanner trusts me—but he's also offered on more than one occasion to handle it himself. As much as I appreciate his eagerness to defend me, causing more issues between Tanner and one of his fraternity brothers isn't something I want, especially with only one semester left until Elijah is out of our hair for good.

"Want me to punch him in the face?" Jenna jokes. At least...I think she's joking.

Oh my God, I hope she's joking.

"Believe it or not, I would actually prefer you not do that," I laugh.

She shrugs. "If you insist, but just remember...I'd do it with very little convincing."

Jenna insists that she and Marcus are fine, but it's hard to ignore the tension between them whenever Elijah's name comes up in conversation.

"Hey Jen, did you order that pizza?" Brendan asks as he rubs his temples, staring down at a textbook that I'm only about fifty percent sure is some kind of high-level calculus.

"Yeah, it should be here any minute," she says, checking her phone. "Actually, they're here."

The doorbell rings right on cue, causing Brendan to jump out of his seat and dart toward the front door. He returns with a stack of three large pizza boxes precariously balanced in his arms, the delicious scent of melted cheese and warm dough filling the air. He starts to eagerly tear open each box until finally reaching the bottom of the stack, where the coveted extra-pepperoni pie awaits.

Tanner joins him, carrying a bundle of paper plates. He grabs two and fills one with three slices of pizza—one of each flavor. On the other plate, he carefully places a single slice covered with pepperoni and pineapple, a small ramekin of ranch dressing on the side. My heart swells with warmth as he hands me the smaller portion and affectionately kisses the top of my head.

I catch Jenna's gaze fixed on me. Her forehead is slightly creased and her lips are pursed, making her expression nearly impossible to read.

"What?" I ask.

Her lips twitch, fighting back a smile as she rolls her eyes. "Ugh, you two are disgustingly cute." She groans playfully.

"Well, get used to it."

CHAPTER FIFTY-ONE

"Oh, I plan to."

FIFTY-TWO

TANNER

Kat fidgets in her seat, her voice laced with impatience. "Seriously, where are we going?"

I suppress a smile as I reply, "You'll see when we get there."

It's only the second time in the past six minutes since we left her mother's house that she's asked about our destination. As we drive on, I watch her out of the corner of my eye, growing more restless with each passing second.

After the snafu of her outerwear situation on Thanksgiving, I warned her before we left for winter break that she would need to bring a coat. She gave me a long lecture about how she is not a child and how she is fully aware that she should bring a coat home for winter break, only to tell me when we were twenty minutes from home that she did indeed forget her coat and we had to stop at Old Navy and buy her a new one.

Either way, at least she's warm.

As we approach the grand and vibrant gates of the

CHAPTER FIFTY-TWO

Columbus Zoo, my heart races with anticipation. I watch as Kat's face transforms into one of pure joy, her eyes widening in childlike wonder as she takes in the first of many extravagant Christmas light displays that decorate the front of the park. The air is filled with an electric buzz, as if every twinkling bulb holds its own special magic waiting to be discovered. I feel like a child again, caught up in the magic of the holiday season.

Her delicate fingertips drum against the warmth of my palm, nestled within the safety of my gloved hand. Despite the cold, she stubbornly refuses to fasten the top of her mittens, leaving her fingertips exposed to the crisp air.

"It ruins the look," she says when I remind her that her mittens have that additional pocket of fabric for a reason.

I chuckle. "Whatever you say, sweetheart."

Despite an irritatingly disengaged professor, I managed to get through finals without having a nervous breakdown. It's hard to consider it a true success when the person grading your work is only there because of tenure, completely disconnected from the real world. But I somehow managed to get an eighty-seven in his class, so I'm more than happy to leave Professor Stanton in the past and look forward to graduation in only a few short months.

We approach the penguin exhibit, our breaths turning into small clouds in the crisp winter air. I can't help but feel a rush of excitement as we pass other exhibits with animals huddling indoors for the season. But we lucked out—the penguins are still here, waddling around and sliding on the ice. The zoo is embellished with beautiful Christmas lights, but nothing compares to watching these incredible creatures in their natural habitats. I could spend hours here, mesmerized by their antics and playful interactions.

"That one kind of looks like the one you drew in your sketchbook." Kat points toward a small penguin near the back of the enclosure, a bit more isolated than the rest of the animals.

"They all pretty much look like that drawing."

Kat has spent an exorbitant amount of time recently going through my old sketchbooks, thanks to my mother, who so kindly showed her some of my older ones from middle school when Kat was over for Thanksgiving.

Thanks, Mom.

"Yeah, but that one has the same black spot on his belly."

"Well, yeah, it is him. Didn't you know? I talk to penguins." I wink, causing her to smack me in the arm.

As snowflakes start to fall, I wrap my fingers tighter around Kat's icy hand and we stand side by side, entranced by the wildlife as a flurry of activity unfolds before our eyes. The black and white birds move in unison, their feathers glistening in the cold winter air. With a whoosh and a splash, they dive into the icy water, their streamlined bodies disappearing beneath the surface before gracefully emerging.

Kat's chin rests softly on my arm as she gazes up at me with her stunning piercing blue eyes. Her lips curl into a small smile as she mumbles, "Thanks for this."

I can't help but grin back down at her and ask, "For what?"

"All of this," Kat says, flailing her free hand around.

"Believe it or not, sweetheart, *despite the rumors*, I did *not* build the Columbus Zoo."

She swats my arm again, but her smile doesn't leave her lips. "Be serious for a second."

CHAPTER FIFTY-TWO

"It's honestly nothing."

She lets out a sigh, her shoulders rising and falling in a familiar gesture that always tugs at my heart. I catch a whiff of vanilla from her freshly washed hair as a gust of wind rushes by us. My grip tightens on her hand, feeling the chill of her skin against mine despite my thick gloves. I guide her toward the entrance of the outdoor elephant exhibit, trying to draw her attention away from whatever thoughts just crossed her mind.

My hands tremble against the blistering cold as I reach for her other hand, gently pulling both into my grasp. I tilt her chin up, softly coaxing her to meet my gaze.

"What?" she laughs, clearly shrugging off the moment.

"You don't have to thank me for the bare minimum, Kat."

"I wasn't." She looks around she clears her throat before her eyes land on mine again. "You didn't have to spend tonight with me—we literally *just* got home for winter break and you haven't seen your parents in weeks."

"Taking you to the zoo lights tonight was my mom's idea."

"Still." Kat's shoulders rise and fall in a dismissive shrug, her attempt to downplay her anxiety. But I can see right through her facade and want no part in allowing it to plague her for a moment longer.

"Prioritizing you will *never* be an inconvenience for me. I completely get what got you thinking that way, but believe me when I say that will *never* be me. There is nothing that matters more to me than spending time with you. I've gotten to spend twenty-two years with my family—they're fine with waiting until tomorrow."

"But—"

"Sweetheart. I love you; my family loves you. Me spending

time with you tonight is not an inconvenience. Okay? Say it, please. *Spending time with you is never an inconvenience.*"

"Spending time with me is never an inconvenience."

"Good girl," I sigh as I press my lips to her forehead, which is almost as frosty as her chilled hands. "Now, let's go see the giraffes, then get some cocoa."

Kat's lips curve upward into a smile as I pull her down the walkway toward the giraffe enclosure. "They're not even outside."

"They still exist in winter, you know," I respond, knocking on the cold metal door marked *"Employees Only."* My knuckles sting as I tap three times.

Suddenly, my cousin Aaron opens the door and greets me with an irritated scowl. "You have ten minutes—after that, you need to get out. I'll get fired if they find you in here."

"Did you say fifteen?"

"Ten." He is not amused.

"Twenty?"

Aaron's arms tense, crossing over his chest as his eyebrows shoot up in irritation. "Zero?"

"Okay, ten minutes."

He holds the door open with his right hand and gestures for Kat and me to go ahead, then he steps outside, pulling the door closed behind him.

Kat's eyes instantly widen with amazement as she stands just a few feet away from a giraffe. The majestic creature towers over her, separated only by a thin netted barrier.

And I know with certainty: nothing that makes her smile like that will ever be an inconvenience.

Despite the joy on her face, there is something in her expression that gives me pause.

CHAPTER FIFTY-TWO

"Are you nervous about tomorrow?" I ask.

"A little," she mumbles, but she doesn't look at me.

"You don't have to see him; you know that, right? No one would judge you if you left him to die in peace without ever knowing you."

"I want to...for me. I need to know."

I press a kiss to her temple, trying desperately to provide her with a sliver of comfort. "Okay, then we'll go."

FIFTY-THREE

KAT

As I stand on the porch of my father's imposing home, my eyes sweep over the grandeur and opulence before me. Pristine white pillars tower above us, framing the massive front door that looks like it could belong to a palace. The gardens are meticulously landscaped, even in the dead of winter, with perfectly trimmed bushes and vibrant flowers peeking out from under a layer of frost. Parked in the driveway is a sleek, expensive sports car, making me painfully aware of my father's wealth.

I clench my fists until my knuckles turn white, fighting the urge to grab the expensive vase by the door and smash it against the wall. The anger bubbling up in me tastes like bile in my throat, as if I could vomit up all of my resentment. That vase is probably worth more than my entire tuition for this semester.

My anxiety threatens to pull me into a downward spiral, but Tanner's large, calming hand presses gently against the small of my back. The warmth and weight of it anchors me.

CHAPTER FIFTY-THREE

"So, you didn't grow up here?" I ask Patrick, who stands at my other side, seemingly just as anxious as I am.

His voice drips with bitterness and resentment as he replies, "No, he got rid of the house last year. Said it reminded him too much of my mom, so he downsized."

I sense a heaviness in his tone and choose not to probe further—I've got enough baggage when it comes to our father; carrying any of Patrick's would pull me under.

"Oh, I'm sorry to hear that." And I mean it. While I might resent her for what she did to my mom, I know Patrick loved his mom more than anything. Losing the home that she raised him in because his dad just didn't want to look at it anymore is a kind of cruelty that no child should have to endure.

"Thanks." Patrick's hand trembles as he punches the code into the keypad, his fingers leaving smudges on the shiny buttons. Once the door is unlocked, he pushes it slowly, the creak of the hinge reverberating through the crisp, stale air.

None of us actually want to be here, but here we are nonetheless—whether out of obligation or fear is hard to tell.

The excessively opulent house is so quiet it's eerie. It's like being in a museum, surrounded by gaudy wealth and excessive decor. But there's no sign of life here, no laughter or bustling servants. It's almost unsettling how empty this place feels. Maybe this is what it means to be rich—living in a huge, empty house that's more a status symbol than a home. Or maybe it's all just for show, like something you'd see in a movie. Either way, I can't shake the creepy feeling washing over me.

The floorboards creak under our weight. It's as if the house is holding its breath, waiting for us to break the bitter silence.

THE VERY FIRST NIGHT

As we cautiously tread deeper into the silent house, a faint chatter fills the air—the sound of a television tuned to the news, emanating from the bedroom at the end of the hallway. The contrast between this solitary source of noise and the rest of the desolate house only adds to the unsettling atmosphere.

A sudden, harsh cough echoes out into the hallway, breaking the tension and catching Patrick's attention. He clears his throat before rapping his knuckles against the partially open door, Tanner and I hanging back in the hall.

Tanner's hand is warm and comforting, resting gently on the small of my back, the only grounding force preventing me from bolting out of this house rather than going into that bedroom.

I thought I was okay with this—I really thought that, with everything that's happened, maybe I was stronger than I thought when it came to my father. But as his voice carries through the air, giving Patrick a cold "Hello" before demanding he grab him more tea from the kitchen, I find myself frozen.

Through the crack in the door, I watch Patrick grab the mug from our father. "There's someone here to see you," he says, his voice shaking.

Typically, knowing someone has come to visit you when you're gravely ill would be a source of comfort, but I've started to realize that my dad may be incapable of that, because that would require a soul.

Our father's expression turns cold and I can feel my stomach drop. "Who?" The bite in the single word causes me to tense.

Tanner pulls me to him, either to provide me comfort or by sheer instinct—I welcome it either way.

CHAPTER FIFTY-THREE

With a pause, Patrick forces my name out of his mouth. "It's Kat."

Silence falls and I find myself questioning if he even heard him, but that would be a much more welcome turn of events than the words that come tumbling out of his mouth.

Cutting through the silence, our father speaks, and his words are like a punch in the gut. "Why would that pitiful girl be here?" His tone is harsh, his eyes filled with disgust as they land on me through the gap in the door.

My heart sinks, and I feel hot tears threaten to escape my eyes.

He turns toward Patrick. "I'm not taking visitors today."

Tanner clenches his jaw and mutters a faint curse under his breath. Without warning, he storms past me and barges into my father's bedroom. He plants himself in front of the TV, blocking my father's view of the news. I can see the tension radiating off Tanner as he faces my father's cold expression, their eyes locking in a silent battle.

Tanner's face twists with anger, his knuckles turning white as he fists his hands tightly at his sides. "Seriously? What the hell is wrong with you?" He inches closer to my father, jutting out a finger in his direction. "Your daughter—who frankly is way better than me for even being willing to see you—comes to visit your sorry ass and that's what you fucking say?" His words are sharp and filled with venom as they fly from his mouth.

My chest heaves with each rapid beat of my heart, the sound filling my ears and drowning out all other noise. I stand rooted to the spot, unable to move as adrenaline courses through me.

My father's lips curl into a cold, threatening snarl as he

narrows his eyes at my boyfriend. He leans in close, speaking with no regard for my presence. "I never had a daughter," he spits, the malice in his tone sending chills down my spine.

When Tanner turns to my brother, who is standing off to the side looking utterly terrified with the mug cradled between his hands for support, his tone shifts from anger to mocking amusement. "Oh, has his memory gone to shit because he's sick?" He turns back to the man who gave me life and says, "Or is he just a fucking degenerate piece of garbage who can't follow through on his commitments?"

My father's face transforms into a mask of fury, his knuckles turning white as he grips the armrests of his chair. He stands up and takes a few unsteady steps toward Tanner, his words slurring from both anger and, I realize, alcohol. "How dare you come in here and lecture me on commitments!" he roars, spittle flying from his mouth.

I rush into the bedroom, my hands shaking with fear and anger. I try to find my voice as I say, "Stop." My eyes dart between the man in front of me and the family photos on the wall behind him—himself, Patrick, and the woman I assume to be Patrick's mother posed against a stark backdrop. He may look like me, his eyes a mirror image of my own, but there is no love or familiarity in them. They belong to a stranger, not my dad.

My heart races as our eyes lock. His expression flashes with a whirlwind of emotions, like a movie reel playing on fast-forward. I see shock, anger, and sadness flit across his face, but there's no hint of regret in his piercing gaze. His jaw tightens and his brow furrows as if trying to make sense of my sudden appearance. "Katarina," he hisses.

"Actually, it's just *Kat*," I grit out through clenched teeth.

CHAPTER FIFTY-THREE

Katarina was his mother's name—or at least that's what my mom told me—and I've spent more of my life than I care to admit trying and failing to make it my own.

His face twists in disgust, his lips curling and eyebrows furrowing. "Ungrateful bitch, just like your mother."

Without even lifting my gaze, I instinctively thrust my arm out to block Tanner's path as he lunges toward my father. He looks at me with concern and love in his eyes, but I know this is something I have to face alone.

My heart pounds in my chest as I steel myself for the conversation that needs to be had.

"What exactly should I be grateful for? You've never done anything."

"I've fulfilled my obligations; I never missed a single child support check."

That is what he considers to be fulfilling his obligations?

As I glare at the man who left me and my mother behind, I can't help but feel a surge of anger. My mother warned me about him in her own way—telling me that we needed to make it on our own without any of his support—but now, as I face down my pathetic excuse for a father, I know what it really was: fear. She never wanted me to hate him; she only wanted to shield me from his wrath, and now I see why. He may share my last name, but there's no denying that we are two completely different people. The thought of our shared blood sickens me.

"I'd hardly call sending a check for half the value of our electric bill every month fulfilling your obligations," I snarl, blatant disgust coating my words.

His voice drips with arrogance as he says, "You may not know much about me, but Patrick here can attest that I never make a bad investment. So why would I send more money when, to be frank, you simply weren't worth it?"

I've spent a large portion of my life believing just that—believing everything he presumably thought about me was right and that I just had to try harder to make my father love me. Send more letters, get better grades, accomplish more... then maybe, just *maybe* he'd see my value.

Now I realize that his approval, his love, has never mattered. All this time, I've been chasing after someone who doesn't deserve my love or attention, and with that realization I finally feel free.

He continues without delay, his snarling voice causing my skin to crawl. "But back then, when you got someone pregnant, you were expected to marry them, so I did. I never loved your mother, but I did the honorable thing anyway and I married her. We'd been casually seeing one another and the bitch trapped me."

It takes everything in me not to retort and say that it takes two to conceive a child and that he was just as responsible as she was, but I refrain, wanting to hear the rest of his tangled web.

"Patrick's mother and I were on a break at the time, but your mother managed to get her jagged little nails in me. I refused to allow her selfishness to stop me from having a family."

"You *had* a family." My voice comes out colder than I've ever heard it.

"You and your mother were never my family. You were an unfortunate result of a horrible mistake. Luckily, Christina forgave me."

Suddenly, so much about him makes sense. Every ignored

CHAPTER FIFTY-THREE

letter, every changed phone number, every effort gone unanswered—it all makes sense now.

Patrick Marritt Sr. is a horrible person.

As I stare up at him, my throat tightens and my stomach churns with anger, but I take a deep breath and force myself to speak. "Okay," I say, my voice trembling with a mixture of sadness and anger.

His ice-blue eyes are as cold as ever, reminding me this is the right choice.

I don't bother to tell him goodbye; I don't force myself to maintain composure long enough to wish him well. I couldn't care less if not caring that he's battling cancer makes me a horrible person.

So, with the last shred of dignity I have left, I hold my head high and walk out.

I'm proud to say that, for the first time in my life, I don't look back.

FIFTY-FOUR

KAT

Janet sits across from me in her cozy office, scribbling notes on her yellow legal pad. It has been a while since our last in-person therapy session, and I am relieved to be back in this familiar space where I can feel seen.

I just finished telling her about seeing my dad yesterday: everything he said and ultimately how I handled it.

"That must be incredibly difficult for you," Janet says gently, her eyes filled with empathy.

I let out a shaky sigh and rub my arms, trying to force away the lingering emotions from seeing my father. It was necessary to face him after years of silence, even though it felt like an emotional nightmare. I've accepted who Patrick Marritt Sr. is, but my heart still struggles to come to terms with it. Last night, I laid in bed, tears streaming down my face as I tried to find solace in sleep.

With a nod, I force a tight-lipped smile. My hand trembles as I grab a tissue and dab at my teary eyes. "It was tough, but necessary," I manage to say, my voice quivering with emotion.

CHAPTER FIFTY-FOUR

"It was brave, Kat. Being hurt by it doesn't make you less brave for facing him."

"I just...I spent over twenty years chasing the love of a father who hates me. I feel stupid," I confess.

"You're not stupid. You have an immense capacity to love others—don't allow your father's inability to see the worth in that to diminish something that makes you so special."

"Well, I'm two for two on loving people who don't love me back, so it's not exactly easy to look at it from a different point of view." I cross my arms over my chest as I look at a framed photo of a cat in needlepoint on the wall behind her, desperately searching for a distraction.

"You're not two for two, though. Yes, your father and Elijah were very hard lessons for you, but—Kat?"

"Hm?"

"Tanner loves you back, and that's not nothing. It's not everything; it can't be everything. But he seems like someone who wants to help you be the best you, and that's not nothing."

"You're right." I bite down on the inside of my cheek.

"Have you had a chance to talk to your mom about what happened yesterday?"

I've been struggling to find the right words to discuss it with her, but ultimately I feel a sense of guilt. For years, I harbored resentment toward my mom for not trying harder with my dad, for not even pushing him to provide more child support. I never could grasp why she would rather work seventy hours a week at the restaurant, missing recitals, parties, and holidays, all to do it on her own. However, now that I've actually met the man, I can understand why she chose to distance herself from him.

"No, not yet."

FIFTY-FIVE

KAT

Christmas morning as a kid was always my favorite day. What kid *doesn't* love Christmas? But more than anything, it was because it was the one day a year that Pip's was closed and the only day I could guarantee my mom wouldn't end up having to pick up a shift. It was always my favorite day.

As I enter the kitchen, the familiar scent of sizzling bacon and bubbling cheese fills my nostrils. My mom stands at the counter with her favorite apron tied around her waist, delicately cracking eggs into a bowl. She turns to smile at me, and I can't help but feel a lump form in my throat as I think about how she makes this egg bake every year without fail—just for me.

"Do you want some coffee?" She steps back from the counter and opens the cabinet, revealing a mismatched collection of mugs and grabbing one with a cartoon cat on it. She pours piping hot coffee, adding a strong splash of hazelnut creamer and a spoonful of sugar before handing it to me without waiting for an answer.

CHAPTER FIFTY-FIVE

I gratefully grasp the hot cup, my fingers tingling with warmth. Setting it on the kitchen counter, I pull her into a warm embrace, feeling her arms wrap tightly around me.

She chuckles in surprise. "What's this for?" she asks.

A small sigh escapes my lips and I'm unable to hold back the tears any longer.

She tilts her head back and looks at me. "What's wrong?" she asks, her voice soft with worry.

"Thank you," I reply shakily. "For being the one who stayed."

Concern morphs to relief as she steps back and squeezes my arm. "Oh, honey, you don't have to thank me for that. I'm your mom; that's what moms do."

"I met Dad," I blurt.

She raises her brows before she walks over and shuts off the burner. "When?"

"A few days ago. Um, Patrick—" She looks at me, confused. "Patrick is his son. He contacted me a few months ago and…"

And so I tell her all of it—I tell her how he found one of my old letters; how he sent me one in return and how at first I thought it was from my dad; how we've seen each other a few times and how I think we could really have a relationship. I tell her that Christina died and my dad has cancer, but I choose to leave out the awful things he said about her.

I know my mom, and the warped perception he has of her could not be further from reality.

"How bad is it?" she asks when I'm done.

"The cancer? I mean, I don't know a ton of details, but I can't imagine Patrick would have asked me to see him if it was good."

She nods as she stares down at the counter, wiping away grime that isn't there. "Are you okay?"

How is it, that amidst everything this man has put her through, she still manages to stay so tight-lipped about it? How can she be so focused on me being okay about the potential death of a man like that?

"He's horrible, Mom." My voice cracks, but I hold my tears at bay—I've cried far too much over the past few days to ruin Christmas by doing it again. "Why did you never tell me?"

She pauses for a moment before her eyes meet mine, a glassy sheen coating them. "A girl should think highly of her father, or at the very least she shouldn't hate him. He's your dad and I never wanted to give you reasons to hate him. Pat is a complicated man and, yes, at times cruel. But...he gave me you."

"I love you, Mom."

My mom reaches for a kitchen towel and dabs away the residual moisture on her waterline. With a wide grin, she playfully nudges me and says, "I love you too, sweetie. Now help me get this damn egg bake in the oven."

As we finish savoring every last bite of the delectable egg bake, my mom and I leisurely make our way to the living room, where a beautiful Christmas tree stands tall and proud, its branches decorated with an eclectic mix of ornaments. Each one holds a special memory, a story to be told over and over again. My eyes light up as I spot the homemade ones I crafted as a child, still proudly displayed on the tree. The twinkling lights and glittering baubles reflect the joy and warmth of the holiday season, filling the room with a sense of nostalgia.

"I can't believe you kept that one—it looks like a turd." I

CHAPTER FIFTY-FIVE

laugh, pointing to one of the homemade ones, a stack of popsicle sticks haphazardly glued together and painted dark brown.

"It's a sled!" she argues.

"It looks like an actual piece of poop."

Her head cocks to the side, her eyes fixated on the old ornament. After studying it for a moment, she turns her attention back to the neatly wrapped presents beneath the tree. With a grin on her face, she plucks a square box from the pile and marches toward me with purpose. "You're right, it does kind of look like a turd." She says it so matter-of-factly as she drops the box into my lap.

I gesture to the brightly wrapped Christmas gift that sits near her usual spot in our cramped living room. "That one is yours."

I tug my legs up onto the couch, crossing them beneath me. I begin to pick at the corner of the Santa wrapping paper, waiting for my mom to eagerly tear into her own gift before I even think about unwrapping mine.

My mom grips the edges of the wrapping paper with determination, her hands steady as she pulls it apart. The small, elongated box is wrapped in a deep burgundy velvet and I can see the jewelry store's metallic gold logo on the side. She sets it down carefully on the coffee table.

"Katarina," she reprimands softly.

"Go ahead, open it," I urge, my excitement bubbling over. I had insisted on making a stop at the jewelry store in town after seeing my dad the other day. Now, seeing the look on her face, I know it was worth it.

Despite the way her hands tremble and her eyes dart back and forth between the box and me, she reaches out to grab it.

THE VERY FIRST NIGHT

With a sharp tug, the lid flies open. A hushed gasp escapes her lips as she lifts out a dainty silver locket. Inside, there is a photo of her holding me as a baby on one side and another from my high school graduation on the other.

Tears well up in her eyes as she gazes down at the sentimental treasure. "It's perfect," she whispers, not prying her eyes away from her newest prized possession until finally she looks at me. "Now open yours."

Excitement pulses through me as I eagerly tear at the wrapping paper, revealing a white box with a glossy image of a camera lens on the side. My heart flutters as I read the familiar letters: EF 70-200mm f/2.8. It's the lens I've been looking at for months, which I was planning to buy for myself as a graduation present.

A wave of guilt washes over me as I realize how much money my mom must have spent on this gift. "Mom, this is too much," I say, gently setting the lens down on the table. "You should take it back."

But she just smiles and shakes her head, insisting that she wanted to get me something special this year since I graduate in the spring.

Tears prick at the corners of my eyes as I realize how much thought and love went into this present. Unable to contain my emotions any longer, I stand up and wrap my arms tightly around her, whispering "Thank you" in her ear.

FIFTY-SIX

KAT

As much as I long to cling to my college years, spring semester flies by faster than I could have imagined. After returning from winter break, every week was packed with exams, projects, and social events. And now, standing in a hotel room forty-five minutes away from campus, just three weeks away from graduation, my throat tightens with an overwhelming sense of nostalgia and fear for the future.

When Tanner first mentioned the formal for his fraternity last month, I imagined a dingy, run-of-the-mill frat house. But as we step inside the beautiful hotel in Cleveland, I'm in awe. A grand chandelier hangs over the entryway, casting a golden glow on the marble floors. The walls are decorated with elegant paintings, and mahogany desks line the left side of the room. As I walk across the sparkling tiles, I can't help but wonder if they're made of actual glitter.

Tanner strides up to the front desk, introducing himself and handing over his ID and credit card. The receptionist hands him a room key. As we make our way to our designated room, I can sense the potential for chaos brewing in the air.

Tanner reaches for the door, but before he can insert his keycard, Elijah comes into view with a petite blonde on his arm, heading toward the room next to ours. My heart sinks as I realize the cosmic joke in store for us: sharing a wall with Elijah Hanas.

"I didn't expect it to be this...fancy," I laugh as I set down my bag inside the door and Tanner closes the door behind him.

"Yeah, well, we have Governor Hanas to thank for that," Tanner replies with a wince, clearly uncomfortable with the situation. He explains how Elijah's father donated money specifically for this event, wanting to make his son's senior year unforgettable.

"Of course he did," I mumble as I move my suitcase to the stand in the corner of the room before sifting through its contents.

Tanner sits on the edge of his bed, already half-dressed and casually sipping a beer. He said we have an hour and a half to get ready before we need to head downstairs, and I'd bet money he only needs ten minutes of that.

After over an hour of primping, I emerge from the bathroom in a cloud of hairspray. My freshly ironed curls cascade down my back, and my makeup is elegant yet understated, thanks to countless YouTube tutorials Jenna has been sending me for the past couple weeks. I step into the room in my bra and underwear in pursuit of my off-the-shoulder cobalt cocktail dress, which I bought especially for this event last week.

CHAPTER FIFTY-SIX

"Sweetheart." Tanner's voice is husky and inviting and I know without looking at him what he's insinuating.

I playfully dodge his reaching hands as I dart forward to grab the dress from on top of my suitcase and pull it on. I know we have to hurry if we want to make it downstairs on time. But damn, that bed looks awfully tempting as I pass him sitting on it.

He takes the hint in stride, keeping his attention on the television and the cold beer in his hand, but I don't miss the way his eyes keep drifting over to me as I pull the stretchy fabric over my frame. Once it's on and I'm almost ready, I sit down on the bed next to him to fasten my heels.

"Let me," he says and sets his beer on the bedside table to kneel in front of me, his button-down shirt open to reveal his toned chest peeking out from the neckline of his undershirt. His eyes scan my body appreciatively before he reaches for my black stiletto heel, running his fingers along the delicate ankle strap. I can feel the heat of his breath against my skin as he leans closer and firmly grasps my ankle in his hand.

"Is this a foot thing?" I crinkle my nose.

A chuckle rolls past his lips before he presses a gentle kiss to my inner ankle, causing goosebumps to erupt over my entire body. "No, it's a you thing."

It takes him no time to fasten the straps around both of my ankles, but he holds my foot in his hand as his eyes meet mine in earnest.

I tense under his scrutiny, despite his intentions never having been nefarious. "What?" I ask.

"I—" He clears his throat, clearly searching for the right words to convey his thoughts. "If you don't want to go down there, be around him, I would understand. We can hang out

THE VERY FIRST NIGHT

here and meet up with our friends in Marcus and Jenna's room later."

While the prospect of doing that sounds preferable to dealing with Elijah, this is Tanner's senior year. I might not understand Greek life, not outside of what I've seen over the past two years, but I know that this is a night he'll never get back if I take him up on his offer.

"I love you for that, but no. We should go—I want to go. Seeing Elijah doesn't matter. It hasn't mattered for a while."

My fingers reach up to brush a stray chestnut-colored strand of hair off Tanner's forehead, and he releases a small sigh of relief. I can see the worry lines on his face relax.

"If you're sure—"

"I'm sure." I smile down at him in an attempt to give him a shred of the comfort he's given me over the past couple years.

With a gentle hand on my calf, he leans forward and presses three soft kisses along my inner thigh, sending shivers down my spine. Then he stops, causing me to groan in frustration, and releases his hold on my leg. He stands up, discreetly adjusting the slight bulge growing in his dress slacks.

"Mean," I huff out.

"Hey, you're the one who doesn't want to stay in the room. Besides, you've been walking around in your underwear for the past twenty minutes—you're lucky I didn't go higher."

"'Lucky' isn't the word I'd use."

Tanner just laughs as he pulls me to my feet and encourages me toward the door.

Once we're downstairs, all my anxiety melts away as Jenna comes barreling toward me. Despite living together, we haven't seen each other much over the last week due to

CHAPTER FIFTY-SIX

Marcus's parents being in town and taking up most of Jenna's time. The two seem to be getting very serious and, while I once might have worried about losing my best friend, I'm confident now in the fact that that won't happen.

"Oh my God, you look amazing!" Jenna squeals as she steps back to admire my outfit, the very one she helped me pick out.

"Thanks," I laugh. "So do you!"

"I know!" she says with confidence, flipping her long golden curls over her shoulder before looping her arm through mine and pushing us into the ballroom.

The ballroom is decorated with mismatched streamers and balloons, a clear indication that the planning committee consisted of inexperienced fraternity brothers. Despite their efforts, the space still lacks the elegance and grandeur of other events I've attended, but it's a steep ask to compare a fraternity formal to any of the weddings I've photographed. Their effort is clear, even if it doesn't quite land in the way they were hoping.

"Is your skin crawling?" I laugh as I turn to Jenna. As an interior design major, she is rather meticulous with design of any sort, so the underwhelming decorations must be causing her distress.

"Very much so. I tried to help, but they insisted." She gives a quick shrug, her arm brushing against mine as she pulls me toward the bar.

I immediately notice Tanner, a drink in hand, leaning against the counter. We had discussed my decision to cut back on drinking and what that meant for this formal at length. Tonight, I've made the choice to indulge a bit, but not too much—no tequila shots or standing on bars for me.

However, a few glasses of champagne are more than welcome.

I eagerly grab the flute of bubbly from the bartender's hand and tug on Tanner's sleeve, giddy with excitement to get the night moving. We weave through the throngs of people toward the center of the ballroom, where the music beckons us to dance.

His deep laugh rumbles as he presses his hand against my lower back, guiding me closer to him. "What's got you so excited all of a sudden?" His other hand holds the frosted beer bottle, and the confident way he balances it shows years of partying and dancing at college parties.

To be honest, I feel relieved. I didn't think I would be so indifferent toward Elijah's presence tonight, and the fact that I can finally say that he no longer holds a place in my heart is freeing. I am truly in love with Tanner, but the lingering fear in the back of my mind over how things ended with my ex has been gnawing at me, making me worry that I will never fully move on from it.

"Can't I just be happy to be here with you?"

"Of course you can." Tanner's warm breath tickles my cheek as he bends down to kiss me, his hand gently cupping the back of my neck.

A rush of tingles spreads through my body as I lean in and savor the softness of his lips against mine. With a blissful sigh, I melt into him, feeling completely at ease as we sway to the music.

After a few hours, I'm very much feeling the effects of the alcohol. Tanner seems to notice and asks, "Do you need to get some air?"

"No, I'm good. I just need to use the restroom." I've been

CHAPTER FIFTY-SIX

fighting the urge to break the seal all night and it's finally caught up with me.

"Sounds good, sweetheart. I'll be right here," he says, backing toward a group of brothers, and I step off the dance floor.

As I emerge from the cramped bathroom stall, my nose is assaulted by the cloying scent of artificial roses and harsh chemicals. Exiting the restroom, I inhale deeply, grateful to be back in the relatively fresh air of the hallway.

"Hey," whispers an unnervingly gentle, familiar voice, causing every hair on my body to stand on end.

I know who it is without even looking, so when I turn and meet Elijah's eyes, I'm instantly filled with dread.

"What?" My voice comes out snippy and short, but I no longer care how he may perceive me.

"C'mon, Kat. It's just me." He stumbles closer, his words slurring and his breath reeking of alcohol.

I look around and notice that we are alone in this empty hallway. My heart rate starts to quicken in my chest as he reaches out for me.

Panic sets in and, while I don't think Elijah would ever cross the line from asshole to predator, it's hard to say with the amount of alcohol he's had. As his fingers wrap around my wrist, pulling me toward him, I find myself scanning the area. His grip tightens as I try to pull away.

"Elijah, that hurts," I grit out through my teeth, trying to pull my arm free.

"You're being dramatic as usual; I'm barely touching you."

"Please, let go of me. You're drunk and—"

"You used to love the way I'd touch you when we were

drunk," he says with an uneven cadence. "The way I'd make you come with your inhibitions down—you used to love it."

I struggle against his grasp, to no avail. "Well, I don't anymore. Let me go," I snarl, but it falls on deaf ears. Reasoning with Elijah sober is one thing, but when drunk, he's impossible to sway.

He says calmly, "Not until you hear me out."

Brendan's voice booms from the doorway of the ballroom, and I feel a surge of relief. His tall frame fills the hallway as he glares at Elijah. Approaching us, his presence is both comforting and intimidating. "Is everything all right out here, Kat?" he asks sternly.

"She's fine. Besides, this doesn't concern you, Wallace." Elijah doesn't pull his gaze away from me as he talks to Brendan.

"Actually, it does." Brendan wraps his fingers around Elijah's hand and squeezes tightly, causing him to release his grasp on my wrist with a wince. "You see, this is my best friend's girl, and you appear to have been touching her without her consent."

Elijah scoffs. "You're just as bad as she is. I was just trying to talk to her."

"Well," Brendan sighs, "looks like you talked. She doesn't care. So I will be taking Kat back into the ballroom now."

Elijah clenches his jaw, his dark eyes flashing with anger before he lets out a string of curses under his breath and storms off to the men's restroom.

Brendan turns to me, gently takes my hand, and drapes it over his arm, leading me away from the tense situation. Back in the ballroom, I let out a relieved sigh as he squeezes my hand and asks, "Are you okay?"

CHAPTER FIFTY-SIX

"Yeah, I'm fine."

FIFTY-SEVEN

KAT

Tanner's jaw tightens and his shoulders tense as he inserts the key card into our hotel room door. I can feel irritation radiating off of him, stemming from his conversation with Brendan about the incident. I had meant to discuss it with Tanner in private, but unfortunately Brendan spilled the beans as soon as we saw Tanner in the ballroom. Knowing how easily Tanner gets heated when it comes to Elijah, I quickly guided him out of the ballroom before he could start a fight with another fraternity brother.

I drop my clutch onto the TV stand in our room, but I wait for Tanner to shut the door before saying anything. Once the door clicks behind him, I let out a sigh.

"I had it handled."

"You shouldn't have to handle it—he shouldn't be cornering you like that." Tanner paces back and forth, undoing the top button of his pressed white dress shirt, revealing the spattering of hair and freckles hidden beneath. He's a bundle

CHAPTER FIFTY-SEVEN

of nervous energy right now and I don't have the slightest idea of how to address it.

I stand in front of Tanner, stopping his pacing, and place my hands on his trembling jaw, forcing him to look into my eyes. "I'm okay," I say firmly, trying to reassure him. When he doesn't seem convinced, I lean in closer and whisper against his lips, "I promise. I'm okay."

His tense body begins to relax, but I can still sense the apprehension in his voice when he speaks. "I could kill him."

"I know, but I'd prefer not to spend the rest of my life with the man I love in prison. Kills the vibe, ya know?" My lips quirk upward, mirrored by a smile finally creeping over his face.

"The rest of your life, huh?" Tanner responds.

I shrink under his intense gaze, my mind instantly racing with regret and self-doubt, wondering if I have ruined everything with my honesty.

Tanner's eyes soften as he notices my inner turmoil, but his smile doesn't fade. "I want that, you know. You, forever."

"Not like, soon. But eventually." I laugh awkwardly. I love him with every fiber of my being, but the nagging fear remains—what if one day he sees through my facade and realizes I'm not the perfect girl he thinks I am?

Tanner laughs. "Kat, I can see your cogs turning. I'm not going to propose any time soon. We're young, but just know...I will, one day."

My heart flutters at his words—at never having heard someone speak about me with such conviction before, never having had someone be so sure about me.

"I love you," I whisper against his lips.

"I love you too," he murmurs. Then, his voice drops to a

low, husky growl as he adds, "Now, take your dress off." He smirks and takes a step back, waiting for me to make the next move.

I've never been the type to enjoy being told what to do, but there is something about Tanner doing it—this man who has spent so much time and effort ensuring I have complete autonomy—that makes me melt under his gaze.

Following his precise directions, I slide my arms out of the delicate straps. The soft blue material clings to my body as I slowly pull it down, savoring the feeling of the fabric against my skin. It pools around my feet, revealing my black strapless bra and matching lacy thong.

"Come to me." His low voice sends shivers down my spine as his gaze travels from the curve of my hips to my exposed collarbone.

I bite my lip and take a few hesitant steps toward him, clad only in lacy undergarments and stiletto heels. The tension between us is palpable as we both feel the heat rising in the room.

I stand in front of him, but he keeps his hands by his sides, leaving me unsure of what to do with my own. In an attempt to break the tension, I tentatively reach out and grab onto his belt buckle, pulling him closer to me. The cold metal presses against my palm as his breath quickens.

"What now?" I whisper, trying and failing to wield control.

"On the bed."

Following his instruction, I slide onto the bed, his eyes locked on me as I crawl over the plush comforter. Every sway of my hips catches his attention, and I can feel his gaze burning into me. My heels clank against the bedframe as I take

CHAPTER FIFTY-SEVEN

my time climbing onto the soft mattress, savoring the anticipation building in my core.

Finally, he approaches, and our eyes meet, causing my heart to race with excitement.

I lay on the bed, propping myself up on my elbows to admire his form. His crisp white shirt is neatly tucked into his tailored pants, but the top two buttons are undone. My eyes follow the line of his body down to the undeniable bulge in his gray slacks. He stands at the foot of the bed, trying to conceal a slight tremble in his hands, biting down on his bottom lip so hard I can see it turn pink. A shiver runs through me, my cheeks flushing with heat under his intense scrutiny.

As he rubs the heel of his hand over his straining erection, I can't help but watch, my gaze lingering on every movement. My mouth waters at the sight of him, my heart swelling with love as he gives me an adoring look.

No one has ever looked at me quite the way Tanner does, and I feel immensely grateful for that in this moment. It's as if this connection—the love we share—is for us and no one else in this world.

"Scoot down," Tanner demands.

I obey and scoot down the soft linen comforter until my legs dangle over the edge of the bed.

However, he seems unsatisfied, and with a sharp yelp of surprise from me, he pulls me even further until my butt is perched on the very edge of the mattress. "Much better," he mumbles.

His lips brush against my ankle, sending shivers up my spine. He moves slowly, trailing kisses up toward my knee as I try to steady my breathing. As he releases my leg, I exhale sharply in annoyance, but his deep laughter rumbles against my skin. He looks at me with a mischievous glint in his eye before taking my other leg and repeating the routine, kissing from my ankle to my knee. This time, he continues his advance past my knee, up my thigh, and I clench in anticipation as the corner of his lips graze the soft lace of my panties before he retreats once more.

I glare at him as he pulls away, my hands balled into fists. All I receive in return is a mischievous grin. He knows exactly what he's doing to me and is thoroughly enjoying it. My heart races and my body quivers, longing for him to really touch me. Every fiber of my being yearns for the pleasure I know he is capable of providing. But right now, he's just playing a game, and I can't fully enjoy it because all I want is for him to move a little higher.

Tanner continues his pattern of teasing me, except this time he inches down to kneel at the edge of the bed and pauses at the seam of my lingerie once more. His fingers dance along the edge of the fabric, teasing and tempting me. His warm breath tickles my skin as he leans closer, his nose grazing the damp fabric before pressing a gentle kiss against the lace. With each passing second, I find my anticipation overwhelming me.

With a gentle tug, Tanner pulls the lace of my panties tight against my sensitive skin. His head dips down and his warm tongue glides slowly over the delicate lace that separates him from my throbbing core. The soft friction sends shivers down my spine and I can't help but gasp as he pushes the fabric between my pussy lips. My body tingles with pleasure as he skillfully uses his tongue to trace circles around my clit.

"Tanner, please," I beg him as the ache between my legs

CHAPTER FIFTY-SEVEN

grows unbearable, trembling as I look up at him with pleading eyes.

He hungrily grabs hold of the panel of lace and slides it aside, revealing my wet and aching core. Without hesitation, he dives in with his tongue, lapping at my damp flesh before nipping at my bundle of nerves. My back arches and I moan his name, overwhelming sensations coursing through my body.

Every lap of his tongue against my sensitive skin sends sparks flying. My body tenses as he expertly works me toward climax, and I grip the bedsheets for support.

He surprises me with a sudden thrust of two fingers inside me just as he sucks on my clit with an intensity that drives me wild. Colors explode behind my closed eyelids as I reach the peak of pleasure, completely lost in this moment with him. Despite my efforts to remain quiet, I scream as my orgasm rocks me.

Tanner's lips trail down my inner thigh, pleasure rippling through my body at each touch. My chest rises and falls rapidly as I try to catch my breath.

The moment he stands and begins to move away from the bed, my eyes snap up to meet his.

"Where are you going?"

He pauses halfway through unbuttoning the cuff of his dress shirt, poised to peel it off his skin. "I thought we could take a shower together." He gives me a soft smile before taking off his shirt to reveal a plain white undershirt. "But I can give you some time if you need it."

I glance at the clock and see that it's almost midnight. "No, I want to. Let's do it."

He steps toward the bathroom and every muscle and curve of his body is illuminated by the bathroom light streaming from behind him. He leans against the doorframe, casually crossing his arms over his chest.

My heart skips a beat at the sight of him. As I take in all of his naked glory, I can't help but smile back at him, feeling overwhelmed with desire and love for him. Tanner nods toward the bathroom before disappearing inside, an unspoken invitation.

Without hesitation, I rush into the bathroom, feeling a little ridiculous standing there in nothing but my lingerie and three-inch heels. My feet are throbbing from hours of dancing, and the buzz from earlier has faded away. All I want is to kick off these torturous shoes.

Tanner turns to me and wordlessly lifts me onto the counter, his strong hands working to unbuckle the strap around my ankle.

Letting out a contented sigh, I say, "Thanks."

He remains silent, but his actions speak louder than words. He leans over and carefully places my high heels on the floor, one by one. His warm lips trail down my neck as he expertly unclasps my strapless bra. My body responds to his touch, aching for more, yet this moment feels far more intimate than just sex.

Sweat beads on my palms as I bite my lip, fighting the urge to blurt out the burning question that has consumed me for weeks. But it escapes before I can stop it: "What's going to happen?"

His brows pinch together. "What do you mean?"

My voice shakes as I try to speak. "After grad."

My mind flashes back to two years ago, when Tanner was just a friend, nothing more. Now, as we approach graduation, he's become my best friend and the love of my life. It's overwhelming how much our relationship has changed. I can feel tears welling up in my eyes as I think about what will happen after we both have our degrees in hand. Will we stay together or drift apart? The uncertainty is terrifying, and I can't stop the thoughts from racing through my mind.

"I meant what I said earlier, Kat. I fully intend to spend the rest of my life with you. The good and the bad, all of it."

"But I know what graduation means. Do you have a job lined up? What if it takes you somewhere other than Ohio? What if you end up on the other side of the country? I'm not made for long distance and I would seriously freak ou—"

"Kat," he says, his voice calm and reassuring.

"Hm?"

"I start at Smith and Paterson at the end of July."

His words carry meaning, real meaning, but my brain takes a minute to catch up. "But the Smith and Paterson Group is in Columbus." He chuckles and it registers. "Oh."

"Yeah, *oh*." He laughs as he presses a gentle kiss to my lips. "Wherever you go, I go. You already told me that you plan to stay with your mom, at least for now. So I started looking at jobs near Columbus."

I bite my inner cheek. "Is that what you want, though? What if in a couple of years you resent me for holding you down in Ohio?"

"I always wanted to stay near my parents. I'm not going to say I was dead set on Columbus, but I always planned to stay in Ohio. This is what I want—you are what I want, okay?"

"Okay." My voice cracks, tears pricking at my eyes.

Tanner leans in and gently presses his lips to the stray tear that escapes down my cheek, sending a warm shiver through my body. He gently cradles my face, our eyes lock, and his words flood my senses. "I love you more than anything, and I would do anything to keep you in my life."

I giggle. "Would you eat a bug for me?"

Tanner grins and nods. "I would eat a bug for you."

I raise an eyebrow playfully. "What about swimming with eels?"

He rolls his eyes but nods again. "I would swim with eels for you."

Before I can think of another silly question, Tanner lifts me off the counter and carries me toward the shower. "That's enough interrogation," he says, stepping under the warm water with me still in his arms.

FIFTY-EIGHT

KAT

As I step through the glass doors of the MAC center, familiar sights and sounds surround me. The basketball court is packed to capacity, the stage is set up for graduation, and a banner hangs, proclaiming *"Congratulations Kent State Graduates!"* But today, everything feels different.

I'm dressed in my oversized blue graduation gown. Even Regina, our resident fashion design student known for her impeccable style, looks out of place in the standard polyester robe, yet we all wear it with pride as we embark on this rite of passage together—becoming Kent State University graduates.

Two years ago, I was driven by one thing and one thing only: making things work with Elijah. It didn't matter if my grades suffered, if I disregarded my friends, if I disregarded myself in the process; it was all to make it work with Elijah.

Looking out at the sea of excited faces, I can't believe how foolish I was to have ever thought this moment wasn't as important as a guy.

Amidst all the cheers and applause, my eyes land on my mom. It's a bit shocking that I'm able to spot her in this chaotic crowd, but there she is with her long brown hair pulled up into a neat bun atop her head. Sitting by her side is someone I never thought I'd see her with: my brother Patrick. Despite all the reasons she could resent him, she has formed a genuine connection with him and never once expressed any ill will. It takes immense strength for her to forgive him for being the product of our father's infidelity, but it only solidifies my belief that my mom possesses superhuman levels of grace.

My attention is soon drawn to Tanner's family. A group of four, they are easy to spot—his beaming mother stands by her husband's side, Larry playfully smacking Theo's head for some shenanigans during the ceremony. Their pride and joy light up the room as they wait for Tanner to walk across the stage to receive his degree.

Suddenly, Marcus approaches the microphone, ready to give his salutatorian speech. I had no idea he had officially achieved this honor until now. Most of our spring semester was spent listening to him go on and on about some girl in the business college who was only .001% ahead of him for the honored title.

"Ladies and gentlemen, esteemed faculty, proud parents, and my fellow graduates," Marcus begins, his hands visibly shaking as he holds his notes between his fingers. "As we stand on the cusp of this momentous occasion, I can't help but reflect on the journey that has led us here. Our time in college has been marked by countless trials and tribulations, moments of doubt, and challenges that seemed insurmountable. Yet, through it all, we persevered."

CHAPTER FIFTY-EIGHT

Despite his clear anxiety, Marcus is a natural-born public speaker, his words eloquent and poised as he addresses the room filled to the brim. He continues, "But amidst the chaos and uncertainty, there has been one constant source of support and strength: our friends. The bonds we've formed during our time in college have been a guiding light, illuminating our path and giving us the courage to press on, even when the road seemed darkest. Together, we've laughed in the face of adversity, shared in each other's triumphs, and lifted each other up when we stumbled and fell. We've formed friendships that will last a lifetime, bonds that transcend the boundaries of time and distance."

Tanner swivels around in the squeaky plastic chair, his graduation cap slightly askew. Jenna, a few rows behind him, turns around in her seat as well and twists her long blonde curls nervously. The weight of Marcus's words hangs in the air between us.

The crowded gym buzzes with excitement and anticipation for the ceremony to begin. As Marcus's speech comes to an end, there is a collective sigh from the graduates. But as we stand to sing the alma mater one last time, a sense of unease settles over us, unsure of what the future holds after leaving these halls that have been our home for four years.

The room echoes with the names of my classmates as I fidget in my seat, trying to maintain composure. Jenna and Tanner have already collected their degrees and sit among the other students, but I remain, waiting patiently for my turn. The anticipation is almost unbearable as I mentally rehearse walking up those steps and accepting my college degree from the dean.

Finally, "Katarina Marritt" rings out through the crowd and I take a deep breath. With as much grace as I can muster, I make my way toward the stage, feeling grateful and relieved as I receive my well-earned degree.

After the ceremony, I step out of the crowded gym.

My mom's eyes shine with tears as she envelops me in a tight embrace, nearly crushing my newly minted degree between us. She whispers, "I'm so proud of you!"

Despite my exhaustion and excitement from just graduating college, I can't help but smile at the joy on her face. For as long as I can remember, she has talked about how important it is for me to earn a degree because she never had the opportunity herself. And now, in this moment, I can feel happiness radiating off of her as she finally gets to experience that dream through me.

"Congratulations, Kat," Patrick says with a small smile. He stands with his hands tucked into the front pockets of his jeans, shifting from one foot to the other in a gesture that reveals his slight discomfort.

We've been navigating things, trying to figure out what our relationship means now that we've distanced ourselves from our father. For me it was simple—he didn't want me around anyway—but I know it's been hard on Patrick to make the decision to cut his toxicity out of his life.

"Kat!" Jenna screams, her long blonde hair bouncing wildly as she runs toward me, her graduation cap clutched tightly under her arm. She reaches me and squeezes me in a bear hug, nearly crushing my ribs. "Can you believe it? We did it!" she exclaims, jumping up and down with such force that I am lifted off the ground.

CHAPTER FIFTY-EIGHT

Amidst the chaos, I feel a pair of strong arms wrap around me from behind. Tanner's breath tickles my ear as he mocks Jenna. "Can you believe it? We did it."

I laugh and lean back into his embrace, turning my head to the side to meet his gaze. "Where are your parents?"

"They're over there with Brendan's parents. They'll be over in a sec."

Gazing around the bustling room, my stomach drops as my eyes lock onto two familiar figures—Elijah's parents. His father works the crowd like a seasoned politician, shaking hands and kissing babies, while his mother stands close by with a forced smile plastered on her face. My stomach churns at the sight of them, memories of past encounters flooding my mind.

Elijah beams with pride as he approaches his parents, clutching his newly earned college degree tightly in his hand. He eagerly holds it out to his father, anticipating praise and recognition, but is met with a dismissive request to give it to his mother without even a glance. The disappointment on Elijah's face is tangible, evoking sympathy within me. It is evident that he has spent his entire life striving for the validation and affection of a man who will never truly value him. From a distance, I can't help but feel empathy for the man I once loved and imagine how lonely and disheartening it must be to constantly seek approval from someone who will never care.

I used to spend every waking moment trying to win the love of someone who constantly made me feel small and insignificant. But now, as I lean into the strong embrace of a man who truly loves me, surrounded by our closest friends and family, I am filled with nothing but love and contentment.

Going back in time to fix things with Elijah is nothing but a distant memory, replaced by new ones full of happiness, warmth, and genuine love.

For the first time in my life, I am eager and excited to look ahead instead of dwelling on the past.

FIFTY-NINE

THREE YEARS LATER

KAT

"Sweetheart, you look amazing." Tanner holds my gold strappy heels up as I fight to get out the door of our hotel room to head down to the wedding of two of our best friends. Despite spending the morning with Jenna, she insisted I go up to my own room to get ready because my nervous energy was going to give her a nervous breakdown.

I glance at the clock and panic sets in. I grab my mascara wand and touch up my already thick lashes. My mom's bracelet glints on the dresser, a reminder of my maid-of-honor duties: Jenna's *something old*. I take one last swig of champagne, hoping it will calm my nerves before heading down to the hotel lobby.

Tanner knows what today is—it's the day we stop rewriting history and start completely anew. Over the past three years, we have built a life together, created new memories and traditions with our families. My mom's warm hugs and his parents' delicious dinners are now a regular part of our routine. Happiness radiates from every corner of our home, and it is a dream I never thought could become a reality. I'm so excited to see what comes next.

My business is booming. I'm now utilizing Cheyeanne in a capacity I was terrified to at first. She's incredibly talented, but I initially struggled to let go of the reins. However, she has proven she's competent and then some, so when I asked if she would like to shoot the wedding I'd booked long before Jenna and Marcus officially set a date by herself, she instantly jumped at the opportunity. Luckily, the bride was completely fine with it.

Once I've fastened my heels, I look down to find a drop from my coffee sitting in the middle of my chest, the red lace of my dress stained a deep brown. "No," I sigh as I pick at the discolored spot, anxiety over potentially ruining Jenna's big day washing over me.

"I'm sure she has a stain remover pen," Tanner says. "Let's go." With every passing second, he grows more irritated by my insistence on not leaving the room.

I turn to him, contemplating my options. "Maybe I should just change?" I suggest, mentally scrolling through the other dresses I brought along for the wedding. Jenna requested an eclectic look when it came to our attire as long as it incorporated shades of pink or red. Since this time there are only two other bridesmaids, changing my dress shouldn't disrupt anything too much.

Tanner lets out a heavy sigh and turns to face me, his frustration barely contained. "If you want to change, do it now. We only have five minutes until we're supposed to be down there," he says sternly. Then his gaze travels up and down my body, taking his time. My pulse quickens as I feel his intense desire for me spark between us. "But honestly, you

CHAPTER FIFTY-NINE

look stunning, even with the small blemish," he adds with a sly smile before stepping closer to me. "Whatever you decide, though, we have to go."

"You're right—I'm sure someone has a Tide pen." I nod, finally pushing out of our hotel room.

As the elevator doors open, my eyes immediately take in the grandeur of the hotel lobby. My gaze is drawn to a massive chandelier made of solid gold hanging from the ceiling, but my focus shifts quickly to the room off to the side of the reception hall, where I'm supposed to meet Jenna.

As I move to walk away from Tanner, he grasps my hand tightly.

"What is it?"

"You actually have an hour," he chuckles nervously, causing me to look down at my phone to reveal that it is indeed an entire hour before I agreed to meet Jenna.

"That was a dirty trick!" I smack his arm.

Tanner flashes me a mischievous grin. "No need to worry, it's just a harmless one," he says before letting go of my hand and playfully swatting my backside. He pushes me toward the bridal suite where Regina is rushing through the door with a sewing kit. "I'm sure she has some stain remover; why don't you take care of that, then we can go for a walk?"

In the bridal suite, my eyes lock on Jenna sitting on the couch against the far wall. "You look stunning," I say, gesturing dramatically toward her.

She rolls her eyes. "Thanks—I looked exactly like this an hour ago," she retorts.

"Oh, right," I reply with a laugh. "Sometimes I forget just how beautiful you are."

Her lips curve up in a small smile. "Flattery will get you far with me."

"I know," I tease before turning to the room. "Anyone have a Tide pen? I spilled coffee on my dress earlier."

"Brown purse, side pocket," Regina responds without looking up from her work.

After quickly fixing my stain, I head toward the door. "I'll be back soon."

"Where are you going?" Jenna asks, a hint of concern in her voice.

"Tanner wanted to take a walk before we need to get you dressed," I explain.

Her face lights up at my words. "Oh, okay! Have fun!"

Suspicious of her response, I step back into the stunning entryway and spot Tanner leaning against the garden door, his tawny suit perfectly tailored to accentuate his broad shoulders and narrow waist. His white button-down shirt is crisp and neatly tucked in, with just a hint of cologne lingering in the air around him. He had fought hard for the groomsmen to wear brown instead of traditional black or blue, and Marcus finally caved when Regina pointed out that it was predicted to be a popular trend in the upcoming bridal season. As always, Marcus prides himself on being just a little bit better than the masses.

"Are you ready?" Tanner whispers.

I rise up onto my tiptoes and give him a soft kiss on the lips. Linking my fingers with his, I smile as I say, "Let's go."

Despite the sunlight, fairy lights are draped below the gazebo set up for the ceremony, their glow significantly duller than they will be in a few hours when Marcus and Jenna stand below it to exchange their vows. As we make our way past

CHAPTER FIFTY-NINE

rows of white chairs, we see florists frantically arranging flowers. The scent of roses, lilies, and hydrangeas fills the air as we reach the back of the setup nestled right behind the historic hotel.

My breath catches in my throat as I gaze at the seemingly endless expanse of vibrant flowers perfectly arranged on the lush green lawn. "It's beautiful," I whisper as a faint memory stirs within me—one of Tanner and me walking through a similar garden at Kent. I shake my head, perplexed as always that I could have ever seen him as just a friend.

"You're right, this view is breathtaking," Tanner whispers, causing my cheeks to flush as his attention never leaves me. He reaches for me, pulling me closer, and his confident demeanor seems to waver. "Come here," he says in a shaky voice.

As I turn to face him, his grip on my hand tightens and he exhales nervously. My heart races with anticipation.

Tanner clears his throat. "I don't remember much of anything from before, when we were here on this exact date, before we went back. I remember what I felt, how much I ached for that to be us but knowing that it more than likely never would be. You saw me as just a friend, and admittedly, I hated it."

"I'm sorry, I—"

He laughs awkwardly. "That's not what I'm saying—I'm glad we did it the way we did. I got to have so many incredible memories with you, before we had to be fully functional members of society, when it was still socially acceptable to go out to a bar and get hammered on a Wednesday night. I'm glad it happened the way it did, even if it meant I had to watch you fall in love with him all over again."

I open my mouth to speak, but Tanner cuts me off. "When

we finally got together, when I finally knew that it was a very real possibility that I would get my wish, that I'd actually be able to spend the rest of my life with you, I knew even then that I intended to ask you to be my wife." A lump catches in my throat as he continues, "And what better day to do that than the first day of the rest of our lives?"

"Wait," I say, trying not to laugh at his shocked expression. "You can't propose on someone else's wedding day, especially when you're part of the bridal party."

A relieved smile spreads across his face as he realizes I am just teasing him. I urge him to stand back up, but he remains kneeling on the ground, a mischievous glint in his eye. "Do you really think I would do this without Jenna and Marcus's blessing? It was actually Jenna's idea." He gestures toward the hotel, where Jenna and Regina are peeking through the blinds of the bridal suite, barely containing their excitement.

The realization hits me like a wave—this is real; Tanner is actually proposing to me.

Tears prick at the corners of my eyes and a deep chuckle escapes him as he reaches into his pocket and pulls out a small maroon velvet box, its purpose unmistakable.

I gasp as he opens the box, revealing a stunning sapphire ring nestled within. The color matches my eyes perfectly, and I feel a rush of emotion at the thought and care Tanner put into choosing it. I extend my hand, trembling slightly as he carefully positions it against the tip of my ring finger.

"Katarina Emma Lyn Marritt, will you do me the honor of being my wife?" His words send a burst of joy and disbelief exploding in my chest.

This moment I've dreamed of is finally happening.

Tears of happiness stream down my cheeks as I nod, my

CHAPTER FIFTY-NINE

voice failing me. A broad smile spreads across Tanner's face as he slides the ring onto my finger, a perfect fit. We both feel the weight of this moment settle over us, surrounded by an atmosphere thick with emotion and love. I throw my arms around him, burying my face in his chest, taking in his familiar scent and feeling the warmth of his embrace.

Through the window, we can hear Jenna's ecstatic cries and see her and Regina pounding against the glass. Any concern about whether they might actually break it is overshadowed by the immense love I am feeling right now and the intense realization of what today is.

The very first night of the rest of our lives.

READ MORE BY NICOLE RYAN

Just Peachy Series

Second Chance Vacation (Just Peachy Book 1)
Gen & Jackson's story
Available now!

Mostly Loathing You (Just Peachy Book 2)
Hannah & Liam's story
Available now!

ABOUT THE AUTHOR

Nicole Ryan is a contemporary romance author that expertly blends slightly inappropriate humor, steam, and heartfelt emotion. Her journey into writing began during her childhood, spending afternoons with her grandmother at the local paper, where her grandmother worked as a copy editor. Nicole further honed her skills through creative writing competitions in school.

Her debut novel, Second Chance Vacation, is especially meaningful, written after the unexpected loss of her youngest sister in 2022. This experience brought profound emotional depth to her storytelling, resonating deeply with readers.

facebook.com/nicoleryanbooks
instagram.com/nicoleryanbooks
tiktok.com/@nicoleryanbooks